T0290204

The Road to Walden North

The Road to Walden North

SHEILA POST

GREEN WRITERS PRESS *Brattleboro, Vermont*

PUBLISHER'S NOTE: This is a work of fiction. Names, characters, places and incidents either are the product of the authors' imaginations or are used fictitiously, and any resemblance to actual persons, living or dead, business establishments, events, or locales is entirely coincidental.

Printed in the United States

10 9 8 7 6 5 4 3 2 1

Green Writers Press is a Vermont-based publisher whose mission is to spread a message of hope and renewal through the words and images we publish. Throughout, we will adhere to our commitment to preserving and protecting the natural resources of the earth. To that end, a percentage of our proceeds will be donated to environmental activist groups. Green Writers Press gratefully acknowledges support from individual donors, friends, and readers to help support the environment and our publishing initiative.

Giving Voice to Writers & Artists Who Will Make the World a Better Place
Green Writers Press | Brattleboro, Vermont
www.greenwriterspress.com

ISBN: 978-0-9961357-6-4

Visit the author's website at: www.silepost.com

PRINTED ON PAPER WITH PULP THAT COMES FROM FSC-CERTIFIED FORESTS, MANAGED FORESTS THAT GUARANTEE RESPONSIBLE ENVIRONMENTAL, SOCIAL, AND ECONOMIC PRACTICES BY LIGHTNING SOURCE ALL WOOD PRODUCT COMPONENTS USED IN BLACK & WHITE, STANDARD COLOR, OR SELECT COLOR PAPERBACK BOOKS, UTILIZING EITHER CREAM OR WHITE BOOKBLOCK PAPER, THAT ARE MANUFACTURED IN THE LAVERGNE, TENNESSEE PRODUCTION CENTER ARE SUSTAINABLE FORESTRY INITIATIVE® (SFI®) CERTIFIED SOURCING

To Tad & Ian—
Cherished travelers along the road
to Walden North

'How many a man[woman]
has dated a new era in his[her] life
from the reading of a book.'

"Students . . . should not play life, or study it merely . . . but earnestly live it . . . by at once trying the experiment of living."

"Will you be a reader, a student merely, or a seer? Read your fate, see what is before you, and walk on into futurity."

"I learned this, at least, by my experiment; that if one advances confidently in the direction of his[her] dreams, and endeavors to live the life which he[she] has imagined, he[she] will meet with a success unexpected in common hours."

—HENRY DAVID THOREAU, *Walden*

The Road to Walden North

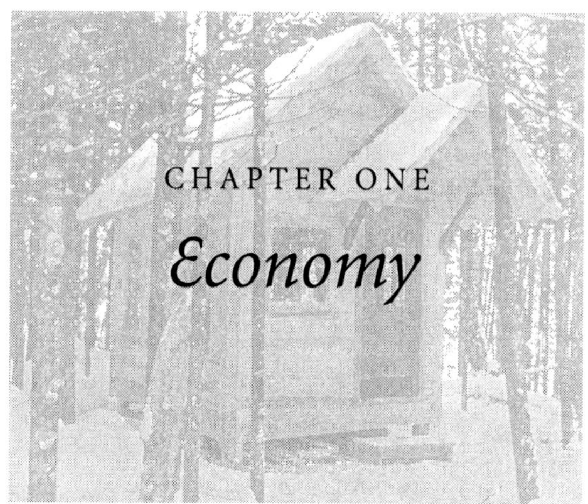

CHAPTER ONE

Economy

BLINDED BY A CERTAIN SLANT OF LIGHT that streamed into her eyes with an oppressive glare, Kate Brown was forced to stop literally in her tracks on the much-traveled, gravel path that wound along the contours of the Mystic River. Suddenly realizing that she had shifted from her usual jogging gait to a full-blown sprint, she bent over to catch her breath. Even from within her huddled position, Kate felt the breaking light reach her face, imposing its unwelcome influence on her now escalating sense of urgency. She raised her head in an effort to slow down her panting, when the swirl of dawn caught her eye—as it spread majestically along the point where the Mystic flowed into the harbor beyond.

Despite the dramatic threads of rose, yellow, and golden light, Kate felt only annoyance. Her time was sacred—particularly now. Though she preferred to run in the afternoon, due to her tendency to work into the night, this morning she deliberately rose before dawn. She was determined to get her run in, before heading to campus for her unexpected and unnerving summons by the adjudicator of her academic fate—the *Dean*.

Turning her back on the now visible sun stretching over the horizon against the iridescent harbor, Kate retreated into the half-light to complete her run, racing all the way back before collapsing in a breathless heap on her front steps in Cambridge. As people rushed by on their way to work, Kate pulled herself up three flights of stairs to prepare for her important day—not realizing that it had already passed before her unseeing eyes.

Intent on reserving a few minutes for last-minute preparation, Kate darted across campus, oblivious to the visible hues of rust and amber spreading throughout the dense, leafy canopy overhead. She would not be late, even if she were forced to jeopardize her carefully prepared appearance—her wrinkle-free new clothes—for timeliness by running.

Just before she opened the heavy glass door of the Arts building, Kate glanced back. A quaint cobblestone path carved its way among ivy-laced stone buildings, along which a few figures scurried from one to the other—like hounds on a scent. Her heart swelled as she realized she could now claim a place, however modest at this point in her career, amid the august setting—her reward for years of painstaking library research. And Harvard, no less—she reminded herself with pride, as she mentally celebrated landing a tenure-track position there.

With pursed lips, the dean's secretary opened a ponderous mahogany door to a vast inner sanctum, beckoning Kate wordlessly to enter. With an expression approaching reverence, Kate gazed wide-eyed at the floor-to-ceiling oak bookcases covering the walls, the richly upholstered leather club chairs, and the enormous, hand-carved desk, behind which sat Dean Edwards, a man who seemed to relish his role as a figure of importance. He appeared the perfect accompaniment—the finishing touch—to the quintessential décor.

Kate looked at him expectantly. Had she been a novelist, she mused, she could not have penned a more appropriate character for the collegiate setting—herringbone jacket, starched blue shirt with a paisley bowtie, and horn-rimmed glasses—all rather stylishly out of date. Stacks of books, papers in towers, and bundles of folders lined his desk.

"All settled in?" The dean looked up briefly from a paper he was reading, which he signed and placed on his desk. She had forgotten his English accent—an Oxford man.

"Yes, thank you, Dean Edwards," she replied, her tone demure.

"In Cambridge, are you?" He surveyed her clothes in one sweeping, critical glance. "Or, perhaps, Somerville."

Squirming involuntarily at the slight, Kate instantly regretted her choice of brightly-colored clothing. Too self-consciously—deliberate. Looking down, unable to meet his judgmental gaze, Kate realized that she should have chosen more dowdy colors. Academic brown, she mentally noted, from this point on.

Inhaling deeply, she forced herself to make eye contact before emitting a smile. "Right here in the heart of Cambridge," she said in as light a tone as she muster, "a short walk from campus."

"Oh?" He studied her with a cold stare.

She looked away. "I purchased."

"Indeed." Leaning back in his swivel chair, the dean peered at her intently—while drumming the desk with his fingers. "Intending to remain with us, then."

"Yes, of course," she replied without thinking, which she instantly regretted. "At least, I certainly hope so, Dean Edwards."

With a muffled snort, he abruptly began sorting through a pile of folders, listing precariously toward the edge. "In that case, you have your work cut out for you." He continued his efforts, before finally retrieving one. "Ah, here we are."

He handed her a memorandum. "The first of my '*Great Expectations*,'" he announced with a stern nod. "I don't suppose you have been with us long enough to have heard the update regarding Prescott's Fulbright."

"No, nothing at all." Kate wondered what she had to do with Prescott, whom she hadn't even met during her campus interview. The world's foremost authority on Thoreau would most likely remain a departmental colleague with whom she would have no contact, out of her reach as a lowly assistant professor. With an instinctive twist of her mouth, she searched the dean's largely impassive countenance for any clue to the purpose of his summons. She waited for some explanation, tapping her knees together in a staccato rhythm.

Dean Edwards rifled through some more papers in the folder before continuing. "Well, then, Ms. Brown, you obviously must be unaware of the consequences for you."

His glance conveyed an ominous mix, it seemed to Kate—a skeptical bemusement. She was sure he was enjoying watching her agonize over the purpose of the meeting.

"For me?" she repeated faintly, unsure of how to proceed. She turned her head slightly, as if to diminish the force of whatever he was about to say. She was sure it would not be positive.

He pushed another document over to her side of the desk. "This will be your new teaching schedule, revised now that Prescott will spend the year at Oxford. The government has released the Fulbright funding, despite the sequester."

Assuming the worst, Kate rapidly scanned the schedule for confirmation of her suspicions. "I am to replace Professor Prescott in his freshman Thoreau seminar?"

Dean Edwards nodded without making eye contact, which Kate interpreted as an indication of his mounting impatience to shift to the next item on his towering pile.

"Yes, yes. Due to Prescott's unanticipated leave for this semester, I have switched around your courses. You will not be teaching an elective on Melville this year, as we had discussed during your interview."

A sinking feeling overcame Kate, as she suddenly felt feverish. "Thoreau is not one of my areas of specialization." She shifted slightly in her chair. "Surely, the students must be expecting one the world's foremost scholars—"

The dean pushed back his chair with an impatient thrust. "Indeed. A level of accomplishment we fully expect you to attain in the not too distant future," he said, peering over at her above his reading glasses, "hence our reason for hiring you."

"Indeed," murmured Kate in a tone of resignation.

Dean Edwards squinted at her, upon noting her anguish. "Your mentor at Northwestern intimated as much." With a grimace, he added, "I should hope you have no intentions of proving him wrong."

Kate squirmed under the emotional weight of the thinly veiled threat. "No, Dean Edwards, of course not," she said. "I have every hope of excelling in my field—Melville studies," she added with a slight emphasis. "I am simply surprised that you wish to replace a Thoreauvian scholar with a Melvillean." She avoided meeting his shrewd stare. "It is certainly a daunting challenge."

His nod was brusque. "That is the reason I have summoned you now. You have three weeks before the semester begins to prepare for your seminar on Thoreau." He offered a sardonic grin. "Actually, it may be less complicated than you think. The focus this year is simply *Walden*—nothing more."

She offered the briefest of smiles. "Daunting enough for someone who hasn't experienced the outdoors, except through the windows of a library these past four years, to teach a book about the joys of living in the midst of nature." She looked away, unable to meet his now penetrating gaze. "I have yet to visit Walden Pond."

"Perhaps you are more Thoreauvian in your outlook than you acknowledge."

"Hardly, I would think." Kate checked his expression to determine whether her comment had been too caustic. He was difficult to read beyond his brusque affect.

The dean replied as he stood, "I believe the young David Henry—as he was then called—said something similar about his own studies here at Harvard, deeming it ironic that his work in navigational science never included being out in an actual boat on the ocean." He peered down at her before pacing through the cavernous office. "Imagine such a preposterous notion."

"Indeed," she uttered in a faint voice, unsure of where the exchange was leading.

With the briefest of nods, Dean Edwards continued. "Isn't that the point of an intellectual education? Theory over practice. Theory is the experience." He turned back to her. "I am confident that you can regale your freshman students with analyses of Thoreau's various philosophical meditations along Walden Pond." With a sidelong glance, he added with a dismissive shrug, "You're a philosopher, after all, of sorts, I suppose."

"Well, yes, Dean, but—"

Pausing to peer at her, he added, "I should think the rhetorical circumstance not unlike that of Ishmael discoursing about whales and life aboard ship." He offered a rare smile, evidently pleased with his comparison. "Your years in the library at Northwestern have more adequately prepared you for this teaching assignment—than could a mere pilgrimage to Walden Pond."

Kate stared at him with increasing concern. "Yes, Dean, I'm sure they have."

Sitting down again in his throne of a chair, he reached over for a folder. "Oh, Ms. Brown. Let me give you Prescott's syllabus for the seminar, which I expect you to follow. He has organized the seminar in this manner: starting with lectures on the doctrine of transcendentalism, followed by a series of chapter-by-chapter analyses of the book, together with an historical overview of the criticism. I believe he then assigns each student to write his seminar paper on a selected critic." He offered a brief smile, followed by a droll, "Quite *simple*, really." He regarded her with expectant eyes.

The statement elicited a brusque nod, before Kate recovered to offer a polite, though terse smile over his literary pun. *Simplify*, indeed, she thought, as she tried to restrain her inclination to bite her lips when disconcerted. She knew there was nothing simple at all about this seminar.

Kate briefly reviewed the syllabus. "I do not see a field trip to Walden Pond here." With an inquisitive glance up at him, she added, "It seems appropriate, given our proximity to the location of the book's setting."

Dean Edwards instantly slanted his eyes, his right eyebrow soaring high onto his forehead, while his mouth turned downward into a decided grimace. "And did you engage in field trips, Ms. Brown, as you referred to them, to the ocean, or perhaps to the South Seas, whilst studying Melville at Northwestern?" he sputtered.

"Well, no, Dean, but we were located in the Midwest, not along the seaboard. Here, Walden Pond is but miles away."

Now openly sneering, Dean Edwards peered stormily at her before offering a retort bordering on outright rebuke. "And this is *Harvard*, Ms. Brown. We do not engage in *field trips*—except perhaps in the School of *Education*."

"But—" she began.

With a slight wave, the dean summarily dismissed her. "Good day, Ms. Brown." Pushing up his reading glasses, which had descended down his nose as he talked, he picked up another folder to continue his work.

"Thank you, Dean," Kate responded demurely, as she picked up her valise. Shaking her head, she fled through the door, mumbling, "Great impression I must have made."

With downcast eyes, she hurried—under the canopy of towering maples, now shimmering in brilliant sunlight—straight for the library. She fully intended to spend the remaining time before the beginning of the semester—sleeping there, if necessary—immersed in the scholarship on *Walden*. After all, she reminded herself, it was

Harvard. They expected nothing less. There was no doubt in her mind that she would put aside everything else in her life in order to live up to the dean's "*Great Expectations*" for her. As she entered the library, she murmured to herself, "Everything else? What am I thinking—Academia *is* my life!"

A thoroughly prepared Dr. Brown entered her classroom at precisely the right moment. Scanning the sea of faces, oddly reminiscent of buoys bobbing guardedly in the harbor, she passed out her multipage syllabus for the course, as she introduced the course.

"Good morning, Everyone. Welcome to Freshman Seminar, the topic of which, this academic year, will be Thoreau's *Walden; or, Life in the Woods*. As you may be aware, the point of this seminar is to rely on this text as a framework for introducing you to the rigors of academic thinking, the processes involved in formulating issues, making arguments, and contributing to existing scholarly research." She looked around, as she nodded pleasantly to the students, before adding as an afterthought, "As well as, of course, reading and deconstructing *Walden*."

Someone spoke out toward the back of the room. "But Professor, isn't *Walden* about living off the land in the woods? How is that academic?" An anticipatory hush reigned, as no one even dared to respond to the forward question.

Kate offered a knowing nod, displaying no irritation over the challenge. "As we will come to see," she said, with a pointed look in the direction of the comment, "and, perhaps, to appreciate, the forest along Walden Pond served as a vantage point from which to analyze and critique the machinations of society."

Assuming the posture of a seasoned lecturer, Kate slowly paced the front of the room as she qualified her statement. "Much of the scholarship focuses upon this very point—research with which you will become more than familiar by the end of the year."

She stopped to face the group of students watching her with impervious expressions. Almost blank—despite their obvious levels of intelligence, she noted, but that will change, once they understand how to think like an academic—a scholar. She offered a tight smile. "As an introduction to your reading for next class, allow me to outline for you the motifs of chapter one, called 'Economy.'"

A fellow dressed in a polo shirt shot out, "What's the economy have to do with living in the woods?"

Kate looked up. "That's precisely the point, as we will see," she said, with a brief glance at the student. Scanning the other faces to gauge their response, she gave a brief nod before pulling out her notes. Walking over to the lectern, she began, "In this chapter, unlike the Jeffersonian celebration of the agrarian life, Thoreau casts a critical eye on what he calls the '*enslavement*' of farmers to their land." With a glance at the impassive faces before her, she continued, reading an excerpt from the chapter:

> "*When I consider my neighbors, the farmers of Concord . . . the man who has actually paid for his farm with labor on it is so rare that every neighbor can point to him.*"

A voice emerged from among the sea of students. "Doesn't he mean that the farmers had attained ownership through inheritance, rather than work?"

Kate glanced up, registering her surprise, before a look of understanding crossed her face. Sizing up the costly laptops, phones, and even more expensive clothes, she wondered how many of the students came from families who didn't know what it was like to work—to toil physically to earn a living.

The polo-attired student nodded at several of his fellow classmates. "That's an attitude some of us grew up with. Nothing wrong with inheriting land and money," he quipped, as he looked around at the others, some who chuckled, while others immediately slunk down in their seats before shifting their attention back to Kate.

Kate met their inquisitive stares. "He's not referring here to inherited wealth, but rather to an economic system that he felt ensnared the participants in endless debt—a situation, perhaps, with which you may not be personally familiar." She looked down again before continuing with her lecture.

Another student interrupted with a question. "But didn't he respect farming, since he lived in the woods himself and grew some of his own food?"

Kate offered a brief nod, followed by a cursory, "Good insight," before launching an explanation. "He describes an economic system among his rural countrymen that required farmers to toil almost forty years, before paying off their mortgages. Indeed, the historical statistics point out that during the 1840s, only one in three actually owned their own farms outright."

With a tight smile, she added, "Not unlike our present system of home ownership, though we have reduced mortgage terms down to thirty—even fifteen—years, thus demonstrating our economic evolution from Thoreau's days."

When no one offered any comments, she glanced up from her notes. "Today, we can choose from a vast array of financing options, including both fixed and variable rates."

Some students merely shrugged their shoulders.

Kate surveyed the impassive faces, before offering a wan smile. "They even give out such mortgages to new college professors saddled with graduate student loans." Isolated chuckles scattered the seminar room.

She flushed, a warm smile spreading across her serious countenance. "Several of his observations and critiques of the society of his times you will find rather quaint. For example, as many who bemoan change, Thoreau complained of the then clamor for '*luxuries*,' as he called them, though to our contemporary way of thinking, absolute necessities, such as plumbing and heating systems—beyond a wood stove, that is." She offered a brief smile.

Kate gazed at the students now typing furiously into their laptops. "Imagine the condition of our lives without plumbing or what we may call the 'global effect'—importation of goods from other countries—another thematic point he ardently criticizes."

Leaning her arms on the podium, Kate relaxed into explanation. "Of course, Thoreau failed to appreciate the vital role that the nascent Industrial Revolution would come to play in the formation of modern society." She glanced around the room before continuing. "Just consider how much society has evolved since Thoreau's day. After all, where would we be without our imported laptops and our cell phones, our clothing, our global foods, and other necessities?" Smiling, she offered a playful shrug.

Gathering her notes, Kate concluded, "Check the syllabus for the particulars of your first assignment. I shall expect your papers on one of the first two chapters to be emailed to me on time." Checking her watch, she turned to leave—only to notice that a few hands waved in the air.

"Sorry, I don't have much time for questions today, but I'll take one or two now." Kate thrust an impatient nod at a studious-looking fellow sitting in front of her. "Yes?"

"So there's no point, really, in trying to apply Thoreau's philosophy to modern life," he commented, "much less trying to live as he lived."

Tilting her head, Kate offered an officious smile. "I suppose we must differentiate between ideals and practical reality as we examine his themes." With a quick glance at her watch, she announced, "Sorry, but I must rush off." Picking up her bag, she offered, "Feel free to submit any questions you might have, either on your reading or from this lecture, along with your assignment."

Just as she turned away, a soft, yet firm voice from the back halted the ensuing flight from the classroom. "It is not only possible to live a lifestyle of simplicity today, but many actually seek it out where I come from."

All heads turned to locate the source of the comment. A female, sporting a long braid and wearing a sweatshirt with the word "Vermont" in dark green letters, added, "I know from personal experience. My father and I live that way in Vermont." She glanced unsmiling from face to face, as if to the underscore the import of her statement.

Kate stared at her in surprise. Composing herself, she nodded to the class, announcing, "The perfect segue way to chapter two, 'Where I Lived and What I Lived For.'"

Gesturing to the student to approach, Kate said kindly as they left the room, "I'm sure we will all be curious to hear about your lifestyle in Vermont." She turned to the unadorned girl. "Your name?"

"Um, Heather. Heather Channing." She looked at Kate through what seemed like sad, though expectant eyes.

Kate offered a warm smile in an attempt to dispel Heather's apparent anxiety. "Well, I'll make a special effort to keep an eye out for your essay." With that, she turned brusquely and hurried out of the building.

Kate bounded across campus in order to arrive on time for the faculty reception, hesitating momentarily before the building. With a nervous tug at any imaginary wrinkles from her brown tweed jacket and sand silk blouse, she worried about whether she had dressed appropriately for her first faculty event. With a sigh, she opened the door to the reception hall, smiling inwardly as she recalled Thoreau's warning regarding any event that necessitated new clothes. How completely *un-Thoreauvian*, she thought with a sly grin. With one last tug at her jacket, she tried to reassure herself that at least her clothes didn't *look* new, her rationale for adding to her mounting credit card debt—another Thoreauvian *faux pas.*

The opulent ambiance of the hall, with its rich leather furniture, ornately carved mahogany chairs and tables, and ponderous velvet draperies lining each of the long, leaded windows struck her as even more Old-Worldly than any of the lavishly decorated banquet halls back at Northwestern.

Kate surveyed the scene before her. A soft murmur echoed throughout the hall, interrupted only by the occasional approximation of mirth. Small clusters of men, interspersed with an occasional woman, stood talking—*discoursing*, more likely, she qualified—as they maneuvered a wine or shot glass in one hand, followed by an appetizer in the other.

Classic-looking servers attired in starched black tuxedos, reminiscent of butlers in some great country estate, roamed through the various groups, offering an endless array of tidbits from sparkling silver trays. Daunted by the scene, Kate took a protective step backward, wishing she could assume a place from which to observe, rather than participate. Retreating to the security of the edge of the room, she feigned great interest in the gilt-framed, massive portraits lining the walls. As she scanned the noble stares of various entitled-looking individuals, she felt as if she couldn't escape their frozen scrutiny.

"I've come to rescue you from your pose as a portrait of a wallflower, albeit, however lovely," announced a British-sounding voice behind her.

Reeling around as if stung, Kate looked with wide eyes at the bemused person standing before her. Definitely English, she surmised, based on his attire: a tweed jacket, cashmere sweater-vest, and a crisp, button-down Oxford shirt, replete with striped tie—most likely, she thought, one of those university-coded ties indicating his elite academic affiliation. She averted her glance when she felt a flush rise in her cheeks.

"My, you look absolutely terrified," the fellow quipped. Pointing to the portraits above them, he asked, "Is it the old fellows," followed by waving his arm in the direction of the hall, "or we '*old boys*' who frighten you?"

Kate offered a shy smile. "All of you, I suppose."

"Ah, we'll grow on you, I should think," he remarked. "Once you get used to us, that is." He offered a self-deprecating smile. "We're a rather dour lot, though quite endearing in our own way," he said, with a slight bow, "if I should say so myself."

Kate surveyed the room, now brimming with intimidating figures. "I'm sure you are all utterly charming," she said, with a slight toss of her head, "each in your own way."

"Charming? Hardly," he sputtered. "Rather intense, I should say—if not outright obsessive."

"That goes with the territory, I would think," she said with a glance at him.

"Indeed," he said amiably. "See? You needn't feel so terrified—you are getting to know us already." He smiled down at her, as he slid his hand under her arm. "Allow me to guide you through the multitudes, navigating you around those to avoid, as well as those to cultivate."

With a gentle tug, he led her away from the wall over to the bar. "Come now, Kate, you simply cannot endure your first faculty reception without a glass of sherry in hand."

Although grateful for his protective assurance, she stopped abruptly. "How do you know my name?" she asked with a start. She hurriedly disengaged her arm from his grasp, as her mouth descended into a half frown.

"Your fame precedes you, I'm afraid." Smiling at her, he added, "You may have noticed only a few representatives of the fairer sex here, so I'm afraid you stand out in the crowd—however much you may try to blend in with the walls."

Leaning in more closely, he whispered knowingly in her ear, "Though if you wish to be taken seriously by these gents, you will need to walk like a cadaver, and keep that lovely red hair of yours restrained in that severe bun you are about to lose."

Kate looked up at him, startled. "Oh, no." She quickly patted her hair to assess the damage, reapplying her hairpins to gather up the loose wisps.

"Actually, those bits are quite becoming, though not, perhaps, for this particular social event." Handing her a sherry, he added, "More suited for a dinner party—mine, in particular." He smiled at her. "Cheers, then," he said, as he clinked his glass to hers. "To a successful year for you."

Toasting him back, she said, "And for you—whoever you may be." She offered a slight smile.

Bowing, he toasted her again. "To us, then."

Kate looked at him with a disconcerting gaze. He seemed astonishingly self-composed, quite at home in the surroundings. She concluded that he must be some important *old boy*. Taking a large sip of her drink, she asked, "Since you apparently know my identity, perhaps it's time for me to know yours."

"Oh, Prentiss, here," he said with a nod.

Kate studied him. "Prentiss, Prentiss. I know the name, but can't place it, exactly." She scrutinized his features, as if trying to siphon out clues to the odd fellow's identity. "Is that your first or last name?"

"Oh, family name." Smiling, he asked, "Then you did not detect a resemblance to any of the esteemed gentlemen's features on the walls, which you seemed to study with such intent focus?"

"Why," she asked carefully, "are you related to one of them?"

He flashed a big smile. "More like a dozen or so, I should think." His eyes twinkling, he added in a tone of mock *ennui*, "I gave up counting ages ago." He waved his hand over to one wall, followed by the other. "Both sides of the family," he said, "or, perhaps more accurately, all sides of the family are represented up there."

"Really?" she said in obvious admiration. "How amazing." She scanned the portraits again. "So who are all of you?"

Finishing his scotch, he hailed a server over. "Another shot of the single malt, if you would." He turned back to Kate.

"Let's see. Some of the family served as past presidents of the college, while those—over there," he said, waving his arm in the opposite direction, "represent the benefactors." He smiled at her. "In more cases than not, of course, they were both."

"That's quite an impressive genealogy," she remarked, with a hint of sarcasm, "but you still haven't told me *your* first name." Emboldened by the warmth of the sherry, she asked dryly, "You do have your *own* name, don't you?"

He gave a hearty guffaw, his voice full of mirth. "Good God, of course not. I follow a long line of names from both sides of the family contending for first-name domination."

Kate smiled. "And who won out?"

"The Prentisses, of course," he quipped. "They always dominate whenever given the opportunity."

He quaffed down his glass. "I apologize for sounding so perverse. Allow me to introduce myself properly. I am Charles Blake Winthrop Prentiss." He offered a charming smile. "But my friends call me Blake—much to the disdain of my good mother, I might add, who prefers to show off her ancestral link to the current royal family."

"Uh-huh," said Kate.

Sizing up her confused expression, he added, "You know, the future king, Prince Charles, and all that."

"Ah, yes, of course." She tried to restrain the smirk she could feel ineluctably spreading across her mouth.

He smiled at her. "I prefer my link with the family *literati*—hence Blake."

She gazed at him with widened eyes. "You mean *the* Blake?" "The very same." He bowed slightly.

"Well, it is good to meet you, Blake—finally." With a slight shake of her head, she added, "I thought we'd never get through the middle names, which were beginning to feel like an interminable Midwestern winter, solidly frozen in time, with no chance for an imminent thaw."

Blake nodded his head in approval. "The lady evinces spirit and wit—two admirable traits," he said, "to display in certain circles—though not, perhaps, among the present gathering."

"And which might those be?" Kate asked.

Blake leaned in toward her. "More overtly social circles, as in the one I am hosting tomorrow evening." Smiling, he added, "I do hope you will join some of my associates and friends for an evening—*chez moi.*" He looked around the room. "An event that promises to be more lively than this esteemed—and decidedly *dull*—gathering." He handed her a card, which she promptly pocketed.

Flustered by the attention, yet delighted to be included, Kate readily accepted. "Well, yes, that sounds wonderful." She hesitated. "But I have nothing to bring except myself, as I have been immolated within the thick walls of the library these last few weeks—not unlike the poor creature in Poe's 'The Cask of Amontillado.'" She offered a rueful grin. "I've barely eaten, let alone spent time cooking." She looked away from him in an attempt to hide her embarrassment over the admission.

Blake's eyes sparkled. "Just as a new assistant professor should spend her time." Nodding his head, he reassured her. "Leave it to me. I have both time and the inclination to cook, now that my most recent publication has guaranteed my promotion."

Kate offered a wide grin. "And I would have thought your pedigree would ensure clear sailing through the process."

Looking sheepish, Blake shrugged. "Well, I admit that my ancestry hasn't hurt my chances—to say the least." He pursed his lips into a pout. "Mother would be most annoyed if I shouldn't become a permanent fixture here, like her father and grandfather before him, back more than several generations."

She offered a sympathetic nod. "Have you no choice in the matter?"

"No, not really." Blake offered a smile full of charm. "Family influence is both pervasive and utterly inescapable, I'm afraid." He shrugged. "But I do well enough on my own, more or less, particularly with my most recent book, which has caused quite an uproar in my field."

She asked politely, "And what is your field?"

"Shakespeare, actually."

"Of course," Kate responded without thinking. *Typical,* she thought with a shrug, as she noted how closely his academic field complemented his status, his attire, and his accent. As she continued to study him, her mind raced through a multitude of book titles. When it came to her, she remarked, her tone reflecting deep admiration, "You must be the author of the multiple Shakespeare book just out."

He bowed. "Yes, indeed."

She nodded. "I hadn't connected the names, although I had read that raving review about your work in *The New York Review of Books.*" She remarked, her tone faintly critical, "You're making quite the name for yourself—in your *own* right."

He offered a slight retort. "Ah, if it were only so."

Realizing with a sudden sense of regret that she may have overstepped, Kate resorted to literary authority for validation. "Remember what Thoreau says in *Walden*—about not becoming enslaved to opinion and to tradition?" She looked at him with a pointed stare.

He laughed. "How very *American Dream*-like of you with your 'work hard and get ahead' resolve. Yes, well, the Brits, among whom I spent much of my childhood through university, weren't as keen. Seems I have stepped on the sacred toes of the mythological Shakespeare."

Kate offered a slight smirk. "In academia, we actually refer to that as '*groundbreaking*.'"

"Not when it comes to the sacred texts of the *old boys*," he responded, as he lightly touched her arm. "Never take on the 'old boys,' as the saying goes." He offered a tight smile. "But being one of them, I have been allowed some measure of toleration, however small, hence the glowing reviews in *The Guardian* and the *TLS*—publications, coincidentally enough, in which the family owns substantial shares." He shrugged, it seemed to Kate, in embarrassment.

With arms folded, she studied him a moment before responding. "Sounds like the situation Thoreau described in first chapter of

Walden hasn't changed here in New England." She met his eye. "You know, the one about the farmers being enslaved to their farms. If I may, you seem enslaved to your pedigree."

Averting his gaze, he swallowed down some scotch, before meeting her stare. "I should think it's more like Coleridge, you know, in *The Rime of the Ancient Mariner.* There are times when I feel as if I am being slowly strangled by the family albatross round my neck." He offered an apologetic smile.

Kate looked at him in dismay. "Surely, you are not saying that your provocative, yet utterly convincing arguments and groundbreaking research amount to nothing more than, well, icing on the cake of pedigree and prestige, or polish on the wooden floor of tradition?" She regretted her outburst, though, when she detected a wave of sadness pass over his face.

Blake offered a taut smile. "How did you manage to preserve such philosophical idealism while surviving the doctoral program at Northwestern?" He shook his head slightly. "Maybe it is the Midwestern in you." He polished off his glass of Scotch. "Well, welcome to the world of New England where old money, status, and family ties prevail."

"Indeed." Kate's voice cracked.

"The sooner you understand the unwritten rules of academia, particularly, Harvard, the better." He looked at her, a sly grin spreading across his bemused face. "If anything," he said, "I should say you just may turn out to be more supportive of the system than the dogged *old boys* themselves."

Kate turned to him. "Indeed. I see nothing wrong with that, actually." She hoped her tone sounded acerbic enough to convey her growing exasperation with the exchange.

"Sorry, Kate, for my jaded attitude. I see that this discussion has hit you hard." He touched her arm gently. "Look at it this way. All you need to do, really, is meet their '*Great Expectations*,' as our dean is so fond of saying, and you will retain your club membership, so to speak."

"I fully intend to do nothing but that," she retorted.

He waved his arm as if to cast off any frowning onlookers. "Henry Adams has nothing on you. But I do monopolize you. You really should be introduced around, so we will conclude chapter one of *The Education of Kate Brown.*" He firmly took her arm. "Allow me."

With that, Blake guided Kate to a small gathering of fellow department members. Excusing himself soon after, he took his leave, though not before whispering in her ear, "Tomorrow night, seven sharp." She nodded, before returning to the conversation.

Soon, Kate found herself involved in a lively intellectual exchange with her new colleagues, much to her delight. Blake's words receded as a new tide of enthusiasm crested. And now, she mentally celebrated, as she momentarily removed herself from the conversation, *I am living the dream.* Everything else—the disconcerting talk with Blake, the stress over wanting to fit in, and her anxiety of performance—faded into the sunset, now streaming rainbows of color through the leaded, stained-glass windows.

Turning her head slightly, Kate caught the magic light of what most assuredly was a radiant sunset outside, now casting an alpine glow throughout the hall, transforming the subdued hues of leather and tweed into shimmering effervescence. She smiled at the simple, yet majestic beauty of the light. The simple joys of everyday life, she thought.

The sunset triggered memories of Thoreau's famous sunrise passage:

Only that day dawns to which we are awake.

She glanced over in the direction of Blake, who appeared to be joking with some colleagues near the door. Her thoughts took a pensive turn. Mulling through the implications of Thoreau's assertion, Kate considered how the statement applied to her current situation. Her challenge lay not only in remaining awake to fulfill the '*Great Expectations*' of the dean, but in knowingly creating her own set, as well. With a deep sigh, she concluded there was nothing '*simple*' in either edition of *Great Expectations.*

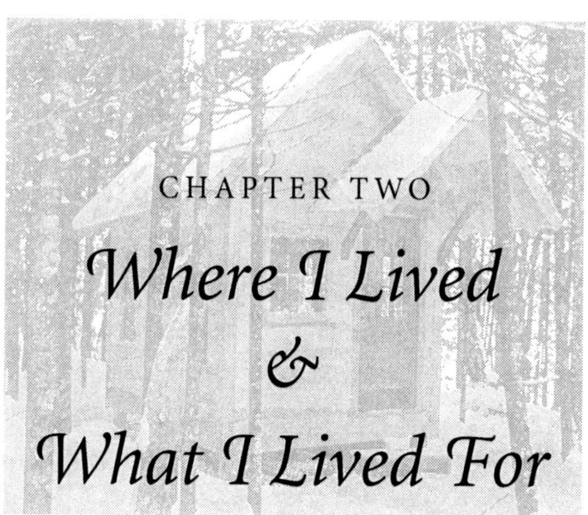

CHAPTER TWO

Where I Lived & What I Lived For

KATE SURVEYED THE REMAINING BOXES OF BOOKS still waiting to be shelved on her new bookcases. Although the college had supplied an impressive set of antique oak cases in her faculty office on campus, she decided to keep her extensive collection of Melville, and now, her Thoreau books, at home—knowing that as a night owl, she would be working late regularly. Better to spend time working here, she reasoned, where she could make a pot of tea and a bite to eat during what was sure to become inexorably long hours.

When deciding on essential furnishings, Kate had opted for bookcases and a desk first, followed by furniture as she could afford it. With each monthly salary check, she was hoping to purchase something new—after paying off a portion of her sizable credit card debt, which had accrued from setting up her new place in Cambridge. She looked around at the sparsely furnished flat, seeing only its potential: a couch and a leather reading chair would fill the empty nook, reserving the best view from the long window for her desk. After all, she reasoned, she would be spending most of her time sitting there.

Kate couldn't believe her luck in being able to purchase a condo so early in her career. The bank had, upon learning she would be a Harvard faculty member, approved a zero-down, adjustable rate mortgage under a first-time homebuyer program, an opportunity at which she jumped. Though her payments, together with her credit card debt, would consume well over half her monthly salary, she justified the expense by knowing she would have virtually no other claims on her income—outside occasional clothing costs—and certainly no travel or entertainment expenses.

She was here to work. *Work hard and get ahead*, as her parents had always urged her. She fully intended to live by the family mantra. *Sure, America is a grand country, altogether*, they would proclaim. *Ye can come clothed in nothing but your dreams, yet rise to the skies above, glittering like stars in the golden clothes of success.*

Kate smiled, thinking how thoroughly her parents' ideals had informed her own, as she made up a pot of tea in her kitchenette. No more than a small counter between the sink and stove, really, but she hadn't planned on spending time preparing gourmet meals. No time for anything but work.

Walking over to her desk, she set her cup of tea down on a trivet, not wanting to leave a stain, and opened up *Walden* to prepare her lecture on chapter two. She noted Thoreau's reasoning carefully:

> *I went to the woods because I wished to live deliberately, to front the essential facts of life.*

Underlining the statement, Kate decided to organize her lecture around the notion of living *deliberately*. She leaned back in her chair as she sipped some tea. She wasn't sure what the expression meant, exactly. Gazing out the window through the branches of a sprawling, thickly truncated maple tree, she could see a flurry of activity two stories below—people walking and jogging along the sidewalk, while others cycled in the street, dodging cars that rushed by. She wondered whether they were all living deliberately. She looked around at her tiny, essentially two-room flat. *Am I?*

The question made her laugh aloud. If living space were a criterion for deliberate living, she thought, then, surely, her place was on a par with Thoreau's 10 x 15 cabin, being not much bigger. Kate sighed before reigning in her anxiety, reminding herself that it was home, and a great start to upward mobility. She found herself dreaming about moving to a bigger place once she got tenure. "Okay—back to living *deliberately*," she admonished herself. She read on through the rest of the chapter to bullet points that supported Thoreau's notion of his chosen lifestyle.

After some time reading, Kate sipped her tea and gazed out the window, her eyes focusing on the leafy branches of the trees outside. She wondered why Thoreau felt compelled to *front the essential facts of life* in the woods, *one mile from any neighbor,* rather than reside among other people in the town. How did living under the pines along the shore of Walden Pond constitute deliberate living? Was it not possible, she conjectured, to *live deliberately* right in the very heart of Cambridge—as she was now doing?

The concept slipped past her intellectual grasp. She considered different analytical perspectives, shifting from Wordsworth's *emotion recollected in tranquility* to the Yeatsian melancholic wistfulness for the simplicity of "The Lake Isle of Innisfree"—while residing among the multitudes of London. She wasn't sure, but there was only one way to find out. *Research.*

After some hours consulting the major criticism on the concept, Kate decided to take a break. Her favorite spot to treat herself was the Coop, the Harvard bookstore, followed by a chai latté at Starbucks. Grabbing her backpack in case she picked up some more books, and putting on her running shoes, she headed off, jogging the several blocks to the bookstore.

Inside, she lingered over the table labeled "Harvard Authors," where dozens upon dozens of new releases stood upright, backed by what seemed like hundreds more books—all written by her new colleagues. As she reverently fingered the covers of various books, Kate felt a deep sense of pride at being considered linked to them, even though she had not yet published her dissertation as a book, a project upon which she worked feverishly, when not preparing her Thoreau seminar. She smiled, as her hand swept along the stacks of books. Someday soon, she promised herself, she would join the list of eminent Harvard authors.

Reading through some of the jackets to learn what type of writing was being done in her new department, she came across an intriguing title: *The Multiple Shakespeare.* Blake's book, she noted with excitement. She picked it up eagerly, scanning the adulation and praise included on the back cover, before perusing the jacket. "My God!" she murmured to herself, "Everyone important has endorsed him."

Building upon the groundbreaking research of a prominent Harvard cognitive psychologist, Blake had applied the theory of the existence of "multiple intelligences" to an analysis of the writing styles of the major plays, demonstrating rather convincingly, she concluded, based on her cursory reading of the reviews, that the plays were, in fact, composed by different authors. Kate suppressed a laugh, impressed by his bold, provocative thesis for an *old boy*. Guess the *young* old boys can get away with openly challenging their elders, she surmised, with more than a slight tinge of envy. She considered how much easier it would be to have a cadre of positioned people behind one, making success a given.

Kate thought about her parents, who had barely graduated from high school in Ireland, let alone procured a college education. In fact, if anything, they had inadvertently hindered her academic goals, aside from offering emotional support, since they had absolutely no understanding of the American educational system. Indeed, their *work hard and succeed* philosophy precluded them from understanding the caste system inherent in American colleges. To them, a college education was simply a college education, whether one went to Harvard or to the local state university. As immigrants, they were completely averse to credit, so taking out student loans to attend a more expensive university was considered wasted money. They would have none of it. Little did they realize that the name of the college was even more important than the actual degree.

Despite her state college education, Kate discovered that her stellar grades, coupled with relentless preparation for the Graduate Admissions Exam, had paid off. She was admitted to Northwestern University, a prestigious institution in its own right, borrowing against her future to study there. To help defray her living expenses, she also taught part-time as a teaching assistant, and later, as an instructor for the freshman composition program. When several of her writing students made their way into the advanced course of the nation's leading Melville scholar, he hired Kate, after a lengthy interview, to work with him on his decades-long project—editing the prestigious scholarly editions of Melville's writings.

Her job of several years' duration, later to evolve into her dissertation, focused on compiling, along with a team of scholars, a definitive edition of the author's *magnum opus, Moby-Dick,* from the disparate and often conflicting first British and American editions. She had entitled her dissertation "The Multiple *Moby-Dicks*: Towards a Theory of the Philosophy of Composition." Her work secured for her the unequivocal endorsement of her dissertation advisor. A few phone calls later, he informed Kate she was to be interviewed for a tenure-track position at his own *alma mater,* Harvard.

Kate gazed at the title as an insight emerged. Perhaps she, in fact, had more in common with old *Charles Blake* than she had thought. Though not as extensive, her support network included the protective wing of her professor, a definitive *old boy*. As she scanned the table of contents and dipped into the introductory section of Blake's book, she became increasingly impressed with the breath and depth of scholarship. She deemed it both rigorous and original—a far cry from the poor-little-rich-boy *ennui* he had portrayed.

Kate skipped around, reading various excerpts from different chapters. A smile emerged from behind the clouds of concentration. She marveled at the striking similarity of their approaches, judging by his book's title and thesis. Intrigued by the notion, she tucked his book under her arm and proceeded to the checkout with her new purchase.

Under a cloudless, brilliantly blue sky, Kate headed down the street towards Starbucks, her nose in her new book. She couldn't help but bump into people who seemed more immersed in reading than in navigating the crowded sidewalks. Whenever she did look up, usually to apologize, she noticed benches filled with people reading. It was no different when she entered the café, which, even on the idyllic Saturday afternoon, overflowed with people buried in books or their tablets. Picking up her chai, she secured the only open table in the house, a lone seat in the back corner. From her vantage point, she surveyed the relatively quiet café, sipping her tea in contemplation. My kind of place, she thought, my kind of people. *This is what I live for.* After dipping into Blake's book for a while, she walked slowly home, deep in thought.

Mindful of the dinner at seven, Kate decided to spend the remainder of the afternoon reading the student papers that were now pouring in through email—even before the ten p.m. deadline she had set. She was eager to know what level of critique the Harvard students would bring to their readings of *Walden*. Despite her extensive teaching experience at Northwestern, Kate never had the opportunity to teach the honors freshman seminar, that amorphous evolution of what used to be called freshman composition into a course that combined textual analysis with disciplinary methodology, cultural studies, and of course, writing.

Kate chose an essay with the intriguing title, "Economy: A Global House," and began reading:

> *The majority of critics seem to focus on the Greek etymology of the chapter title, as in 'keeping one's house in order,' rather than*

on its modern reference to a monetary system used to produce and purchase goods in a given society. In today's way of thinking, Thoreau seems to be making an argument for what we would call a 'local' economy, independent of global forces.

But we live in a global world, and for better or worse, the global dominates over any local attempt at self-sufficiency. Indeed, the world has evolved dramatically since Thoreau's days. Far from the 'it takes a village to make a world' attitude, we now live in an age in which it takes the global to ensure the viability of the village.

How would Third World countries survive without the pharmaceuticals of the Western world, or, for that matter, sophisticated cultures without their Third World ethnic foods?

Global interdependence, not independence, is the new paradigm. Poor Thoreau must be turning in his grave at the ring and buzz of now over a billion cell phones, or the incessant click of keys on computer keyboards globally, too numerous to even count.

Kate was impressed by the argument. "(Global) food for thought here," she wrote, chuckling over her rather clever pun.

After reading a few others, she scrolled down through the various titles, when she abruptly clicked on one that particularly struck her:

Walden North: A Vermont Lifestyle; or,
Where I Live and What I Live For

She gazed out the window at nothing in particular as her mind raced. Walden *North*? In Vermont? *Is* there such a place?

Returning to the essay, she found her eyes racing along the lines with more rapidity than her brain could process:

Reading Walden, for me, is like reading pages from the diary of my life. I live with my father, a self-proclaimed disciple of Thoreau—who, I remain convinced, is Thoreau reincarnated—in a simple, hand-crafted, log cabin in the woods, along a pond, in a place, appropriately enough, called Walden North, Vermont.

So there *is* such a place, Kate thought, as she sat back in her chair—*unless it's fiction.* She rapidly scanned down through the remainder of the essay to assess its veridicality:

While my father has long lived his life according to the dictates of his master, adopting a lifestyle of 'simplicity'—you know, 'simplify, simplify,' (sung to me growing up as an endless refrain)—over his earlier life of urban luxury, I have followed his example.

Until now. Being here at Harvard, my father's own alma mater, has loosened the philosophical roots entwined around my psyche. Here, I feel confused, disconcerted, unsure. Where do I live? In an 8x10 room amid a luxurious historical palace rich in ideas. What do I live for?

I am here to learn the answer to that question. Maybe like Thoreau, who also lived and studied here once, I'll return to my childhood home in Walden North. But then again, maybe my own path follows the beat of a distant drummer—however far away.

"Poignantly written," Kate typed, though she concluded that Heather sounded really confused. She closed the file, realizing that there was no time to deal with the affective issues in the entry. Leaning forward again, she immediately switched screens and conducted a search for the name of the alleged Vermont town. She was astonished to discover Walden North up in what was called the "Northeast Kingdom" of Vermont, close to the Canadian border.

She leaned back, turning gently from side to side in her swivel chair, as she stared with a pensive gaze at the maple outside. In the late afternoon sunlight, its leaves now shimmered in vivid hues of gold and red, something she had not noticed until that moment. Her thoughts swirled, not unlike some of the leaves she watched cascading down to the ground below. Was there a connection between the two places? Her thoughts hummed the poetic refrain, *Walden Pond and Walden North.* The notion of some underlying link struck her as utterly intriguing.

Kate instinctively checked her watch, a habit she performed repeatedly throughout the day. She was alarmed to discover that the time had slipped by much more rapidly than she had imagined. With just over one hour to the appointed time for dinner, she reluctantly shut down her computer. She smiled as she rose from her chair, declaring to herself that Walden North would have to wait until after Beacon Hill.

Unsure of the level of formality of the dinner, Kate decided to give Blake a call to ask what type of dinner party he was hosting.

"Hello, Blake?" she began.

"Don't tell me, Katie, you are calling to send regrets on your promise to join my little soirée this evening."

Kate couldn't help but laugh. "No, Blake. I'm calling with a rather silly question—how fancy is this dinner of yours?"

Blake bantered back, "So there *is* a girl who lurks underneath all that rigorous intellectual exterior, after all."

"Yes, yes, of course," she retorted, her tone defensive.

"Hung up on what to wear, are you?" he asked with obvious enjoyment.

Uncomfortable with being found out, she muttered, "Well, yes, actually. I was wondering—"

"Oh, put on something wickedly seductive, Katie, so I can't take my eyes off you all evening and repeatedly lose my train of thought."

"Oh, Blake, that's not what I meant. How formal is the dinner?"

"Quite laid back, I should say."

"Uh-huh."

"What is that supposed to mean?" he demanded.

"I am having a hard time imagining you all 'laid back,' as you say. I'm wearing a skirt."

He moaned into the phone. "Oh, *no*, Katie dear. Not academic *drab*, for God's sake. Don't you have any slinky jeans?"

"You really are incorrigible, Blake," she protested, feeling more relaxed with him.

"I practice hard at it, Kate, honest I do. Jeans, *please.*"

"Jeans it is," she agreed with a sigh. "God help you if your soirée turns out to be an elegant affair."

"You'll be fine. It's time you learn about Harvard *chic* for after hours. It's quite common among the younger faculty. You know, slinky jeans, boots, and silk—always silk, Katie, or season dependent, cashmere."

She laughed again. "Yes, I get the picture. I'll try not to disappoint, though I'm having a difficult time imagining you in boots and slinky jeans yourself." She paused, before adding in a caustic tone, "Are you sure you're the author of the *Multiple Shakespeare* book? Somehow, I am having a difficult time reconciling the exacting scholarship of that book with this particular exchange over my attire."

"I am exacting on both fronts, Katie—research and fashion. I am simply displaying my understanding of the multiple intelligence theory."

"As I said, you really are incorrigible."

"But extremely lovable, really, Katie. Now, can you be ready in twenty minutes?"

"Of course. I'm not dying my hair for the occasion, but I need directions. I've never been to Beacon Hill."

"Good, I love the red locks just the way they are. Go downstairs in twenty. I'm sending my driver to collect you."

"Your *driver*?" she asked, her tone an octave higher than usual.

"Yes, my driver. He'll be waiting outside your door."

"I can catch a cab," she said, resisting the offer. "I'd drive myself, but I don't know where I'm going. I lost track of time while reading my first group of student essays. Besides, you don't know where I live."

"Not at all on both counts. Do tell—let me impress you," he persisted.

"I am already impressed—by your book."

"Oh?" His tone sounded hopeful. "Have you been reading me, then?"

"I have indeed, and I must say, it's quite extraordinary, well deserving of the mountain of praise it has received—on its *own* intrinsic merits."

"I do hope you will come to find the author as extraordinary as the contents of his book," he volleyed back. "We have lots to discuss then, so we must get you to hurry on, not waste precious time in trying to find me. Now, where shall I send the driver?"

With a sigh, she acquiesced. After providing her address, she paused. "Oh, and thanks."

"Not at all, Katie. Looking forward to cooking for you."

The existence of a "driver" made her rethink her wardrobe for the evening, despite Blake's expressed preference for jeans. What he really meant was *slinky*, she concluded with a playful smile. Abandoning the idea of jeans, she chose instead a pair of jean-styled silk pants—just in case.

When Kate arrived at the car, a sleek black Jaguar, the driver was already standing at attention, ready to open the door for her.

"Good evening, Dr. Brown. May I?" he said in a polished English accent.

"Oh, yes. Thank you, Sir," she responded. *Jesus,* she wondered, as they sped along Riverside Drive, does everyone sport an English accent here in Boston—or is it just the Harvard crowd?

They arrived at a tree-lined street filled with elegant-looking stone townhouses, which were accented by richly colorful flower gardens, encased within ornately scrolled, wrought-iron fencing. More British than American, she noted. It was so different from the Midwest, even with the elegance of the North Shore. Another world entirely, she realized. *Old-World* America.

Escorting her from the car, the driver opened an oversized hand-carved mahogany door with a large brass knocker. Kate entered timidly, wondering where to go next. Just then, Blake jogged down the ornately carved stairway dressed in cords and a stiff-collared shirt.

"Oh, good! You've arrived, then," he said, offering a big smile. "I see you intuited the slinky look—even if you are not clad in jeans," he added with clear admiration.

"Oh, Blake, thank you. Really, you needn't be so charming," she said with a frown. "Besides, I don't take compliments well." Turning, she scanned the various closed doors lining the long marble foyer. "Which floor are you on, then?"

He came over to her and brushed her cheek with a kiss. "All of them, actually, Katie dear," he said with a ready smile.

"Well, thank God for family money, since you'd never be able to afford these digs on an assistant professor's salary—even at Harvard," she said with a grin. "I was able to manage only two rooms, not an entire house."

"Perfectly in keeping with your teaching assignment," he remarked in a flippant tone, as he opened the double French doors leading to a magnificent parlor. "You know, Thoreauvian *simplicity* and all that."

"Something about which you clearly know little," Kate responded dryly, as she gazed round at the elegant décor. "Where is everyone?"

"We'll be dining out in the back garden," he said evasively, as he placed his hand under her arm, gently guiding her through a stately dining hall to the enormous kitchen.

Kate gazed around in awe at the spectacular kitchen, with its long line of antique cabinets, soapstone counters, and a cooking enclave, replete with two Agas on each side of a wood-burning baking oven, over which hung an enormous, hand-hammered copper hood. She glanced over to the washing-up area, where a series of soapstone sinks cascaded underneath a stand of multicolored, leaded windows, which opened out to what looked like a lush back garden.

Kate looked back in astonishment at Blake, who was observing her with twinkling eyes. "It's just amazing," she said, her voice hushed. "Although I have been in some utterly fantastic Arts &

Crafts residences—even a Frank Lloyd Wright home—in Evanston, I have never witnessed anything quite like this splendor," she said.

"Old World, New World, you know," Blake said in an off-hand tone. "It is based on 18th-century English Georgian architecture and décor—with a bit of 19th-century interior fashion thrown in by some latecomers to the family history." He smiled at her. "There's a bit or two of the early Arts & Crafts, English Gothic style, you know."

"How lovely," she murmured.

Blake waved his arm in the direction of the magnificent hood, as well as an original Craftsman glass and copper chandelier, poised over a hand-carved, butcher-block island. "Those pieces, along with some other William Morris furniture." He walked over to a full-sized wine cooler and chose a bottle of champagne.

"I see," Kate said, as she rapidly attempted to translate the various architectural allusions.

"Actually, I prefer that look myself," said Blake, as he sauntered over to her, "along with Elizabethan Tudor, of course, so I should think I would enjoy the architecture in your Prairie-style city."

Uncorking the bottle, he gathered two crystal champagne glasses, and filling both, said, "I thought we might start with a bit of the bubbly—for our celebration." With a boyish smile, he handed her a glass.

"What are we celebrating?" she asked, looking puzzled.

"Harvard's and my great fortune in having you as a colleague, of course," Blake said as he clinked glasses with her. "Cheers."

"Yes, cheers, as all you Brits say," she said. "Somehow I hadn't expected Harvard to be so, well, *English*, in culture."

He sipped some more champagne before responding. "It *is* called *New* England, you know, for a reason," he remarked in his droll tone. "But aren't you of British stock yourself, with a name like Kate Brown? Brown is an old aristocratic British name—Norman in origin, as surely, you must know."

Blake used the opportunity to study her features, before flashing a big smile. "Unless, of course, you are the devastating descendant of the Great Catherine of Russia—or perhaps more recent French nobility."

"Russian, I am not. I suppose you were closer with the French link, and only ancestrally linked to nobility." She sipped her champagne. "I would think you have enough blue blood running through your veins for the two of us," she added.

"Well, then?" he said. "If you choose not to enlighten me as to your cultural origins, let us adjourn to the garden terrace, where I have *hors d'oeuvres* ready to sample. I hope you like seafood. I've made some delectable lobster paté." He refilled her glass before leading her out to the garden.

"Where are your other guests?" Kate asked, once they were seated round a table under a massive pergola, which overlooked a garden brimming in flowers. She looked around, taking in the magnificent setting, while waiting for his response. The table sat on large, irregular slabs of stone, interlaced with spreading thyme, while rustic hand-hewn beams covered in flowering vines added a charming air to the setting.

"I rain-dated them all," he said with a sly smile, before blurting, "Oh, Katie, I had to keep you all for myself."

"Oh, really? A set-up, was it?" she asked lightly, before changing the subject. "Everything is so beautiful out here. Just as I imagined a real English garden to look like." She slipped him a sly look. "Even if it is *New* England, as you say."

He glanced over at her. "Well, perhaps, you might see a true English garden soon—should you join me at our residence in Stratford. The gardens there are quite magnificent. My mother's specialty, actually."

"You don't mean Stratford, as in Stratford–upon-Avon, do you?" As she posed the question, a knowing look crossed her face. "Of course, you must. The Shakespeare connection, as well as the preference for Elizabethan Tudor, no doubt." Kate twisted the stem of her crystal champagne glass.

He responded with a proud nod. "The very same." He popped a lobster aperitif in his mouth before continuing. "We moved to the ancestral home of my mother's family outside of Stratford, when I was just a young lad—where I spent several years, through post-grad studies, actually." He took a sip of champagne. "It was in Stratford, of course, where I developed my insatiable passion for Shakespeare." With eyes twinkling, he bantered, "It didn't hurt to reside in a true Elizabethan Tudor, either."

"That explains the English overtones to your accent and speech," Kate remarked with a nod, before adding dryly, "besides, of course, your overtly charming manner, which exudes all things British."

"Odd, you should say that." He rubbed his glass, displaying a usually well-hidden anxiety. "My school chums, and later university pals, all treated me as some exotic example of an uncultured cowboy Yank from the *Colonies*, as they referred to America."

She arched her eyebrow, surprised by his admission. She had conjured up in her mind a characterization of him as stereotypically elite. "I can easily imagine the attitude you are describing," she said. "I've heard more than my share of the cultural snobbery of the British." She peered at him, her expression quizzical. "But even toward you—with all those eminent ancestors of yours?"

He looked away. "I never felt really as if I belonged," he said quietly, before adding, "despite my distinctly *blue* blood, which, of course, is one reason why I developed a passion for Shakespeare."

"Really? And why Shakespeare?" She leaned forward, placing her fingers over the rim of her glass.

"When you really think about some of his plays, particularly the historicals," he said, swirling his champagne, "he wrote from an outsider's perspective—at least, one of the authors collectively known as Shakespeare."

Kate urged him on. "Continue. I am really interested, truly intrigued. You intimate, but do not offer, this level of detailed background in your book—at least, not as far as I have read."

He gave a brief wave of his hand. "Oh, it's all in there," he said, with a dismissive shrug.

She gazed at him with renewed interest. "So you came up with your theory based on your own sense of cultural alienation, thereby more easily detecting it in others."

"Indeed." He offered a gentle smile. "As I have perceived it in you."

Kate looked briefly away, before meeting his stare. "I admit that I am just a bit overwhelmed by being part of the Harvard scene," she admitted. "It is such a different world here from what I left behind at Northwestern."

"Yes, yes, indeed. New England, particularly Brahmin Boston and Harvard, are entire worlds unto themselves."

"I was beginning to wonder whether the famed American Revolution was yet another mythology embedded into accounts of American history with all the Brits around me." She flashed a smile. "I thought the Loyalists had all fled to Canada."

Blake responded with a gracious snort. "You're quite spot-on there. My mother's ancestors were ardent Loyalists who returned to England." Leaning forward, he teased, "If I didn't know any better, I would say there lurks a sub-textual criticism of British culture behind your admiration."

Kate laughed, now more at ease with him. "Well, let's just say that I inherited some culturally-biased genes."

"Ah," he said, with a definitive nod. "You're a Highland Scot, then," he surmised, and continuing to gaze at her features, added, "Or, perhaps, Welsh." He rattled on. "No, not with that hair. Actually, I should think you are Irish." He leaned back, an expression of surprise spreading across his face. "But Catherine is not an Irish name, nor is Brown, as far as I know."

She looked away again and said nothing.

"So you will not enlighten me? Are you ashamed of who you are? You shouldn't be," he said softly.

"I am a mix, really," she admitted, "as are many Irish, some of us with conflicting ancestries wresting for dominance."

He nodded slowly. "I am enchanted. Do continue," he urged, as he gently placed his hand over hers.

Kate studied him a moment before speaking, but the champagne had loosened her reticence, which she felt slipping away in her interest to communicate openly with Blake. She had been on guard since arriving in Cambridge. "I am Irish, yes." She shrugged. "Both sides, actually, though from radically different Irish ancestries."

He whistled softly as he sat back in his chair. "So I mistook your name Kate as short for Catherine, when it is not?" he said.

She frowned briefly. "In a manner of speaking, if you are thinking along British cultural norms." Relaxing her expression into a smile, she explained, "Actually, my name is Cáitlín—spelled the Irish Gaelic way—but pronounced the American way, as in Kate-lin, hence Kate."

"How intriguing," he said. "And the Brown? Shouldn't your last name start with an O, or a Mc?" He suddenly looked worried, instinctively removing his hand from hers. "You haven't married someone named Brown, have you?"

Kate laughed, her inhibitions now removed by his easy acceptance of her as an Irish Catholic. Well, he doesn't know the last bit yet, she thought, as an involuntary shudder revealed itself in her gestures. "No, I remain unmarried. Too much academic work to do, I'm afraid."

"Well, then?" He gazed at her, prompting her with his insistent expression.

Kate uttered a deep sigh. "Well, the long and short of it is that I decided for academic reasons to alter my name slightly, shall we say."

"From?" He urged her on.

"If you must know, from Cáitlín Browne O'Neill to Kate Brown." She finally made eye contact with him. "Browne—with an 'e'—was my maternal grandfather's name, and yes, it is the same family as the revered English Brownes, as in Sir Thomas Browne, *Religio Medici*."

"Aha," he exclaimed with a sly nod. "You sport your own pedigree, after all."

She looked away again. "Since his work is considered an exemplar of the melancholy tradition established by Donne and Burton, we in the family always assumed he had written that as a confessional account of the experiences of his relatives once they had moved to Ireland."

He snorted, before erupting into a hearty laugh. "Good one, that."

Kate twisted her mouth into a half-grin. "In short, the Earl of Kenmare's granddaughter married the descendant of the great Celtic royal clan, the O'Neills of Connemara, and an uneasy truce has existed ever since."

"I can just imagine." He studied her a moment before speaking. "So if I am to deduce from what is not being said here, you were afraid of being viewed in less than the luminous intellectual light you deserve, should your cultural affiliations, say, being Irish, and I presume, Catholic, cloud one's perception and acceptance of you."

She finished her glass. "There you have it, all hazy elements comprising one indistinguishable photo."

"You could always sport your British Sir Thomas Browne affiliation," he suggested, his tone hopeful.

She shrugged. "I believe that's the subtle point of my Kate Brown nomenclature, much to the chagrin of my Irish parents—particularly, my father."

Pouring her some more champagne, Blake gently touched her shoulder. "It means that much to you to succeed in academia?"

Her gaze was unwavering in its steely determination. "Absolutely." She shrugged, as her formerly bright smile transformed into a decided frown. "It's my entire life."

He gulped down his glass. "Well, you certainly have come to the right place, Kate Browne, truly with an 'e' and no 'o.' As I have intimated, based on my own sad tale of trying to be accepted in England, I empathize."

He leaned over to touch her hand again, giving her a gentle squeeze. "Your secret is safe with me."

She looked away. "It's not really some dark and dirty little secret," she said with a faint tone of protest in her voice. "It's just that I would like to be accepted."

"You were perfectly right to change your name, not that it isn't lovely, but at Harvard," he hesitated as he searched for the right words, "if your name does not end in Kennedy—"

"I completely understand," she interjected. "The *old boys'* club."

"Well, Kate, they do admit women, as you have seen for yourself, and lucky for you that you chose Melville to work on, and of course, now Thoreau," he smiled, "as long as you pronounce the latter's name—not as you folks in the Midwest with your French influence—but as we stalwart expatriated Brits do here in New England."

Kate grinned. "I have to remind myself of that each time before I refer to him." She felt relieved to discover that he was easy to talk to and confide in—not so much an *old boy*, after all.

Blake nodded smugly. "We're so protective of our cultural origins while still maintaining a pride in being New Englanders. Quite pathological, really."

"Oddly enough, I do get that."

"By the way," he said, "How are you faring with Thoreau?"

"It's a bit of a stretch for me," she admitted, "both in terms of my areas of interest and my own philosophy." With a dismissive toss, she said, "Imagine being against mortgages. It's the American path to upward mobility."

"I don't have a mortgage." He pursed his lips into a playful pout.

Kate tapped his arm playfully. "That's because you are landed gentry, you elitist. You don't need a mortgage—most likely, for any of your many houses."

Blake looked down. "Family money." He gazed at her. "You are much more impressive, since you are attempting to make it on your own."

"Whether impressive or foolhardy, I cannot say," she countered. "All I know is that Thoreau must be turning over in his grave to think that a mortgage holder doling out 50% of her salary is teaching *Walden*—at his *alma mater,* no less."

"Ah, yes. Simplify, simplify, and all that. No mortgages, no drink, and no fish." He swallowed his drink before popping another lobster puff into his mouth. "How utterly dull."

Kate looked around. "Yes, I can see how the philosophy of *simplicity* hasn't reared its proselytizing head here." She smiled at him. "But in being forced to focus on its minute details, I'm finding it an intriguing book in its own way."

"Indeed," he said in a non-committal tone. "Have you yet visited Walden Pond?"

"No, not yet." With a grimace, she recounted her exchange with the dean regarding hosting a field trip to Walden. "Perhaps you might come with me, sometime," she said with a glance in his direction, "though I promise to keep your visit a secret."

"I should be happy to take you," he said, "but the estimable Dean Edwards may know best. Walden has become quite the tourist trap, a far cry from your man Henry's days."

Kate smiled amiably. "Yes, perhaps. By the way, speaking of Walden," she said, as she remembered what she had wanted to ask him, "Have you ever been to Walden North, Vermont?"

"Good God, no," Blake exclaimed. "Now that is simply *too* primal for me. It is way up north—I make it a rule not to go farther north than Woodstock."

"Woodstock? As in the concert?" she asked.

"No, Katie, Woodstock, Vermont. Quite the opposite. Very *hoity toity*, altogether—settled by the Rockefellers. We have a country house there. Mother summers there, though I much prefer it during the autumn and winter months—while Mother winters in England. Quite charming. You must come with me to take in the peak."

"The peak—you wish to go mountain climbing?" She tilted her head, trying in vain to imagine him trudging up a mountain trail.

"Leaves, Kate. The point at which the change in the maples is the most vibrant is called the *peak*." He touched her hand. "You're so, how should I put it—so *Midwestern*."

"Well, we tend to have more oaks than maples in Chicago," she said, removing her hand. "What I know of maples I learned from observing them through the windows of the library at Northwestern."

"Spoken like a true academic!" He snorted contemptuously. "And *you* are teaching *Walden*?"

They both shook their heads.

"Yes, I'm more inclined to 'talk the talk' than 'walk the walk,'" she said, as she offered a smile, "but I am quite interested in going out to Walden Pond—if I can figure out where it is, exactly."

"I suppose I could take you, Katie. We'll make a picnic of it."

She wagged her finger in his direction. "Only if you bring the foods Thoreau would have eaten there."

Blake sighed. "Didn't he drink only water and eat beans, along with unleavened bread?" he asked, before adding, with a wink, "With the exception of the woodchuck he roasted, of course." With a brisk shake of his head, he remarked, "It's really no wonder the man was so dour." He stood up. "But enough of Thoreau—let's feast on the sumptuous meal I have prepared for you."

After lingering over dinner, Kate finally called it an evening, saying she needed to return to her papers and class preparation—however reluctantly. As they stood in the foyer, waiting for the driver to walk up the steps, Blake gave her the briefest of kisses on her cheek, saying, "I am here for you, Katie."

With one look back, she waved, as he closed the door to his world.

After some moments recalling specific aspects of her evening, Kate made a cup of tea before returning to her student essays. As she waited for her computer to load, she suddenly realized that, seduced by the elegance of the Beacon Hill experience, the charming ways of its host, and his highly enticing invitation to his Vermont family country house, she had completely neglected to pursue the topic of Walden North. In the excitement of the moment, Walden North had been cast aside for Beacon Hill and Woodstock, Vermont—distinctions, she realized, she did not yet fully appreciate.

Kate shook her head, as if to cast off the spell the evening seemed to conjure in her. She didn't know whether she was so easily lured by the glimmer of inherited wealth and the protection that it offered, or simply preferred not thinking too hard about the implications of Thoreauvian ideals on her own life. "Like Bartleby, '*I prefer not to*,'" she told herself.

The excitement of being part of the Harvard scene was simply too seductive to consider any change in attitude. She felt more than content with *talking the talk*. The realization prompted her to recall what it was the dean had asserted as the essence of academia, before remembering—the primacy of intellectual reflection over experience. She found herself agreeing with his formulation.

With a sigh of contentment, Kate decided to return to her work. Though planning to resume reading Heather's essay on Walden North, she was so intrigued by exploring a possible connection between the Vermont and Massachusetts locations, she opted, instead, to continue with her research. Combing through the scholarship on the name of the pond along which Thoreau had lived, she could not find any mention of the Vermont town. She leaned forward in her chair and went to work researching the history of Walden North, Vermont.

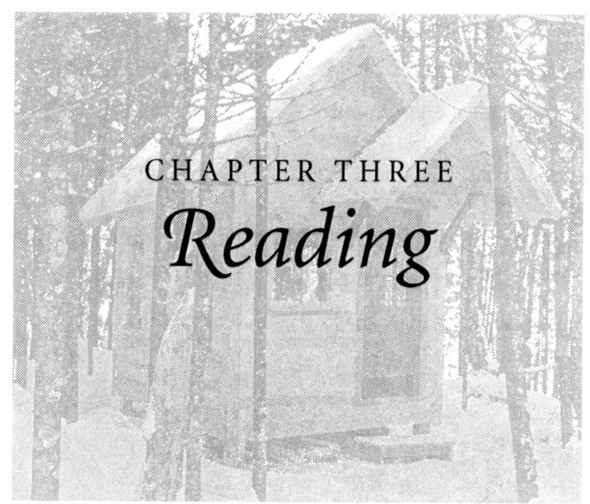

CHAPTER THREE

Reading

KATE READ LONG INTO THE NIGHT, completely intrigued by the historical accounts of Walden North. She perused the town website, apparently created by a local shop owner, a history buff. She found herself particularly impressed over the woman's proud claim:

> *My family has resided here for more than eight generations, all the way back to the mid-18th century.*

Kate admired the charming photos of the quaint country store, perched along the shore of an evergreen-clad pond. She shook her head in wonderment—*another Walden Pond.*

Kate sat back in her swivel chair, gently swaying from side to side, lost in thought. The name of the Vermont hamlet triggered her recollection of Thoreau's proclamation:

> *In wildness is the preservation of the world.*

Whether "wald" or "wild," she surmised, their etymologies suggested to her that Thoreau must have conflated both meanings in the title of his book. She shook her head over his cleverness, immediately wondering whether anyone had written about this point—besides Heather.

Kate spent some time thumbing through a tower of books on *Walden.* Reading an article on the possible sources for the pond's name, she threw down the book in disgust. "'Walled in,'" she scoffed out loud, "You've got to be kidding."

She pushed back her chair before standing up. If anything, she thought with a defiant shrug, Walden Pond connotes just the opposite—*freedom.* She plopped down again. Opening her laptop, she started to record her thoughts:

> *Freedom from the economic system—for those who deliberately adopt a life of simplicity.*

She looked up briefly to glance out the window. Branches rustled softly. She typed again:

> *Freedom for.*

Kate stopped abruptly, as her mind raced to connect Thoreau's philosophical beliefs with his anti-slavery sentiments. Continuing her research, she discovered that Walden North, Vermont had served as a hotbed of abolitionist activity, inspiring the state, one of the first in the nation, to declare slavery illegal. Kate shook her head, as she silently commended Thoreau for his subtle brilliance. Leaning back in her chair, she contemplated the possibility that there was much more to Thoreau and to *Walden*—as well as Walden North, Vermont—than she had initially assumed.

She hurriedly made up a pot of tea before returning to her reading. After a bit, she found a site that discussed Vermont history.

During the colonial period, apparently, King George of England "bestowed" the lands of Vermont upon one of his loyal subjects. "Nice euphemism, that," she muttered. She read on with an acute skepticism, yet intrigued by a place she had never visited. The king "bequeathed" large sections of Ireland to one brother, while granting parts of Vermont to the other. Suddenly, she sat up straight, her eyes racing. Browne? The Brownes were the first family of Vermont? *My* Brownes?

Glancing at her watch, Kate decided to call her mother, despite the late hour, her motivations decidedly more emotional than scholarly. She tried to stifle the rising excitement over the thought of being connected through her own bloodlines to the settlement of Vermont.

"Hi there, Mum," she began.

"Has something happened, Cáitlín?" her mother interrupted. "'Tis awfully late to be ringing."

Kate grimaced. "Sorry, Mum, but I came across something I wanted to ask you about."

"So nothing's wrong, then," her mother rushed. Kate could hear her sigh with relief.

"No, no, Mum. Not to worry. I just wanted to ask you about the Browne side of the family."

"The Browne side," her mother repeated in a clipped tone.

Undeterred, Kate persisted. "In some reading I am doing for my course preparation, I came across—"

"Sure, you're not extending the tale about your supposed name, now, are you, Cáitlín? Didn't I tell you there's no shame in calling yourself by your rightful last name. You're an O'Neill—and should be proud of it. Isn't it a Celtic royal name, after all?"

"Yes, I know, Mum, but—"

"But nothing now, Cáitlín. Just because you're at Harvard, doesn't mean you should be ashamed of being Irish. After all, didn't the Kennedy lads study there?"

Kate sighed and tried to respond as lightly as she could. "Yes, Mum, they did, but they were *Kennedys*, after all, and I—"

"And you are an *O'Neill!* Your poor father is still shaking from the insult of you changing your name for your job. He says it's as bad as the days when the bloody Brits demanded we Irish anglicize our Gaelic names."

"Oh, Mum, you just don't understand about the subtle discrimination here."

She imagined her mother's scowl emerging from her downturned mouth, as she assuredly wagged her finger into the phone.

"You needn't tell me about discrimination, now, Cáitlín. I know all about it, from the ways the bloody Brits treated the Irish."

Kate felt a long-suppressed sense of regret rise within her, upon realizing that she had reopened the cultural floodgates. Trying to compose herself, she regained control of the exchange.

"Mum, I have a very specific question," she said firmly, before launching in. "Have you ever heard of a Sir Robert Browne, as well as his sons, Robert and Valentine?"

"Valentine Browne," her mother repeated, a tendency she had when she tried to recall something. "Ah, yes, Valentine Browne. Sure, wasn't he my great, great grandfather, or is it three great grandfathers, I'm not sure, now."

"So he is the one who was granted the lands in County Kerry—the father of Sir Thomas Browne?" Kate asked timidly.

"Yes, he was, indeed—granted the high and mighty title 'Earl of Kenmare,' don't you know," her mother sneered, before continuing in a whisper, "though, mind you, we don't discuss that in front of your father."

Kate sighed. "Yes, Mum, I know, but I'd like to discuss his brother. What do you know of him?"

"What, your father's brother, is it?"

"No, Mum, Valentine Browne's brother. Was he granted any lands, like his brother—from the King?" Kate asked gingerly, knowing all too well that anything related to England could set her mother off on a tirade against the *bloody Brits*, as they were commonly referred to in their household. Kate held her breath, twisting her mouth first in one direction, then another, as she waited for her mother's response.

After a pause, her mother remarked, "You must be referring to Robert. He wasn't as lucky as our Valentine, as he had to go off to America for his land parcel."

"Vermont, was it, Mum?"

Her mother was silent a few moments. "Yes, somewhere over there."

"*Here*, Mum," Kate corrected.

"Here where?"

Kate twisted her mouth in frustration, before explaining. "You said *over there*, and I said *here*. You said it as if we were back in Ireland."

"What matter," her mother muttered, followed by a curt, "Why do you wish to know?"

"I came across a reference this evening to the Brownes of Vermont, and not knowing we had any ancestors who had settled here—in America—before you and Da', I wanted to find out, is all."

"He would be your third grand uncle, so." Her mother sighed deeply, before whispering again into the phone. "It's not something we're proud of, you know, Cáitlín, being given land from the bloody King, as if he had the authority to hand over other people's land to still others. It makes us seem, well, less *Irish*, if you know what I mean."

It was Kate's turn to sigh. She had forgotten how deeply entrenched *Republicanism* flowed through her Irish family—even through her mother's ancestral Norman side. She shook her head with an impatient thrust.

"Yes, Mum, I understand, but I do find it interesting to know that we have ancestors who emigrated here to New England. It makes me seem less, less—*dare I say it*—less, well, more *American*, I guess."

"Yes, I suppose it does, Kate," she said softly, using Kate's American name. "We just hope that you aren't ashamed of us. Sure, there's nothing to be ashamed of in being Irish, you know."

"Oh, I know, Mum," Kate reassured her in an easy tone. "I am proud of my heritage. It's just that they are rather snobby here." She groaned. "They all speak with a practically English accent, for heaven's sake!"

"It's not called New *England* for nothing, you know, Cáitlín."

Kate sighed, noting her mother's different emphasis on the region's name from Blake's. "Thank you, Shakespeare," she mentally called out. *What's in a name,* indeed.

"Yes, Mum, I know. Okay, I'm back to the books."

"Right, then, Cáitlín. Don't ever forget who you are, and where you come from."

Kate smiled happily, as she filled up her teacup before returning to her desk, immediately warming to the discovery that she possessed her own ancestral links to New England. With a raised eyebrow, she exclaimed aloud, "Won't Blake be impressed!"

She researched the Browne side of the family late into the night—before literally falling asleep among the layers of books, now scattered everywhere over her desk.

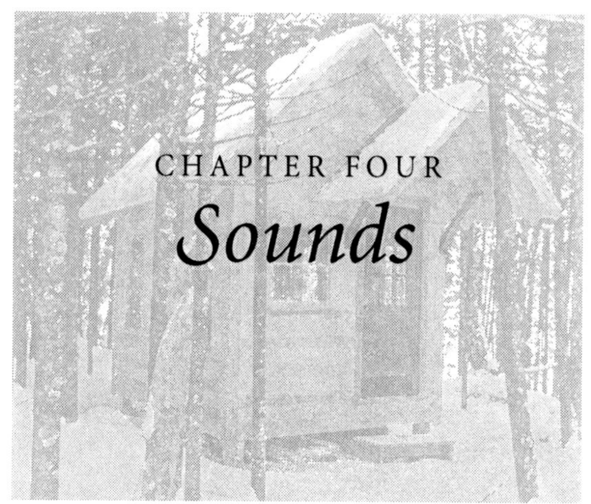

CHAPTER FOUR
Sounds

KATE WOKE WITH A START, peering into the darkness of the room around her, only dimly illuminated from the shine of the streetlights outside. Silence. No, she corrected herself, as she sat up and stretched—*tranquility*. She was coming to enjoy the relative stillness of the city late at night, as the symphonic hum of traffic shifted to the solemnity of a minor key—like waves, which, after a raging sea storm, gently cascade to shore. A thought crossed her mind that her newfound sense of tranquility must be what Thoreau had meant by the transcendence of sounds.

With an instinctive glance at her watch, she was stunned to discover that she had slept the greater part of the night on her desk. Standing up groggily, she walked over to make some tea, trying to remember what it was she had been reading before she fell asleep.

Now fully awake, Kate decided to go for a run before dawn. She soon found herself along the Charles River, noting that she hadn't been to the riverwalk since first moving to Boston back in July. She had spent the fourth watching the fireworks from along the park there, not knowing a soul, yet internalizing the excitement of the moment—the celebratory sounds of laughter and crackling booms, as sparkling colors illuminated the night sky. This is the land of the Boston Tea Party, after all, she remembered thinking. No wonder they take Independence Day so seriously here. As she watched the magnificent display and listened to the patriotic notes of the *1812 Overture* resounding through the night air, Kate felt at one with her new home. It was her independence, as well. She hugged her arms around her knees, overjoyed with the realization that she, too, was free to start a new life. That acknowledgment inspired her to stand up and cheer with the crowds around her as the Boston Symphony performed the grand *finale*—cannons booming in time with the dazzling display of dozens of rockets and firecrackers.

Stepping on a rock jolted Kate's thoughts back to the present. She admonished herself for daydreaming, when not focusing on the moment could result in a broken leg. Looking around, she noticed that despite the early hour, a surprising amount of activity hummed about her.

A seemingly continuous stream of rowers in long, narrow boats sailed by, their oars creating a regular beat in the water, followed by a rhythmic trickle of waves, gently lapping against the riverbank. The sounds seemed to blend with her thoughts. Imperceptibly at first, as she focused on the undulations, she became increasingly conscious of her mind chanting the words of Yeats to the beat of the lapping waves and the soft tread of her own steps:

I will arise and go now,
And go to Innisfree,
And a small cabin build there,
of clay and wattles made . . .
Lapping with low sounds by the shore . . .
I hear it in the deep heart's core.

As she raced on, she felt the *zone* flow through her—that transcendent sense of being at one with the landscape—where *Time* and *Place* melded into one. Her heart felt light, her mind calm, as all sounds hummed in unison.

Kate stopped to watch the sun rise. As it appeared over the edge of the river in the distance, birds began to sing—first one, then another—swelling into a symphony of birdsong. Somewhere in the distance, a church bell chimed the hour, while even more scullers rowed by, the sounds of the dipping oars blending with the symphonic sounds of the landscape. She shook her head in admiration, as she mentally declared both the setting and the experience as New England transcendentalism at its best. So Emersonian, she thought, as she reluctantly broke the spell by getting up. No, she qualified. Thoreauvian—*Waldenesque,* even.

As Kate resumed her jogging, with the rising sun now shining yellow light on the rippling blue waters, she again recounted the words of Thoreau:

Only that day dawns to which we are awake.

Stretching, her arms extended as if to touch the brightening sky above, she found herself thinking how *transcendent* it seemed to be so in tune with the world around her. It was definitely a new feeling—a new attitude, even, for her.

On her way back, Kate impulsively stopped at the local market. She walked slowly through the yard goods section, stopping before an array of birdfeeders. Attracted by a simple, unadorned one, she touched it softly, as she wondered whether she should buy it.

A fellow from behind her announced, "That's the best one. Produced by the Wildlife Conservancy, so it's made from sustainable wood and contains nothing to harm the birds." Kate looked at him, saying nothing.

He studied her a moment before asking, "Is this the kind you were looking for?"

"Never had one before," Kate admitted. "What do they eat—besides bread crumbs?" she asked, looking up at him, revealing her shy hesitance.

He shrugged. "Depends on the types of birds you wish to attract." He eyed his customer. "You live here in Cambridge," he asked, though to Kate, he said it more as a statement, than a question.

She squirmed slightly. "Is it that obvious?"

He briefly scanned her up and down. "Yes, it is." Noting the blush rising on Kate's cheeks, he pulled out a bag of black-striped sunflower seeds. "You should use this," he said, "you know, for the birds around here."

Shrugging, she said only, "Okay, sure." She picked up the bird feeder, and reaching for a bag of seeds, struggled with its weight. She turned back to the man. "Do I really need this much seed?"

He smiled coyly. "Depends on how many birds you would like to attract."

Returning his smile, she said, "An entire chorus of them, I hope."

"Well, then, get ready for your bird symphony. That seed will draw them in, and then some, but here, take this smaller bag." He glanced at her with questioning eyes.

She picked up her bird feeder, and after paying, headed for the door. He followed behind with the bird feed.

"May I put this in your car for you?" he asked politely.

Kate offered a wide grin in response, as she pointed to her feet. "These are my ride." Taking the bag from the man and slinging it over her shoulder, she said, "I'll take it from here. The birds are waiting."

Leaning against the door, the man watched her depart. When she turned to glance back at him, he seemed to Kate as if he were thinking, *some of these Harvard types are human, after all. Taking time to feed the birds. There's hope for them.* She felt his glance following the last of her, before the crowds enveloped her completely.

Despite the weight of the sack on her shoulders, Kate trotted home, eager to set up her bird feeder. She leaned out to place it on the maple branch that brushed against her window. The act filled her with a sense of contentment. She found herself eagerly looking forward to the sounds of birds chirping away. Replacing the screen, she stood back in the shadows, waiting impatiently for the birds to discover their new dining hall. This is silly, she thought with a sigh. *Back to work.*

Some hours later, after reading and preparing for her next lecture on chapter four of *Walden*, Kate stopped typing and listened. A radiant smile broke out on her face, not unlike the sun reappearing between the clouds on a late autumn afternoon. *Birds!* Afraid of scaring them away, she turned slowly toward the window, surveying the scene outside.

Two birds sat on the rung of the feeder, picking up sunflower seeds, before darting away to a higher branch—only to be followed by a trio clamoring for food. *Chick a dee, dee, dee. Chick a. Dee dee.*

Kate sat listening to the sonorous birdsong echoing through the room. Delighted over the notion that they were keeping her company, she started to hum in tune with the birdcalls. Catching herself, she noted with some surprise how lighthearted she felt. She shook her head in surprise that a simple bird song could bring such joy. A look of recognition lit up her face—*the simple joys of Nature.*

With that insight, she returned to her laptop. Soon, the sounds of her keyboard and the songs outside blended into a harmonious melody in her ears. As she became aware of the transcendence of sound, she murmured to herself, "*The vibration of the universal lyre.* Remarkable." She continued with her work, feeling more than content.

Kate worked for hours, while afternoon slipped into early evening. As she put the finishing touches to her lecture, she stopped and gazed outside to a bevy of birds, now picking the seeds, one after one, as the light cast golden shadows through the branches. Leaning back in her chair, she sipped her cup of tea, thinking how much Thoreau's words resonated with her. She now realized that feelings of loneliness could not co-exist with such blissful solitude.

Watching the last of the birds depart for the night, Kate closed her laptop, turned on her desk lamp, and walked over to sit on the windowsill to listen to the sounds of the coming night. A sense of serenity oozed through her. Leaning back, she absorbed the tranquility of the night. *It is a delicious evening,* she quoted mentally, *when the whole body is one sense and imbibes delight through every pore.* She sat there a long time, taking in the evening, before rousing herself into action.

Returning to her desk after night had fallen, Kate continued reading the journals of her students. This time, however, she scanned down the list to find the most recent entry from Heather. With each submission, Kate felt a rising intrigue slowly replacing her initial reaction of bemusement over what had seemed like a quirky lifestyle. The account of the Vermonters' Thoreauvian *experiment in living,* chronicled by one whose life seemed a perfect blend of thought and action, now made her pause.

Wood Song

> *Since I basically grew up roaming around by myself in the woods—my version of an urban playground—I have gotten to know the sounds of the forest pretty well. Just by listening, I can not only tell which animals are talking, actually communicating, but* <u>*what*</u> *they are saying. I guess listening, really listening, to the sounds of the forest is like knowing several different human languages. You speak French and German—I speak Bird, Bear, and Deer.*

Kate sat back, laughing softly. Sipping some tea, she shook her head, as she imagined Heather telling someone at Harvard that, well, rather than French, she spoke Bear, Bird, and Deer. She returned to the entry with heightened curiosity.

We locals find it kind of amusing when flatlanders talk about the sounds of the forest. There seems to be a pervasive belief among them (by the way, 'flatlanders' are people from places like Massachusetts and Connecticut, or New York) about various sounds they claim to hear there. One of the funniest to me, as well as to most locals, is the insistence by flatlanders that bears 'hoot.' In fact, one of my father's friends actually wrote a book about flatlander myths of life in the North Woods, which he called, Bears Don't Hoot, and Owls Aren't Wise.

Anyone who has been up close and personal with a black bear—which I have been too many times to count—knows they do not 'hoot.' They do make many different sounds, ranging from high-pitched screeching to guttural sounds and snorts when communicating with each other, but hooting is definitely not part of their language. The more time I spend around different animals, like bears, the more I come to understand their distinct language. This is true for any animal. (My father claims it is true for plants, as well, but it takes a special ear to hear the sounds and language of plants.)

I really liked this chapter of Walden. It made me homesick for the woods in my own Walden up north. I used to love to sit and listen to what I called, 'woodsong.' It's a special moment when all of the sounds of the forest blend into one barely perceptible hum, just like Thoreau said about his Walden woods.

But I guess the most beautiful part of life in Walden North is listening to the sounds of silence. As I sit here typing this, my head pounding, (trying in vain to tune out the blaring music of my dorm mate, along with the constant honking of cars, the screams of sirens, and the squeal of car alarms), I try to conjure up the tranquility and true joy I used to experience when being, just being, in the middle of a great, vast, silence. But this is where experience supersedes theory. I need to be there, actually listening to the woodsong—and the silence.

This is probably difficult for you to relate to. You just have to be there, and experience it, to understand what I am trying to communicate.

Imagine, if you can, a place so quiet that the soft sound of an occasional bird's wing flap can be heard in still air. Better yet, go experience the sounds of silence for yourself.

Kate slumped back in her chair, shifting her gaze to the night outside. She tried to imagine hearing only the occasional flap of birdwings in the air. She shook her head. She couldn't ever recall hearing that. She twisted her mouth into a grimace.

She reread the entry again to take in some of Heather's points. Bear language? Animals with sophisticated linguistic systems akin to humans? She continued reading. And plants, as well? The notion seemed preposterous, yet she wondered whether it was due to the inability of urban dwellers living surrounded in noise to experience what Heather had described. She reread the last line:

Go experience the sounds of silence for yourself.

Kate felt a tremor of excitement stir in her. *I'd like to take her up on that challenge.*

Closing down her computer, she got up to call Blake.

"How about a midnight snack?" she asked.

Blake moaned slyly into the phone. "And what type of snack have you in mind?"

Kate sighed. "Oh, Blake, not that kind—a real one. I've been reading student essays all evening, and I'm famished. Thought we could meet up at one of the cafés here in Cambridge." She stopped. "Or is that taking you too much out of your way?"

"Not at all, if you don't mind me holding out hope for a spicy dessert," he retorted. "I'll pop by to collect you."

"Not necessary, Blake," she countered. "Anyway, I could use a little fresh air."

As Kate walked down the streets in the direction of the restaurant, she focused on listening to the various sounds she was hearing in the night air. *Hmm. No flapping of bird wings.* The sudden screech of a car alarm just ahead made her jump. She was dismayed to discover that nothing around her sounded very natural at all.

"Okay—try harder," she admonished herself. Tuning out the drone of the cars sweeping by, she strained her ears for any sound of nature. "Ah, there we are," she murmured, "a dog." Not exactly a *bear,* though, she thought in dismay. The thought triggered an involuntary shudder, as she wondered what Heather had meant by getting up close and personal with a bear. And what did she mean, exactly, by bear language? She shook her head as she arrived at the restaurant. *Intriguing place, that Walden North.*

Blake had chosen his favorite café in Cambridge. As usual, thought Kate with an involuntary scowl. Though she grudgingly admitted to herself that he did have great taste in food, she wished he would request—if even just once—her preference for a restaurant of choice.

"So, Katie, love, what have you a taste for this evening—besides *me*, that is."

Kate felt herself wince. "Actually, I was thinking of something less definitive, more adventurous."

Blake looked crestfallen. "Am I so dull?"

She glanced at him before looking away. "Oh, Blake, I didn't mean it that way. I just meant that I would like to try something new, experience a new flavor."

"A bit chancy, that, lest you choose something not to your liking." He scanned down the menu. "That's why I always go for the tried and true."

Kate nodded. "I'm sure you do," before instantly regretting her comment. Realizing how it must have sounded, she explained, "As do I, usually, but tonight, well, I'd really like to experience something new."

"Well, then, Kate, on to a new culinary adventure," he announced. Leaning over, he asked with a wink, "May I offer some recommendations?"

She exhaled a quiet sigh. "Sure, Blake. Go ahead."

Reading quickly, he looked up with excitement in his eyes. "Have you tried duck *confit*? It's simply *incroyable* here."

Kate crinkled her nose in rejection. "Oh, no duck, thank you. I've just been reading through an elegiac celebration of the sound of bird wings in the air." She smiled at him. "I'd like to continue envisioning birds intact with their wings in flight, rather than as a dinner entrée."

"It'll be quite dead, I can assure you," Blake said in a droll tone, chuckling at his cleverness.

"Thank you, but something vegetarian."

"Well, something exotic, then." He looked over at her with a sensual smile playing at his mouth. "Unless, you'd like to save exotic flavors for—"

Kate put her hand up in the air. "I'm good on that part." Looking down her own menu, she said, "I'll choose something myself, thanks." Over a glass of wine, she tried to share with Blake her experience of reading her student's essay on the world of Walden North.

"Sorry, Kate, can't hear you, love." The sound of people at the next tables laughing and talking, together with the music playing in the background, drowned out her attempts at communication. They ate in silence, unable to talk without shouting.

Once outside, Kate sighed with relief. "Well, that was deafening."

Blake smiled. "Oh, it's part of the *ambiance* of the place. The noise makes it feel like it's the place to eat and be seen, hence the crowds—even at this time of night."

Kate shrugged. "Seems a bit oxymoronic. Doesn't *ambiance* suggest something a little more sonorous and soothing—quiet, even?"

"Well, sometimes, I suppose." He shrugged. "What is it you wished to say to me in there?" Blake took her arm. "Were you inviting me for that promised dessert *chez vous*?"

Kate disentangled herself from his grasp. "You certainly are relentless."

"That's how I get ahead in academia," he said dryly, "Being single-mindedly determined."

Kate offered a sly smile. "Oh, and I thought your success was due to your social status as a young old boy."

"*Touché*. A point for Kate."

Returning the conversation back, she said, "Speaking of being relentless, I was wondering if we could get away this weekend, perhaps go up to your Vermont house?"

He looked at her. "You have been saying you'd like to visit there."

"Yes, I would—very much." She smiled at him. "I am intrigued." Flashing a charming smile, he took her hand, pressed it to his lips and said, "I do have a lot of work to get done, as I'm sure you do, as well, but perhaps we might combine interests, then. Dessert after a weekend of work in Woodstock."

Kate laughed. "Absolutely incorrigible, you are. Sure, you can think of it that way, if you must. I'd really like to experience Vermont."

"And I—you," he whispered into her ear. "Until then."

Turning down his offer of a ride, Kate walked home alone. As she slipped down the dimly lit streets, she focused on listening to the sounds around her, hoping to rejoice in the song of the owl. *At least, I'll know it's not a bear*. She softly chuckled.

Once in bed, she closed her eyes, trying to imagine the sound of silence. Instead, an exchange with Heather flowed through her thoughts:

"We academics truly believe in the primacy of thought over action, or perhaps more particularly, theory over practice, requiring

convincing assertions, postulates, or arguments, rather than experience."

"But what about experimentation, as in scientific experiments?" Heather asked.

Kate shrugged. "Experiments serve mainly to justify the legitimacy of the theory, rather than the other way around."

Just as she was dropping into sleep, Kate heard an owl hooting into the night, *Who cooks for you? Who cooks for you?* A radiant smile slowly spread across her slumbering face, much like the dawning sun shining brilliant beams of light—where there had been darkness.

CHAPTER FIVE

Solitude

LONG, GANGLY TRUNKS OF TREES leaned out over the rounded shoreline, their needled limbs bending down, as if to caress the lapping water below. Sitting down beside the bank, Kate watched a solitary spider skim along a delicate thread of webbing that connected two alternating twigs along a bending branch. As she gazed around, she noticed that the branches softly waved and folded into one another, creating a gentle undulation that seemed to pass through the forest. *Everything is interconnected here.* She took a long, slow, deep breath to inhale this new insight—a tranquil *wholeness.*

Leaning back against the rounded trunk of an aged cedar, Kate watched a ballet of branches shifting, waving, dipping, as an earthy scent wafted through the air around her. Glimpses of soft, yellow light cascaded among the maples and beech, sending waves of gold and emerald tones into the air—before settling down into a blanket of green. She sank back into the comfort of the trunk and sighed contentedly. She felt at one with the place, as if she melded right into the primeval, timeless setting.

Closing her eyes, Kate listened intently to the subtle sounds of the forest around her, as a sonorous refrain, a blend of Heather's and Thoreau's words, seemed to lap in harmony with the soft waves:

The sound of silence.
Alone—but not lonely.
Solitude.

She had found the forest bordering Walden North Pond.

After some coaxing, Kate had finally managed to slip away from Woodstock, saying she wanted to go see Walden North for herself. She and Blake were staying in the guest cottage, formerly the blacksmith's cottage, situated along the perimeter of his mother's Vermont country estate.

"Bit of a bother has come up," Blake had announced with a sigh the night before they were to leave for Woodstock.

"What's that?" Kate asked with concern. She noted the worried expression on his face. "We can still go to Vermont, can't we?"

"Yes, yes, of course, but if we're to make a long weekend of it, I'm afraid that we'll need to hole up in one of the cottages in the back woods along the outskirts of the property, as Mother is preparing for and hosting her grand farewell party. No privacy among that crowd."

Kate visibly relaxed. "That's perfectly fine with me." With a bright smile, she added, "I actually prefer being out of the way. *Solitude*, you know. It's the subject of the chapter I'm teaching next."

"Well, we will be on our own the first two nights, but we simply must join in on the festivities on Saturday evening," he insisted. He regarded her with a pleading expression in his eyes. "You must meet Mother, or I shall never hear the end of it."

"Of course," she said, turning away in fear that her sense of trepidation over meeting "Mother" might be revealed in her expression.

He gently rubbed her shoulder. "But after this weekend, we'll have the main house to ourselves the entire winter."

"It doesn't matter to me," said Kate. "I'm more than fine with staying in a guest cottage."

He responded apologetically. "Are you certain?"

She smiled, her eyes glistening. "Absolutely. I'm just so grateful to be able to get up to Vermont and see it all for myself."

Blake studied her facial expression with concern, as if trying to discern her underlying motivations. "Why are you so taken with the idea of Vermont?"

Suddenly, Kate touched his arm. "Oh, I forgot to tell you something about my family history that I've only recently learned!"

"What is that?" He looked at her as he leaned into her touch.

"I have ancestors here—*blueblood* ancestry, actually," she announced, her tone proud. "In Vermont."

His face elongated, jaw thrust out, as whenever he showed deep interest in a subject. "Oh, do tell, Katie." He grasped her hand tightly.

Letting her hand remain in his, she related the story of her Browne ancestors.

Blake cut in excitedly. "Oh, I know those Brownes," he proclaimed.

"Really?" exclaimed Kate. Was this co-incidence, she wondered.

"They are friends of Mother's, actually," he said with a big smile of relief, as if that were all that mattered. "They both enjoy country estates in Vermont, as well as neighboring ancestral seats in England."

"Well, that makes sense, since the family originated from England," she said excitedly.

He shook his head. "I had never thought to make the connection, as you claimed direct ancestry from Ireland." He glanced over at her. "The Brownes I know are decidedly—and thoroughly—British."

"Well, yes, I suppose they would be. It was one of the ancestral brothers who took up residence in Ireland."

Relinquishing her hand, Blake paced the room as he talked. "In fact, I shouldn't be surprised if one or more of them attend Mother's gala."

"Really?" Kate said. "It would be interesting to meet them."

Blake turned to her, his face flushed. "Indeed," he said absently, still apparently lost in thought, as he continued his pacing.

Abruptly stopping, he snapped his fingers, turning an excited gaze her way. "The perfect introduction to Mother." Squeezing her shoulder, he suggested, "Perhaps we'll call on them, once they learn of your shared ancestry."

"Hmm," murmured Kate. "There's an idea."

Later, as they were driving up to Vermont, Blake glanced over at Kate. "You know, Katie, love, if I am not mistaken, I do believe you may have *inherited* that rapidly evolving transcendental spirit of yours."

She squinted at him. "What do you mean?"

"While I usually do not listen to Mother's precise litany of bloodlines among her social circle, I seem to recall that the Vermont Brownes were, in turn, the direct ancestors of, or at least closely related to some of the transcendental group."

Raising her eyebrow, she asked, "Who, exactly?"

With a dismissive wave of his hand, he said, "Oh, the precise link doesn't matter, really, as much as the general association, but I do believe some then famous transcendentalist member of the family hosted Thoreau on his walks throughout the north here, somewhere near Brattleboro, if I recall."

Kate's eyes lit up. "Really?" she asked in a tone of reverence.

He shrugged and glanced at her. "It doesn't matter which one precisely—as long as you *do* have that connection."

Her only response was to eye him warily, her instincts on high alert.

Blake seemed relieved as he exhaled slowly. "How utterly fortuitous!" He glanced at her again. "I can't wait to introduce you to

Mother as one of the transcendentalist descendants—and a Browne, to boot."

Biting her lip, Kate gazed at Blake with a frown, thinking before she spoke. "Is it that important to you I have elite blood flowing through my veins?"

His expression turned serious, as he pursed his lips to reveal his annoyance. "Never underestimate the cultural power of ancestry," he warned, "particularly in our circles." His eyes assumed a translucent glare.

Kate just shook her head, before turning to gaze out the window at the forested hills. Whatever happened to the idea of success based on one's work, she wondered. She hadn't realized how extensively, even still, the doctrine of predestination pervaded the New England psyche.

Her thoughts shifted to Emerson. Turning back to Blake, she asked, "Whatever happened to the Emersonian urge to repudiate tradition?"

Blake glanced at her, his own thoughts obviously elsewhere. "Yes, Katie, maybe it was Emerson's family, after all, to whom you are related."

Kate just sighed, shifting her attention back to the scenery outside.

Blake had driven in the back way to avoid alerting "Mother" to their arrival. They made their way through a dense stand of immense maples, before passing a hay field, where a towering, ancient barn, more than four stories high, proudly stood.

"We're just behind that barn," he announced, as he drove slowly along a dirt road that meandered around the antique structure.

Situated against the tapestry of maples sat an English-style stone cottage with slate shingles, long windows with shutters, and a thick oak door with a massive wrought-iron handle.

"How absolutely charming," exclaimed Kate excitedly, "like something out of the English countryside."

"Quite rustic, I'm afraid," Blake said, his tone apologetic, "but I have transformed the interior into one grand study of sorts." He glanced over at her briefly. "I come here to write, when the main house, is shall we say, too festive for deep thought."

"You mean to seek *solitude*," she qualified, before breaking out into a wide grin. "I'm beginning to find icons of Thoreau everywhere I look."

Blake waved a finger towards her. "Now don't you go turning yourself into some woodswoman, like that woman in the Adirondacks who, upon reading *Walden*, gave up her wonderful life. She lives in utter isolation from the world, offering a book every few years, chronicling her meager existence."

Kate turned to him in surprise. "Really? I haven't heard of her. I'll have to look her up."

She thought a minute before adding, "But in a way, isn't your blacksmith cottage a version of the same experience—a desire for solitude?"

"Ah, but *Vive le différence!* I have not chosen to live in poverty." He shuddered. "Ghastly notion."

Kate understood immediately upon entering the lavishly restored cottage. Two rooms of equal size conjoined the stone foyer, each decorated in sumptuous leather and mahogany.

"I see what you mean," she said in a tone of reverence. "This place is just beautiful—like those scenes of posh men's clubs in London one sees in various films."

"Precisely the look I had sought," said Blake with a nod, as he gestured toward the room to the right. "I had one of Mother's staff set up a desk for you, as well, so we each may work without discomfort."

Kate scanned the room, which featured a large stone fireplace with a crackling fire, bordered by bookcases cascading round the entire room under a series of leaded windows. What struck her particularly, though, was the position of two immense hand-carved desks in front of the fireplace, yet facing opposite directions.

She turned to him in surprise. "An odd sort of desk placement, isn't it?"

"Oh, Katie, if I were to face you, my mind would wander to various parts of your lovely body."

Kate instantly blushed before turning away.

"This way, we can each gaze at the fire, but feel as if we are alone with our thoughts." He walked over to his desk and set down his computer bag, along with an armful of books.

She revealed a knowing smile. "Yes, that sense of *solitude* again."

Blake looked up, his expression displaying an obvious trace of annoyance. "One must be practical, you know. We are scholars first, lovers, second." He gestured over to the other desk. "That'll be yours. Go ahead and get set up, before I show you round the rest of the place."

He immediately busied himself, arranging his books just so. "Oh, by the way," he said, looking up briefly, "should you need anything, do let me know, though I did have the housekeeper fill your drawers with notepads and other bits I thought you might like."

"Oh, thanks," said Kate. "I'm sure I'll be fine." She brushed her hand along the shiny desk and touched the leather desk cover. "It's absolutely gorgeous, like nothing I've ever seen, really, except maybe in the dean's office."

Busy at his keyboard, Blake didn't look up. "Oh, it's some antique," he said with a dismissive wave of his hand, "I don't know, 18th-century England, I believe. Mother picks up this stuff on her annual pilgrimage there and ships over a container each year."

Typing with a staccato rhythm on his keyboard, Blake looked over with a cursory nod. "Right then, I've turned on the wireless so we can access the Internet." He walked over to her desk. "Let me set yours up, and while I'm standing, why don't we have a quick look around—before settling down to work?"

Taking her hand, Blake led Kate into the adjoining room. While an identical stone fireplace stood majestically in the center of the outer wall, rather than bookcases, pairs of long, leaded French casements flanked either side, offering a view out to the maple forest. She turned round to take in the room. Tall bookcases lined the interior walls, sumptuous leather club-style chairs with ottomans sat scattered around the fireplace, and a long leather couch completed the tranquil setting.

"Reading *salon*," Blake announced, "for *après* work."

"Just beautiful," Kate murmured, as she followed meekly along behind.

He smiled, as he proudly led her through the adjoining room, in the rear of the cottage. "I almost never dine in here, preferring pub grub to nibble on in the *salon*."

They entered a cheery kitchen with soft buttercream cabinets, a large Aga, and an antique maple island. Blake rushed over to one of the ovens in the range, and opening one after another, exclaimed, "Oh good! Supper is already prepared." Turning to her, he asked, "Hungry?"

"Not quite yet, actually," said Kate. "I'm too busy taking in all this elegant charm."

He took her arm, leading her back to the study. "Right then, shall we get to work for a bit—before retiring to the *salon* for a bite and some reading?" He didn't wait for a response, ushering her back to her desk.

Kate sat quietly for some time, gazing alternatively at the fire, followed by the view outside. As the darkness spread over the landscape, the ancient maples transformed into tall silhouettes, exuding a silent majesty. Kate felt the view extinguish her motivation to tackle the mountains of work waiting for her, kindling, instead, a flaming desire to visit Walden North.

She rationalized her feelings by declaring the act of experiencing Walden North *part* of her work—a Thoreauvian *experiment in living*.

She smiled to herself as she laughed mentally over the thought—can't say *that* to the dean. With a soft sigh, Kate turned back to her keyboard and typed away for what seemed like hours.

After some time, they shifted to the *salon*, eating supper round the fire in silence, as each read. Kate had brought along *Walden* to reread the chapter she would present next, before turning to the student reading journals, wondering in particular how Heather had responded to the chapter. She glanced out into the dim evening, the woods offering only shadows here and there. *Solitude.*

When Blake hadn't stirred after completing dinner, Kate stood up, stretched, and began clearing away their dishes. She glanced over at him, realizing with a grimace that he probably never bothered doing dishes with all the butlers hovering about.

"Mind if I make some tea?" she asked.

"Hmm?" With a brief glance up, he murmured, "Oh, sure, Katie, whatever you like."

He watched her walk away. Calling after her, he added, "I wouldn't mind a sniff of the single malt to accompany the tea, love."

"Okay, sure." As she looked back at him, Kate noted that his eyes had returned automatically to the pages of his book.

Blake was so immersed in his reading that he didn't even look up when she re-entered the room. She quietly set down the tea and scotch glass without generating any acknowledgment from him. She peered at him with a caustic look, when the realization hit her that he most likely assumed she was one of the servants. Shaking her head slightly, she sat down without a word and resumed her reading.

Solitude: Alone, but not Lonely

As I write this, sitting alone here at my desk in what feels like a jail full of cells, I must admit that I am feeling both alone and lonely. Thoreau said it perfectly, which made me laugh, despite my sense of despair:

'The really diligent student in one of the crowded hives of Cambridge College is as solitary as a dervish in the desert.'

How is it that this self-proclaimed 'community' of scholars feels so alienating? I watch students and professors racing around campus, almost knocking one another over in their seeming desperation to get to their next lecture or the library. Though, when I first arrived here, I used to say hello to each person who passed me, I have long given up on that—no one ever responded. Instead, I got the once-over, and realizing they didn't know me, simply raced on. Just like Thoreau said in this chapter:

> *'We live thick and are in each other's way, and stumble over one another, and I think we lose some respect for one another . . . We are for the most part more lonely when we go abroad among men than when we stay in our chambers.'*

Yet, despite my intense feeling of loneliness here—the sense of feeling truly alone in an uncaring world—I found myself renewed upon reading 'Solitude.' His descriptions of being in the woods and the sense of rejuvenation it gave him to be there brought back again that sense of <u>*centeredness*</u>*—the feeling I have when I roam the woods back home.*

You'll probably find this hard to believe, coming from a city, and being a professor and all, but there, among the pines and maple, the deer and the bears, I feel what Thoreau describes, 'alone, but not lonely.' The simple joys of solitude.

My father always says that one can never feel lonely in solitude—if we live close to the earth, surrounded in nature. He would quote 'the prophet' declaring:

> *'There can be no very black melancholy to him*
> *who lives in the midst of Nature.'*

I look out of my cell in the 'Cambridge hive' over the campus lights and buildings with people scurrying about like ants. Nature feels very far away—worlds away—from here. No wonder my father chose life in the north woods over this.

Solitude. You have to experience it to understand its nurturing energy.

After reading Heather's entry, Kate sat back. With a slight shake of her head, she let out a heavy sigh. Heather wrote so movingly. She glanced over at Blake, who noticed neither her shift in movement, nor her sigh. She realized that she was feeling a bit lonely herself, despite his presence. Well, she qualified, more like a *detached* presence.

Closing down her laptop, Kate sunk down to relax in the chair, placing each arm on the down-filled armrests. She thought about her reading as she looked around, shifting her attention to Blake, who sat immobile, riveted to his book. He seemed to enjoy his solitude, with his aptitude for such single-minded resolution and focus. She mused over whether he could be anywhere working, such as in the middle of a great forest, or did he require the comforts—Thoreau's *necessary luxuries*—of his privileged lifestyle?

Kate gazed pensively into the fire. Questions floated by in her sea of thoughts. Is solitude a metaphor for a state of mind, a way of being alone with one's thoughts, she wondered, or is it a feeling that emerges upon directly experiencing the vastness, majesty, and tranquility of Nature? She shook her head, as a feeling of sadness overcame her. I don't know. *I am grounded in theory, not experience.*

She closed her eyes, imagining the scenes described by Heather, of walking along seemingly endless, needled paths amid huge trunks, past the pond, before ascending into higher terrain. Her imagination carried her past beaver ponds, winding past maples and beeches, to a forest of softwoods—spruce and fir. Not that she could really distinguish those types of trees, but she so loved imagining the pristine setting. As she nodded off, she felt a sense of tranquility sweep through her. With her last wavering conscious thought, she promised herself that she would experience solitude—alone—in the forest of Walden North. *Tomorrow.*

When Kate awoke the next morning at daybreak, she found Blake hard at work at his desk, a cup of tea by his side. He was so immersed in his writing that he did not hear Kate enter.

"Good morning," she said, nodding to him.

"Ah, sleeping beauty has at last arisen." He blew her a kiss before returning to his keyboard.

She watched him for a few minutes before going over to her desk to check her watch, which she had left there. "It's just after six," she announced, surprised. "What time did you wake up?"

He offered her a charming smile, before bending back over his computer screen. "Oh, hours ago. You know how my insomnia wakens me, so I usually just get up."

He motioned with a brief flourish in the direction behind him. "There are tea and scones in the kitchen. Help yourself," he mumbled, already re-immersed in his work.

She watched him. "Oh, thanks. What are you working on?"

He looked up, revealing a sense of annoyance through his tight expression. "Must get this book review completed and sent out by the end of this weekend, Kate. I'm afraid I'm not much fun," he admitted, shifting his gaze back to his work, "but we did say, with the exception of Mother's gala, we would spend the weekend working."

"Oh, no problem at all," she said lightly. "I have mountains of work to do myself, of course."

After helping herself to a scone and tea, Kate settled down at her computer. Rather than write or read, however, she consulted the Vermont *Gazetteer* to locate the village of Walden North, as well as all the places there to which Heather had referred. Kate planned to make a day of it, visiting the general store, followed by a walk along the pond. If she could manage it, she hoped to find that path leading up to Heather's family cabin.

After jotting down the directions, she got up, tiptoed over to Blake, and whispered, "Blake, mind if I use the car?" She was hoping for an absent nod.

He glanced up her with a look of surprise. "Why, Kate? Do you need something? I can send out—"

"No, it's not that," she countered. "I want to drive up to Walden North. Want to come?" she asked, while turning away, hoping he would say no. She strongly felt that the trip was something she needed to embark on—*alone.*

When Kate turned to face him, she read disapproval written into his grimaced expression.

"Oh, Katie, whatever on earth for? Just a bunch of gun-slinging vets hiding out in the woods up there." He turned back to his writing.

"I need to see for myself what the attraction is," she replied. "My student writes constantly about her life up in Walden North, and now I am more than intrigued."

With a sigh, Blake reluctantly agreed to her proposal. "Well, you might as well go and get this fascination for the place out of your system, once and for all."

With a wide smile, Kate glanced outside. "Plus, it's a beautiful day—perfect for a leisurely stroll along the pond."

He looked up with a frown. "Be careful in the woods, Katie, lest a bear decides to make you his meal, or a hunter his target. They shoot anything and everything that moves up there, so I've been told."

Kate grinned. "Not to worry. My student says that black bears do not attack people unless cornered or provoked."

"Well, I wouldn't want you to get close enough to find out." He offered his boyish smile. "I want to keep you for myself."

Patting his back, she planted a light kiss on the top of his head. "So I've gathered."

Walking over to a bureau, he pulled out a set of keys. "You had better take the jeep. You're apt to need four-wheel drive on those back roads." He turned back to the desk. "It's parked in the carriage house."

What Blake didn't say, of course, was that the jeep was a hundred thousand dollar plus Mercedes. "Some jeep," she muttered, as she saw it glistening in the light, realizing that she would stick out like a sore thumb. She sighed, as she sped along the drive to the main road. Once she hit the interstate, a radiant smile broke through her clouded expression. She was finally doing it—she was heading to Walden North.

And now, thought Kate triumphantly, as she jumped out of the jeep and walked briskly in the direction of the sign pointing to the pond, I'll get to experience Walden North for myself—*at last*. Following along a twisted path through maples and conifers, she arrived at the pond, lined in clusters of billowing evergreens. From her vantage point, it appeared more like a long, narrow lake than an actual pond. The famed Walden North. Standing at the edge of the shoreline, she gazed out over the water. Not unlike Thoreau's descriptions of his own Walden, she observed happily—with its shimmering effervescence of blue and green.

Noticing the general store at the head, together with a few cottages scattered along the more populated section of the pond, Kate headed in the opposite direction, mindful of Heather's directions. Walking along the shoreline, she soon found herself under a canopy of dense growth, some sort of evergreen with small needles she could not identify. It felt so peaceful to her, almost like the sense of sleeping under a mountain of down. The path meandered through different sections of what seemed like an endless forest, where the downy evergreens blended into stands of huge maples, followed by even taller pines. She walked and walked—enjoying the solitude.

At last, like a ship mysteriously appearing through waves of impenetrable fog, the silhouette of a structure faintly emerged among the thick pines. Certainly a more enchanting setting than the photos she had seen of the replica of Thoreau's cabin, located in the parking lot at Walden Woods, Kate thought with a grumble. This seemed to her like the real thing.

She continued stepping slowly around the hefty trunks, as she slowly made her way toward the cabin, now seemingly beckoning her forward in welcome respite from the miles of dense forest. She marveled over how much more remote this place seemed than the description of Thoreau's cabin along the shores of Walden Pond. She shook her head, thinking that Heather's father sure took the *solitude* motif seriously. A line from *Walden* surfaced, as she tried mentally to calculate whether he had taken Thoreau's advice to heart, placing his cabin a *full square mile* from his nearest neighbor.

All she knew was that she felt alone in a magical place—*a world elsewhere*—yet oddly, she noted with delight, not lonely.

Solitude!

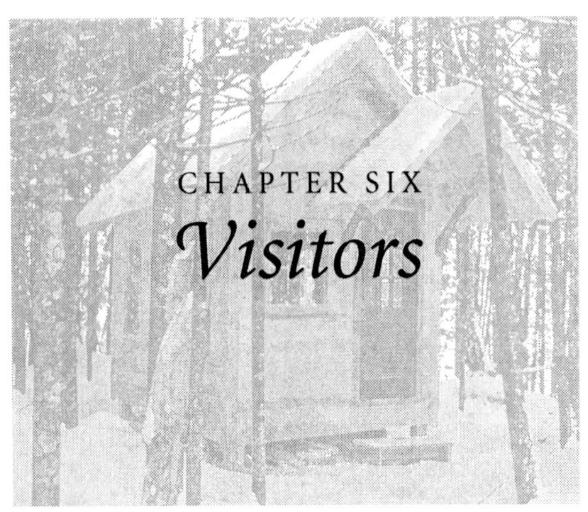

CHAPTER SIX
Visitors

ASIDE FROM THE FLUTED BIRDSONG echoing through the woods all about her, Kate witnessed no signs of active life. She faltered, wondering whether to venture forward and knock on the door. Drawn to the spot at the edge of the woods, she stood gazing around. *So peaceful here.*

Noticing some large pinecones laying half-submerged among a sea of pine needles, she walked over to look at them more closely. Marveling at their size, she realized she had never seen ones of such immensity. After collecting a half dozen or so, she simply stood, looking up along the enormous trunks whose top branches seemed to brush the sky. Their majestic size spoke to their antiquity, but their age, she couldn't even begin to estimate. On impulse, she walked to the base of one of them, carefully laid down her collection, and wrapped her arms around it. She tried to recall the impressions recorded by the Puritans, upon discovering the old-growth forests of New England. As she reached around the trunk without being able to connect her fingertips from each hand, it came to her. It took the girth of seven men's arms to wrap around one solitary trunk. Noting she covered about a quarter of the diameter, she leaned into it and placed her ear against its trunk, as if a seashell, hoping to hear the soft sounds of the woods. Instead, she heard a man's stern voice behind her.

"You've come all this way onto my property to hug my trees," and noting the collection of pinecones, added, "and to collect pinecones?" He studied the enigmatic young woman before him. Folding his arms across his chest, he waited for an explanation.

"Oh, hi," said Kate, as she whirled around, offering a shy smile. "I hope I didn't disturb."

The fellow looked her over as if sizing her up. "I suppose in a manner of speaking," he said, but turning away slightly, he added, "but no harm done."

Kate blushed. "I beg your pardon?"

His brief smile conveyed his meaning. "I guess I should welcome any intrepid visitor who braves what I thought were rather daunting 'no trespassing,' 'private property,' and 'beware of guard dogs' signs."

She looked down.

"Yes, I did notice those signs, and most decidedly yes, they produced their intended effect," she said, before adding dryly, "if fear and trembling were the anticipated outcomes, that is."

"But not enough to deter *you*, I see," he said with a chuckle, as he stuck his hands into his faded jean pockets. As she observed him size her up, he remarked, "You must be more rugged in character than first appearances—and your coordinating urban outfitter attire—indicate."

She grinned. "Yes, my audacity surprises even me."

Trying to hide a smile from involuntarily emerging on his stern face, he added, "And not even a gun to defend yourself against the wild beasts and men who roam these woods."

"A *gun?* Good God, of course not." Meeting his steady gaze, she said evenly, "Besides, we all know, even we, *urban* types, that black bears do not wantonly attack humans just walking through the woods."

He stared at her in surprise. "Well, yes, that is true."

With a tight smile, she added, "And as for the wild men, I think I can fend them off with my lashing tongue."

"Indeed," he said, looking startled. He turned almost as red as his plaid shirt.

She offered a twisted grin. "I thought all you wild men up here were too busy sitting around contemplating nature to bother with other human beings."

"I see you know our ways a bit better than first impressions—like brazenly walking past 'Keep out' signs—would suggest." He gazed at her, waiting.

Again, she locked eyes with him. "I guess you don't know who I am."

He shot back, "Well, if you're the new lister aiming to increase my taxes, you should have thought twice before coming out here without your gun."

Kate shook her head. "A lister? I don't even know what or who that is, so I suppose I am not."

He continued to gaze at her, though his expression revealed a tint of curiosity mixed with intrigue, Kate noticed, despite that he seemed to be trying hard to hide it. "Well, then, what is the reason for your visit?"

She met his gaze. "Gee, even Thoreau was more welcoming of the odd visitor to his abode in the woods. I thought you were a disciple. Don't you remember from *Walden,* his claim that living—'*withdrawn so far in the sea of solitude*'—" Glancing at his rustic cabin, she said pointedly, with a slight toss of her head, "This setting certainly fits that description."

"'*That few came to see me on trivial business*', you mean," completing her reference. He peered at her unsmiling. "So if you're not the lister, then who, exactly, are you? What nontrivial business brings you here? And how do you know of my interest in Thoreau?"

Kate grinned despite herself. "That last one's rather obvious, don't you think?"

He studied her some minutes, before concluding, "I am quite sure that our paths have never crossed until now, as I do believe I would have remembered you."

"Not sure whether that is a compliment or a critique," Kate said with a smile. "No, while we have not met, I suppose it's fair to say that I know a bit about your self-fashioned life of simplicity."

"Did you come all the way here to criticize my lifestyle?" He squinted at her. "How would you know anything about me, seeing we have never met—unless you're from one of the ashrams." He studied her through intense eyes. "No, can't think that you are, as you wouldn't be so critical, and as I said, I would have remembered you."

"Don't mistake intrigue for criticism," she quipped. Noting that he did not apparently see the humor of his question, she added hastily, "I know about you from your daughter, Heather."

He instantly turned away with a groan. "I'm fine with my life the way it is. I've told her repeatedly to stop trying to fix me up—"

"Excuse me," Kate retorted, as she peered at him, "but I can *assure* you, that is not my purpose here." She shook her head and muttered, "a bit presumptuous, don't you think?"

He actually looked embarrassed. "Sorry for the insinuation," he said. "You wouldn't believe all the times, she—well, no matter. So how do you know my daughter?"

"I'm her English professor," she said to a blank stare. When her comment didn't elicit a response, she nervously added, "You know, from Harvard. Hasn't she told you about the freshman seminar on *Walden*, Thoreau's *Walden,* that is, she is taking with me?"

A look of recognition spread over his face. "Yes, of course," he said, "though somehow I had imagined some crusty, old gent in a weathered, tweed jacket discoursing about Thoreauvian philosophy, not some Patagonia-clad female roaming my woods." His somber expression shifted to a slight smile.

"Those would be my colleagues," she said dryly, with a self-deprecating smile, "*all* of them, actually."

"And how did you end up with such a jaded group?" With a decided frown he declared, "Connections, no doubt."

Kate shook her head, offering a lopsided grin. "No, actually, just my research as a female scholar on an *ol' boy* author—Melville, to be exact."

He snorted. "Well, if it's the sea you are seeking, you took a wrong turn," he said caustically, "Somewhere back on Huntington Avenue in Boston."

"I was asked to replace the Thoreau expert who left suddenly on a Fulbright to England," she said with a shrug, "So here I am."

"I see," he said, with a slight bow. "Well, I understand that you are teaching Thoreau, but why, exactly, are you *here* in Walden North, Vermont?" He studied her intently for a moment. "They did tell you, didn't they, those old boys, that Walden was located outside Concord, in *Massachusetts*?"

"Yes, yes, of course," she countered, her tone betraying her rising irritation and disappointment with the exchange. "I guess this was a mistake," she said, turning away. "I'm sorry for bothering you—and for trespassing."

"Which, in particular?" he asked, ignoring the last part of her statement. "Was a mistake for you, that is." He stared, waiting.

Kate looked at him through clearly distressed eyes. "Well, Heather has been writing such poignant entries in her reading journal about her life up in Walden North, that, I was, well, more than intrigued—and wanted, perhaps, *needed*—to experience it for myself," Kate blurted, before blushing. "Hence, my trespassing."

"Reading journals—at Harvard?" He stroked his graying beard, as he studied her with what she considered a mischievous glint. "So Heather has been writing about our life here—in detail?"

Kate smiled, before offering a grin. "Yes, in gory detail."

His taut smile appeared bitter. "She's rejected her childhood already, has she, after a few weeks among the pretentious, culture snobs of Harvard?" With a slight bow, he added, "Present company obviously excluded, of course."

Kate gazed at him in surprise. "No, actually, quite the opposite," she said, ignoring his wise crack, choosing instead, to shift the tenor of the exchange back to Heather. "I think she is longing for her life here and struggling with navigating between the two worlds."

"Ah." His expression softened considerably. "I was afraid of that," he said, with a slight shake of his head.

Noting the pain on his face, Kate felt compelled to reassure him. "Oh, she is fine, really," she said, with a bright smile, "just busy considering her new world at Harvard, along with some of its implications, through what might be called, different—sometimes competing—philosophical lenses."

He bowed, placing his fingers together in what appeared like prayer. "Please, forgive my incivilities. I have truly misjudged the reasons behind your presence here." Straightening up, he looked at Kate with a kind expression. "Most unlike me to sound so rude. You have come a long way to experience Heather's lifestyle, her own *Walden*, literally and metaphorically. Would you care for a cup of tea?"

Kate smiled sweetly at him. "That would be lovely," she said, immediately forgiving him for grilling her. "I didn't bring any water, not realizing that the walk would be so long."

"Of course," he said, with a slight bow. Ushering her into the cabin, he said, "Come this way."

Inside, Kate looked around, noting various details of the interior, just like Heather had described it. She tried to hide her burgeoning smile, when she noticed the chairs.

"What is it you find so amusing?" he asked soberly, as he followed her gaze, before pouring out hot water from a large kettle sitting atop an antique cook stove.

She glanced over at him with a wide smile. "You have the requisite number of chairs, I see," she said, turning to him, "'*One for solitude, two for friendship, three for society*'."

He chuckled. "So that's how you know about my avocation for Thoreau," he said, as he handed her a mug of tea.

"Pretty obvious, don't you think?" Kate bantered, "Though you seem to live farther than '*one mile from any neighbor*.'"

Indicating one of the chairs for her to sit in, he nodded in agreement. "I decided to base my relation to the rest of humanity on his insight that it's best to live separated by one *square* mile."

Kate looked at him with a searching expression. "How big, exactly, is a square mile?" Shrugging her shoulders, she added, "I was trying to do the math as I walked here, but couldn't figure it out."

"Sixty-nine acres," he said.

"My God, that's huge!" Kate exclaimed. "I don't think there's even a quarter acre separating my neighbors in the city." She shook her head. "What am I saying? I live sandwiched in between two neighbors above and below—a matter of feet only."

He nodded grimly. "Ah, yes. I remember all too well."

"How many acres do you live on here?"

"Just over three hundred," he said with a nod.

"No wonder Heather called it her 'extensive playground.'" She looked at him with a sheepish expression. "I'm having real trouble imagining the size of 300 acres."

He smiled at her. "If you came up here by way of the pond, you walked about two miles, through about 100 acres."

Kate's eyes widened. "That's amazing," she remarked in real admiration. "It is just incredible here." She looked over at him with a shy smile. "I've never walked so far in such an untouched and wild landscape."

He half-smiled. "City girl, are you?"

Nodding, she took a sip of tea. "No wonder Thoreau said that freedom lies in preserving the wild."

He smiled. "Yes. '*All good things are wild and free.*'" Leaning slightly toward her, he asked, "Speaking of wild and free, can you tell me how Heather is doing? I know what social challenges she must be facing."

Kate thought his tone sounded bitter.

"Well," she said carefully, "She has trouble tuning out all the noise." Kate smiled. "We're working on how to transcend particular noises, blending them into one sonorous hum from Thoreau's '*universal lyre*'—since we just completed 'Sounds.'"

He nodded sincerely. "That would be helpful. I always found the incessant explosion of car alarms disruptive to my internal tranquility."

Kate glanced out a window to the forest beyond. "I was so entranced by Heather's account of the '*woodsong*,' as she put it, that I came here to listen."

"She wrote about that, did she?" he asked, his tone hopeful.

Kate shifted her gaze back to him. "That's how I knew about black bears, actually." She added as her cheeks reddened, "I would have been scared to death to walk out here alone, otherwise." She shook her head. "You might know that we city girls think of remote areas as potential crime scenes."

He nodded, though suppressing a laugh.

"But," Kate added, "Instead of being afraid, I have been feeling really at peace here." She offered her shy smile. "The place *oozes* tranquility."

He leaned back in his chair. "That's one of the reasons I left everything behind and decided to live up here." He stared at her. "But you probably already know that about me, don't you, having in insider's view of our life here."

Kate instantly blushed. "Oh, not at all. It's not a diary she's writing, after all. It's a reading response journal to the various themes of each chapter." She offered a rueful grin. "I just realized that despite all the time we have been talking, I don't even know your name—or you mine, for that matter—since I only know you by the appellation, 'dad.'"

He now openly laughed. "I seem to have left my social skills behind in Boston." He stood up and walking over to her, extended his hand to shake hers. "How do you do. Welcome to my humble abode, Professor. My name is William, William Channing, though I go by Channing. And yours?"

Smiling, she said, "I'm delighted to meet you, Channing. I am Kate, Kate Brown."

"Nice to make your acquaintance," Channing said, with a slight bow that appeared almost instinctual. "Would you like some more tea?" he asked.

"No, no thank you, though it is really delicious." She turned to him. "What is it?"

"Red raspberry leaf from the raspberries in the woods here."

"Of course!" she said, taking one last sip. "Now that you say that, I can taste the flavor of raspberry. Much more poignant than the boxed teas." She looked at him briefly, before turning away. "If I'm not taking up too much of your time, I'd love another cup, actually."

"Of course," Channing said, his tone formal. He poured her more tea, while commenting, "One of the advantages of life here is wild crafting, as well as growing one's own food. Nothing more fresh or succulent than that."

Kate nodded. "I can just imagine." After drinking down her tea, she stood up. "Speaking of which, though, I must get back," she said, glancing at her watch, "I'd love to walk back through your growing fields. Heather has written about them, though I didn't see any on my way here."

"Of course," he said easily. "I'll accompany you part of the way to your car, while you tell me more about Heather's experiences there." He shrugged. "Without Internet, phone, or cell, I must wait until she returns home to hear about her life."

Looking surprised, Kate said, "Sure. That would be great." She gazed at him silently for a minute, before adding, "In turn, I would love to know more about how you chose to live here and how you enjoy your life—if that's not too personal a request."

Clearing away the teacups, Channing said with a grin, "Sounds like an exchange fit for a philosopher and a wood-chopper."

Kate chuckled. "You really do know your *Walden*. Perhaps you should be teaching it, instead of me."

He looked at her in curiosity. "I may be equipped through disposition and experience, but my doctoral training is in linguistics, as you must know."

Kate gazed at him in awe. "You have a doctorate?" she blurted. "I wouldn't have known—"

He directed a bemused look at her. "You remind me a bit of old Henry David yourself. If you remember your *Walden*, particularly the chapter, 'Visitors,' you might recall Thoreau's astonishment that a simple-looking woodchopper could wax poetically and philosophically to rival Homer."

"I didn't mean—" Kate turned away.

He smiled pointedly, before quoting, "'*There might be men of genius in the lowest grades of life*'."

Kate's cheeks blushed beet red. "I didn't mean to suggest that you seemed ignorant." She turned to look at him. "Did you ever do anything with your doctorate?"

He gazed at her somberly. "Yes, I moved here."

She looked away, choking on her words. "What I meant was, did you teach or conduct research?"

He looked at her without speaking. Finally, he said quietly, "I taught at Harvard—like yourself."

Kate stopped abruptly. "You *did*?" She instantly regretted her tone, but her sense of complete astonishment overwhelmed her sense of decorum. She didn't want to insult him, however odd he seemed to her.

"Well, you needn't sound so surprised," Channing protested. "Don't I look the part?" He gave a half shrug. "I see that Heather hasn't provided you with all the details of our life here, after all."

"Um, not exactly," she said. With a brief glance at him, Kate shot back, "Haven't seen too many ripped plaid-shirted, faded jean-clad, wildly long-bearded men among my colleagues." She twisted her mouth into a wry grin. "You must be from a different department—maybe the theological school?"

Snorting, he countered. "Well stated."

"Well?" she asked, her tone more serious. "I'd really like to know."

Glancing over at her, Channing said, "All right, then. I was a Harvard undergrad, who went to MIT for my doctorate, before returning to Harvard to teach."

She looked at him, her eyebrow arching involuntarily. "Really?"

Channing glanced at her a trifle annoyed. "Well, yes," he countered. "I have a joint doctorate in linguistics and biochemistry, of all things."

Kate studied him a moment, before shaking her head slowly. "Can't figure that one out. How are they connected?" she asked.

"I did my dissertation, under a world-renowned linguist there, on the linguistic systems of plants."

Kate's eyes widened, as a look of recognition spread across her face. "Oh, that explains your talking to plants, then," she remarked.

He turned to her, offering a bemused smile. "Oh, so you do know about that?"

She smiled back, trying to smother a rising laugh. "Only that you talk to plants in some Native American-like way that results in highly bountiful yields."

Snorting, he folded his arms across his chest, while nodding his head back and forth. "I suppose that's one way of referring to my work."

Studying him a moment, Kate said, "Somehow, I don't picture you, or your research, at Harvard."

"That is one of the reasons I am here," he said, nodding grimly, "though I have written extensively about plant communication."

The information triggered some memory in Kate. "Oh, that's right," she exclaimed. "Didn't you help start up some sort of botanical meditation center in the Berkshires—after spending time in northern Scotland at that renowned spiritual retreat for gardeners?"

His laugh was deep, yet warm, despite his attempts at restraint around his bold visitor. "I've never heard it described in quite those terms, exactly, but yes, I did on both accounts." Averting his gaze, he exclaimed in a somber tone, "That is where I met Heather's um, mother, in the Berkshires, I mean, where she was doing a spiritual retreat at the neighboring ashram." Shrugging, he added, "The rest is history—on all counts."

Kate averted his gaze. The conversation was taking a more personal turn than she had expected. Suddenly, she turned back to face him. "Oh, I remember now what Heather said."

Channing looked at her with a stern expression, as if to ward off any painful comment that might emerge. "Yes?"

Kate smiled at him. "She said you started up a spiritual retreat to meditate away bugs and other garden pests."

He burst out laughing. "Well, that would be her child-like perspective on our work there," he said, with a shake of his head. "I remember how she used to try to catch the beetles flying away after a meditation session. She was even born there."

"I had no idea such things existed."

Opening the door for her, Channing returned her glance with his own amused expression. "Hey, don't forget your collection of pinecones," he counseled, waving his arm towards their location under the pines.

"Oh, thanks," Kate said, her cheeks flushing a soft pink. "I've never seen ones so big."

Channing suppressed a smile while he watched her scurry over to collect them. "Not unlike a squirrel," he mumbled in amusement.

When she returned, clearly delighted over her find, Channing couldn't help himself. "You do remind me of the various visitors to Thoreau's cabin, who took such simple delight in collecting pinecones, like you, or rust-colored maple leaves." He peered at her with eyes that seemed to penetrate her thoughts.

Looking away, Kate said with in an airy tone, "The simple joys of Nature, I guess. Rather medicinal—therapeutic even—this being in the woods."

"I call it *transcendent*."

She responded with amusement. "Of course you do. I wouldn't expect anything else."

He shot her a guarded look of curiosity, mixed with begrudging respect. "Perhaps you have internalized the teachings of *Walden* more than you acknowledge."

Surprised, she looked at him with a searching gaze, as if to identify what he was seeing in her. "Um, perhaps—oddly enough, my dean said as much."

Along a winding path blanketed in pine needles, they walked in silence, each sorting through the various threads of their conversation.

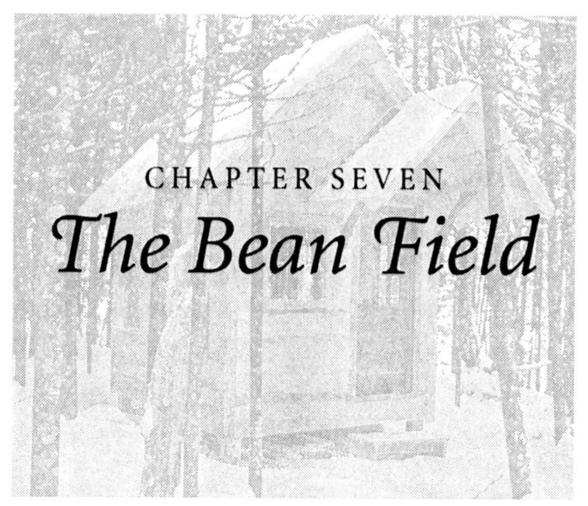

CHAPTER SEVEN

The Bean Field

THEY SOON ARRIVED AT AN EXPANSIVE CLEARING. It stretched, for what seemed like to Kate, miles in every direction. She looked over at Channing in awe.

"These are all your vegetables?" She shook her head as she gazed out over the field. "My God! It's huge!"

He only smiled, saying nothing. Glancing from his field to her, he said, "Not really. Only about twenty acres."

Kate scanned the field, trying to identify the various crops growing there. "What are they?" she asked, before grinning, "Don't tell me." She looked at him with an earnest, though bemused glance. "It wouldn't be *beans*, now would it?"

Channing shot her a sharp glance that cut short her mirth. He was nothing if not serious about his *experiment in living*.

"Yes, of course." He glanced at her again, though less severely, before turning away. "Several different kinds. Started the season with about a dozen or so different types—though now," he said with a wave of his hand, "this time of year just a few, including edamame, for fall harvest." He bent over, gently touching some plants.

Kate was surprised to discover that the implacably stern air of detachment, she had so far experienced with him, had suddenly transformed into a soft tenderness. His glance appeared loving, as he assessed their growth. "They're still coming along well," he said more to himself than to her. "Unusually warm autumn." He nodded. "Indisputable proof of global warming, I'm afraid."

"Really?" she asked. "It must be a daunting task to grow so many vegetables—in any climate." She studied the lines on his face and the way his hair seemed bleached from the sun. "How do you do it all yourself?" She looked back over the field. "Looks like a lot of work."

His glance was somber. "It's not work," he said, turning his back to her. "It's a *lifestyle*."

Kate turned to him, silently studying his back. "A lifestyle? I never thought of growing beans that way."

She walked over to him, and when she met his eye, offered a bemused expression. "Actually, I don't think I have ever thought about growing beans in *any* way at all—until now."

Channing studied her a minute, before responding, looking as if he were deciding whether to bother explaining—or take the risk. At last, he shrugged and remarked, "Why would you? You teach at Harvard and probably buy your vegetables at some franchised grocery store."

Her response was immediate. "I do teach *Walden*, you know," she shot back, her tone clipped. "I am expected to know all aspects of the book."

Channing seemed amused by her comment. "Oh, I doubt the ol' boys expect you to know about growing beans." He waved his hand in the direction of his field. "They most likely assumed Thoreau thought of beans as a *metaphor*, not as something actually planted, grown, harvested, eaten, and preserved."

Kate offered a sheepish grin. "Most likely." She thought back to her exchange with the dean. "Yes, I believe I was informed about what my dean called '*the primacy of theory over experience.*'"

Channing nodded his head curtly. "It was precisely such attitudes that drove me to seek out an alternative lifestyle—this one," he added, as he glanced at Kate, "one grounded in literal, not metaphorical, nature."

A gentle breeze grazed the rows of beans, now resembling ripples of waves in an undulating, green sea. He turned to her. "Actually, it was 'The Bean Field' chapter, if I remember correctly, that inspired me to start up my line of research, eventually resulting in my leaving everything behind to come north."

She peered intently at him, as if trying to read in his expression the source of his motivation. "What about it, exactly?" Before he could respond, she quipped, "Intrigued by a dinner of roasted woodchuck, were you?" She offered a pointed smile.

He laughed, despite his stern affect. "I suppose it was related to the woodchuck incident," he said, before qualifying his statement, "though, of course, I am a vegetarian." He shot her a knowing look.

"Of course you are," Kate rejoined, trying to hide the smile that she was sure circled her mouth. "You'd be missing out on a large part of Thoreau's—and your own—*experiment of living*," she said, "if you weren't."

Kate watched him size her up to discern whether she was mocking him, but apparently convinced of her sincerity, he continued. "I decided that an alternative to acting against one's philosophy, as in the case of Thoreau, was to simply meditate the woodchuck away."

She turned to gauge his seriousness. "And did it work?"

Smiling, Channing said, "Well, yes—eventually."

Kate shook her head. "Amazing."

"No, not really. It's not so difficult communicating with other organisms when one learns how."

Her tone reflected the wonder she was feeling. "Tell me more about your *experiment in living,*" she urged him. When he didn't respond, she added softly, "I'd really like to know."

"Well, perhaps we should add some beans to your souvenirs of pinecones to take with you as we talk," Channing said with a shy glance at her, before turning to pick some beans.

"Sure," Kate agreed enthusiastically. "I've never picked beans. Can't wait to share this experience with my students when we get to 'The Bean Field' chapter."

Channing gazed over the field. "I think about that chapter each season when I plant the beans, as well as harvest them," he said softly. "The idea of digging into the soil as people have done for thousands upon thousands of years, being part of an annual tradition of growing one's own food, well," he said, with a furtive glance back at Kate, "it's one of those life experiences that is truly transcendental."

Kate studied him a minute or so before speaking. Tilting her head slightly, she said, "I am trying to imagine it."

"It's not easily imagined, nor can its transformative power be reduced to metaphor. You have to experience firsthand—the sweat, the taxing physicality of preparing the fields, coupled with the simple hope," he glanced over at her, as he nodded, "the 'faith in a seed,' as it were, followed by the joy of discovering myriads of green shoots stretching into the air, the absolute feeling of responsibility to caretake, nurture, and encourage growth; well, I could go on and on," he said with a rare, almost self-deprecating smile, "much like the elegiac passages of Thoreau's homage to beans."

Kate smiled at him in admiration. "You definitely speak his language." She looked at him with a growing sense of respect. "It's very admirable—inspirational even," she murmured.

Turning away from him, she looked out over the field, lost in thought for some minutes, before turning to him again. "Speaking of Thoreau's language, can you tell me more about your research on the language of plants?" With a slight blush, she admitted, "I never thought anything like that was possible."

He glanced down at her. "There exist entire levels of life, of which the majority of humans are unaware today," he started, "though such understanding once formed an integral part of our human interaction with the world around us."

She nodded, silently urging him on.

"Bits of this knowledge and understanding can still be found amid different cultural groups, even today," he said, turning toward her. "Surely, you have read about Native American claims that at a previous period in our collective history, humans were able to communicate easily with other animals, or about the ability to heal others remotely, Tibetan monks engaged in levitation, and other mystical accounts." Channing gave a brief shrug. "In short, knowledge that has survived in bits and pieces through the ages."

Kate looked at him with a searching expression, her head tilted slightly to one side. "Yes, but I never realized that one could communicate with plants."

"That's where the biochemistry comes in," he explained with a nod. "There's an entire world of extra-species communication that occurs among plants, insects, animals, and even the fungal kingdoms, not unlike how humans speak to one another, though more complex, and, I would argue, significantly more sophisticated, than our own meager vocalizations and body signs. We humans have barely tapped into our cognitive and spiritual abilities to communicate telepathically through such channels with one another, let alone with other life forms, such as plants." He spoke in a torrent, not unlike a stream in spring overflowing from snowmelt.

She stared at him as if transfixed. "Utterly fascinating. Go on."

Glancing at her briefly, Channing resumed his gaze over his field.

"When I read about some people along the barren sand dunes of the North Sea in northern Scotland, who were not only growing plants in a location thought impossible, but grew vegetables, like cabbages, for example, yielding 40 lbs. in weight," he said, taking a quick breath, before continuing, "by communicating with the plants through *meditation,* I knew I had to learn more. I wrote up my dissertation proposal and spent the next few years researching and living at the intentional community called Findhorn."

Kate revealed her confusion over following his explanation. "What's an 'intentional community'?"

Offering a curt nod, he said, "Not part of the Harvard vocabulary, is it?"

She smiled shyly. "No, I should think not. It sounds a bit too grounded in experience—you know, too *intentional.*"

Channing shook his head, if somewhat sadly. "Yes, I know precisely what you mean." He resumed picking beans. "Intentional communities are also known as communes, but not necessarily your understanding of that term, as in a '60s free love sort of way."

Kate suppressed a smile upon imagining this stern man in a free-love commune.

"They are communities created largely for a group of like-minded souls to live according to some expressed philosophies, such as social justice, harmony with nature, or the like."

Channing glanced over at Kate to gauge her reaction to the concept. Apparently satisfied, he continued, "In the case of Findhorn, the community was founded upon insights into the spiritual nature of life and our ability as humans to communicate with the spiritual essence of other organisms—even the divine itself."

As he turned to her, his look, Kate noticed, revealed a palpable fear that his ideas must surely sound too unconventional for the urban academic listening to him. His question confirmed her intuition.

"Shall I continue?" He continued to look at her guardedly.

"That's a lot to take in," confessed Kate. "I don't know what to think, but sure, tell me more."

As they walked slowly down the rows, picking beans here and there, Channing continued talking, explaining his research in simple terms. "Surely, you have experienced how a plant, placed near a window, for example, will grow toward the light emanating from it."

Kate nodded. "Yes. Yes, I have, of course." She wondered whether he considered her completely ignorant of botanical truisms. She twisted her mouth into a wry grin. "We did have plants inside the library, you know, and yes, they grew toward the light outside."

With an audible snort, Channing glanced at her before continuing. "Well, plants also have the ability to grow toward sounds they like, such as soft harmonic music or sonorous voices, as well as grow away from those they do not."

"Really?" She stared at him.

He briefly met her gaze, before averting his once again. "Yes, actually, they do." He bent over to pick some more beans, before resuming his explanation. "In fact, plants communicate with others in the same room—warning them, for example, when danger is approaching, as in a human picking something from them, or even worse, when a branch is about to get cut."

Kate stopped. "But how do they do that?"

He looked over at her. "It's rather complicated, but basically, through a combination of chemical and electromagnetic signals that they instantaneously emit to the others, as well as, perhaps, of course, through telepathy."

"I had no idea." Kate stared in wonderment over the novel ideas.

Channing offered a brief smile. "Oh, that's just the most basic of their abilities," he said with a brief nod. "They can size you up to determine whether you are friend or foe, based on the type of energy you emit, and move in toward you or away from you, depending on your intent. Trees in a forest, for example, do that often."

"Is that really possible?" Kate wasn't sure about how much credibility to grant the fellow, despite his MIT education. His account of the life of plants was like nothing she had ever heard or studied.

He gave her the briefest of nods. "Their communicative abilities are more extraordinary than you can imagine," he said in a clipped tone. "And I haven't yet explained their communication underground, which is truly incredible."

"So how do you communicate with them?" Kate asked.

"Through meditation," he responded. "Plants and animals have the ability to read our minds as well as communicate directly with us, as we can with them." He looked at her with a searching glance before speaking. "If you have ever had a dog with whom you bonded, you would understand how dogs can intuit when you are planning to leave them, before you even begin preparations for departure." He added with a nod, "They simply read your mind."

Kate shook her head. "Although I have heard of that from some dog lover friends, I have never personally experienced it." She stood looking at him. "So, what you are saying is that humans can engage in mental telepathy with dogs, with plants, and with things like bugs?"

He smiled at her. "Yes, and with bears, and deer, and birds. In short, with all of creation—including water."

"Amazing," she said softly, with a sidelong glance, "though difficult to believe."

"It isn't a matter of belief." He looked at her with a stern expression. "It is not a matter of theology; it is actual *science*—biology, chemistry, physics, and psychology—with a bit of metaphysics thrown in."

Kate gazed at him, while she shook her head gently. "Absolutely incredible."

Channing smiled at her, while extending his hand to give her some beans. "And that, in short, is what we do up here. We talk to our plants, we meditate away pests, we commune with our trees—in short, we 'walk the walk.'"

Kate shook her head. "I had absolutely no idea such a lifestyle existed." She smiled at him. "I am completely in awe."

He studied her with a sober expression. "Ready to 'walk the walk,' are you, then?"

"No, my job is to 'talk the talk,'" she countered, offering him an apologetic smile, before turning away to hide her growing sense of embarrassment—or shame—she was feeling. She didn't know which.

His tone sounded terse. "I thought as much."

With a shake of her head, Kate looked back at him. "Besides, I've bought into the very economic system against which Thoreau rails in his first chapter." With a slight flush and a toss of her head, she said, "I'm mortgaged to the hilt, maxed out on my credit cards, and paying on a car loan."

"Indeed, all to which you voluntarily 'enslave' yourself, in order to teach students at Harvard the philosophies of Thoreau!" The downturn of his mouth spoke volumes to her.

With a decided shake of her head, Kate admitted, "It does sound rather contradictory, doesn't it?" She turned away with a burgeoning sense of her own despair over the ineluctable truths of his analysis.

Channing nodded slightly, and noticing her embarrassment, said more gently than usual, "The economic system of leveraging, together with a philosophy that posits luxuries as necessities, are so deeply embedded in our cultural psyche that we find it almost impossible to stand outside of it to critique it—unless we read, *really* read, commentators like Thoreau, who describe the '*lives of quiet desperation*' that result from economic systems like ours."

Kate regarded him with a deeply pensive expression. "Until this enlightening conversation, I had never considered that a lifestyle such as yours would be a conscious, um, positive choice."

Channing gave a brief shrug. "There are plenty of us deliberately holed up in the woods to sow the literal—and the metaphorical—seeds of a Walden North lifestyle."

Kate gave him a warm smile. "It's gratifying to know that some people exist out here, like you, and many of your neighbors, it sounds like, who actually do both—'walk the walk,' as well as 'talk the talk'—that is."

He gazed over at her with a knowing look. "Watch out—'*way leads onto way*'—as the good poet said. Perhaps you will come to give up talking for walking."

Kate offered a sly grin. "Sounds like you already have more than enough self-styled Thoreauvians up here, living in log cabins in the woods without me adding to the mix." Shaking her head, she added, "Besides, I couldn't swing an axe if my life depended on it."

Channing shot her another pained look. "There's always a chainsaw." He shrugged again. "Anyway, our lifestyle up here has been labeled a 'local food movement' by mainstream media."

Kate offered a bright smile. "That sounds rather *ground-breaking*."

Channing gave a snort. "Clever pun," he said with a nod, before redirecting his thoughts, signaled through a downward turn of his mouth. "Many of us found it rather amusing when celebrity journalists, reporters, and even renowned chefs flocked to our little world here to announce the new movement on the six o'clock news and in the *New York Times*."

"Really?" Kate asked, her tone betraying her astonishment.

"Even the *Wall Street Journal* covered the story." He shook his head in disdain.

"That's pretty impressive," Kate said with a nod.

As he opened a bag that he had slung around his shoulder, filling it with beans, he continued. "With Dewey College in the next village, students and others interested in getting back to the land have been settling here for generations, actually. Everyone around me is organic, as well as largely food independent—actions that have no allegiance to the political attitudes of 'preppers.'"

Flicking his arm, he indicated to her to help pick some more beans. "And what we might not grow or raise ourselves, we get in exchange through a sort of informal bartering system."

Kate stopped dead in her tracks. "You mean without money? How intriguing—and *Thoreauvian*."

"Yes, indeed." Channing nodded in agreement. "We even host a seed exchange each year, where we can barter different seeds, as well as cultivars, and for those who raise animals, select breeds."

"Sounds like you all are quite organized." She smiled. "No wonder it's called a 'movement.'"

"Oh, I think people in rural areas have been doing such things for hundreds of generations," he said, nonplussed, "though here in Walden North, it started as a 'buyers' club,' so to speak, an attempt to bring in high-quality foods, we either couldn't get in the stores, or needed to buy more inexpensively." Channing shrugged. "Though we may be rich in wholesome organic foods, we don't have much money or luxurious lifestyles."

Kate noticed that he was starting to relax with her, most likely over her patently sincere interest in his lifestyle.

Channing offered a sheepish grin. "I admit I occasionally relish a good hot shower, plumbing, and bright lights overhead."

She looked at him in surprise. "You don't have electricity or plumbing—even with the high price for organic foods?"

His tone reflected a tinge of impatience. "As I said, it's a lifestyle."

A look of understanding descended upon her. "So it's not a matter of money?" She stopped to rephrase her idea. "Rather, a sort of Thoreauvian *simplicity*?"

He shrugged his shoulders. "Well, perhaps originally for more than a few of my neighbors and friends, money was an issue, but it quickly evolved into a way of life. You know, alternative energy, an alternative lifestyle."

"Really?" Kate asked with a shake of her head. "Even *today*?"

"Well, yes," Channing said in a tone that betrayed more than a hint of irritation. "Some of my friends who run financially successful organic businesses have opted to remain with their wood-fired ranges, from which they do all their cooking, as well as heat water for bathing, for example. They also rely on outhouses or composting toilets, rather than bother with the complexities of plumbing."

"You sound like you've started a Church of Thoreau, taking a *Waldenesque* vow abstaining from central plumbing." She grinned over her clever hyperbole.

Channing was not amused. "Spoken like a true academic," he snapped. "You are intrigued by the *idea* of something, but not its reality."

Kate turned away from him and sighed. "I suppose you're right. As my dean proclaimed, we live a life that celebrates the 'primacy of theory over experience.'" She turned back to meet his eye. "It's just that your, your lifestyle, well, it sounds rather *extreme*."

Channing studied her before speaking. "I don't suppose you have ever considered central plumbing and electricity as political acts that carry, to use your word, *extreme* ramifications."

Her green eyes flashed red as she countered. "And how is that, exactly?"

"Quite *simple*, really," he batted back. "Central plumbing relies on petrochemicals in its construction and its ability to function. Electricity and electrical grids, likewise. And in order to have petrochemicals to operate these systems, the country involves itself in controlling, if not outright destroying, other countries rich in petroleum, so that you can turn on a light switch at will."

Kate stared at him, now wide-eyed, but saying nothing.

Channing turned to look at her. "And for those petrochemicals that do not originate from countries we have forcefully subdued in order to supply our country with cheap oil, we simply poison our own land by shooting toxic chemicals into the ground, resulting in increased earthquakes and poisoned water supplies, in order to extract shale oil, so you can have central plumbing." He frowned, as he stared at her through steely eyes. "Up here in Walden North, we would call *those* extreme acts."

Kate shook her head. "I admit; I have never, *ever*, thought of electricity and plumbing in those ways."

He smiled. "It seems both less extreme and a hell of a lot simpler to heat your water on a woodstove, and use a composting toilet."

She turned away slightly. "And I thought his comments about living without plumbing, eating locally, and living a simple life were antiquated—quaint ideas for a *previous* century—not this one."

"I wouldn't repeat that too loudly up here," he remarked sharply.

Kate picked beans, saying nothing.

He continued harvesting as he spoke, his back now to her. "And I should think *extreme* is an adjective that aptly characterizes the economic system in which you are embroiled, one that involves a precarious balance between spending and debt, luring you into economic servitude—with the promise that in thirty years' time, you will be economically unencumbered, through finally owning your own house outright—of course, after having paid out in interest, three times its value to some bank."

"Oh, my God," she exclaimed. "I've never really considered those points."

He glanced back at her. "Not so different from the economic circumstances Thoreau described in chapter one of *Walden*, he aptly called 'Economy.'"

Kate stopped picking, to gaze at him. "Well, I'm beginning to see that there's an entire worldview associated with growing your own food." She shook her head. "So much to think about."

"Might I suggest something," Channing said with a smile. "Why don't you take a walk down some of the rows of beans, and experience, firsthand, what it is like to stroll down a twenty-acre field of beans, imagining the generations and generations of people before you, who have walked those very fields, sowing their bean seeds." He shrugged, while displaying a playful frown. "It may help you to process some of my rant."

"Well, sure," she said, "that sounds like a good idea."

He almost looked charming in that rare moment of self-deprecation. "Besides, I'm sure you'd like to ensure that I have left the weeds growing among the beans, as the bean guru had encouraged."

"Of course," she bantered. "I won't bother looking out for any woodchucks, though, since I know you have already meditated them away."

When he grimaced, Kate added hastily with a grin, "Sorry, couldn't resist. But I know that you have sown the metaphorical seeds of truth and sincerity among the various bean seeds here."

Channing offered only a curt nod in response.

Smiling amiably, Kate asserted, "Of that, I am absolutely convinced."

"Thank you," he finally said, in a tone of humility. "We certainly do try to live according to the ideals of *simplicity* and all that comes with it."

Kate gave an enthusiastic nod. "That is really obvious." Glancing at her watch, she gasped, "Oh, I must leave—I have a function, I absolutely must attend."

"Oh?" he asked, with a slight tilt of his head.

She looked up at him. "Funny, how time has just flown by here. This is the first I've checked my watch."

He nodded, his mouth now taut. "Yes, and in that one glance, the world of social expectations came crashing down upon you—like lava from a volcanic eruption."

"Well," she said, looking down.

He gazed at her flushed cheeks. "I can see the stress already clouding your sunny expression."

Kate put her hand to her face. "Is it that obvious?"

He shook his head slowly as he spoke in a gentle tone. "Yes, it is. Up until this moment, you have been '*living as deliberately as Nature*' for one day of your life. Your expression has radiated the sense of simple joy you have been experiencing, in discovering your pinecones, for example, in walking under the trees—even taking in this field."

Kate looked at him, surprised by his observation. "Really?"

He offered a brief smile. "If you lived here, you would soon discard that watch, learning, instead, to experience time in a different way."

"How is time different here?" she asked, intrigued by the notion.

Nodding, he added, "Remember the words of the great teacher: '*Time is but a stream. I would drink deeper*'. You would soon soak in Nature's time, not the time of social appointments."

"Ah." Kate gave an apologetic frown. "I never take off my watch, even while I'm sleeping."

Channing folded his arms across his chest. "Don't tell me you also sleep with your cell phone on next to your bed."

Turning to meet his eye, she said, "I can't imagine my life without my watch and cell phone."

Shaking his head slightly, he commented, "As I said, this is a lifestyle, as well as a life philosophy."

"Yes, I am beginning to see that."

With a sigh, as if in a class full of students counting the minutes until the end of the session, Channing said with resignation in his voice, "Well, perhaps you can think about Time as you saunter through the bean field. You can follow the path back to your car at the end of it. Just a short distance to the parking lot near the pond." He gave her the bag of beans. "Here is a souvenir of your trip to Walden North."

Kate smiled brightly. "Well, thank you. I don't think I've ever had so many beans. They'll make many a dinner for me."

He looked at her briefly, before turning slightly. "So you're rushing back to Cambridge? At this time of day?"

"No, actually, to a town called Woodstock where I am staying."

Turning, he held up his hand to stop her. "You needn't tell me more. I get the picture of the type of 'function' you will be attending. Worlds apart from here." His tone had settled into one of obvious irritation.

She rolled her eyes and said with obvious sarcasm, "Now that's an understatement, if ever I heard one."

"Well, good-bye then." Bowing slightly, Channing joined his fingertips from each hand. "Please say hello to my daughter for me and urge her to come home soon," he said, his tone turning wistful. "I miss her terribly."

Kate felt sorry for him in that moment. "I'm sure you do," she said tenderly, "but if it's any consolation to you, Heather seems to be adhering to the principles by which you reared her."

"I know what she is up against," he said, his mouth a grim line. "It's a tough balance to navigate between living according to principles grounded in a philosophy of simplicity and the lure of social status and luxury."

He flicked his hand. "As someone leaving here for socializing in Woodstock, you might know of which I speak." He looked hard at her.

Shaking her head involuntarily, as if to ward off his disapproving stare, Kate responded, "Well, I'll make sure to share with her my truly insightful experience here, talking with you."

Channing hesitated before speaking. "I appreciate your looking out quietly for her. Um, thank you." He bent slightly and folded his hands, his fingers again projecting upward.

Kate smiled, her eyes bright. "No, thank you, for your time, your insights, and your . . . well, patience, with what must have been for you, highly irritating questions."

Channing only nodded, as if to dismiss her, and with one wave before turning, said, "Good luck on the tightrope between talking and walking."

And with that, Kate walked in respectful awe along what felt like endless rows of beans, as bits of their exchange floated along through her memory. She smiled over her remark about his sowing the seeds about which Thoreau had written—actual beans, as well as the seeds of *sincerity, truth, and simplicity.*

Kate glanced back once more, before entering the woodland path along the pond. Channing remained in his field, tending to his beans. As she looked at him a final time, she found herself thinking, such sincerity and commitment to an almost arcane philosophy were more than impressive—they were truly *inspirational.*

She walked back along the pond—deep in thought.

CHAPTER EIGHT

The Village

AN ELABORATELY SCROLLED SIGN announced the entrance to the village. Kate drove slowly along the road, eager to see what Woodstock offered, since she and Blake had arrived at the country estate from along a back road. She glanced in both directions to take in the array of charming buildings, faced with even more attractive storefronts. People thronged the sidewalks, carrying shopping bags of merchandise likely purchased from the staggering array of clothing, artisanal, and antique shops that lined the road. She found herself so intrigued by the place, that she decided to stop at one of the cafés for a quick chai.

Stirring her tea with a slow, deliberate movement, Kate glanced surreptitiously around at the other tables, noting the sophisticated level of fashion adorning each patron. Diamond rings and highlighted hair glittered in the sunlight, while elegantly attired men and women, looking as if they had just come off the golf course or tennis court, leaned back leisurely, many with sweaters tied round their necks.

She imagined them chatting about their matches—and their latest investment returns. She smiled to herself, as she leaned forward. So *this* is Woodstock, she thought. It all felt so seductively enticing—a world apart from Walden North and the bean field.

Reluctantly finishing her drink, Kate headed back to her car. She made her way along the road into the postcard-perfect countryside, following the directions Blake had given her. Not long after, she arrived at a set of stone pillars with a massive wrought-iron gate. She pressed the buzzer, only to see the gate slowly open. Before her, a winding drive wrapped around stately maples and late-season flowers. Continuing along the road for almost a mile, she glimpsed the residence up ahead. "Some country house," she muttered. As she reached the stone-pillared portico, a tuxedo-attired man opened her door, saying he would park her auto, while another similarly clad man opened the front door. Kate could hear the faint sound of laughter and conversation.

Inhaling deeply, she walked hesitantly into the grand entrance foyer, unsure of how to proceed. Through a series of cascading drawing rooms, she glimpsed, through glass French doors, groups of people flowing outside onto a stone terrace. She looked down at her hiking boots, vest, and jeans, realizing that she couldn't possibly join the party looking like she did, and wondering where and into what, exactly, she should change. With a nervous glance, she gazed at the scene outside. She felt rooted to the floor.

Kate was startled when, someone from behind her, cleared his throat. Turning around, she saw the butler bending down to retrieve her bag from her clenched hand.

"Dr. Brown, if you would be so kind as to follow me, I shall direct you to your suite. Perhaps Mademoiselle might like to freshen up before joining the festivities?"

Without waiting for her response, he strode up the staircase, beckoning her with his hand to follow. When they arrived at her appointed room, he laid down her bag, opened a set of French doors leading to a balcony, and swiftly left the room, after announcing, "I shall notify Monsieur Prentiss of your arrival."

Glancing around at the original artwork of classical pastoral scenes, the period cherry furniture, the billowy, cushioned sofas and chairs, and the four-poster canopy bed, Kate slumped down on the ornately patterned Persian and leaned against a bedpost. Does this prosperity have no limits? she wondered with a deep sigh. Closing her eyes, she envisioned the field with its rows of beans, seemingly flowing into eternity. She was so immersed in her thoughts, that she did not hear her door open.

"You've made it this far, then," said Blake, looking down at her. "I feared you might turn back."

She gazed up at him. "What, not fancy enough for me, is it?"

He grinned. "Bit of a culture shock, I should think, after your trip to Walden North." Leaning over, he held out a hand to help her up.

"To say the least." Brushing herself off, she added, "Though which lifestyle is more shocking, I can't really say."

"Oh, do tell me all about your trip to the Arctic reaches, Katie darling, but only after you've showered and dolled up," said Blake, as he led her by the hand to the bathroom. Turning to her, he offered a sly smile. "Something seductively slinky, I hope. I want to show you off."

Despite herself, Kate laughed, giving him a brief kiss on his cheek. "You really are so charming—even when acting like the utter sexist snob that you are."

Turning to leave, Blake said, "In case you didn't think about dressing for dinner, Katie, I took the liberty of gathering a few things for you. We'll keep them here for socializing on our various trips back. I think you'll find them all hanging in the walk-in, closet, that is."

She turned to him in surprise. "Now you're *dressing* me?"

He almost pleaded. "Ah, Katie, love, this is the last of Mother's summer *gatherings*, a farewell gala for herself before she goes off to

England for the winter season." Blake shrugged. "Quite hoity toity, you know. Mustn't look like you've just come," with a quick glance at her clothing, "well, from *Walden North*, for God's sake." He offered a playful grin. "And not to worry, I've added a few *sweet nothings* for our own gathering later." With that, he closed the door behind him.

"I can just imagine," she muttered. Sighing, she turned on the water in the shower room, watching a cluster of vapor jets stream in various directions. She was soon submersed in the soothing, warm water, which seemed to wash away her rising apprehensions over the party below, together with Channing's lecture on indoor plumbing. Before the shower was over, Kate wondered only what kind of clothes awaited her in the closet.

As she opened the doors, she took an involuntary gasp—the closet was filled with lavish dresses, shoes, smart little jackets, silk blouses, skirts, and a variety of silky, patently French-laced *négligées*. Shaking her head, she muttered, "So much for '*Beware of any enterprise that requires new clothes*'!" Her hand brushed through the variety of clothing, stopping to touch a particularly soft silk fabric, here and there. The lush feel to the velvety silks of the undergarments made her pause, as she struggled to recall what memories they were triggering. She closed her eyes momentarily.

Images of the faded, ripped jeans, and the threadbare plaid shirt worn by Channing appeared. She suddenly opened her eyes when a jolt of understanding flowed through her. Yes, of course, she realized. I'm experiencing a *'Paradise of Bachelors, Tartarus of Maids' moment.* She turned away from the closet, to glance out the windows down to the gathering below. Both worlds existed almost contiguously. She couldn't help but wonder whether one served to support the other.

After some hesitancy, Kate settled on demure over seductive—despite Blake's urgings. She rationalized her decision by reminding herself that she was meeting *Mother*, hoping a more modest appearance might help subdue her rising anxiety over the level of snobbery she was about to encounter. With a heavy sigh, Kate slipped on the dress, followed by a light cashmere jacket. She was becoming accustomed to dealing with social status as an indicator of personal merit in New England. Her thoughts turned to Melville—no wonder he placed his call for social equality in the intrinsically more democratic setting of the sea!

When she reached the bottom of the graciously winding stairs, Blake came rushing over. "Oh, there you are, Katie," he said, taking her arm. "Looking captivating as usual," he remarked, as his glance sized her up and down. "I see everything fits beautifully." He leaned in closely towards and whispered, "Looking forward to seeing the fit of what's *under* those clothes this evening."

Kate smiled. "It seems you have sized me up perfectly."

"Indeed," he said absently, as he searched through the throngs of guests, "one of my specialties."

Kate found the comment vaguely disturbing, certainly much too confident, but given the circumstances, decided to refrain from addressing her concern. "Indeed," she echoed.

"Ah, here we go," he said as he redirected Kate. "Let me introduce you to Mother."

They made their way through the French doors to the terrace, where an older group of men and women, bearing a striking resemblance to the people at the café in town, Kate noted, stood talking, drinks in hand. At the center, stood a strikingly elegant woman, holding court, surrounded by attentive admirers. She was exquisitely dressed and lavishly decked out in jewelry to rival any British aristocrat: a series of heavy, gold bracelets, together with a stunning, sapphire and emerald necklace with matching earrings. Kate felt herself slump in trepidation at the sight of the woman, assuredly the famed, *Mother*.

As they approached, Blake bent down to whisper into her ear, "Now, let me do all the talking, Katie." Then standing up straight, he led her to his mother.

The group stepped back to make room for Blake and his guest. "Mother, dear," Blake said gallantly, as he leaned in to plant a gentle kiss on her cheek. "This is my guest, the lovely Dr. Kate Brown, of Harvard."

Though beaming at the introduction, Kate noted the stilted tone of his voice.

Blake's mother sized up Kate in one curt glance, before quipping, "We are *all* from Harvard, Charles darling."

A soft ripple of laughter rose among the onlookers.

Blake's mother nodded. "How do you do, my dear." She extended her hand, her bracelets clinking from their weight. "Charles has spoken almost exclusively of you these last few weeks."

Kate thought she detected a lurking cynicism in her tone. "How unfortunate for the listeners. I had no idea my research was fascinating to anyone, but myself," she said with a pleasant nod. "A pleasure to meet you, Mrs. Prentiss." She offered the grand woman before her a shy smile. "How gracious of you to invite me."

Kate could feel Blake's mother eyes scrutinizing her. "Though Charles refers to you as from Harvard, dear, who are your *actual* people?" She turned a bracelet on her arm, waiting.

Blake intervened before the now patently flustered Kate could respond. "Oh, Mother, did I not tell you? She is one of the Vermont Brownes, of course."

His mother stared at her. "What a pity," she said. "They have already departed for the season."

Blake smiled confidently at Kate, before continuing. "Kate hails from the direct line of Sir Thomas Browne, whose uncle was, of course, Sir Robert Browne, the fellow to whom valiant King George granted the Vermont seat." He smiled graciously at his mother. "But you know your peerage better than I, Mother."

"Indeed." Mrs. Prentiss nodded. "An old Norman family. They are among my social circle in Britain." She glanced at Kate. "I know them quite well, actually."

"Then you, surely, must know they are related to the Unitarians of Concord, as well, don't you, Mother?" He offered a charming smile. "Harvardites, like ourselves."

"Indeed." Through slightly turned lips, Mrs. Prentiss exclaimed, "Well, then, dear, we must continue this utterly fascinating account of your genealogical peerage when there aren't so many guests around."

Without another word, she turned towards one of the men standing near her. "You were saying, James?"

"Right," said Blake, as he guided Kate away. "We've been summarily dismissed." He sighed. "But I think it went well, don't you, Katie dear?"

Kate looked up at him as she twisted her mouth. "I wouldn't know." She looked away. "I was a bit taken aback at the introduction of my *people.*" With a scowl, she said bitterly, "And my *peerage.*"

"Ah, yes, I rather thought you would. Mother is all about social status, I'm afraid." He drew his lips into a pout.

Kate nodded, her cheeks reddening. "I see now, firsthand, what you mean, that being associated with Harvard is only part of the story."

"Indeed," said Blake, a bit too perfunctorily, thought Kate, as he suddenly steered her in a different direction. "Let me introduce you to some of the neighboring summer people."

The remainder of the waning afternoon found Kate wearing a perfunctory smile, as she was paraded through what felt like endless waves of guests. By early evening, she was exhausted. Excusing herself, she hurried up the rounded staircase to her room. Leaving the light off, she walked over to the open window and gazed down at the scene below. Slowly shaking her head, she turned away with a sigh—and an even heavier heart. The themes of Melville's tale regarding the non-intersecting social worlds of New England resonated powerfully through her. *Paradise of Bachelors and Tartarus of Maids, indeed.*

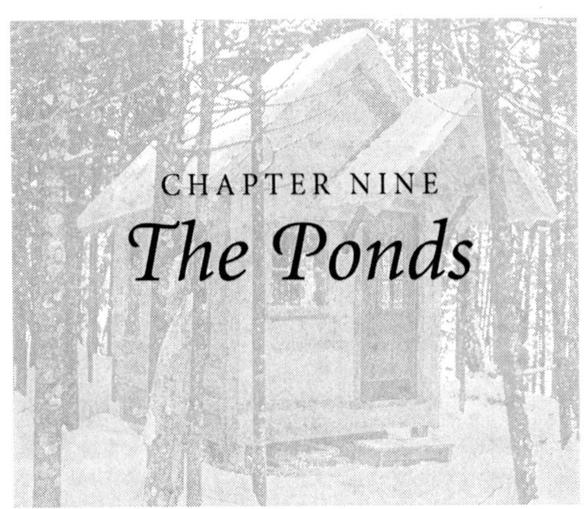

CHAPTER NINE
The Ponds

EVEN FROM BENEATH THE QUILT, Kate could sense the dawning of a quintessential autumnal day. Hopping from bed, she rang up Blake. "Hey, how about an outing?"

Blake groaned into the phone. "You mean beyond my desk? I have so much work to complete this weekend. There's that article still hanging over my head—not to mention the conference paper."

Kate sighed. "I know. I have mountains of work, as well, but it promises to be a gorgeous day, and I haven't yet visited Walden Pond."

"Oh, Katie," he protested. "It will be filled with starry-eyed idealists this time of year, taking in the leaf color and sipping water from plastic bottles."

She laughed. "I can just imagine," she said, "but I really need to see the place. Besides, I'm about to teach a chapter called 'The Ponds.' How can I do that when I haven't ever seen them myself, much less hiked around Walden Pond?"

Blake's tone bristled with disapproval. "Now, don't tell me you expect me to walk around the whole bloody thing. That will take hours."

"Actually, I was thinking of taking a run around it." With a sigh, Kate caved. "All right, then. I'll go myself."

"Besides," continued Blake, continuing to dissuade her, "what happened to the 'primacy of theory over experience'? One trip to Walden North has transformed you into an Ansella Adams?"

"No, nothing like that," she assured him. "But it feels silly not to at least go *visit* the place."

"Have a look at the photos on the website," Blake suggested.

Kate was firm. "No, I am going. After all, I am writing up an article about the two Waldens. I should get into their library and have a look around for any useful material."

"Thatta girl!" Blake exclaimed. "I want my scholar back, not the nature girl who returns home all muddy and laden in pine cones, of all things, ranting on about cabins without plumbing and talking to bugs."

"Well, you're the one with a home in the 'country,'" she retorted.

"Yes, but not to commune with the trees," Blake said, his tone caustic. "It's all very civilized. Stylized gardens. Nature in its place, and all that sort of thing."

"Yes, yes, it's all quite beautiful, really." Kate tried to re-assure him. "Listen, this isn't a life-altering experience. I just would like to see Walden Pond for myself."

"Right, then. You go off and swing by on your way back for a bite." He said, in a deliberately jaded tone, "I am so looking forward to hearing about your '*experience*.'"

"Oh, Blake," she said, with resignation in her voice. "I'll see you later."

Kate stomped to the kitchen to get some water for her hike. He could be so *maddening* at times. After all, she thought, it's just a simple visit to a pond. She didn't understand the reason for his resistance. After searching for some receptacle to bring with her, she shrugged, realizing that she could soon be labeled as one of Blake's starry idealists with her plastic water bottle.

Checking her e-mail one last time before going, she saw a note just sent from Heather. An impulse shot through her, as she recalled her promise to Channing to look out after his daughter. No better way to engage her, Kate reasoned, than while taking a walk in her world. She bent over her desk to write to her.

Want to leave the '*hive*' for awhile?
How about a hike around Walden Pond today?
If so, meet me at Starbucks at noon.

After figuring out her route, she closed her computer, changed into her running clothes, and gathered her copy of *Walden*, thinking she just may be inspired to read it by the pond. She broke out in a radiant smile.

Despite her e-mail, Kate was surprised to see Heather waiting for her at Starbucks. "Well, *hi* Heather," Kate said, flashing her a wide smile, "I'm so glad you could come."

Heather looked at her momentarily, before turning slightly. "I had to get out of my dorm," she said, "and the few trees on campus were not giving me the right setting for reading *Walden.*"

Kate smiled at her. "I know what you mean," she concurred. "But before we take off to explore the wonders of Walden Pond, let me get a chai to go. What can I get you?"

Heather patted a canteen she had slung over her shoulder. "Thanks, I'm good," she said with a shy smile. "I made some iced tea from some raspberry leaves I brought from home."

Kate offered an enthusiastic nod. "Oh, that tea is absolutely delicious," she exclaimed. "Your father brewed me some. You can really taste the raspberry flavor."

Heather stared at her in astonishment. "You know my father?"

Kate chuckled. "Oh, yes. He almost succeeded in converting me to a life of simplicity."

"But when and where?" Heather asked, her eyes wide orbs.

Smiling, Kate said, "I'll tell you all about my trip to Walden North on the way to Walden Pond. Let me just get my chai and some water for the trip, and we'll be off."

Shortly after, as they drove along the highway to Concord, Kate related bits about her visit. "You know," she said, glancing over at Heather, "I have been so intrigued—and impressed—by your reading journal entries, that I just had to see the place for myself."

Heather looked over at her with a shy half-smile. "Really?"

"Absolutely," Kate assured her. "Your perspective on *Walden* has been so insightful. You know, due to your lifestyle up there, you see things differently, and through your philosophical lens, bring a level of understanding and analysis that the rest of us find difficult to achieve."

Heather turned away, gazing out at the blurred views. "Sometimes, I feel so weird in class, talking about my life." She shrugged her shoulders. "As if I live on a different planet than the other students."

Kate cast a concerned glance at Heather, her mouth registering a sympathetic grimace. "Is it that bad for you?"

"Yep, definitely sometimes," said Heather with a shrug. She gazed at Kate, as she shook her head. "And my roommates," she said, as she rolled her eyes, "Absolutely *shudder* over the idea that I grew up not shaving my legs and arms—and whatever else."

Kate burst out laughing. "I can just imagine."

Heather turned away to gaze out the window. "It's so discouraging—the pressure to conform."

Kate nodded. "Your father was afraid of that."

Heather now fully turned in her seat to stare. "Afraid of what?"

Glancing over, Kate smiled before responding. "Oh, well, that you might feel out of place." She hesitated before adding, "and perhaps give in to their ways of acting and living."

Heather turned to face the roadway. Crossing her arms over her chest, she said in a terse tone, "Not a chance." She shook her head as she stared moodily out the window. "Did he really think I was so pliable?"

Kate turned and lightly placed her hand in a soothing gesture over the girl's folded ones. "Not at all, as far as I could tell," she said firmly to re-assure Heather. "But he did say that you must find your own way." She smiled, and with a gentle grip before releasing her hand, said, "You know, *follow the beat* of your own drum, *'however distant or far away'*."

Heather nodded knowingly and smiled, now more visibly relaxed. Looking over at Kate, she said, "Yeah, he always did say that I didn't need to choose between my mother's and his different lifestyles, but experiencing both would inspire me to create my own beat." Heather grinned. "Guess I know now, what he meant. Should have known it came from Thoreau."

They both laughed.

"Exactly." Kate nodded. "He's nothing if not the ardent disciple of the philosophy of *simplicity*." Glancing over at Heather, she added with a quick nod, "Lots to be said about that, though, particularly as we make our way through this bloody traffic—and on a Saturday, no less!"

Heather cast a sidelong glance at Kate, before asking, "I'm really intrigued. How was your visit with my father?"

Kate smiled easily at her. "Why? Having a hard time imagining me up in Walden North, Vermont, hiking through the woods alone, and drinking raspberry leaf tea from a bucket of water collected from a spring?" She took a sip from her chai latté.

"Well, um, yes, I guess so." Squirming a bit in her seat, Heather admitted, "When you went on in your first lecture about how outdated Thoreau's attitudes were about criticizing the 'need' for indoor plumbing and mortgages, I figured you wouldn't get the way I was brought up."

Kate glanced over with a bemused expression. "So I seem more like your mother than your father?"

Heather shook her head. "Um, not exactly." Glancing over at Kate, she rolled her eyes before speaking. "My mother's idea of simplifying is to collect rose hips around her family cottage on the Vineyard."

Kate looked over at her. "Oh? She has a summer cottage? I suppose that serves as an ode to basic living."

Heather just shook her head. "Hardly," she sputtered. "Guess you've never been to the Vineyard."

"No, the closest I came was to New Bedford." Kate looked over at her. "*Moby-Dick* country, you know."

"Well, on the Vineyard," Heather explained, "A cottage means, well, it's like a euphemism for an estate—a mansion with a ton of rooms." She gave a little laugh. "My dad's cabin would fit with lots of room to spare inside her front foyer."

Kate grinned. "Ah, I get the picture."

"Oh, it's much worse, I can tell you," said Heather with a laugh. "My mother thinks she lives the life of simplicity by leading Buddhist retreats in the woods, or by the sea, but only to 'retreat' back, so to speak, to some super elegant retreat center, costing thousands and thousands of dollars for a week of *simplicity*." She looked over at Kate and shrugged. "Drives my dad crazy."

Kate nodded and smiled at Heather. "I can imagine. He was pretty rough on me with my—how did he put it—my '*urban outfitter apparel*'!"

"Yep, that's Dad. A stickler for philosophical detail."

They grinned at one another.

As they drove west in silence for some minutes, house-lined roads gave way to canopies of trees, before Heather exclaimed in obvious relief, "Trees at last! I've really missed being among them."

Kate looked over at her in surprise. "But don't you think the campus is laden in trees?"

Heather darted a look of disappointment. "They're just plantings, really. I mean look around here," she urged, as she gazed out the window. "This feels like a real forest."

Kate glanced out the window. "Yes, I guess I see what you mean," she admitted. "I suppose coming from a city, I am grateful for any large tree cover, planted or not. I never really thought to consider the *amount* of trees before."

Heather turned toward Kate, tucking up one leg under her, and with her back leaning against the door, studied her professor a minute before speaking. "So you haven't really told me what you thought of your experience up at my house." Shaking her head gently, she added, "It must have been a real shocker for you."

Kate met Heather's curious gaze. "The enormity of it all was a bit overwhelming."

Heather's eyes widened. "Enormity? I would have thought you considered it small—to say the least."

"I'm not referring necessarily to the actual size of your cabin, er, home," she said, correcting her terminology in order not to offend, "but to the enormity of the life represented by the cabin in a sea of trees, in the middle of a deep, dark forest that seemed to extend for miles and miles in every direction."

"Oh, it's huge, all right," affirmed Heather, her tone wistful. She glanced out the window. "That's what I mean by missing *real* trees."

Kate nodded. "But it was also overwhelming in the philosophical sense. For someone like me to adopt that lifestyle," she hesitated, before continuing, "well, it would mean completely changing my life, everything I have worked for, dreamt, and accomplished."

"Uh-huh," Heather said noncommittally. "My dad often talks about how he had to make those kind of decisions." With a glance at Kate, she added, "And how glad he is that he chose life in Walden North."

"Really?" Glancing over at Heather, Kate added in a soft voice, "I mean, I can't even *begin* to imagine changing my life in that way."

Heather smiled, with just a hint of a smirk emerging. "Didn't the wise Prophet say, if you '*Live the life you have imagined*', you will '*meet with a success unexpected*'?" She groaned. "Can't tell you how many times I've heard that one."

Kate nudged her playfully. "Hey, you, we haven't gotten to that chapter yet." She chuckled. "I'm still taking in the enormous implications of growing my own beans, like you and your dad."

Heather giggled. "Did he give you the line, 'it's not work'—"

Kate chimed in. "'It's a *lifestyle,*' you mean?" she said with a wide grin. "He sure did."

Heather returned her smile. "He used to say that to me whenever I complained about the bugs as I weeded or picked the beans." She sighed. "My mother would say that it was my dad's form of a Buddhist mantra." She added with a chuckle, "You know, instead of 'ommmm,' indefinitely, it would be that saying." She gazed out the window. "Now, *that* drove my mother crazy."

Kate looked over with a sympathetic expression. "Must have been hard for you to experience such radically different approaches to life."

Nodding, Heather said, "That's why I'm here—at Harvard, I mean. It's the only place their opposing lifestyles truly converged."

"That must be a bit overwhelming in its own way." Kate looked over at her. "Trying to navigate between the two worlds."

Heather nodded sadly. "Yeah, and where I go from Harvard, I have no idea." Shrugging her shoulders, she turned to face the window. "If I *make* it through Harvard, that is."

Kate was adamant in her response. Giving Heather a gentle swat against her arm, she retorted, "But of *course*, you will survive, and even thrive, through the experience!"

"Oh, I don't know if I can take another semester, let alone three more years." Heather shook her head.

Kate thought she detected tears glistening in her eyes. With a vigorous nod, she said, "Listen, you *understand* firsthand the attitudes of the elite at Harvard, particularly, if you have spent any time with your mother, and from what I gather, summers on the Vineyard. You've actually *lived* it yourself. In fact, it's part of you, though perhaps not as deeply engrained or even as heartfelt, as is the Walden North lifestyle."

Kate could read in Heather's tear-brimmed eyes a sense of wistfulness, hoping to be understood, as she looked shyly over at her.

Wiping her eyes, Heather admitted, "I suppose you're right. After all, my mother's family money, and mine, too, I suppose, is exponentially more vast than most of those snobs in our class."

Kate looked over at her with unrestrained curiosity. "Really? How can you tell?"

Heather rolled her eyes, before slumping down in her seat. Thrusting her legs up on the dashboard, she admitted, "Oh, there are all sorts of subtle ways to detect whether someone is *old* money, *new* money, or—" with a sidelong glance at Kate, as if to gauge how she was reacting to the cultural lesson, "*no* money at all."

Kate whistled slightly, followed by uttering an involuntary, "Phew! I had no idea!" She glanced over at her student, who seemed, not only completely relaxed, but entirely in her element. "Another lesson in the sub-textual layers of New England society," she exclaimed, with a sad shake of her head.

"What do you mean?" Heather gazed at her.

"Oh, never mind me," said Kate with a smile. "I'm just being perverse." She nudged Heather. "Go on. It's fascinating."

"Oh, there are all kinds of clues, really," said Heather in a matter-of-fact tone. "My mother has taught me the signals ever since I was a little girl," she added candidly, with a guarded glance over at Kate, before resuming her gaze forward. "She always used to say how important it was to protect our family from what my grandparents called 'the impudent *upstarts*.'" She giggled.

Kate nodded slowly. "How interesting," she said in a vacant tone. "Wonder how your father took all that."

Heather turned to her listener and responded immediately. "Oh, he intuitively understood that. It was part of his family too, after all."

Kate almost jammed on the brakes. "Really?" she asked in a tone that revealed her emotional reaction to the information.

Heather smirked. "Well, of course!" She turned to face Kate. "How else do you think he could manage his '*life in the woods*,' so to speak?" She turned back, and folded her arms across her chest. Thrusting her legs back up on the dashboard, she admitted, "He's a trust-fund baby, just like my Mom." She looked out pensively for a moment before resuming her explanation. "Only differences are, one, the source, since my mother's comes from an active, highly successful corporation," and glancing over at Kate to ensure she was keeping up with the inside story, added, "and two, how they choose to live their lives based on that inherited money." She flicked her hand in the air. "Guess you can work out the rest."

"How utterly fascinating." Kate felt so humbled by the information, she could think of nothing else to say. She drove in silence for several minutes before speaking. "I guess that puts a different spin on your father's lifestyle."

Heather smiled and offered, "He always used to say that even Thoreau came from a factory owner's family." Turning in her seat, she added, "But the money doesn't matter on my father's side since he doesn't touch it—at least, not since he got out of graduate school."

Kate turned towards her. "So he really does live off the proceeds from his beans and the like?"

"Oh, yeah. There were times when we really could have used some additional money, but he completely refused."

Kate just glanced over at her and nodded, urging her to continue. Heather became quite chatty. "Says he's waiting for the right time to rely on it, like organizing some kind of 'Walden Woods North' foundation for conserving huge tracts of Vermont forests and farms."

"Oh?"

Looking over at Kate, she explained. "I don't know, something like that, or a Findhorn, Vermont, though minus the overtly Buddhist aspects of both the original place in Scotland and the one he and my mother had started up in the Berkshires."

"Hmm. Interesting ideas."

Heather nodded knowingly. "There are enough organic growers up where we live to support a 'Findhorn, Vermont,' he thinks. They could all come and learn from my dad how to meditate away their potato beetles." She giggled, eliciting from Kate a wide smile.

"It sure sounds like a 'world elsewhere' up there in Walden, Vermont," she said with a chuckle, as they turned into the parking lot of Walden Woods. "Who would have thought Thoreau's message could have resonated so powerfully among people of this generation?"

"Oh, look!" exclaimed Heather, as she pointed to a small structure along the edge of the parking lot. "Did Thoreau live *here* in the parking lot?" She turned her wide eyes on Kate.

"No, silly. They didn't have parking lots back then, except perhaps, for one's horse and buggy. That's the famous replica."

"But why isn't it at the location of where he actually lived, you know, by the pond?" Heather asked.

Kate nodded. "Yes, one would think that would be more historically accurate," she said as they left the car. "But since this is now a park, or some such designation, they made the cabin replica physically accessible for all."

Heather looked around at the lot filled with cars and people walking by with fishing rods or picnic baskets, as well as joggers and cyclists decked out in their sporting gear. "Wonder whether all these people have read *Walden*?" She glanced back at Kate with questioning eyes.

Kate smiled as she grabbed the two bottles of water she had brought for the hike, before closing up her car. "That would make a great *Walden* project, wouldn't it? To assess to what extent and ways in which people's reading of Thoreau dictate their use of Walden Woods."

"Yeah, maybe."

As they started walking over to the cabin, Kate added, "You could share your insights with the Walden Woods people, or use it, perhaps, as a way to help your father with his 'Findhorn, Vermont' project."

"Hmm," said Heather.

Glancing over at Heather, she continued, now taken with the idea. "You know, as a way of determining contemporary interpretations and applications of the original impetus guiding Thoreau's, as well as the Findhorn founders', *experiments in living*."

Heather paused thinking. "That sounds interesting. I could make it a comparative study."

Kate shot her a look of surprise. "But that would entail going to Findhorn. Isn't that up somewhere in northern Scotland?"

"Yep." Heather nodded. "I've been there a lot, as you might imagine, given the interests of both my parents. My mother would send me, no problem, since it deals with Buddhist meditation, though my father might object since, well, she would endorse it."

Kate shook her head. "I'm beginning to appreciate the complexities involved in navigating the two worlds of your parents, even though they seem to intersect at some key points."

Heather retorted sharply, "It's the differences between their lifestyles that are the difficult paths to navigate. Kind of like tiptoeing across a philosophical minefield."

They exchanged knowing glances.

"So," Kate said, as they stood in front of the cabin replica, "feel at home?"

Heather smirked. "Hardly, with all these cars and people." She walked around the cabin, studying its features. "My dad definitely used this as a model for our house, though."

Going inside, they gazed around at the wood stove and the sparse furnishings in a reverential silence. "It's like going into a church," murmured Kate.

Heather glanced at her. "I wouldn't know. But it certainly has the respectful command of a Buddhist shrine."

Kate stood at the doorway, lost in thought. "I'm trying to recall what he said about sitting in the doorway, watching the birds, or simply taking in the woods all about him. Guess that's why he didn't need a larger house—the woods and the pond were part of his sense of home."

Heather turned towards her. "That's what my dad always said, as well, whenever I complained about not having enough space," she said, with a shrug. "'Our home is 300 acres of woods,' he would say."

Kate offered a sympathetic smile. "In those woods of yours, any bigger house would feel like it was imposing itself on the landscape. The way you live must always remind you that you form only a small part of the '*vastness of nature*' as Thoreau called it." She gazed solemnly round the cabin. "Something rather intriguing about that idea," she murmured, as she reluctantly stepped outside.

Heather studied Kate, while a wry grin spreading across her face. "That's what my father always says." She chuckled. "You must have spent too much time with him."

Kate decided to sidestep the reference to her father. "Oh, not really," she said in an off-handed tone. "Shall we get to the pond?"

Heather walked over to a wooden box near the cabin. "Here are some maps of the place."

They stood waiting, while a near constant stream of cars whizzed by on the busy roadway, which separated the parking lot from the actual pond.

"Wonder what Thoreau would think of this highway near his beloved pond?" Heather asked with a shrug.

"Probably the same as your father would about one near his house," retorted Kate.

Heather rolled her eyes, as they crossed the road. "Ah, that wouldn't go over too well." She gave a quick laugh. "You should see him when someone trespasses onto the property." She glanced at Kate with a smirk. "He goes ballistic. He really likes his *solitude*, as he calls it."

Kate grinned. "Oh, I know firsthand what he's like, since that was my first encounter with him." She looked at Heather with a big smile. "He thought I was the tax lady coming to raise his taxes."

"Oh, I bet you were terrified of him, then," said Heather, with a laugh. "He can seem really menacing when wielding his shotgun and interrogating you."

Kate offered a rueful smile. "Oh, I was pretty taken aback, though he was actually much worse, once he realized I was your professor."

Heather turned to her. "Really?"

Kate directed them over to the path that meandered around the pond. "Let's just say that there's no love lost over having left Harvard."

"Yeah, he begged me to go to MIT instead, but in the end, I listened to my mother's advice there."

Kate just shrugged, before turning to study the map. "In honor of your father and his beans, shall we take this path? It apparently leads us to the location of Thoreau's original cabin site, as well as to the legendary bean field."

Heather grimaced. "Too bad he doesn't have a cell phone. We could snap a few photos and text him."

Kate looked at her with horror. "From my few brief moments around him, I'd say that would not go over very well."

"Oh, I'm only kidding." She smiled. "I really love my dad and his ways. It's just that, at times, they can feel, well, a bit stifling."

"Come on, then. Let's go for an *expansive* hike."

As they ambled along a mulched path under a canopy of pines and colorful maples, Kate asked, "You would know better than I, Heather. In 'The Ponds' chapter, Thoreau talks about finding wild blueberries and huckleberries on Fair Haven Hill." She looked over at Heather, who seemed at home in the forested setting. "Is it the season for finding such berries now?"

Heather shrugged her shoulders. "Well, we are farther south here, than where I live up north." After noticing her professor's blank face, she explained, "That means it is warmer here. There may be the stray berry left, since it is still September—you know, no killing frost yet in this location."

Kate offered a self-deprecating smile. "Guess you intuited that your urban professor is not an expert on the botanical details of Walden Pond."

"No worries," said Heather, shrugging. "Since I grew up roaming the forest and ponds like this one, I can show you a few things about how Mother Nature operates in the wild." She looked around at some joggers running by. "If you call this 'the wild,' that is."

Smiling, Kate said, "Guess it's a matter of perspective, really. To me, this is pretty wild."

They continued along the path, until it opened suddenly to a distant view of the pond, having avoided an alternative course, which led to the beachside setting on the eastern end. They both stopped abruptly at the tranquil sight, gazing at the pond before them, cradled in trees and hills beyond.

Standing in awed silence for some minutes, Kate broke the spell by exclaiming, "I now see why Thoreau called Walden Pond '*the earth's eye*,' which, by looking into it, he said, we can gauge the depth of our *own natures*." She stood silently, staring out over the shining, green waters.

Even Heather seemed impressed by the scene. She wrapped her arms around herself and with head back, breathed in deeply, before slowly exhaling, as she set her gaze out over the translucent water. "The color is amazing, isn't it?" She looked over at Kate. "So green, like the Caribbean."

Kate nodded slowly in agreement. "He claimed the sandy bottom creates what he called the '*vitreous greenish blue*' when viewed from this perspective, but a cerulean blue, when viewed from atop the northern hills over there." She shook her head slowly, saying in a soft voice barely above a whisper, "It's absolutely gorgeous. Utterly breathtaking."

"I see now why they call my home town Walden North," said Heather with a respectful nod.

Kate looked over at her. "Yes, Walden North does exude that feel of the wild, doesn't it?"

Heather smirked. "Oh, much more wild. This is, well, like a postcard."

Kate redirected her attention to the pond. "It looks just like Thoreau described it!" Not knowing whether Heather had actually read the chapter, she explained, "He wrote about the northern side of the pond." She waved her hand in one direction. With a glance over at Heather, she continued. "Anyway, he wrote about that hill over there," she said, pointing, "where some Native Americans were having a powwow. After what sounded like an earthquake, only Walden, one of the women, survived, after whom the pond was reputedly named."

Heather smiled. "I like the idea that Walden is named after a Native American woman. You know, it's not so different from the stories about the origins of my Walden North."

"Really?" Kate glanced over her with a smile. "I began researching the history of your place up there, but didn't get as far as I had hoped—yet." She looked away, as she added, "I've been thinking of writing an article about the two Waldens."

Heather looked over at with a sly smile. "So Walden North *resonated* with you, as you would say."

Kate chuckled over her mimicry. "Do I use that verb often?"

Heather rolled her eyes. "Uh, *yeah*! So much so that it has unintentionally become part of my own vocabulary."

"Well, at least, I am having an effect."

They both chuckled, as they continued their way on the path along the pond. After walking along the deeply ridged path, which wound its way through a stand of pines, they emerged right along the shore.

"'*Skywater,*'" Heather whispered.

"Yes, indeed," said Kate, nodding, as she smiled warmly at her. She marveled at the level of insight Heather evinced, wondering whether it was her upbringing in the woods that had given her such wisdom at her age. She gently shook her head, as she gazed at the young sage.

Kate studied the map. "This must be where Thoreau came to collect water and to bathe, since the actual cabin site is just over through there." She waved her hand in a direction away from the shoreline.

They stood again in silence, as they gazed out reverentially over the pond.

Heather squatted down, peering into the water before speaking. "I'm pretty impressed that it is so clear."

Kate turned to look at her in surprise. "Really, why?"

"With all the people who come here. Hasn't it been a historical site for almost a hundred years?"

Kate nodded. "Yes, I suppose so—actually longer." She bent down alongside of Heather. "What are you checking out, exactly? It really is crystal clear, isn't it?"

Heather pointed to the water lapping along the shoreline. "Usually in ponds I have seen, there is a muddy bottom layered in silt, which houses frogs, and depending on the site, either lily pads, or wild irises." She looked over at Kate, who was peering intently into the water. "This pond has a sandy bottom. Just like Thoreau described."

Kate admired the few stones glistening in the sun. "I love how the water shimmers in the sunlight—transforming into a brilliant blue." She looked over at Heather.

"Yep. Skywater."

Kate continued, her professorial tendencies on high alert. "Now that you and your father have introduced me to a world without plumbing, I've been rereading the chapter where he, Thoreau, that is, discusses his antipathy toward what he called the 'luxury' of it. He claimed that Walden was unique in its water quality, so pure that pumping it out would be like emptying the Ganges of its holy water to wash dishes in." Glancing over at Heather, she added, "the sacred river—"

"In India. Yes, I've been there," said Heather, with a shake of her head. "Not at all as clear as Walden."

Kate looked at her in surprise. "You certainly are well-traveled."

Heather smiled. "Oh, I've visited most of the world's sacred sites."

"Really? With your—"

"Mom, largely, though almost annual pilgrimages to Scotland—and Stonehenge, naturally," she said, as she grinned, "with my dad."

Kate smothered a rising giggle. "Of course," she said in as nonchalant a tone as she could manage.

Heather shrugged. "I know how it must sound."

Regaining her composure, Kate continued. "Not to worry. Anyway, if I'm not mistaken, he, Thoreau, that is, also claims that it is not only the sandy bottom of the pond, and the hidden subterranean spring somewhere that replenishes it, but the presence of the dense stands of trees alongside of it, that make Walden so pure—unique among the many ponds he used to visit in the area."

Glancing over to gauge Heather's level of interest, Kate added, "So Walden assumes a level of importance, both literally as a rare natural specimen, and metaphorically, as an ideal." She looked back at the pond. "And I thought he meant it all as metaphorical. It really *is* pure." She shook her head in awe. "Wouldn't have known that unless I came here—to see for myself."

"That's why I am so glad to see there are lots of trees here," said Heather, with a nod.

Kate stood and looked out over the pond. "Yes, I can appreciate now the importance of protecting this idyllic spot."

"My dad always says that the different parts of nature co-exist in a sort of interdependent way, kind of like birds needing trees. We need the purity of Walden Pond to be maintained as much as the trees surrounding it."

With a glance at Kate, Heather continued. "So to compromise one, like by cutting the trees, or tapping into the water as a water supply, would be to destroy the community that keeps both alive and thriving."

Noting Kate's blank expression, she asked, "You probably don't know about mycorrhizae, right?"

Kate smirked. "Right."

"Well, it turns out that plants, like beans, grow really well in the presence of this special microbe that lives under the soil, nourishing their roots." She smiled at Kate.

"Hmm. Speaking of which, shall we continue walking to the original bean field, as we talk?" Kate suggested.

Heather continued, as they resumed their expedition. "As my dad explains it, different trees in an area create a community of interdependence where each shares and/or offers nutrients for the other types, and this community is enhanced by the presence of a pond like Walden."

"Like an ecosystem," volunteered Kate.

Heather tossed her head from side to side. "Well, maybe." She shrugged. "I don't know—to me, 'system' sounds pretty lifeless."

Kate looked at her in obvious surprise. "You know, I don't recall ever thinking about that connotation before."

Heather nodded. "That's it, I guess," she said, glancing at Kate with an animated expression. "What I am talking about is all alive—conscious—even, actively and intelligibly communicating with one another, though different cultivars and species."

"Hmm. How fascinating." Kate glanced at her. "I really had no idea."

Heather stopped abruptly. "Wait, doesn't Thoreau describe Walden as *alive*?" She searched Kate's expression. "I know my dad," she added excitedly, "always said that since ponds and forests have consciousness, 'intelligence,' I guess you could call it, they communicate with one another, as well as with us."

Kate glanced over at her. "Yes, I believe your dad said something like that to me, though I didn't quite get it." She offered a sheepish grin.

Heather thought a minute or two before expanding her thoughts. "To put it into an urban context, it's more like a multi-cultural neighborhood, where different ethnic groups share their cultural traditions, forming a larger unit dependent on each of the parts. Cut out one or more, and you have destroyed the ideal, as well as the reality, of cultural diversity."

"Hmm. Never thought of nature like that before," admitted Kate, as she slowly shook her head. "How absolutely fascinating."

Heather nodded. "That's why even selective cutting hurts the forests, or in this case, would harm the pond, if the trees here were cut away."

"Yes, Thoreau laments and rails against the practice back then of leveling the trees, saying that the pond needed them to flourish." Kate gazed around. "A very powerful environmental message, his homage to Walden."

"Yep."

Kate turned her gaze on Heather. "While I have always thought of his themes in a philosophical sense, I can now see that the philosophy is *grounded*," she said with a shrug, "so to speak, in actual science—ecology, in this case."

Heather nodded. "That's what my father does. He studies the science of the environment to learn its secrets, and from those insights, forms his philosophy of living." She looked directly at Kate. "Once you get that the pond is alive—possessing memory, feelings, and the ability to communicate with humans—it is very hard to take advantage of it through, for example, the 'luxury' as Thoreau called it, of siphoning it off for plumbing."

Kate nodded pensively. "Yes, I can see how your philosophy evolves from that construct."

Heather continued in an earnest tone. "I think that's why Thoreau was so much against it. Having lived here, he knew what was at stake, by damming ponds and rivers—draining them of their course of life and purity."

Kate shook her head. "Back to where we started. I had no idea that plumbing was such a multi-valenced philosophical statement!"

"Well, that's why we don't have it, as convenient as it is. *Living in harmony with the natural world*, as my father calls it."

"But didn't he cut trees to build your cab, er, house?"

Heather smirked, as she shook her head. "Not my dad," she proclaimed, "He took only felled or standing dead trees." She smiled. "He really tries to leave as little a human footprint as possible."

"Impressive." Turning away, Kate motioned at the small, wooden sign. "Well, here we are, the original bean field, now all overgrown in trees." She smiled. "Thoreau would be happy, since he ended his chapter detailing his experiment of growing beans, you might recall, by saying how he preferred wild nature over his beans."

Heather giggled. "Yeah, that's where he and my dad part ways." She looked at Kate. "He hates weeds in between his precious beans, though he leaves some for philosophical reasons, he says."

"Of course." Kate looked around at the pines. "Imagine having to cut this all down by hand, remove the trunks and stumps, and then start the arduous process of creating a field in which to grow beans." She shook her head. "It's incredibly hard work producing food!"

Heather smirked. "No, it's a—"

"'*Lifestyle*,'" they chimed in unison. They looked at one another and broke out laughing.

"Well, I am truly beginning to appreciate what goes into eating, drinking water, and residing in a house." Kate looked around, her expression reflecting her deepening admiration. "This certainly has been an eye-opening experience," she murmured, with a slight shake of her head.

"See? You have communicated with the '*earth's eye*' of Walden

Pond, which has, in turn, opened your own." Heather shrugged. "At least, that's what my dad would say if he were here with us."

Kate gazed at her with a sober expression. "He may well be onto something."

They walked slowly away from the former bean field to the site of the original cabin, marked only by a simple plaque.

Kate looked slowly around. "Imagine living here."

"This feels like home," said Heather in a whisper.

Kate glanced over at her. "It certainly is tranquil."

"You have no idea." Looking at Kate, she qualified, "Well, you have the idea, but not the actual experience." Her expression assumed a dream-like trance. "Peacefulness just flows all through you when living surrounded in trees and by a pond."

Kate gazed out over the water—green in some spots, with shimmering blue hues toward the middle. As she stood silently looking, her thoughts flowed into one another, like the water ever so gently lapping into shore and back again. Excerpts from her now two favorite authors reverberated through her consciousness:

> *Like silent sentinels they stand gazing out from the farthest reaches of the land to the sea.*
> *Skywater.*
> *Lakes of light.*

She closed her eyes for a moment. *What am I learning from this experience?*

Turning briefly to look at Heather, Kate finally spoke. "It's like Ishmael says in *Moby-Dick.* Scenery can be utterly charming, but the presence of water in the landscape takes it to an entirely new level of beauty—what the Romantics called the 'sublime.'" Her smile shifted to a sheepish grin. "Now I know why I used to be so content after going for long jogs along the lakefront back home. Guess I took it for granted without really thinking. There's something about the water and the land, the point at which they meet, which is so inspirational." She turned back to continue her gaze. "As Ishmael said: '*There's magic—and meaning—in it.*'"

Heather nodded silently. Shaking her bowed head, she said, "Being here, I really miss home."

Kate offered a sympathetic look. "I can imagine how big of an adjustment it is for you." She looked out through the trees to the pond.

"Say," she said, turning to Heather, "I'm actually planning a trip up to your Walden one of these next weekends for my article. Why don't you come, and I'll drop you off at your house?"

Heather turned to her with bright eyes. "Really? That would be great!"

Kate smiled. "Sure. In the meantime," she said, "why not practice a little transcendentalism?"

Heather squinted her eyes. "What do you mean? How?"

"Well, I came across a poem once written by Emerson, or perhaps one of the other transcendentalists, that discussed the importance of internalizing a setting—like this one—steeped in tranquility, and relying on that internal photo, so to speak, after returning to the stresses of city life."

"Kind of like meditation," Heather said, nodding. "I have some photos of scenes from home around my desk and bed, so when I get lonesome or upset, I meditate while looking at them." She looked away. "It makes me feel as if I am there."

Kate smiled amiably. "I guess it's all part of the '*one great whole*,' as Emerson said." She looked around. "Although I have never meditated, I think I'll retain in my '*mind's eye*' as one of them said, this utter peacefulness and simple beauty."

They walked slowly back along the path, each immersed in her own thoughts.

As they drove back to Cambridge, Kate admitted, "I didn't really expect to discover what we found at Walden Pond today."

Heather looked at her. "What did you expect?"

Kate smiled, before laughing softly. "Oh, I thought it would be more like going to a museum, for example, where one sees a lot of different items in an exhibition, remarks on their qualities, and leaves." With a shrug, she added, "You know, more culturally entertaining, than fundamentally thought-provoking—as this trip has been."

Heather nodded. "More like going on a pilgrimage to Mecca—"

Kate shot her a sharp look. "Which you have done, no doubt."

Heather shrugged, as she admitted, "Well, yes, of the many pilgrimages I have been taken on." She turned to Kate. "So what was it about this experience, in particular?"

Kate smiled at the turn of tables, since she was used to being the one who helped others clarify and articulate their thoughts. "Well," she started, as she hugged the steering wheel, "I feel as if I had gotten '*lost in the landscape*', to borrow the words of an Irish poet—a humbling experience to say the least." She stopped. "A bit of a shock, really."

"In what way?"

"Well, in academia," she began, glancing over at Heather, "we try to compartmentalize and thus assume expertise of—or perhaps *over*—our subjects, but I simply cannot imagine being an expert over those incredible scenes."

"Yep, sounds right to me."

She looked over at Heather with a sheepish grin. "That idea is the humbling part."

"And the shocking part?"

"That I could be so *moved* by the experience."

"Yeah? Go on." Heather twisted in her seat to sit with her back against the door. She looked at Kate, waiting expectantly.

"You know, well, actually, maybe you don't, there is a famous collection of essays about the Walden Woods Project that a renowned rock singer, Don Henderson, organized, called, *Heaven is Under our Feet*, a quotation—"

"*Walden.* Yes. I know."

Kate looked sharply at her. "Your father's influence again?"

Heather offered a slight smirk. "Ah, yep."

Kate shook her head. "Well, anyway, I read that collection from cover to cover, and afterwards, found myself agreeing with the theory that the forests here should be preserved from real estate development as even Thoreau hinted at in his book."

"Go on."

"But it wasn't until I actually stood there, along the shore of Walden Pond, getting lost in the landscape, as I said before, that I truly felt, no, *experienced*, the transformative power of a natural setting." She shook her head, as if in disbelief. "It felt like being truly altered in a fundamental way."

Heather looked at her with questioning eyes. "Is that a unique experience for you?"

Kate nodded vigorously. "Exactly." She gazed over at Heather. "I don't know if you'll get the irony of this, but I experienced firsthand, *the primacy of experience over theory.*"

"And?"

Kate produced a radiant smile. "It was amazing—transcendental, actually." She shook her head with an introspective shake. "Now, I understand what Ishmael meant, hmm, as well as Thoreau, come to think of it, when each described feeling lost in the landscape."

"Yep. I know what you mean," Heather said with a nod.

Kate offered a sheepish shrug. "Guess that's my new expression based on this Walden experience." She glanced over at Heather with a big smile. "*Resonate* with you, does it?"

They both laughed.

"Great!" said Heather excitedly. "Some new expressions to use!"

They soon arrived outside of Heather's dorm. "This was a remarkable day on many counts," said Kate. "Thanks so much for accompanying me to Walden."

"Oh, thank you for taking me. I feel so much better about my 'path,' so to speak, here at Harvard." Heather smiled sweetly, her eyes now clear.

Kate looked at her sharply. "Oh?"

Heather offered a shy smile. "I guess I don't feel so out of place anymore, despite my lifestyle differences with the rest of them." Tossing her head, she added, "After all, we are studying *Walden* for an entire year, and I have firsthand, personal experience of '*life in the woods*.'"

Kate nodded. "That's right. You and Thoreau are the real experts here."

Heather searched her professor's eyes, before speaking. "I guess, too, I would have to say that watching you respond to Walden Pond, made me realize how important my experiences have been." She looked away. "I mean, since you, my Harvard professor, was so blown away by just going to Walden." She smiled before shrugging. "I have lived it my entire life."

She turned around, without waiting for Kate to respond. "If you were impressed by the experience, well, there must be something to my lifestyle that others, if they only understood it, would come to really appreciate and respect."

Kate nodded. "That's exactly it. I have gained a deep respect for the lifestyle and the philosophical tenets it entails by having just spent one afternoon there," she said, gazing earnestly at Heather, "though perhaps that experience today was deepened by my trip to Walden North, talking—" she qualified with a bright smile, "well, more like *listening*, to your father discuss his and other's lives there, coupled with reading your entries and talking with you." She chuckled. "The '*one great whole*' re-surfacing again, it seems."

Heather smiled back. "Guess you'll know better after your next trip up to my Walden."

Kate smiled. "An amazing day all round, then, and another wonderful experience to which to look forward." With a nod, she asked, "Perhaps next weekend, then, since it is a long one?"

"Awesome. See ya." With that, Heather turned and disappeared into her hive, while Kate slowly drove along the canopied streets to her own 'wooden cabin', as she now enjoyed calling her building.

Sitting on the window ledge, she sat back and listened to the last of the sparrows, as the light of early evening lingered—before inevitably succumbing to night.

Going to her desk, she opened up her laptop, searching for the Walden Woods Project website, where she read into the early hours of the continuing efforts to protect forever the forests from real estate "development."

"After all," she murmured to her closing screen, "as Thoreau warned us:

How can you expect the birds to sing,
when their groves are cut down?"

Sitting back with her eyes closed, she felt her thoughts drifting along the sparkling, clear blue waters of Walden Pond—adorned in undulating shades of green.

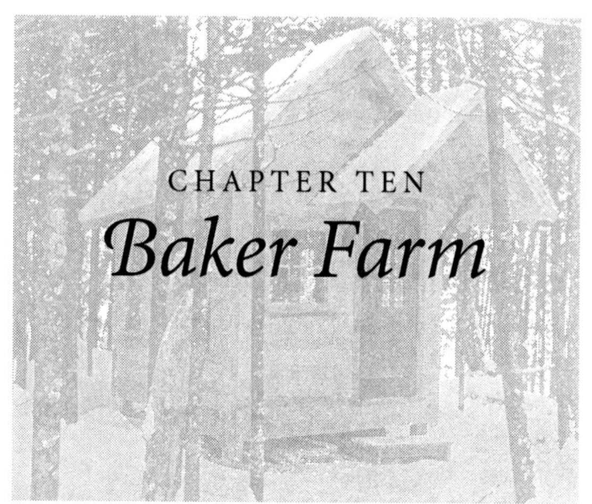

CHAPTER TEN
Baker Farm

AS CLASS ENDED, and Kate leisurely stuffed her bag full of notes and books she had used for her lecture, Heather approached—looking more than uncertain. Noticing her expression, Kate asked with concern, "Is everything all right?"

"Well," Heather stammered. "Something's come up."

Kate looked at her, disappointment spreading across her own countenance. "Oh, you can't go up north this weekend?" With a forced smile, she added, "We can always make it another time."

Heather couldn't meet her eyes. "Well, that's not it, exactly."

Kate studied her a moment before responding. "Are you nervous about going with me, or is it something else?"

Heather responded with sincerity, "Oh no, not at all! I was really looking forward to going with you and showing you more of my Walden, but—"

"But?" interjected Kate. "Too much homework this weekend?" Glancing briefly at Kate, before averting her eyes, she mumbled, "My dad is coming to visit."

Kate's eyes widened. "Really?" Registering her disbelief, she qualified, "Here, you mean—to Cambridge?"

Heather smiled. "I see you're as surprised by the news as I am."

"Well, he did make his feelings about our ivory castle here rather clear," she quipped.

"I never thought he'd *ever* come here to see me." Kate thought Heather's voice sounded wistful.

She responded with a rush of warmth. "Well, of course, he'll visit you here. He misses you!" She offered a big smile. "That's great news!"

Heather glanced at her for a second before once again averting her eyes. "Well, um, there's more."

Kate ushered her out the door. "Come on, we can talk while we walk."

They sauntered along the stone pathway under a rainbow of color. Kate glanced up remarking, "Beautiful fall day, isn't it?"

Heather looked at Kate before responding. "Yep, it sure is." She gazed around at the maples and oaks dressed in an array of color. "I've always loved this season."

With a somber glance at Heather, Kate asked, "So what's the other part you are having a difficult time asking?"

Heather offered a shy smile. "Well, I don't know really how to say this—so I guess I'll just try it!"

Kate stopped and gazed at her student with concern. "Is something wrong?"

"No, not really, I guess," said Heather with a shrug. "It's just that my dad asked me to ask you if we could come visit you."

Kate raised her eyebrow. "Oh, so that's it!" She looked at Heather and said evenly, "Sure, we can meet up while he is here." She thought a minute and added, "In my office or a café?"

Heather vigorously shook her head. "Oh, he'd never do that in a million years!" Glancing shyly over at Kate, she added in a soft tone, "He would like to visit you at your place."

Kate stared at her with surprise. "Oh, really? Well, sure, you both can come see my 'wooden cabin' as I now call it." She offered a half-smile. "Not much to look at, I'm afraid."

Heather met Kate's curious eyes. "He said something about wanting to visit your '*Baker Farm.*'"

Kate chuckled as she shook her head. "My, that's clever. That speaks volumes, or at least chapters! My '*Baker Farm,*' indeed." Glancing over at Heather, she said with a rueful smile, "You go on and read 'Baker Farm' so you can appreciate the multi—"

"Valenced levels?" interjected Heather, her eyes twinkling.

Kate smiled and retorted, her tone dry, "Actually, I was going to say multi-*textual* levels of your father's comments, but, multi-valenced would do nicely, as well."

They both smiled.

"So when is he coming?" Kate asked, as they reached a fork in the path. "I'm off this way."

"I think Saturday, but he could always surprise us." Heather rolled her eyes in her typical manner. "He's not one prone to keeping a schedule."

Kate laughed outright. "I bet." Stopping, she pulled out a post-it and scribbled on it saying, "Okay, then, Heather, here's my address. I guess I'll see you both sometime—starting now."

Heather giggled. "Yep. I see you get how my father operates."

"Not really," Kate said with a shrug. "I've never met anyone quite like him to tell you the truth." She glanced hurriedly at Heather and added, her tone full of concern, "I don't mean that in a bad way, you know. He's just so—" She stopped, searching for the right word.

Heather smiled. "That's because Thoreau has been dead, for what, 150 years."

Kate smiled back. "That's it. He's so *Thoreauvian.*"

Heather turned to leave. "Yep. Thoreauvian. Another new vocabulary word to add to the list." Smiling she said, "See ya!"

"Yes, see you soon, I guess." She smiled as she watched Heather walk away. *An amazing kid.* No, she corrected herself, she's an amazing person, with the wisdom of a lifetime of transformational experience stored within.

Turning away, Kate pursued a less-trodden path that led toward an unusually dense stand of trees in a side courtyard. Seemingly oblivious to the time, Kate sauntered, deep in contemplation, along the cobblestones, as a growing sense of awareness seemed to rise within her consciousness. Noticing some long roots intersecting the path, she focused her gaze on them. Following one particularly gnarled root back along the ground, she discovered its source—a trunk of a tree that stretched in every direction. Its majestic size struck her with awe. Stopping, she twirled slowly, enjoying the experience of standing amid the grove of mature trees. The words from "Baker Farm" filtered through the tangled boughs of her memory:

> *Sometimes I rambled to pine groves . . . so soft and green and shady that the Druids would have forsaken their oaks to worship in them.*

With a knowing smile, Kate readily agreed with Thoreau's conjecture. As a modern-day descendant of the Druids, she would willingly forsake her Chicago oaks of stately grandeur to stand among such primeval pines. As a breeze whistled through the needles, she thought it resembled the tranquil sound of waves gently brushing over a pebbled beach. It was so enjoyable that she decided to extend the special moment. Glancing at her watch, she sighed. *So much for working*, she thought, as she threw her bag of books on the ground and plunked down herself, leaning against the immense trunk. Gazing up through the canopy, Kate tried to discern which types of trees grew there.

She soon lost count of the different types of leafy and coniferous specimens. A deep sense of regret—a feeling surprising to her—descended upon her over the fact that she didn't really know one type of tree from another. She shook her head in dismay. Content with declaring them all pines for the moment, she vowed to buy a book on tree identification. There was so much to learn. She gazed up through the maze of needles and leaves, repeating to herself phrases from *Walden*.

Wavy boughs . . . rippling with light.

She felt her eyes drifting shut, lulled by the tranquility of the largely unpopulated part of the campus. *This is so nice.*

Her thoughts drifted along to the pine forest in Walden North. She saw herself walking along the meandering path under the towering pines, awed by their majesty, their sense of timelessness, their simplicity. *Alone, but not lonely. Tranquility.* Her thoughts bobbed along the gentle rolls lapping ashore on Walden Pond. *Kate. Kate. Kate. Kate.*

Kate slowly opened her eyes to discover someone leaning over her. Her eyes widened in disbelief, unsure of whether she was still asleep.

"I see you have internalized your visit to Walden North," said the deep voice above her. "Keeping your appointment with some trees again, are you?" Smiling, Channing stood with his hands stuck in each pocket of his jeans.

Kate's vision focused on the man standing over her, a wave of surprise breaking upon her consciousness. "You're here already?" she asked in a stupor. "Heather mentioned Saturday," she said while trying to stifle a yawn. "Have I been sleeping that long?"

Channing offered a pointed smile. "Some people slumber their entire lives."

"I can't believe I actually fell asleep." She continued gazing at him in surprise. "How on earth did you find me here?" She searched his face for an explanation. "I've actually never done this before."

"And I thought you spent your time in the library researching or exchanging intellectual insights with your colleagues." He regarded her with curiosity; his head tilted slightly.

Now fully awake, Kate retorted, "'*Instead of calling on some scholar, I pay many visits to particular trees.*'" She leaned her head back against the trunk. "This old fellow being my newfound favorite."

"So *Walden* is having some impact on you," he said with a nod. "Heather intimated as much." He sat down across from her.

Kate looked at him with an expression brimming in skepticism. "Oh? And I thought you shunned all contemporary modes of communication except for personal contact." She offered a wry grin. "Since I left Heather just, hmm," checking her watch, continued, "my, just over an hour ago, I can't imagine how you have communicated with her."

Averting his eyes, he mumbled, "I admit to relying on e-mail on the rare occasion."

"Ah," she said nonchalantly, noting his discomfort around the subject.

Looking back at her, he explained, his tone chastened. "Your visit to my humble abode has awakened me, as it were, to my responsibility to check in with Heather regularly while she is here."

Kate smiled. "That's good—for both of you, I would think."

"Indeed." He offered a slight smile, rather shy, noted Kate.

"It is sometimes necessary to engage with certain aspects of life—even if they occasionally conflict with one's philosophy."

With a broad smile, Kate said, "Oh, really? You have Internet now in the cab, er, house?"

He shook his head, as he leaned over towards her. "Oh, I wouldn't go to that extreme." With a wry grin, he said, "No self-aggrandizing Thoreauvian could bring himself to install Internet."

Kate dropped her gaze, coughing slightly, before looking at him. "I see Heather filled you in on the vocabulary lesson she has been having with me."

The slight curve of his mouth blossomed into a full smile. "She has, indeed. I hear you had a transformational experience at Walden—Thoreau's Walden, I mean," he said, before looking away.

"Oh, my visits to both Waldens have been working their transcendental magic on me, hence the site of my new office," she said, waving her arm around.

"That will go over big with your colleagues," he commented, his tone sarcastic, "though your students are bound to love it."

Squinting, Kate eyed him with curiosity. "Heather did say that you abhor schedules, but aren't you a day or two early?" With a nod, she said, "I don't think she is expecting you until Saturday."

He nodded in agreement. "My board work ended early, so I thought to come visit her before heading back home." With an involuntary shudder, he admitted, "I can't take being down here for too long. Too many people, too much pretension." He shrugged his shoulders. "I've transformed into quite a backwoodsman."

Kate regarded him silently before speaking. "Given your aversion to Harvard and crowds—at least of *people*, anyway," she said with a slight smirk, "what kind of board work would drag even you down here from the idylls of Walden North?"

Channing looked over at her with an earnest expression. "I am still on the board for the intentional community I helped established with, um, my, um—"

"You mean Heather's mother?" she offered.

He looked away. "Well, yes."

"Ah."

Looking back again, he shifted slightly, turning his head to the side. "But actually, the bulk of my time here has been dedicated to setting up a new foundation."

"Oh?" Kate asked. "What type of foundation?"

"I'm starting up a new meditative retreat and school—in Vermont," he said in a rush, "only tangentially related to my, um, work in the Berkshires."

"Hmm," Kate said, nodding. "Tell me about it." Smiling, she added coyly, "I don't suppose it has to do with talking to plants and meditating away pests?" She twisted her mouth into a wide grin.

"You think my work too speculative, I see," he said, looking down, "too far gone along the road of a '*different drummer*' from the rest of you Harvardites."

Kate rushed to assure him. "Oh, not at all. I'm truly interested." She offered a sincere smile. "I have been fascinated by the bits that Heather has shared with me—through her reading response journals, mainly."

With a brusque nod, he said, "On that note, I was quite surprised to learn of such an assignment."

"Why is that?" Kate looked at him expectantly.

Channing explained, glancing at her from time to time. "The Harvard I remember was famous for the formidable term paper. No one thought to ask how the students actually navigated through the reading of various assigned texts—requiring, instead, their intellectual engagement with the criticism."

Kate smiled easily. "Oh, I've had to explain myself to my dean for such assignments, though in this case," she said with a shrug, "I simply relied on Thoreau's own language to back me up:

> *Will you be students merely or seers actively engaged in the business of life?"*

She offered a self-deprecating smile. "I used that passage to make a case for reading response journals."

Channing crossed his arms. "I imagine that did not go over very well."

With a quick nod, she said, "When I inquired about taking a field trip to Walden Pond, he informed me in no uncertain terms that I was not teaching in the School of Education, but in the esteemed College of Arts & Sciences."

They both smiled grimly.

"Anyway, I was about to tell you that my work begins where Thoreau's left off," Channing said, his voice animated. "The notion of a conscious intelligence inherent in Walden Pond, and by extension, in all organic forms, led me to consider whether such intelligences are able to communicate proactively with other organisms, and we, in turn, with them."

"You intimated as much when we last spoke." She thought a moment. "Like Findhorn, then?"

Channing nodded. "Exactly. Its name will reference the Scottish Findhorn. I'm calling it Findhorn-Vermont."

"Will you be associated with them, then?"

He looked at her soberly. "Yes. As a board member there, I have been able to fashion a collaboration."

"Hmm. Interesting." Kate silently regarded him, processing his ideas, before speaking. "And what of the school you mentioned?"

He spoke eagerly, his tone flowing. "Yes, that is my contribution. Given the unique culture of Vermont that overwhelmingly supports organic and local foods, I believe a school offering courses, seminars, camps, and serious study for both children and adults would be very helpful in spreading the knowledge and the practices we espouse."

Kate leaned towards him. "That certainly sounds ambitious," she said, without thinking, but after glancing at his changed expression, added, "though quite achievable."

"Indeed." His gaze had become impenetrable.

She smiled at him. "Your dedication to Thoreauvian philosophy is truly admirable—noble, actually." Gently shaking her head, she added, "What a novel idea."

Channing studied her a moment before responding. "My goal is less ideas, actually, and more, useful practice."

Kate felt chastened. "Yes, of course. How silly of me."

He gave her a sharp nod. "You can't help yourself. You, like the majority of academics, fly with ideas, when you could walk—grounded in practice."

Kate looked away. "Yes, I suppose."

A new voice suddenly broke through the intensity of their exchange. "Well, what have we here? A private *tête à tête* under the trees?" He glanced from one to another. "Such an unusual setting for a discussion."

Surprised, both Kate and Channing turned in the direction of the voice emanating from behind them. So immersed in their exchange, neither had noticed the sound of approaching footsteps.

Kate flew to her feet, her face flustered. "Oh, Blake. Hello." Turning to Channing, who slowly stood, she swallowed before saying in a hollow tone, "Channing, this is Blake Prentiss, my colleague."

"Oh, Katie, dear, I certainly hope I am more than just a colleague to you," Blake protested, his voice approximating a whine.

Briefly glancing over at Channing, she noticed he was staring hard at her.

"Yes, of course, Blake," she snapped.

"More like a version of kissing cousins," he said, giving Channing the once over, "you know, kissing colleagues." He pursed his lips into a decided pout.

Kate turned to Blake, her cheeks radiating an embarrassing red. "This is Dr. William Channing, the father of one of my students."

"Oh?" Blake sized him up in one glance. "You don't mean, as in William *Ellery* Channing? A direct descendant, are you?"

Kate immediately flushed, before turning an astonished gaze on Channing. She had not made the connection in her head to the famous transcendentalist figure.

With a brief, concerned glance, Channing noted Kate's altered expression with some dismay. Both the expression and the shrug he offered were solemn, before turning to Blake.

"Well, yes, to both actually, depending on whether you are referencing the theologian or the poet; however, in the spirit of Emerson, I tend to abrogate tradition—particularly family legacies."

Channing's steady stare did not have the intended effect upon Blake, who appeared enervated by the news. "Oh, impossible among our circles, truly," Blake said, extending his hand. "A pleasure to meet one of the esteemed descendants of one of our Harvard elders. You should rest assured that your child is in good hands under the direction of our newest addition to the faculty. We're quite proud of our Katie," he said, smiling, as he nodded in her direction.

Channing only partially concealed his irritation with the outstretched hand, returning it with a curt, perfunctory shake. "Indeed, Dr. Brown's erudition and pedagogical skills, both in reaching and inspiring the students, are more than impressive."

Upon sensing the now palpable and rapidly escalating tension between the men, Kate forcefully intervened. "Blake, we're actually holding a meeting right now," she said pointedly, before turning away from him.

"Oh, indeed?" he protested faintly.

Ignoring him, Kate redirected her attention to Channing. "Dr. Channing, perhaps we might reconvene to my office, where we could continue our assessment of your daughter's work—without any further interruption?"

With a slight glance over at Channing, Blake asked, "Are we on for our own little meeting over dinner this evening, then, Katie?"

"Actually, Blake," she hesitated, glancing from him to Channing, "I'm meant to meet with my student and her father."

"Indeed," said Blake coldly.

"Yes," said Kate, glancing briefly at Channing, "our meeting for Saturday has been shifted to today—due to an unforeseen change in Dr. Channing's schedule."

Blake glanced from Channing to Kate. "How unusual to meet outdoors," he remarked, before turning to Channing. "I should think my fair colleague's teaching duties are affecting her judgment."

Channing didn't miss a beat. "Actually, Dr. Prentiss, we were discussing the particulars of a chapter in *Walden*, and since it concerns trees, what better setting than this," he said, with a gesture toward the trees, "to discuss my daughter's work?"

Blake almost scowled at Channing, his expression revealing his inner thoughts. "Actually, here at Harvard we prefer to theorize philosophy."

Channing countered the notion with one, curt, dismissive nod. "Yes, I remember all too well, which is why I resigned from my position here."

Blake stared at him in unrestrained surprise. "Oh, indeed?"

Glancing at Kate, Channing said evenly, "Yes, I now live out my philosophical premises, rather than posit theories, as I was conveying to Dr. Brown here."

A knowing look of understanding spread across Blake's face. "Daughter, did you say? You wouldn't be the fellow who lives in a cabin without plumbing and electricity in Walden, Vermont, now, would you?" He looked hard from Channing to Kate.

"Yes, most certainly," Channing said evenly, meeting Blake's eye, "as you most assuredly were the host of Dr. Brown's visit to Woodstock?"

Without waiting for Blake to respond, Channing turned to Kate. "Yes, Dr. Brown, we should continue our discussion in your office before we are joined by my daughter."

Kate nodded without saying a word. Gathering her bag, she offered a perfunctory nod to Blake, before turning to leaving with Channing.

Kate glanced sideways at him as they walked along the stone path toward the main part of campus. "I'm terribly sorry about that."

Channing regarded at her with what felt like pity. "I have a short fuse when it comes to such attitudes of, shall we say, the 'entitled.'" Looking away, he added almost apologetically, "I hope I did not, um, *interfere.*"

"Not at all," Kate said, as she shook her head. "I feel oddly relieved." Casting a sidelong glance at him, she added, "I admit that after so many years striving to get my doctorate, I really enjoyed hearing you use my title." She looked away. "Katie sounds a bit too, well, *girlish*."

Channing's expression turned grim. "Yes, I remember how anti-climactic it felt to reach the academic summit by earning a PhD, only to avalanche down the slope to the base status of 'Assistant Professor'—acknowledged solely by the designation of *Mr.*"

Kate cast a searching glance at her companion, wondering whether she could open up to him. She took the risk. "Actually, it is much more dramatic for me."

He stared at her in surprise. "In what way?"

With a sheepish grin, she admitted, "I actually changed my name for my academic career."

Channing studied her a moment before speaking. "As much as I have wished to change my own," he said, with a flick of his hand in the direction from which they came, "and have unofficially, as you know, by calling myself simply Channing, to disassociate myself from precisely the kind of elitism we have just witnessed, I am rather surprised to hear it was that important to you to be accepted in academia—or perhaps, particularly here at Harvard."

Kate looked away. "Yes, it was, er, *is*."

He turned to her, gazing at her before responding. "And what was your birth name, Dr. Brown, if I might ask?"

Looking down, Kate said simply, "Cáitlín O'Neill."

Nodding, he said, "Ah, a Celt." He gave her a quizzical half-smile. "If I recall my history, the O'Neill clan reigned as one of the high kings of Ireland in the Celtic era." He nodded at her. "Something to be rather proud of, I should think."

Tilting her head, she glanced at him in surprise. "Yes, that's right, actually." She offered the briefest of smiles. "But since my name is not Kennedy, I feared being considered—" she admitted, with a sidelong glance at him, "well, a second-class citizen. It's bad enough I was the lone female in the Americanist program, but to admit to being the daughter of Irish immigrants with an impossibly spelled Gaelic name?"

"Indeed?" He seemed to study her, his curiosity clearly registered in his flickering gaze.

She flung her head in an adamant shake. "I used the Americanized version of my Irish name—Kate-lin—and relied on my mother's maiden name which happens to be my middle name." She looked away before turning back to add, "without an 'e.'"

He nodded, Kate thought, sadly. "You felt the need to change your cultural identity to assume your rightful place in academia." He said it more as a statement than a question. "Not surprising, if I might add, given the attitudes of some of your colleagues." His jaw hardened. "But you needn't have, you know, all the same."

Kate shrugged. Looking back at him, she met his stare. "After all, look at the demeaning way even Thoreau wrote about the Irish immigrants he encountered at Walden." She studied his face.

Channing nodded, "Ah, back to our discussion of 'Baker Farm.'"

Kate arched her eyebrow. "In what way?"

Noting her confusion, he explained. "Well, let's see. We began this encounter by referring to Thoreau's elegy to trees in the opening passages of the chapter, followed by your own expressed preference for communicating with trees over your scholarly colleagues." Emitting a slight scowl, he added, "Having met one of them, I can enthusiastically endorse your preference for the more noble species—the trees."

Kate cast a nervous glance in his direction, which he returned with his all too-somber expression.

"One of the reasons I had hoped we could meet was to discuss that very chapter in detail."

She gazed at him in surprise. "Really? Why?"

Shaking his head slowly, he remarked more to himself than to her, "I felt when you left after our last encounter, there was more, perhaps much more, to be said."

"Oh," she said, unsure of what to add.

Channing continued in his serious tone. "Little did I realize how profoundly this chapter addressed your life choices." Turning his head slightly in her direction, he added, "Or perhaps, I intuited it without consciously realizing it." He met her gaze. "Must be synchronicity at work."

Kate looked at him in wonderment, coupled—she was sure—with blazing cheeks. "Well, I'd invite you for a chai or a coffee, but Heather said you refuse to frequent cafés, hence your reason for asking to visit me."

Shrugging, he said, "I might make an exception in this case, though I would much prefer to visit your abode in the spirit of Thoreau's visit to Baker Farm." He tapped on his bag. "I've brought a batch of raspberry leaf tea."

Nodding in agreement, Kate asked, "Shall I e-mail Heather now to notify her that we'll be gathering at my apartment?" She was surprised to see Channing shake his head.

"Not just yet," he said. "If you don't mind, I would prefer to speak with you alone before my daughter joins us." He offered a half-smile. "Since I am here in Cambridge, I might as well continue to break my pledges and offer to take both of you to dinner this evening," he said, glancing at her, before turning away to complete his thought, "particularly since my presence has thwarted your um, previous dinner arrangements." He looked back at her.

Kate smiled, coughed, and said, "Well, sure, that would be nice." She braved a big smile, despite a sense of disquiet she could not grasp.

Studying her with a curious expression, he said, as if he were reading her mind, "I thought I might confer with you regarding the pedagogical aspects of my Findhorn-Vermont school, while in return, I might offer some insights into academic life here at Harvard."

Kate regarded him with surprise. "That sounds like a spirited exchange," she said, "though I am puzzled by your interest in my ideas about teaching."

He met her gaze. "Why is that? Heather raves about your pedagogical practices."

Kate felt surprise, both by the compliment and the actual information, radiate through her. "Really? Is that so?" She smiled briefly, in spite of trying to contain her feelings.

He offered a quiet smile in return. "She says you are an island refuge in a sea of sharks."

Kate couldn't help but laugh. "My, that's a formidable metaphor." She gave a wry grin. "And I thought she was starting to enjoy the place."

They walked through the streets of Cambridge engrossed in their conversation, interrupted only by Channing's periodic interjections, "downy woodpecker," "oriole," "linden," "Norway spruce." With each identification, Kate felt the tide change, as her initial response of amusement shifted to admiration. As they sauntered along the way, she stole a curious glance at him from time to time. Though he seemed a bit strange, she found him more than fascinating—truly unlike anyone she had ever encountered.

Kate stopped below a large maple tree. She turned and smiled at him. "My turn," she said.

Channing bent his head slightly. "Yes?" he said, as she flicked her hand toward the tree. "Sugar maple."

"Actually, it's *my* maple," she corrected him with a smile. "Here we are. Home Sweet Home." She waved her arm. "This is my wooden cabin, so to speak."

Channing stood and peered at the clapboarded building in front of him. "A triple decker?"

Kate offered a wry smile. "More like a *quintuple* decker, actually."

"Oh?' he said, as he turned back to her.

"I, along with some of my neighbors, each occupy half a floor." She opened the door, saying, "Straight up the stairs there. I'm on the top floor."

Just as she unlocked the door to her apartment, Kate abruptly turned to Channing with a shy smile.

"You are my first visitor," she announced.

He gazed upon her with a serene smile. "Ah, '*the visitor at the door*,' perhaps?"

"Yes, perhaps you are," she admitted, with a hesitant, yet hopeful glance as she met his gaze.

Upon entering, Kate looked around in dismay. "I'm afraid your visit has taken me by surprise," she admitted, as she moved away some piles of books from the table.

Channing offered a knowing look in response. "As did yours to me." With a cursory glance around the room, he smiled broadly when he noticed the maple occupying the view outside the window. "I see now why you call it *your* maple." Walking over, he said, "It conveys the sense of a tree house."

She gave an awkward smile. "I've spent quite a bit of time sitting on that window ledge." Looking at him, she admitted, "I decided to pay more money for this unit due to the view of that tree."

He shot her a sharp look. "You mean you *borrowed* more money, don't you?"

"Well, yes," she acknowledged. "Yes, that's true, from your perspective on economics—"

"And Thoreau's," he interjected.

Kate shrugged. "Yes, right again." She placed the kettle on her stovetop. "Tea, then?"

"Yes, thank you," he said with a slight bow.

She hurriedly moved some smaller stacks of books covering her pine café table to her desk. Turning back to look at him, she said with a smile, "Sometimes, when I get tired of sitting at my desk until all hours of the night, I switch things up a bit by sitting here."

Removing a mason jar from his bag, Channing offered it to Kate.

"Heather tells me you really enjoyed our raspberry tea, so here you are."

"Oh, great, thanks!" Turning back to the now whistling kettle, she said, "I'll make us some tea from it."

As Kate busily prepared the tea and hunted for some clean cups, Channing walked around and stood for some minutes studying the empty corner space with a blanket on the floor, before turning to her. "Ah, you meditate."

Kate looked up surprised. "No, actually, I don't."

Walking over to the table now set with tea mugs, he asked, "Then what is the purpose of that empty corner—with the prayer mat?" He looked at her with a steady gaze.

"Oh, that," Kate said, as she glanced away. "Sometime, most likely later, rather than sooner, that space will be occupied by a brand new brown leather sofa and matching reading chair," she said with a shy twist of her mouth. "In the meantime, I sit on the blanket, imagining it my future couch." She shrugged. "With all the expenses associated with moving and working here, I just couldn't afford to rack up any more debt."

"I see," he said.

Taking a sip, she exclaimed, "Yum, delicious." She offered a warm smile. "Something to look forward to—after I get my dissertation published, that is."

"How are they connected?" Channing regarded her through narrowed eyes.

Kate looked at him in surprise. "Don't you remember how salary increases are based on one's publication record?"

Shaking his head, he said wryly, "I didn't stick around long enough to get that far."

Kate grinned. "No, I can't imagine that you did."

Channing studied her before speaking, appearing even more serious than usual. She felt herself bracing for his next comment.

"Since I am not an academic, shall I call you by your birth name, Cáitlín?" He gazed at her with a searching look.

With a defiant toss of her head, she retorted, "If you don't mind me calling you after your own, *William.*"

His laugh was clipped. "Point well taken." With a furtive glance at her, he said, "I suppose since each of us has renamed ourself, we should respect that name-giving." Sitting up straight, he continued, "Right then, Kate," he began.

Kate cut in. "Oh, it's fine with me." She studied his face a moment, before offering a smile. "Actually, I prefer if you call me Cáitlín, as I sometimes miss hearing my name aloud." She looked away, before admitting with a shudder, "I detest Katie."

Channing nodded, side-stepping the reference. "Right, then, Cáitlín, tell me about your life here and your aspirations. I'm curious to know about the current economics of academic life."

Kate sighed, before turning her head to gaze out the window. "It's trying at times, I must admit," she started.

"Academically or economically?" he asked.

"Both, actually," she said with a nod. "I underestimated how costly it would be to live the life of a Harvard faculty member."

"Oh?" He looked at her, waiting.

"Well, for starters, there's the condo mortgage, which takes up half of my monthly income, excluding the fees and utilities." She looked away. "And food is much more expensive here than the Midwest." Turning to meet his steady gaze, she remarked, "Not much left for books and other necessities, like clothes."

"Clothes?" He looked confused before shifting to a knowing look. "Ah, your urban-outfitter wear."

She shook her head. "No, it's just that we dress differently in the Midwest at the university, brighter colors and that sort of thing. I've been told here to dress in, well, the academic *dowdy* look."

He raised his eyebrow in surprise. "Indeed?"

With a smirk, Kate added, "But even dowdy clothes such as Harris tweeds are quite costly here."

Channing leaned back in his chair. "Ah, yes, it's coming back to me now."

Taking a sip of her tea, she continued. "So, in order to earn more income, I need to get my research published." She waved her arm around the room. "Hence the endless piles of books."

"Ah, enslaved to the books—like Thoreau's farmers to their fields." He gazed around at the heaping towers of books scattered throughout the apartment. "You appear to have your work cut out for you."

"As my immigrant parents were so fond of saying of the American experience, 'work hard and get ahead.'"

Channing leaned toward her. "You do recall Thoreau's take on this ideology, don't you?" Without waiting for her to respond, he quoted:

> *"The only true America is that country where you are at liberty to pursue such a mode of life as may enable you to do without . . . "*

With a hard stare, he explained. "He called them luxuries, 'superfluous expenses'—such as yours."

Kate smiled at him, resting her arm against the back of her chair. "Yes, I remember that passage. I admit sometimes my life feels like a treadmill, but I do love my work, as well as my teaching."

"You know what mortgage means historically, I'm sure," Channing remarked, as he set down his mug. "The death contract—'till death do us part—not unlike the forty-year mortgages on farms to which Thoreau alluded in his chapter 'Economy.'" He gazed pointedly at her.

She threw her head back. "Well, thank God, I have only a thirty year," she said with a grimace, "though, I admit with shame, an adjustable rate."

"'*Let not to get a living be thy trade, but thy sport.*'" He gazed at her. "Do you recall the remainder of the passage?"

She shook her head gently. "I probably read it close to mortgage payment day and decided to skim it, lest it shook up my world too much," she said, her tone reflecting her embarrassment.

He nodded sympathetically before quoting:

> "*Through want of enterprise men are where they are, buying and selling and spending their lives like serfs.*"

He glanced around. "This is your 'Baker Farm.'"

Kate gazed at him in silence, realizing that he was just trying to help, however painful the attempt. She stared somberly into his eyes, trying to decide how to respond. "You know, if it were anyone but you saying such things, I would most likely argue against them in a defiant fit of rage, but knowing how you have deliberately chosen to, well, '*simplify*,' your lifestyle, I understand you speak from raw, sometimes hard experience."

Channing studied her expression before speaking. "You must remember that I observed you in the forest happy and carefree as a young girl while you collected pinecones."

She smiled and looked away.

He continued unabated. "Not only did I see in you the joy of what Thoreau calls '*discovery*,' but I sense in you—even here—a spirit currently subdued by your economic responsibilities and your current life path."

Kate nodded, wondering whether he could detect the depth of sadness that suddenly overcame her. "Perhaps."

He shook his head in what seemed like genuine sorrow. "And to think you changed an essential part of yourself—your name—in order to be accepted here." Shaking his head again and with downcast eyes, he said softly, "It makes me very sad for you, Cáitlín."

Though she thought she detected an emphasis on her name, she shook her head with a dismissive flourish. "Oh, it's not so bad." Smiling, she said as an afterthought, "It is Harvard, after all! I feel fortunate to be part of it."

Looking up briefly, Channing locked eyes with her. "I pass on to you Thoreau's advice, that is, '*grow wild according your nature.*'"

Kate turned to face him. "Speaking of wildness, why don't you tell me a bit more about your lifestyle?"

"Well stated," he said with a nod. "Oh, that reminds me," he added. Reaching into his bag, he pulled out a book. "Thought you might like to read this—as it explains both the theory and the practice of simplifying." He nodded. "It might give you additional insight into Thoreauvian economics."

Kate took the book, saying, "Why, thank you." She read from the title. *Agrarian Economics.* "Hmm," she said with a smile, "perhaps in my next life, I'll take up farming."

"It's more than that, actually," he said with a slight grimace. "It explains how little income one really requires in order to live." He looked away before, redirecting his gaze. "Shall we do some comparative economics as an exercise?" With a shy smile, he added, "An '*experiment in living*,' as it were."

Kate smiled amiably. "Sure, why not?" She looked down momentarily before admitting, "I seem to have told you everything else about my life already. Why not dig a little more deeply?"

Channing sought to re-assure her. "Oh, it will be a mutual excavation." He looked around. "We'll need some paper and pens."

Once she gave him the requisite items, he explained the exercise. "Why don't we use Thoreau's own categories of 'food, shelter, clothing, heat.'" He stopped, nodded, and said curtly, "Under heat, you might think to add your water bills for plumbing and other utility bills."

He gave her a sheet of paper and a pen. "Just write down in one column your monthly income, while on the right, your monthly expenses, and I'll do the same."

Kate took a sheet of paper and asked, "Sure, okay."

Both began jotting down numbers. Looking over at hers, Channing said, "It would be more helpful, though, for our comparison, for both of us to write down the types of items we are purchasing, such as under food, so we might understand more clearly the nature of each of our expenditures."

When each had completed the itemizations, Channing said, "Let's begin with you."

Kate scrutinized her accounting and sighed. "It sure adds up rather quickly in my case," she said softly. "No wonder I am having a difficult time maintaining." She pushed her sheet over to him.

"So," he said as he scanned her columns, "Although you make $52,000—"

"Which I once thought was a fortune," she interjected, with a shake of her head. "Before moving here, that is."

"You spend—" he remarked, as he performed some calculations, "Let's see, 50% of that on your mortgage & taxes, 10% on utilities, 15% on credit card payments & interest, 5% on clothing and almost 20% on food." He looked at her and smiled. "You must have some beautiful Harris tweed suits for that clothing expenditure."

Kate shook her head. "Yes, Thoreau must be turning in his grave to think that someone who is teaching his book about simplifying, not only has overlooked his advice to '*beware of any enterprise that requires new clothes*,' but requires so much of, well, *everything* to be in the position to teach his themes."

He made a short bow. "Yes, precisely so."

Fondling her mug before taking a sip, Kate gazed at him. "Seems ironic, if not outright hypocritical, doesn't it?" she asked with a shrug.

He nodded in assent. "Yes, this is the power of such an exercise—" he said, as he tapped the book he brought her, "and the point of this particular book."

Returning her expense sheet, Channing suggested, "Let's delve a bit more deeply, shall we?"

Kate groaned. "Why, do you wish to depress me completely?"

He looked hard at her. "No, not at all, but insight enkindles a corresponding call to action. Perhaps there are ways, even with your lifestyle of indebtedness, that you might simplify." He scanned the numbers. "Take food, for example."

Kate studied the food column. "Yes, I am rather shocked at the amount of food I am consuming." Her cheeks flushed, as she admitted, "No wonder I am having a hard time fitting into my old clothes."

Channing sidestepped the reference to her figure before continuing. "I was referring to your penchant for chai lattés and their corresponding costs." He glanced at her. "See, look here. One chai per day, at roughly $5, comes to $35 weekly, not counting any pastry, sandwich, or muffin."

"Oh, I drink at least two per day and consume a muffin each morning," she admitted. Looking away to hide her embarrassment, she added, "With the occasional sugar-filled pastry thrown in for diversity, as well as a cookie in the afternoon."

He erased his figuring. "Well, in that case, you are spending," he stopped to calculate, "with the muffins and/or pastry, cookies and two chais daily, a whopping $20 daily, or $140 weekly, $560 monthly, $6700 annually." He stared hard at her. "That equals more than 10% of your annual income in sugar, tea, and milk." He sat back to assess the effect.

"Oh, my God!" Kate exclaimed. "That's even more than my clothing!" She sat back in her seat. "I had no idea it could add up so quickly."

"Well," he said with an earnest look, "if you could manage to get off your addiction to caffeine, and switch to water, which you are already paying for at exorbitant rates, I might add, you could save 10% right there." He scanned the figures again. "Not to mention that chai lattés occupy the majority of your food expenses." Looking startled, he said with a rush, "Oh, I almost neglected to give you the other items I brought for you."

Removing several jars from his bag, Channing placed an assortment of food in front of her. "Beans, both dried and fermented, in memory of your visit to my bean field," he said with a smile, "some raspberry preserves made with birch and maple extracts, in memory of your '*appointment with a birch*,' some honey and maple syrup—in lieu of sugar—for your raspberry tea, and some pine and birch tinctures, for cold and flu season, in memory of your intuitive pine cone gathering."

"My God! These are all amazing!" She picked up one of the tinctures. "You made all these yourself?" she asked in awe.

With a brusque nod, he said, "Not many medical clinics up my way in the north woods, and the very few that are scattered about the larger region, I would never frequent anyway."

"You certainly do live a unique lifestyle." She peered at him. "Doesn't it seem that we live in different hemispheres?"

He nodded, meeting her searching gaze. "Indeed, it does, a sense all the more palpable by this visit to your 'Baker Farm.'"

She studied him in silence.

Picking up his sheet, he said, "Speaking of different hemispheres, shall we have a look at the economics of a Walden North lifestyle?"

"Sure," Kate said, standing. "I'm more than intrigued." Picking up the teapot, she said, "I'll refresh our tea."

Anticipating her next move, Channing announced, "By the way, those raspberry leaves, unlike black tea which becomes embittered, actually maintain their flavor, so no need to dispose of those for new ones." He gestured toward the half-gallon jar. "That should last you until my next visit—next month—even if you substitute the raspberry tea for all those chais you consume."

She turned to look at him. "Oh, really? That's interesting."

"As for leftover tea, you can simply add it to a pitcher for iced tea—to take with you to campus each day in lieu of purchasing the lattés."

"That's a great idea." She filled her kettle with water. "Simplifying." She turned back to him with a big smile and said, "I like it."

"Yes, well, speaking of which, have a look at my figures and expenses." He leaned back in his seat, watching her.

As Kate scanned his numbers and categories, her eyes widened in disbelief. "You pay less taxes than I do!"

He nodded silently.

She looked up at him. "Almost half! How is that possible?" Shaking her head, she said, "You have what, 300 acres, wasn't it, and I," she said, looking around her apartment, "have about 300 square feet."

"You live in a 'high-rent' district, as they say," he said. "You are paying through the nose for the honor of teaching at Harvard."

With a disbelieving shake of her head, she resumed her reading. "There must be some mistake here under food."

"No, no mistake," he said, his tone nonchalant, though his eyes reflected a rare sparkle.

Kate glanced up. "But it says you spend only $500 for food." She stared hard at him. "Don't you mean monthly, not annually?"

He gently shook his head. "Annually, actually, though with my new commitment to Heather to visit monthly, I suppose I shall need to increase that amount another $1000 or so to cover taking her to dinner monthly—assuming just over $100 per dinner during the academic year."

Kate tossed her own with an insistent shake. "But even so, how can you spend so little on food?" Reaching over for her sheet, she noted, "I spend almost *twenty times* that amount." She looked at him in confusion.

"Your high food bills result from purchasing food," he glanced around at her kitchen shelves, "most likely processed foods, here in Cambridge, as well as going out for meals."

She gave a slight shrug. "Yes, that's true. With my work, I rely on ready-made foods for the most part, or eating out."

With a curt nod, he countered, "Hence your high food expenses."

He leaned forward. "In my case, most of my $500 expenditure is for renewing or adding to my seed supply, as well as for purchasing grains I do not grow myself."

Kate shook her head with vigor. "But still, how is that possible?" She looked at him in disbelief. "To eat so little?"

"It's not that I consume little food," he said with a smile. "Believe me, I have a hearty appetite, particularly given all of the taxing, physical labor I engage in." He looked at her with an earnest expression. "It's that growing one's own food, supplemented by gleaning, is very inexpensive."

"Gleaning?" She looked up at him, perplexed by the unknown term she assumed was an agricultural allusion.

He gazed at her with a tranquil expression and said quietly, "That's the practice of finding foods in the wild, such as our raspberry tea."

"Oh, you don't grow raspberry bushes?" She looked at him confused.

Channing actually laughed. "Why would I, with thousands of them growing wild throughout my forests? No, there's no need for me to grow any fruits when they are so readily available all around me."

Kate looked at him as a light of recognition illuminated within. "Ah, yes, '*live in each season and eat the fruits of each.*' I bet you never eat out of season either." A slight smirk formed on her lips.

He smiled. "Only my preserved fruits and vegetables in the winter."

"It really is amazing," she said as she studied his figures. "You need almost no money at all to live up there."

He regarded her through patient eyes. "It's due to my lifestyle more than my location, but I admit the two complement one another."

Kate shook her head. "I wouldn't last a day on my own up there."

With a pointed look, he responded, "Hence the purpose of my school, to show others how they might jump off the economic treadmill, remove the shackles of economic indebtedness, and live a life free to '*explore new continents within,*' as well as in nature, as Thoreau espoused."

"Incredible." Kate stared at him blankly, her mind racing through the implications of his ideas. "Almost overwhelming."

"I understand," he said quietly, "I really understand." Standing up, he took their mugs and moved them to her sink, carefully washing out each, before setting them on her drain board.

"Oh, you don't need to do that," she protested.

She carried over the teapot, which he removed from her grasp, before setting it down on the table. Reaching out for an empty mason jar he had left there, Channing gave it to her. "Now if you just pour the remainder of the tea with the leaves in this, add a little honey," and giving her a sharp look, added, "to wean you off your dependence on sugar, and just leave it, you'll have a refreshing drink to bring with you to campus."

She smiled, meeting his gaze, before turning away, under the pretense of refrigerating the leftover tea. She shook her head to dispel the curious effect of Channing's visit. "Shall we go meet up with Heather now?" she asked brightly.

With a summative nod, he said in his easygoing manner, "Yes, I was about to suggest that. I assume you have had your fill of economics for the moment."

She turned away, hoping not to offend him.

"May we switch to sociology?" he asked behind her as she gathered her things. "I'd really like to hear your impressions of Heather's involvement and work in your course."

Kate turned, surprised by the seamless shift in their exchange. With a bright smile, she said, "Sure. We can talk on the way back to campus."

As they walked down the street, Kate glanced over at him. "Besides the shock of Heather's roommates over her cultural predilections for fashion, as well as her food choices, she seems to be getting along rather well with them."

He nodded, it seemed to Kate, sadly. "I'm sure it's a culture shock for her, despite her, um, visits to her mother's world."

"Apparently," Kate said. "Judging from what Heather has re-ported, I don't think she was quite prepared for the philosophical attitudes of her elite classmates." Attempting to contain her grin, she said, "You could hear a pin drop in my classroom when she admitted that your lack of interior plumbing was a lifestyle preference, rather than an economic necessity!"

"I can just imagine," he frowned. "Though, I am quite impressed she shared that with the class."

Kate offered a re-assuring smile. "Oh, once she gets rolling, she approximates the speed of sound. I think she feels the need, particularly given the intellectual context, to educate them on the advantages of '*simplifying*.'"

"And how are they taking her efforts?" His brief glance conveyed a mix of curiosity and concern.

"Once she related the story of the Vermont snow-board Olympic champion, refusing Oprah's offer on national television to plumb his house," she said with a laugh, "I think some of them started to grasp the concept of a lifestyle choice."

"I'm sure it has never occurred to them to think critically about their own lifestyles and corresponding ideologies," he said, his tone crusty.

Glancing at him, she offered a wry grin. "We'll know when I start getting calls from their parents—wondering why their children are requesting outhouses on their estates."

Throwing his head back, Channing laughed heartily before turning to her. "And you wondered why I wished to speak to you about my school?"

"What do you mean?" she asked innocently. "I'm just teaching *Walden*, a book I don't know very well myself."

He stopped to gaze at her intently. "Actually, you are engaged in what an internationally renowned educator called, '*transformational pedagogy.*'"

Kate smiled. "I'm just not sure who is doing the transforming—the students or me."

He gave her a brief nod. "The point is, of course, that transformation should occur within all of you."

"Well, something is happening to me, all right, though I'm not sure what to call it," she acknowledged.

They resumed their walk. "You might pick up a few of Freire's books, some of which he wrote here while teaching at Harvard."

"Really?" she asked wide-eyed. "We had a world-famous educator here?"

"School of Education, of course," Channing said, his tone sarcastic. "It's doubtful that Freire would have taught in the esteemed College of Arts & Sciences."

Looking sideways at one another, they both smiled.

When Heather spotted them making their way toward her dorm, she shouted out the window and waved, "Dad! Dad!"

Kate grinned before saying, "Do you hear that absolute joy in seeing you again? Don't think for a minute she has forgotten you, or your life together in Walden North."

With the colossal doors slamming behind her, Heather ran to her father and hugged him tightly. "I'm so happy to see you—and here!" He gave her a hug, followed by wrapping his arm around her shoulder as they walked. "I just can't believe you came down here to visit me!"

He smiled at her enthusiasm. "I'll be combining my board meetings with visits to campus here to see you on a regular basis," he said quietly. "If you'd like."

Heather looked over at Kate. "Told you he might show up anytime!"

"He certainly surprised me," she admitted.

Heather gazed from Kate to her father. "I told him where to find you—in your office."

Kate smiled. "Oh, I wasn't there at all. After we parted company, I did something utterly uncharacteristic for me. I simply sat in a courtyard."

Heather looked surprised. "But you seemed in such a hurry."

With a wide grin, Kate said, "I was, actually, until I came across a tree."

Turning to her father, Heather asked, "How did you find her?" With a furtive glance at Kate, he turned to his daughter and replied simply, "Not finding her in her office, I just meditated on her location, and when a vision came to me of an old Norway spruce, I walked around until I found it."

Kate turned to stare at him in awe. "You *did*?"

Channing just shrugged. "That's what I do." He dashed a quick look at her. "Not so difficult really, once you tune into the energies of the universe—and other people."

Heather giggled and squeezed her father's arm. "It's so good to have you here! I haven't heard anyone since I came to Harvard speak like you do."

Despite her efforts to reign in internal waves of merriment, Kate burst out laughing. "Now that's an understatement if ever I heard one!"

Heather turned to glance at Kate. "Well, she comes close at times to sounding like you, but she's right, there's no one else."

Channing shot Kate a sharp look that quickly subdued her. "Perhaps you should frequent the School of Theology. You might find some spiritually inclined folks there."

Kate smiled. "I don't think I'm allowed to frequent other colleges here other than my own." She looked at Channing. "I meant no harm, but you must admit your Thoreauvian lifestyle is not something one expects to find sauntering around these theoretical grounds."

He smiled back. "No offense taken." With a slight sigh, more involuntary than deliberate, he said, "I am aware of how strange my ways may seem to you, though in other circles, they would be taken for granted."

Heather chimed in. "That's right," she said turning to Kate. "You should see him at the retreat center. People revere him, hanging on to his every word."

"Really," Kate said, with a slight toss of her head. "I can only imagine."

Turning to her, Channing said in his serious tone, "Perhaps, sometime you will experience the reality."

Looking at him in surprise, she said, "Yes, maybe."

Once they emerged from the campus, Heather turned to her father. "So where are we going for dinner, Dad?"

He looked from Heather to Kate. "Well, if you two don't mind, there is a local foods restaurant run by some people from the Berkshire Center that has just recently opened. Shall we try that?"

Both nodding in agreement, they proceeded down the street until they reached the town center, lined in storefronts.

"It is one of these here," he said, scanning the names.

"What's the name of the place?" asked Kate.

"'Local Foods, Global Fare,' I believe."

Kate grinned. "It's all-encompassing, at least."

Heather smiled at Kate. "Maybe it's that Emersonian concept you told me about—the '*Great Whole*'—or something like that."

Kate nodded. "Yes, perhaps."

Looking over at Channing she said, "See? Your daughter is really on top of things."

Heather beamed. "Glad you think so."

Kate smiled at Channing. "She is not unlike the transcendentalists, with her remarkable ability to synthesize disparate bits of knowledge—applying her insights to a new context."

Channing looked fondly at Heather before making eye contact with Kate. "It's her meditative training. It helps one see into the realm of the larger whole, often invisible to the uni-dimensional."

Kate gave Heather a big smile. "Very impressive, Heather."

"Oh, it's my dad's influence, really," she admitted, before jogging ahead to locate the restaurant. About halfway down the block, she stopped and turned, calling out to them, "Here it is!"

Just before they entered the restaurant, Channing turned to Kate, and briefly touching her arm, said in a low voice, "Your interest in Heather has made all the difference to her level of contentment here." With a folding of his hands and a long bow, he said, "Um, thank you."

Kate smiled at him. "Actually, I think it's mutual. Although our lives seem worlds apart, we seem to enjoy our little exchanges." She shrugged before whispering, "I think we bond over both being 'outsiders,' as it were."

He looked at her through impenetrable eyes. "Each of us is ultimately alone in the universe. The challenge—as well as the inner joy—emerges in discovering and exploring our points of intersection."

Kate nodded. "Profound." *As always.*

Unlike the majority of Cambridge cafés with their largely two-top, and occasionally four-top tables, three long harvest tables comprised the seating. Larger than life photos adorned the walls, depicting various vegetables, plots, and urban gardens, alternating with floor to ceiling scenes of trees and forests—making the place feel more like an art gallery than a restaurant. Quiet mood music—Kate could think of no other name for it—quietly filtered through the air, offering the sounds of waves, birds, and the occasional whale, interspersed with harp, flute, and soft piano. Kate stifled a grin as the thought passed her mind that everything seemed different in Channing's presence, almost like a parallel universe.

"Let's dine in the back where it will be quieter," he suggested, "if that suits you both." Amused by his comment, Kate looked around at the church-like restaurant, observing people engaged in what seemed like reverential eating, or in barely audible conversation.

"This differs considerably from the bustling bistros I have been frequenting here," she remarked. With a smile, she added, "More like a nature refuge than an urban eatery."

He nodded, as a small smile emerged, before receding again. "I thought this more appropriate for our dinner than anywhere else here in Cambridge," he said.

As Channing led them to a table near the back, Kate noticed some people smiling at him in what seemed like recognition. As she turned in surprise to him, she observed him making a slight bow to one couple, while pressing the tips of his fingers of each hand together.

When they arrived at his seating choice, Channing indicated for Kate to sit across from Heather and him, who sat with their backs to the wall. As she sat down, her eyes immediately were drawn to the wall photo behind, which caused her to gasp involuntarily.

"It feels so familiar," she said, leaning over to Channing, as she gazed at the scene of a deep, pine forest.

Channing smiled at her. "It should."

Heather turned to look back, reeling around to face her father. "Dad, it's one of yours, isn't it?" She gave him a hug. "Thanks. It really feels like home here. It's my new '*local*'!"

They all chuckled at the double entêndre.

Channing touched the shoulder of his daughter. "You are welcome to eat here anytime. I have already bartered for your expenses."

Kate looked from one to the other. "Then it is the scene from your place! I knew it felt familiar, but I just didn't expect to see your setting on the walls of a Cambridge restaurant." She shook her head slowly. "This is all quite amazing, if not uncanny, really."

Heather offered a big smile. "Oh, we call it *synchronicity*," she said, as she glanced at her father. "You know, part of that Emersonian '*great whole*' again."

Kate smiled as she shook her head. "No wonder you remember that notion so vividly. You actually live it!"

Heather and Channing both smiled, as he said, "Yes, we do."

Kate looked at him, intrigued. "So what is your connection to this restaurant, exactly?"

"Oh, some of us from the Center had each invested some money into the startup," he said in an offhanded tone.

Kate shot him a pointed look. "I didn't notice that on your expense sheet."

He regarded her through stoical eyes. "I believe it was under 'miscellaneous.'"

Heather peered from one to the other. "What are you guys talking about? What expense sheet?"

Channing nodded gently, his eyes now soft. "Oh, we were discussing the finer points of Thoreauvian economics through examining a comparative model."

Heather giggled. "See, Kate? He is using our new term as well." Leaning on her elbows, she said playfully to her father, "Be careful—or all kinds of statements by her will start *resonating* with you."

"Too late," he said, nodding, with the briefest of sidelong glances at Kate. "They already have."

Kate looked away. "I wasn't aware that I was having such an influence." She glanced at Heather, before settling on Channing.

Nodding somberly, he murmured, "Awareness is the key to enlightenment, to the '*higher laws*' of our consciousness."

Heather turned to him with bright eyes. "Hey, that's the chapter we are just starting to read."

"Yes," he said with a nod. "Perhaps the most profound of the book."

Patting her dad's shoulder, Heather added, "It's been great for me, Kate, since your trip up to our place, because whatever you said to him has led Dad to e-mail me regularly, asking about my studies. It's awesome to have a father whom I can talk to about *Walden*. I mean, I know we live like Thoreau, but I didn't realize, really, until this course, how much his philosophy resonates with Thoreau's." She nodded. "Pretty awesome."

"Oh, really?" Kate said lightly, before glancing at Channing, who was now staring steadily at her.

"You have awakened me to the experience I was missing—participating more actively in Heather's learning."

Kate's eyes widened. "Oh? But how do you do that, exactly, with no Internet?"

"Oh, I go to the Walden library and use theirs," he said. With a rare smile, he added, "I now look forward to a report of each class with you. Quite intriguing, I must say."

"But surely you know the motifs from each chapter by heart, since you actually live them," she said in faint protest.

He waved his hand. "Perhaps it is less the themes, as how the various members of your class, from different walks of life, respond to and interact with both Thoreauvian insights and one another." With a shrug, he said, "As someone involved with meditative retreats, I suppose I have a bit of the educator in me, as well."

"I'm sure you do," she rejoined.

He leaned over to touch Heather's arm. "And to read Heather's journal entries chronicling her journey of discovery, not only of her reading, but her classmates, and the campus at large, is such an uplifting experience—if not transformational, for her, and I admit, for me."

Kate looked searchingly from one to another. "I had no idea."

Channing fixed a steady gaze on Kate. "You have consciously chosen, in your teaching at Harvard, to walk along the '*road less traveled*,' through relying on such a unique course assignment, and yet one that makes '*all the difference*,' so to speak." He leaned forward. "Surely, you are stirring, from their long slumbers, the intellects and souls of your students."

Kate nodded. "It has been quite an '*awakening*,' to use your term—once I decided to begin each class with reading some excerpts from selected journal responses to serve as a basis for class discussion." Shrugging, she admitted, "Before, I was a hopeless and dull lecturer. Besides, I dwell in theory. What do I know about *simplicity*, really?"

"Perhaps more than you realize," said Channing.

She smiled at Heather. "She's the real expert, so borrowing from some pedagogical techniques we used in teaching writing at Northwestern, I shifted the class focus from me to the students."

Heather spoke with pride in her voice. "I've gone from feeling like an outsider, to an expert on Thoreau's lifestyle." She smiled at Kate. "And it has been interesting to hear about the ways other people live—even if I don't necessarily agree."

Channing nodded, his expression serious. "A healthy respect for differences, as well as an active encouragement to engage with new perspectives," he announced, glancing at Kate, "form the basis of our center."

"And the new one, as well, I presume," said Kate.

"Yes, indeed," he responded. Again leaning toward her as he passed on a menu, he asked, "Am I correct to assume the next stage in the learning journey is to engage with '*experiments in living*'?"

"Absolutely!" Turning to Heather, she said, "If you can keep a secret, I'll let you in on one such '*experiment*'—to experience the dawn." With a grin, she qualified, "and I don't mean by staying up all night."

Heather rolled her eyes. "I don't think that will go over well."

"Oh, I bet," said Kate, "but to experience Thoreau's meanings, one needs to *rise*, not go to sleep, at dawn."

The conversation soon shifted to a discussion of their food choices. Motioning to the menu, Channing said, "Cáitlín, I thought you might be particularly intrigued by one of the dishes featured here."

She immediately flashed the palm of her hand at him and commanded, "Wait—don't tell me. Let me guess!"

She quickly scanned down the list of entrées before exclaiming, "My God, '*The Bean Field*'?" Shaking her head in awe, she read, "Thoreau, with a Vermont flavor." Dropping the menu on the table, she wagged her finger at him. "Aha! I bet they're *your* beans!"

Channing actually laughed. "Well, yes, actually, they are. As the grower, I was able to name the entrée myself, hence the particular description." His expression was soft. "I thought you'd be pleased."

Heather waved her hand. "See, Kate? Synchronicity at work again. It's everywhere." She looked over at her father. "Right, Dad?"

"So it seems, so it seems." With the briefest of glances at Kate, he focused again on the menu.

Resuming her reading, Kate was particularly struck by the categories under which the various food items were arranged. She shook her head, before looking over at Channing through quizzical eyes—only to discover a twinkle in his own.

"*Resonate* with you, does it?" he asked with a chuckle.

Heather began to laugh. "Hey, this is like reading *Walden*!" She began to read from the menu. "'Local, Natural, and Simple are the key concepts around which we create our food offerings, with a healthy respect for culturally diverse modes of preparation.'"

Kate smiled. "Well, except for that last bit." She scanned the menu herself with increasing fascination. "How clever," she remarked, "rather than the term 'entrées,' they have adopted the reference from *Walden*—'Higher Laws.'" She looked over at Channing. "Why is that, I wonder?"

Kate could see from his face that he was relishing the dining experience. He couldn't help but smile, as she waited for his explanation. Suddenly, it dawned on her. She dropped her eyes back to the menu, rapidly rereading the various choices, before looking over at both of them. "Of course! It's vegetarian." She took a sip of her water. "Very clever."

"We decided to organize the menu around some of the culinary and associated spiritual principles espoused in *Walden*, since they, in turn, resonate—there is that word again—with Buddhist practices at our center."

"Such as?" Kate asked. Smiling, she added, "Shouldn't we be dining on beans, water, and flatbread?"

Channing nodded. "In a manner of speaking, yes, but have a look and see for yourself."

Kate offered a sly smile. "You don't wish to order for us?" She couldn't help but contrast him in her mind to Blake, who most certainly would have done so in this situation. With a slight grimace, she pushed him out of her thoughts.

Channing shook his head firmly. "I would never think to subsume to my own preferences, the possibilities that may emerge from shaping your own experience." With a nod, he suggested, "Perhaps we may each choose something that appeals, and if you like, we can all share."

Well-stated, thought Kate, with a sense of admiration.

After they had reviewed the menus, Kate remarked, "This is certainly a new experience for me."

"Oh?" Channing asked quietly.

She looked from one to the other with a slight grimace. "It may be hard for you to imagine, given the fact that you grow your own food, but for me, coming from a city of some eight million people, I don't remember the last time I saw a farmer's field." She nodded. "Except for yours, of course, which afterwards, caused me to think through the many degrees of separation between most food consumers and the food we eat." She gave a shy smile. "This is a real treat—in so many ways."

Heather asked, "Are you a vegetarian?"

Kate gazed a bit sadly at her. "You know, Heather, I have spent most of my adult life marooned in the library working. I never thought to consider developing a philosophy toward the food I consumed."

With a slight bow, Channing said, "The culinary journey of ten thousand meals begins with a single, knowing bite."

Kate studied him quietly for a moment before looking down. "This is unique in every respect, and, perhaps, for me, the beginning of such a journey."

Heather turned in excitement to her father. "Hey, Dad, speaking of journeys, did Kate tell you we are coming home next weekend?" Motioning to Kate, she explained, "Kate offered me a ride since she is spending time in the Walden library doing research."

Channing looked surprised. "No, but what a perfect opportunity to explore further the concept of 'Higher Laws.'"

"What do you mean?" Kate asked, as she tilted her head slightly.

"At our house, you will have the opportunity to experience directly Thoreau's insights regarding an intelligent consciousness that resides in other life forms."

"Oh?" She glanced from one to the other in surprise, waiting for an explanation.

"The experience of interacting with animals from the wild to the domesticated opens our minds and hearts to the 'higher laws,' as it were, of our beings—to act respectfully towards them as fellow creatures sharing the planet."

Heather smiled at her father before addressing Kate. "I think he means we'll go animal watching—you know, deer, moose, and bears, with some spotted cows thrown in for the domesticated examples."

Kate laughed. "Well, that sounds fun, Heather. I am more than intrigued after reading and hearing your accounts of bears, among other wild animals, in the forest. I'd love to see them in action." She glanced over at Channing. "Though, perhaps, at first, from a respectful distance."

She grinned at them both as the server made her way to their table. Dressed in a brightly colored sari, she bowed deeply at Channing, smiled, and greeted him. "Welcome to our opening."

"Thank you, Deesha," Channing said, with a slight bow in return. "You remember Heather, I should think, and this is Cáitlín, a colleague in spirit," he said with a slight glance at Kate.

"Fascinating restaurant," Kate said with a smile.

Deesha bowed slightly and said in a singsong voice, "Thank you for your kind words."

Looking at Kate, Channing asked, "Shall we start with your choice, Cáitlín?"

"In honor of this evening's company and your opening, I would like to try 'The Bean Field,' please."

Deesha smiled, her entire expression radiating happiness. "A choice close to home," she said, before turning to bow before Channing.

Arching her eyebrow slightly at the woman's statement, Kate felt the flush from her blushing cheeks.

Heather jumped in. "I'd like the Vishnu squash, please." Leaning on her elbows, she smiled at Kate. "Wait 'til you try it—it's delicious."

"Can't wait," said Kate pleasantly, shifting her gaze.

Heather turned to her father. "Hey, Dad, remember we used to order it when we stayed at that Buddhist retreat in India?" She shook her head. "It was always my favorite."

"My, you sure get around, Heather," said Kate with admiration.

"And for you, Channing?" inquired Deesha sweetly, with a slight bow.

"Boxty colcannon cakes, please, to start," he said, glancing at Kate, "in honor of our special Irish guest, with 'Grown Wild,' please."

After Deesha poured out some herbal tea and left, Kate leaned over to Channing. "What is boxty? I've never heard of it."

"It's a traditional dish from the north of Ireland, I believe, made from vegetables and herbs found in abundance all over the country—kale, onions, potatoes, wild leeks, and parsley."

When the food arrived, Kate gazed in admiration at the various dishes, not having ever tried the choices her companions had ordered. They dined over a resplendent meal of various heirloom and gleaned vegetables steamed, fried, and baked, tossed in flaxseed and sunflower oils from northern New England, yet prepared according to some of the world's most treasured culinary traditions.

As they lingered over the last remaining bites, Channing remarked, "How have you enjoyed your meal, Cáitlín?"

"Very much." She offered an enthusiastic nod, coupled with a bright smile. "I had no idea vegetables could be so good—and so filling!"

Channing smiled in response. "To conclude our discussion of 'Baker Farm,' I might mention that vegetable buying would trim your food budget significantly over the purchase of prepared meals and meats as well as processed foods."

Kate smiled at him, as she finished the last of her beans and garlic set on a bed of herbed spinach. "I might try out that suggestion as my own '*experiment in living.*'" she said with a chuckle. "The students are bound to enjoy that."

As they said good night outside the restaurant, Kate turned to Channing, looking up at him with a serious expression. "Thank you on so many levels," she said, her tone ringing with sincerity, "so much to think about."

He bowed long and low. "And thank you, Cáitlín, for resurrecting my bond with Heather, as well as for all the good energy you share with her—both in the classroom and out."

Heather gave Kate a brief hug. "I hope this is okay, hugging my professor," she gushed, "but it has been so wonderful for me to spend time with you and Dad together."

Kate smiled at her. "Well, Heather, now we know of a great place to eat besides the dining room on campus—and Starbucks."

"Until next week, then," said Kate, with a glance at Channing, "on to Walden North and the *higher laws* of our natures."

She walked lightly away, though steeped in deep thought.

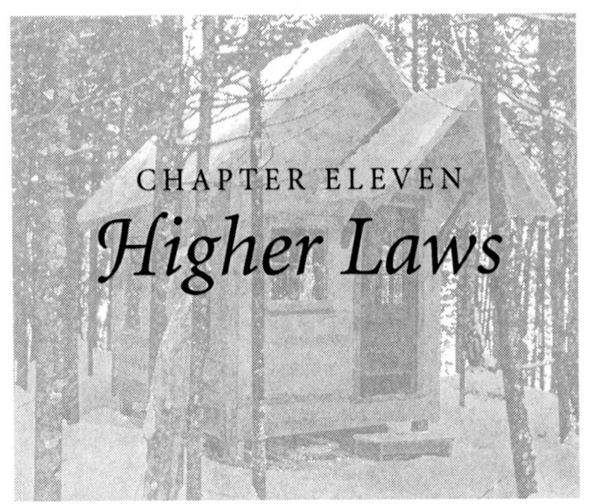

CHAPTER ELEVEN
Higher Laws

THE FARTHER NORTH KATE AND HEATHER DROVE FROM BOSTON, the more spectacular the landscape. Though trying to focus on the road with its bumper-to-bumper traffic, Kate couldn't help but shift her gaze to the miles of spruce-green forests, seemingly ablaze in dramatic flames of red, orange, and yellow.

"My God, it's so beautiful!" Kate swooned. "The contrast against the green really augments the effect."

Heather smiled knowingly. "Ah, yep. "

Kate glanced over at her companion. "Ishmael describes something like this effect in *Moby-Dick,* when he states that one cannot truly appreciate something—until first experiencing its antithesis." With a nod, she concluded, "I guess something similar is at work on our senses in this case."

Heather glanced out the window, before looking over at her driver with a bemused expression. "Oh, it gets even more beautiful—wait until we reach the mountains."

"Can't imagine."

Heather stared at her through slanted eyes. "But don't you remember from your last trip?"

Kate glanced over before explaining. "No, I don't really. When I drive, my mind is usually absorbed with whatever ideas I have been working on, so miles pass by without any conscious acknowledgment of the scenery."

"My dad says it's better to be in the moment."

"Oh, probably," Kate said lightly, before offering a self-deprecating smile. "That is not something that comes easily to me."

Heather chuckled. "I can imagine."

With a slight frown, Kate continued. "Actually, I don't think I came this way last time. At least, not the highway going through the mountains." She peered out her side window. "It really is gorgeous, though."

Heather squinted. "Well, maybe you should try to be 'more in the moment' as my dad would say, and oh, speaking of him, wasn't it Thoreau who said something about the '*journey being as important as the destination*'?" Rolling her eyes, she said with a smile, "I know my father always says that whenever we travel."

With a quick glance, Kate grinned at her. "Well, it's often attributed to him, but it's actually a paraphrase from Emerson."

"Really?" Heather said. "I'll have to tell my dad that. He thinks it's from Thoreau."

"Most people do," said Kate. With a sidelong glance, she remarked, "I've been a destination type person myself, I guess, never too interested in the journey part." She added with a shrug, "You know, goal-directed, driven, that sort of thing." She stared straight ahead, thinking before speaking. "But this feels good, this focusing on the journey aspect of the destination."

Heather responded dryly, "I think Thoreau and Emerson are getting under your skin."

Kate emitted a wide grin. "Oh, most likely, given my near complete focus on *Walden* these days."

Heather gazed out the side window at the endless line of trees. "For me, it's so great to get out of the city. I feel like I can start breathing again."

Kate shot her a concerned glance. "Why, you feel claustrophobic in the city?"

Heather shrugged and looked over. "I guess I feel constrained by the presence of all those buildings, as well as all the people, with their attitudes and expectations." She turned away to focus on the trees outside. "I feel really alive and free in the woods."

Kate studied her a moment. "And you're not afraid to walk alone in those big forests up there?"

"Afraid? In the woods?" Heather turned, revealing her surprise by the question. "No, not at all. If you really want to know, I'm afraid in the city."

"But what about the animals in the forest?" Kate glanced over. "You're really not afraid of being attacked by some wild creature? I know you have written about some of your animal friends and neighbors, but I figured you were relying on poetic license."

Heather shrugged. "Oh, they won't hurt you. I'd be more afraid of humans anytime over a moose or bear."

Kate's eyes widened. "Really? But what about all those bear attacks?" She turned to look at Heather. "I know you mentioned in one of your journal entries that bears won't attack you unless feeling seriously threatened, which is what kept me going as I walked through your forest up there, but can one really count on that while alone in an immense forest?"

Heather offered an emphatic nod. "You must be thinking of all those grim stories about grizzlies." She put her feet up against the dashboard. "Black bears, as I was saying, are absolutely incredible animals. I've basically grown up with entire families of them."

Kate looked over, her sense of horror conveyed in her taut expression. "What do you mean—grew up with them? Surely, you didn't interact with them as playmates?"

Noting Kate's expression, Heather nodded. "Guess it sounds weird, or even really dangerous, but yes, I did." She offered a wide smile. "The cubs are the most fun, though the mothers are pretty playful as well."

Kate almost slammed on the brakes. "What?" She turned her full gaze on Heather. "You played with *cubs*?" she asked, her tone increasing in pitch. "With their mothers standing right there?"

Heather smiled in amusement. "Yep. Guess it sounds pretty exotic to a girl from the city, huh?"

Kate just shook her head. "Does your father know about this?"

"Of course!" Heather grinned. "He's the one who introduced me to my first bears when I was little." She leaned back, glancing sideways at Kate. "By now, we've had, I don't know, several successive generations of bears."

"Oh, my God." Kate gripped the steering wheel.

Sizing up her listener's horrified expression, Heather explained. "First, some adult bears appeared, followed the next spring, by their cubs, who, in turn, when they became mothers a few years later, arrived with their cubs, and so on, down through the generations."

She stopped talking as a sudden realization swept through her. "Come to think of it, I've had more bear friends than human ones."

"I can't even begin to imagine." Kate responded, her tone hollow. With a terse shake of her head, she realized that she had greatly underestimated Channing's level of eccentricity. She could not understand how anyone, let alone a parent, would allow a little girl to play with bears.

Heather smiled at her. "Oh, you will when we get home. I'm sure you'll be introduced to our furry friends. I think that's what my dad meant by experiencing the 'higher laws.'"

Kate shot her a sharp look. "You're kidding. What's 'higher' about getting mauled to death?"

Heather said matter-of-factly, "Oh, they won't hurt you—unless you try to hurt them, I guess." Smiling, she added, "And since I can't imagine you walking around with a gun slung over your shoulder ready to pounce on some poor bear, I think you'll be perfectly safe." With a sly look, she said, "Think of it as an '*experiment in living*.'"

Kate stared at her. "I think I'll pass on this experience in favor of the theory."

Heather turned away to gaze out the windows. "For me—and for my dad, at least, when you get to know wild animals, such as bears, deer, and moose, like we do, we find it unthinkable to consider eating them."

Kate nodded. "I wouldn't think of eating them either, but I don't need to risk my life wrestling with them in my backyard to decide that."

Heather glanced sideways. "And what about cows and pigs?"

Kate met her glance. "Domesticated animals, you mean? Well, they're different."

Unwavering in her gaze, Heather pressed, "In what way?"

"Well," said Kate, returning to focus on the highway, "they are bred for human consumption."

"Tell that to a mother cow who has just given birth to her newborn—" said Heather, sitting up and turning directly to Kate, "only to have it taken away from her forcibly, watching in agony as the poor, crying baby gets shoved into a calf shed, a plastic jail no bigger than the poor calf itself. And to add to the injustice of it all, Mom is forced to give away her mother's milk, intended for her newborn, to the farmer instead—so he can sell it to us to drink in our lattés."

"I have to admit, I've never thought about milk in that way," Kate said, her voice hushed.

Heather stared at her. "You should see the look in the mother cows' eyes when they hear their babies crying out in distress over their separation." She shuddered. "It's really awful."

Kate drove silently for some time before speaking. "But isn't that what they call animal instinct, rather than true feelings, like humans have?"

Heather nodded and said, "When you experience animals up close and personal, you discover that they do have feelings, the same as you and me." She looked over at Kate. "I think some animals are way more intelligent than we humans," she said with a shrug. "They see, hear, move, and act better than we do."

"Really?" She pursed her lips into silence, as her own question triggered her memory of passages from *Moby-Dick*. "You remind me a bit of Ishmael," she admitted in a sheepish tone, "though I assumed Melville was relying on personification as a technique to make his reader enjoy his accounts of whales."

Heather smirked. "Well, thanks—I think." Raising her feet back up along the dashboard, she hugged her raised knees. "Haven't you ever heard or read about those stories of dogs finding their way home after being left hundreds of miles away—"

"But that could be pure instinct," Kate interjected. "As I assumed are the whale migrations."

"Okay, I'll give you two really good examples. Wanna hear?" she asked, glancing over at Kate.

Kate shrugged her shoulders and said with a nod, "Sure. I'm open. Go ahead."

Heather smiled. "Well, the first story is about a bear. A *black* bear—and a female to boot."

"Oh," said Kate with an involuntary shudder. "Sounds like the opening scene of a horror film."

Heather turned to her, her eyes sparkling. "This story is just incredible. It happened to a friend of my dad's." With a sardonic smile, she added, "Ready?"

Kate smiled. "Fire away."

Heather turned to her in surprise. "You don't know how close you are." She studied Kate a minute. "Are you empathic?"

Kate glanced at her in amusement. "Not that I know of."

Heather sunk down in her seat. "Well, anyway. So Fred was writing for the local paper in the next town over, after moving up to Walden North from some flatland area."

"Flatland?" Kate looked over with a mystified expression.

Heather waved her hand dismissive gesture. "Oh, didn't I explain that before in one of my journal entries?" She glanced over at Kate, who just shrugged her shoulders.

"Sorry, don't remember," Kate said, offered apologetically.

"Well, whatever. It's just a term we locals use for outsiders, '*flatlanders*', we call them, who move into our mountainous area of Vermont."

Kate sighed. "Sorry I asked. Go on."

Heather settled into her seat, gently swaying her bent knees sideways. "So, this guy, Fred, moved to Walden North. One day, he walked out onto his back deck and saw a bear eating from his bird feeder—just at the edge of the deck."

Kate looked at her, now clearly startled. "You mean, right there, just a couple feet away from him?"

Nodding, Heather continued. "Yep. So he freaked out and yelled at the bear to stop, as he banged together whatever he could find to make a noise, before running back into the house."

"What did the bear do?"

Heather glanced over at her. "She ran away, of course." With a shrug, she added, "Who wants to eat, when some strange guy is yelling and screaming at you with threatening gestures?"

Kate chuckled. "There's that, I guess. Even a bear might not enjoy such clamor while trying to eat."

Heather looked sharply at her. "Especially a bear. They're very quiet eaters."

Kate glanced at her with a bemused expression. "Yes, I guess you would know." Returning her attention to the road, she said, "So continue on with your story. What happened next?"

"Well," said Heather, giving Kate a quick glance, before staring ahead herself, "Fred refilled the bear feeder, thinking that he'd scared away the bear successfully, but that evening, as he went out to enjoy the sunset, he saw her sitting, just down the deck from him, eating away at the seeds."

"Oh, my God." Kate felt riveted by fear herself.

Heather continued, undeterred by the interruption. "So, he decided, 'I'll outsmart this damn bear.' He then said to her, the bear, that is, 'Look, if you leave my bird feeder alone, I'll give you your own bowl of sunflower seeds—but away from the house.' With that, he made a hasty retreat back inside."

Kate smiled in relief.

"The next day, he set out a large bowl, brimming with sunflower seeds, at the edge of his mowed yard—far enough away to feel safe from the bear, but close enough that he could watch what happened."

"Did the bear return?" Kate asked with rising anticipation.

Heather turned to her and smiled. "Yep, but this time, the bear went for the bowl of seeds, not the bird feeder, as Fred had asked her."

Kate looked sideways at her. "So, don't tell me you think the bear was respecting the fellow's request, rather than responding to an inner instinct: '*Eat from here. There's more of it*'?"

Heather nodded firmly. "Ah, yep, as you'll see by the rest of the story."

Kate sighed. "Okay—continue, please."

"So this became a daily occurrence, Fred providing sunflower seeds and the bear coming to eat, to the point that the guy, writing for the paper, as I said—"

She stopped, glancing at Kate. "Are you with me?"

Kate smiled. "Yes, go on."

"So he decided to write a weekly column about 'his' bear. He took photos of her and published them along with accounts of his bear watching, followed by later, in more articles, about talking to the bear, continuing his account until hibernation."

"Umm," said Kate.

Casting a sidelong look, before turning excitedly to Kate, Heather asked, "Guess what happened that next spring?"

"She returned," said Kate with a quick glance.

Heather offered her a big smile. "Not only did she return, but she arrived—accompanied by three little cubs!"

Kate's eyes widened. "Oh, no, he didn't *play* with them, did he—like you?"

Turning to meet her gaze, Heather grinned. "Well, not yet, anyway."

"So?"

"So, Fred appealed to his readership for sunflower seed donations, since it was getting pretty expensive in seeds. An organic farmer who grew them started to contribute huge bags of seeds, about 100 lbs. weekly in the beginning of the summer. Well, the cubs grew up that summer, going from looking like small Pekinese dogs to good-sized German shepherds by fall."

Kate looked scared. "That big?"

"Yep." Heather nodded. "And Fred started to lose his fear, talking to them more and more—even naming each of the cubs."

Kate interjected, "He didn't play with them, did he?"

"Don't be so worried," Heather chided. "No, but he wrote about them and clearly started really caring for them. He got to the point where he could recognize each of the three cubs."

"*Really.*"

"So one morning in late fall, after the first snows came, he woke up to a gun shot, really close by."

Kate looks over at her in dismay. "Oh, no, don't tell me."

Heather met her stare. "It's not what you think. She bit her lip before continuing. "Actually, it's worse."

Kate groaned. "Oh, God, all right. Tell me."

With a quick glance, Heather continued. "He got up, grabbed his coat, and ran outside—only to see one of the cubs bleeding to death, as a hunter stood with his gun pointed down on top of her. Fred shouted at the hunter to stop, as he ran down toward him and the poor bear, but the only response was another gun shot, with the dead bear cub lying on the ground."

"Oh, my God, how incredibly sad," moaned Kate.

Heather shot her a look. "Oh, it gets worse." With a shake of her head, she continued. "From out of the woods, came the mother bear, whom Fred had named Sparky—due to her *sparky* personality." She looked over at Kate. "She used to get riled easily, Fred said, hence the name."

"Uh-huh, okay, go on, then."

"So, from out of the woods, Sparky came charging, and before the hunter could do anything, Sparky ran him down and swatted her big hand right across his face, sending him sprawling to the ground, then turned to her beloved cub, and—"

Heather stopped and gulped, as she wiped away some tears that started to trickle down her cheeks. "This part always gets me," she admitted.

Kate clenched the steering wheel. "What *happened*?"

"She bent over her dead cub, licking the blood off the wounds, picked up the little one, cradling it in her arms, and started to *cry*." Heather broke down in tears. Trying to compose herself, she turned to Kate with tear-brimmed eyes. "She *cried*, Kate, just like humans, real tears, sobbing away for her murdered child."

Kate wiped away some tears of her own that inevitably flowed from her eyes.

Heather continued. "She just held her child, rocking back and forth, moaning."

Kate shook her head. "How incredibly sad." She looked over at Heather. "What about Fred? What did he do?"

Heather turned, and placing her left leg under her, continued. "This is the really, really, incredible part."

Kate groaned. "Oh, my God, there's more drama?"

"Fred was so moved by the situation and Sparky's grieving, that he walked over to her, and said, through his own tears, 'I'm so sorry, Sparky, I'm so sorry this happened,' and he touched Sparky's arm."

Kate's eyes widened. "What did she do?"

"Oh, she just kept moaning. Then, he turned, went into his shed, brought out a shovel, and dug a hole—to bury the cub in."

Kate turned to her in surprise. "But how would the bear, Sparky, know what he was going to do?"

Heather smirked at her. "What? You don't think bears bury their own dead—just like humans?"

Chastened, Kate returned to her wheel and the highway. "Oh, how ignorant of me, of course." Shaking her head, she urged her on.

"So after about an hour of holding her dead cub, Sparky walked over to the excavated hole, and carefully," she said, glancing at Kate, "gently placed the cub in it, and sat there while Fred covered it up."

Kate twisted her mouth into a grimace. "It's a great story, but how do we know all this really happened?"

Heather glanced at her with glittering eyes. "His wife documented the entire thing in photos."

Kate's eyes widened. "Oh, my God."

"So, here's the last incredible bit to the story. After Fred finished covering the body, he touched Sparky again, telling her how sorry he was, and—"

Kate interrupted. "Hey, what happened to the hunter?"

Heather grinned slyly. "Oh, he was escorted off the premises by the Game Warden, called in by Fred's wife." She glanced over at Kate. "Hunting out of season is really frowned on where I come from." With a toss of her head, she added, "And you're not supposed to kill cubs."

Kate glanced at her. "Sorry for interrupting. I had forgotten about him."

Heather smirked. "Well, he has some scars left over to remind him of his awful behavior."

Kate nodded, saying nothing.

"So, anyway, Fred went up to sit on his deck to process what had happened and to drown his sorrows in a beer, since he felt directly responsible for the cub's death."

Kate looked at her in surprise.

Noticing, Heather retorted, "Well, it was his newspaper columns that had alerted the hunter to a constant supply of bear meat in Fred's back yard."

Kate turned her lip. "Oh, disgusting."

Heather nodded. "Exactly. So anyway, he sat there with his head down in his arms, which were resting against the deck railing, and thinking how he had caused the entire tragedy. He actually started to cry." She glanced at Kate. "You see, he had lost one of his own teenage children in a car accident, so he felt doubly traumatized by what had happened to Sparky."

Kate looked over with sad eyes. "How tragic."

"Yep. So anyway, he just sat huddled over, gently crying, feeling really, really sad and bad, when all of a sudden, he felt these arms wrap around him and hug him."

"The wife coming to console him, I suppose," Kate said with a nod.

Heather glanced over at Kate. "Yes, he assumed the same thing. So thinking it was his wife, he said, 'Oh, I'll be all right. I just feel so bad,'" and reached out with a finger or two to touch her arm, when he realized," she said, turning fully to face Kate, "it was *furry!*"

Kate's eyes transformed into huge orbs. "*What?*"

"Yep. Sparky had come back to console Fred! She was giving him a true bear hug!"

Kate shook her head in awe. "Oh, my God. How absolutely amazing."

"The photo the wife took of Sparky hugging Fred went viral on the Internet," said Heather, nodding. "My dad says his articles and excerpts from his book, *My Five Summers with the Bears,* now appear in major papers around the country."

Kate just shook her head. "That is one incredible story."

Heather pushed out her leg over the top of the dashboard. "Well, that's one example of how intelligent, thinking, and feeling bears are. And all other animals I have met are just the same." She looked over at Kate. "That's why we don't eat meat in my family. How could we—with such wonderful animal neighbors and friends?"

Kate shook her head gently. "As always, around you and your father, a lot to contemplate."

Heather gazed out the window. "We're coming to the Whites now," she said with excitement. Glancing over at Kate, only to notice her quizzical expression, she explained, "The White Mountains."

Bending over toward the windshield, Kate peered up at the series of steep, rocky, sharp-edged mountains. "Why are they called 'the Whites'?" She looked over at Heather. "They're not snow-covered."

Heather said easily, "Oh, I bet Washington, since it holds the record for the coldest temperatures on earth, is already covered in snow, but that's not the reason for their name."

"Really? Where is Washington?"

"It's beyond the Franconia Range here in the Notch, which is this place, forming the end of the Presidentials." Heather smiled at her, and sitting up straight, explained, "The color comes from the Abenaki name for these peaks, which, when they saw them from a distance, called them 'Waumbek,' roughly translated, I guess, as 'glistening foreheads.'" She beamed at Kate.

Kate nodded and smiled. "You are quite the tour guide," she said with clear admiration in her voice. "Very impressive, though I still don't get why they saw them as glistening." She glanced up again. "To me, they look dark and gray."

Heather leaned back to look up through the sunroof. "Oh, that's just because we are driving along this tiny little valley through their base. From a distance, since they are made from white granite, they glisten and look white."

Kate nodded slowly. "Aha, interesting. Again, our understanding is guided by our perspectives, or," glancing with an authoritative nod at Heather, "as Ishmael suggested, '*look at this matter in every light.*'"

"Interesting," murmured Heather, non-committally.

Undeterred, Kate kept her eyes on the curvy road as it wound through the notch. "Melville seemed to be claiming in *Moby-Dick*, that only after considering things in every light, can we gain true understanding into life and its frequent ambiguities."

Heather grinned, as she rolled her eyes in Kate's direction. "Always the professor."

Kate offered an apologetic smile. "Oh, don't mind me. I can't help myself," she admitted with a shrug, "but you would make a wonderful instructor yourself, or even a writer, particularly with all of the world travels you have seen and experiences you have gained."

"Maybe, but I think my dad wants me to help run his Center."

"But is that what you would like to do?" Kate glanced at her. "It's your life, after all."

Heather shrugged. "Maybe I could combine all three into one," she said with a bright smile.

Looking past Kate, she exclaimed, "Oh, look! I just love this view!"

Having emerged from the glen-like notch with its sheer walls of rock, they gazed at the view, which opened out for scores of miles in almost every direction. Layer after layer of successively smaller mountains, followed by rolling hills, cascaded into the distance, before a series of taller, steeper mountains, encased in dark blue, framed the horizon. Billowing white and dark gray clouds swirled above the landscape, interspersed only by rays of yellow sun—radiating down upon the scene before them.

"It's enchanting," exclaimed Kate with a gasp.

Heather smiled happily. "That's why they call that area the 'Kingdom,'" she explained with pride in her voice. "That's my part of Vermont we're looking at."

"It's so majestic," said Kate with true admiration.

Heather pointed, saying, "Walden North lies about there, just past all that farmland, at the base of where the mountains start to grow tall again." Glancing at Kate, she said, "See?"

"Yes, I think so." She squinted through the rays of light and cloud cover. "How exactly do we get there from here?"

Heather whistled softly. "It's a bit complicated, but once we drive down from the mountains here, we end up at the reservoir which borders the Connecticut River. Once we cross it, we're in Vermont." She looked at Kate.

"And then?" Kate was trying to follow the description on her navigation system.

"Well," said Heather slowly, as she tried to reconstruct the journey from her memory. "We drive past some really big dairy farms until we get to some huge stone boulders, where we turn to get to the Danville Road—unless you prefer to go up and over the mountain, since Walden is just on the other side." She looked at Kate, waiting for her decision.

Sighing, Kate pressed various buttons on the nav. "Do you realize that all of your directions have been organized by *place* rather than by routes, street names, and number of miles from one point to the other?" She glanced at her with clenched lips. "I can't make sense of them."

Heather smiled. "You know, I never even thought of that before, but I think you're right. We never say, 'Oh, drive five miles west before taking Route 14 north ten miles.' We use places one passes as guideposts." She chuckled. "Oh, well, I'll just tell you when to turn. No worries."

Kate turned to Heather and asked with a sardonic smile, "So, which highway are we on now?"

Heather shrugged her shoulders, looked out the window and announced, "I have no idea, but we've just crossed over the river now—we're in Vermont." Something about her ready smile conveyed to Kate the level of pride she was apparently feeling.

Returning a warm smile, Kate rejoined, "Well, that's good enough for me!" Turning off the navigation system, she instructed good-naturedly, "Take us to Walden North, Heather!"

At last, they arrived at the rutted dirt lane, marking the entrance to Heather's homestead. Jumping out and jogging over, Heather leaned in the driver's window, looking at Kate with searching eyes. "Are you sure you don't want to come with me?" She asked one last time. "It wouldn't be any bother at all. I can share my room with you, if you feel, um, uncomfortable."

Kate shook her head firmly. "Thank you, Heather, but no. Your father must be really looking forward to spending time with you alone, without my hanging about the place." She shrugged. "Besides, I have a lot of research to do in three days."

"But where are you going to stay?" Heather looked concerned. "There aren't too many places to stay up here, you know."

Smiling, Kate reassured her. "Actually, it will be kind of fun. The owner of the general store, who wrote the pamphlet about the history of Walden North, has rented me some renowned historical pioneer cottage on her property overlooking the pond." With a toss of her head, she said with enthusiasm, "A new '*experiment in living*' for me!"

"Well, okay, then," said Heather with obvious disappointment. "But I can tell you that my dad will be very disappointed, as well."

Kate tried to sound upbeat. "If I finish my work earlier than expected, I'll hike over. Otherwise, I'll see you on Monday afternoon, anyway."

"Okay," said Heather with a downcast expression. "I really hope you'll come visit."

"I'm sure I will," said Kate with a bright smile. "*No worries*, as you say."

With one last backward glance and a wave, Heather headed down her dirt lane. Kate smiled, as she watched her silhouette become gradually enveloped by what seemed like maternal boughs of maples, anxious to tuck a daughter of Nature back into the landscape.

Driving past the landmarks Heather had recited—an historical 'little red school house' on the right, a maple sugar farm on the left, down from the black angus fields across from the pond, Kate spotted the place for which she was searching. At the corner of two small crossroads at the beginning of the pond sat the old store, more wooden than painted, with a long, covered porch filled with rocking chairs. A hand-painted sign listing sideways—not unlike the building itself—announced the location, *Walden North General Store*. Kate smiled, deeming it charmingly quaint.

The squeaky steps, creaking floorboards, and tinkling bell announced her entrance into the store, where she was greeted by a round woman with a big smile.

"Welcome to Walden North General," she said pleasantly. "Traveling through, are you? Maybe a freshly baked maple cupcake to accompany you—just frosted." With a proud toss of her head, she boasted, "They're our specialty."

Smiling back, Kate readily agreed to a cupcake, while the woman said, "Well now, I should keep you company while you enjoy that cupcake," and reaching for another one for herself, stuffed part of it in her mouth and kept talking. "My, are those delicious," she said, nodding, "though we'll need some milk to go along with them." Without waiting for Kate's response, she rushed over to the dairy case, and removing two small glass bottles, gave one to Kate. "This is out best milk. Organic and raw—straight from the cow down the road."

Once the woman understood Kate was the researcher for whom she waited, she broke out in a litany of information. As Kate nibbled on the treat, the proprietor, who introduced herself as Elizabeth Hill, hustled Kate over to a huge, antique oak desk with an overhead bookcase. She pulled down various books and pamphlets, saying, "You'll need this one," before reaching for another, "this one, and, oh, let's not forget the journal of one of the original founders of Walden North." By the time she finished pulling down books, Kate had two large armfuls.

"I see I have my work cut out for me," said Kate with a shy smile. "This is just wonderful. I can't wait to dig into them."

"Well, now," said Elizabeth, "we first need to get you settled in the camp, so you may begin your reading."

Kate looked at her with a confused expression. "Camp?" She shook her head. "I thought I was to rent a cottage from you. With all my research, I'm afraid I won't be good company to the others at the camp." Shrugging, she added, "Besides, I didn't bring a tent."

Elizabeth broke out in what Kate could only describe as merry laughter, her rolls of flab on her cheeks, neck, and waist bouncing gently up and down with each peal. "Now, aren't you too funny?" She gazed at Kate, who stood before her, now openly confused. "You sure aren't from around here, and I'd say, not even a New Englander." She nodded, while continuing her laughter.

"No, actually, I'm from the Midwest. So does 'camp' mean something different here?" Kate asked, now clearly mystified.

"Yes, dearie, a camp is a cottage, usually located along the water or in the woods." Placing her hands on her hips, she said, "Oh, wait 'til I tell Harvey this one. He'll just eat it up."

"Yes, my attitudes seem to serve as an endless source of amusement to New Englanders," she said with a twist of her mouth.

"Oh, it's all in good fun, I'm sure," said Elizabeth in a soothing tone, afraid she might have insulted her new tenant. Walking over behind the counter, she rummaged through a series of keys. "Oh, here we are."

"It's not far?" Kate asked, suddenly feeling tired.

Beckoning her over with a wave of her hand, Elizabeth countered, "Not at all. It's easy to find. Just follow this road here along the pond, past the Unitarian church on the right, with the parking lot and beach on your left, 'til you see a small, little road winding in among the trees. That would be the one you follow on down to the end—and don't mind the road on the left. Just keep going on the right until you come to a log camp, er, cottage, under some large old pines."

Looking confused, but eager, Kate warmly thanked her and asked if there were any restaurants nearby where she could grab a bite to eat.

Elizabeth guffawed heartily over that. "This is it, dearie. That's why we're called Walden North *General* Store," she said. "We sell everything you could possibly need to live or stay up here in Walden North." Nodding, she added, "You just go over there," pointing to a glass case, "and pick yourself out some dinner. Tonight's specials include: maple-roasted chicken, with rosemary potatoes, green beans, and salad sides; chicken pot pie with biscuit; beef stew with rolls and salad, and fried fish and chips."

"Thanks," said Kate with a backwards glance at the proprietor. With a slight toss of her head, Kate scanned the meat-themed dinner choices, finding it interesting to note that not everyone was vegetarian in Walden North.

Ten minutes later, she arrived at the cottage. The log antique was surprisingly tall, thought Kate, for being so old. "Injun Joe was a tall, tall man," Elizabeth had recounted with an authoritative nod. When Kate had asked about its history, Elizabeth replied in long sentences, interspersed with short breaths. "The story goes around here, that the first moment he saw Molly, he fell completely for her. Her father, being white, don't you know, was against the union, but when Joe saved his life, after finding him under a large old maple that had come down atop of him when logging," she said, followed by a quick breath, "and knowing Injun Joe could've just walked away and left him there, and Molly would have been all his, he said, 'Joe, though red you be, you have a good heart and an even better soul to match, so you may have my Molly, just as long as you agree to stop your Injun ways and live here.' Injun Joe took that big ol' maple, sawed it into flat-sawn logs, hauled them up top—to the very site where you will be staying—and built Molly and himself the cottage overlooking the pond." She inhaled deeply and proceeded. "Molly and Joe lived a good long life there, until well into their nineties, they say. They became such a part of the land here, that the pond was called Molly and Joe's Pond by some—even to this very day." She nodded with a wide smile. "And there you have it, dearie."

Kate thought the setting perfect. Just what she expected a cottage in Walden North to look like—surrounded in pines, with some other evergreens she didn't know, with a few flame-red and sunset-orange maples, their long boughs sweeping in among the needled pines. A spicy fragrance filled the air, something earthy enough to be called a scent, though she couldn't place it. She made a mental note to ask Heather about the air there.

She stood gazing through the trees to the pond beyond. The water glistened in the late afternoon sun, its small laps shimmering blue, then green—appearing to waltz under a sheer gauze of yellow light. It felt to her as if Time stood still there. She couldn't imagine that the setting had changed much since Molly and Joe's time. She tried to imagine ninety-something years of marking the days and seasons by the sun and moon, the changes in pond and trees. She shook her head slightly, realizing that, until that moment, she had rarely experienced such a serene setting. She continued her gaze, feeling rooted to the spot, tranquility seeping through her like a spring, forging a new course from its original source.

Almost reluctantly, she turned to look at the cottage. Straight logs of enormous width set horizontally—flat-sawn, Elizabeth had called the style—comprised the siding, with two windows on either side of a wooden Dutch door, offered views to the pond. What seemed like antlers of various types decorated the tops of the windows and door. Gazing at them, wondering about their significance, Kate concluded they must represent a regional equivalent of gargoyles, perhaps. With a shrug, she tried the knob, finding it unlocked. She smiled to think how unusual, in her experience it was to find a door completely unsecured, intrigued by the idea of living in a place without fear of burglary. She entered eagerly.

One amply sized room greeted her, and she looked with interest from one side to the other. A large stone fireplace fitted with an iron hook and a black cauldron occupied one wall. The other side held what she presumed was some sort of a metal cookstove, set between two wooden tables serving as counters, she figured. Above them, some rough, wooden shelves lined the wall, filled with wooden plates and earthenware. While her first impression characterized the interior as primitive, she soon realized it was, in fact, authentic. Her thoughts turned to Thoreau. *Simplicity.*

After setting down her packaged dinner, Kate caught a glimpse of a disquieting image from the corner of her eye. Reeling around, she stood facing the fireplace, noticing for the first time, an enormous head of an antlered moose stuck against the log wall above the timbered mantle. It seemed to stare pointedly at her, even from its lifeless eyes. She gazed at it through her own widened eyes, a sense of horror and revulsion sweeping through her. What a magnificent animal it must have been. She wondered how anyone could, not only kill it, but endure its vacant rebuke day after day. She felt an involuntary shudder ripple through her. As she shifted her gaze, she noticed with increased dismay other animal heads hanging along the walls. Several deer heads, both large and small, hung through the room, with what seemed like stuffed speckled fish on coarse boards in between.

Abruptly leaving the room, Kate strode briskly into the small adjoining bedroom, as if to seek refuge from the gallery of stuffed heads that seemed to watch her with an accusatory stare. Tossing her bag on the bed, she sat down to focus on the tranquility outside. What an anomaly, she thought, between the peaceful setting outdoors and the shrine of violence inside. She shook her head vigorously as if to dispel the sense of revulsion she was experiencing.

As she stood up to unpack her things, she turned away from the bed, looking behind her for any kind of dresser—only to gawk in complete horror at the sight before her. A tall, statue-like stuffed bear, with its arms and claws extended in a menacing stance, stood at attention in the corner.

"Oh, my God!" she shrieked, running from the room as if the bear were alive and ready to attack.

Kate stumbled down the embankment to the pond, not stopping until she reached the shoreline. She crouched, her arms hugging her raised knees, as she gazed out over the water. She agonized over what to do, resolving at once that she could not stay there. She shook her head sadly over what she felt as a stark contradiction between the pristine setting, and to her, a base way of interacting with the natural world. Rocking gently back and forth, she continued to absorb the tranquility around her, as she watched small folds of water gently splash against the shoreline. After a bit, the rhythmic motion of the water sent a sense of calm through her. She felt her breath lengthen, her former tranquility gently filling in the void left by her most recent experience.

A shrill, cackling laugh broke through the silence. Peering in the direction of the sound, Kate observed, apparently a duck, sailing through the water mid-pond, before diving down underneath the water. Waiting for it to re-surface, she was soon rewarded. It was the oddest–looking duck she had ever seen. She assumed it must be a New England native, since the ones back in the midwest tended toward brown and green coloration. She noticed that it had a long neck, ringed in white, though sporting a jet-black head. She thought she detected some black and white spots on its back when it flicked its wings, before settling into a wading pattern.

This time the silence was broken, not by duck calls, but by a low, husky voice behind her.

"Thought I might find you here." She turned around abruptly, both startled and instantly relieved to find Channing standing there. Sitting down next to her without a word, he pointed silently in the direction of the duck. Leaning over, he whispered, "Your lucky day to experience a loon. See there?"

She looked at him surprised. "Is that what it is?" She shifted her gaze out to the loon. "I have never seen one. And such a haunting call it has."

"I startled the loon as I walked here along the edge of the pond, hence its frantic call. They are always on the lookout." He turned to her and smiled. "You know, very few people on this earth ever get to see a loon, let alone experience its mystical song."

Nodding, Kate said, "I can't tell you how wonderful it is to see a wild animal *alive* here." She found herself shuddering again.

Channing smiled grimly. "That is why I am here to check in with you. After Heather told me where you were staying, well, I figured you might not enjoy the particular type of 'nature' experience that you would encounter in that cottage."

Kate shook her head vehemently. "There's nothing natural about it," she said angrily, "to decapitate those gorgeous, wild animals in order to string them along your walls." Shuddering again, she said softly, "and that poor, poor bear."

He nodded slowly. "This camp is famous—or *in*famous, depending on one's perspective on the issue—with hunters and environmentalists alike."

She looked at him through downcast eyes. "I haven't been able to eat a thing since witnessing that, that, *violence* against nature." She turned her lip. "I just can't bring myself to eat the beef stew I bought from the store. And, as you know," she admitted with a grim twist of her mouth, "I am not exactly philosophically *enlightened* when it comes to such matters."

Channing studied her a few minutes before speaking. "Actually, I would say you have connected with the '*higher laws*' of your own nature through this experience." Nodding, he added, "Not unlike Thoreau's account of the reasons why he stopped fishing."

Turning to him, Kate asked, "Why do I feel as if I keep experiencing the motifs from the various chapters I am teaching?" She gazed at him curiously, as if combing through the inner recesses of his mind for insight. As she waited for his response, she flicked her hand and commanded, "No, don't tell me." She smiled. "Synchronicity at work, yet again, is it?"

He offered a somber nod. "Yes, I would say it is." Standing up, he said, "Speaking of which, I came over to invite you to stay at our place this weekend, assuming you would not be able to work inside the camp here, and it's getting on in the evening." He tilted his head to the lowered sun, now radiating flames of ochre in every direction.

Kate's glance rested on him briefly, before looking away. "I don't want to interfere with your time with Heather. From what I gather, it would be great for both of you to spend time alone with one another." She turned to look at him again. "I am supposed to be working this weekend, focusing on researching the history of Walden North—my reason for coming here."

Channing smiled before speaking, his tone resolute. "I have the perfect solution for everyone involved. You are welcome to stay in my meditation cabin down from ours in the woods, right along the pond. I think you will find that it possesses the requisite atmosphere, conducive to deep thought that you, perhaps, had hoped to experience here. We would be very pleased if you joined us for meals, and, um, any other time you wish." He stopped, hesitating before continuing. "Though there is plenty of food in the cabin to sustain you, should you prefer solitude."

Kate immediately felt her body relax. "Oh, thank you!" she exclaimed. "I am so relieved," then stopped mid-sentence.

"Truly, it's not inconvenient or intrusive at all," he qualified, apparently sensing her ambivalence.

She tossed her head slightly to the side, as she gazed at him. "How is it you seem to know my inner thoughts?"

Shrugging, he said in his quiet tone, "No, not always." He glanced at her, before indicating they should walk up to the cottage. "You are an interesting mixture, not easy to discern."

Kate chuckled. "Oh, that comes from my years of studying Melville's '*mixed form*' narratives." She looked at him slyly from the corner of her eye. "I've become, particularly since moving here to New England, teaching Thoreau, and, possibly since meeting you and Heather, a '*mixed form*' myself—a sort of '*philosophy in whales, poetry in blubber*' sort of person." She looked away and paused, saying more to herself than to him, "Actually, these days I am not sure who I am exactly, or where I am heading."

Channing studied her carefully. "You may recall that one of Thoreau's most powerful insights speaks to your own feelings." With a slight smile, he quoted from *Walden:*

> *"Not til we have lost the world do we begin to find ourselves, and realize where we are and the infinite extent of our relations."*

"Hmm. Interesting." Kate gazed at him with a searching look. "I've often wondered each time I have encountered that passage in *Walden*, how, exactly, that would be possible." She shrugged. "I mean if one is lost, then how can one find one's inner self, which I assume it refers to?"

He glanced at her with a bemused expression while crossing his arms across his chest. "I take it you have seldom felt lost in life, then?"

"Never," she responded with a firm shake of her head. "Unsure, yes; lost, no." She shrugged. "I suppose that I'm too much of a planner."

He studied her firm jaw and flashing eyes before speaking. "And if the plan doesn't work out, as in the present case with your cottage rental?" he asked gently.

"Something else turns up," she said, "as you know yourself, by the present example." Glancing at him, she added, "Everything works out in the end."

He nodded to her, before offering a slight smile. "That sounds like a principle particularly grounded in the immigrant experience, almost like '*work hard and succeed*.'"

Kate grinned. "It is certainly a favorite in my immigrant family." With a wry smile, she added, "Not unlike 'part of the great whole' or 'synchronicity.'"

Channing smiled. "Point well-taken."

She turned to face him. "But you must let me pay you for staying in your cabin."

He bowed slightly, with both hands clasped together. "You have already paid more than you realize, by showing such kindness and interest in Heather's learning." He looked up at her, his eyes now translucent. "You may avail of the cabin anytime you wish to stay here in Walden North."

"Well, thank you," she said shyly. "It certainly sounds interesting—a 'meditation' cabin."

He read in her brimming smile, her sense of delight at the unexpected opportunity. "Truly an '*experiment in living*,'" he said with a smile.

"I'm so intrigued!" Kate's expression reflected her enthusiasm.

He offered a warm, though shy smile in return. "It's a very special place, protected by ancient pines."

With a sideways glance, Kate said, "Maybe you can tell me more about it, while we make our way there."

They had reached the rental camp. Channing graciously offered to go in and retrieve her things, while she took them from him at the door and loaded her car. Within minutes, they were driving back down the driveway, back to the general store.

Kate went in to notify Elizabeth that she had made other plans. "The animal heads didn't agree with you?" she asked with her hands on her hips.

Kate grimaced. "Not at all. I was completely spooked by the experience." She shook her head. "Decapitating heads of wild animals and sticking them on trophy plaques is not something I readily understand."

Elizabeth nodded. "City girl. Hard to understand the ways of the woods." She peered outside. "Oh, you're staying with that fellow who talks to bugs?"

Kate reddened slightly. "No, not really. In a cabin he lets out."

Elizabeth looked her up and down. "Didn't take you for a hippie type."

Kate stood straight. "Not at all," she countered. "I am a college professor. I teach Heather, the daughter, at *Harvard*."

"Ah, I see." Elizabeth nodded. "Well, in that case, you may keep the books for the weekend. Maybe you'd like to have a chat about your reading. I've done quite a bit of research myself—even wrote one of those pamphlets I gave you to read," she said, with a proud toss of her head.

"Wonderful," said Kate agreeably. "Perhaps Monday, on my way back?"

"I'll be here."

Not long after leaving her car at the end of his lane, Channing and Kate walked along a path in his vast woods, at last reaching the meditation cabin.

"Oh, my, it's so charming," she said in awe.

He smiled as he looked at her. "It's my tribute to Thoreau, actually. I constructed it based on the dimensions, shape, and framing of his original, though in keeping with his notion of relying on recycled materials, I used wooden planks, rather than shingles for the siding." With a brief nod, he continued. "I see it as a retreat for deep thought, and, perhaps, transcendence."

"I'm sure you do." Kate returned the smile. "Both seem to guide your actions and involvement in life."

"As it does yours, I should think," he responded.

Kate glanced at him. "Oh, I remain within the confines of deep thought, not venturing out into real action—unless you call academic writing active."

"Hardly," he said with a snort. "But one can always hope for transformation in that genre of writing."

With a lop-sided grin, Kate admitted, "Yes, it can be rather dry reading, but thought and theorizing often set the framework for worthwhile action."

He looked at her with a somber expression. "And what brings you to Walden North—in your academic writing, that is?"

Tilting her head, she said, "I am very intrigued by the existence of these two places, both with the same name, and I'm sure, intersecting histories. I thought it would be interesting to explore those connections and write about them as a way of understanding the draw for people, with, well, *convictions*."

"I have some books that may help you in your research there in the cabin. I have collected them for years."

She looked at him with curiosity. "Oh?"

"Yes," he said, "and what has not yet been codified in book form, I can tell you through personal accounts of the various people who have sought out Walden North, at least." He gazed at her. "It is quite a fascinating history."

Smiling, she said, "Great. I look forward to hearing about them all, though after I do some book work."

"Of course. You shall be undisturbed while residing in the meditation cabin. It is an unwritten rule."

"Thank you," she said looking at him, "I really appreciate your generosity and support."

"I'll leave you to explore for yourself," he said with a glance at her, "though perhaps you might like some instruction on maintaining the woodstove?"

With a slight roll of her eyes, Kate admitted, "I haven't a clue about woodstoves." She gave a shrug. "Remember, I'm a city girl—" she began.

"About to experience transformation," he finished for her.

After instructing her on the ways of woodstove cooking and heating, Channing stood at the door. "How fitting that you have come here on Columbus Day weekend."

"Oh?" she asked, "Why is that?"

He looked at her. "Perhaps you recall the last chapter of *Walden* where Thoreau urges his readers to '*be a Columbus to whole new worlds and continents within you.*'" Nodding, he said, "What better place to '*explore thyself* than a simple cabin in the middle of a forest, along a pristine pond?"

Kate grinned. "Might have to save the self-exploration for another weekend," she said with a toss of her head. "Academic duty calls. 'Publish or perish,' you know," she said lightly. She gazed around at the wall-to-wall books. "Looks like I have my reading cut out for me!"

Bowing, Channing said, "You shall be undisturbed. If we do not see you for meals, for which you are welcome to join, as I said, they will be brought down and left on your doorstep." With a nod, he added, "And of course, help yourself to any food here."

Kate whirled around to face him. "Thank you, so very much, Channing," she said with great sincerity, "I can't tell you how much I appreciate your kindness and consideration."

He tilted his head. "My pleasure." As he turned to go, he suddenly swung back. "Remember that you are deep in the north woods. Do not be alarmed if some of our wild animals come calling, as they are apt to do from curiosity and habit. Do not be afraid."

"You mean right up to the cabin?" Kate asked wide-eyed.

He offered a half-smile. "Well, perhaps, or you could always initiate the conversation yourself based on Thoreau's example. Remember what he said," he advised, before lapsing into another passage:

> *"You only need to sit still long enough in some attractive spot in the woods that all its inhabitants might exhibit themselves to you by turns."*

She looked at him with awe. "Do you know the book by heart?"

Channing responded quietly, "I *live* it by heart."

"Yes, you certainly do," she murmured.

With an unwavering gaze, he said, "Enjoy your '*tonic of wildness*'," and with a departing smile, added, "perhaps even the experience of growing '*wild*' yourself '*according to your nature*.'"

Kate soon found herself settled into the meditation cabin. Aptly named, she immediately decided. Floor-to-ceiling bookcases lined each wall between the evenly spaced windows, while a worn reading chair covered with a woven throw, in addition to a desk, obviously hand-crafted, sat positioned under a window overlooking the pond.

She stood, gazing out at the series of massive deep-brown trunks, standing like Ishmael's 'silent sentinels' engaged in water reveries. The image triggered her exchange with Channing. Set within a dense spruce grove, he had said.

"I'll take your word for it," she had responded when he announced the type of trees. *"Haven't yet graduated beyond the pine,"* she admitted.

He nodded. "*That's because you haven't spent enough time yet in Vermont. We're largely a spruce state.*"

Yet, he had said, she realized in hindsight, implying more trips there. She looked around with a pensive gaze, feeling she could get used to the getaway. *My Walden,* she thought, with a wistful glance around.

The last light of the day was coming to an end, the pond gradually deepening in the ensuing darkness. Realizing that she was now quite hungry, Kate looked over the various jars of preserved foods lined on a shelf near the woodstove. She thought how easy it would be to hole up there for a while with such provisions. She stopped when she came to maple squash apple soup. With a grin, she decided it sounded like the quintessential Vermont soup. Heating the jar in a pot of water simmering on the stove, she continued looking around. Peering into the warm oven, she discovered to her amazement that a loaf of bread awaited her. How did he know that she would end up staying there?

Sitting at the desk, Kate started in on her dinner. She hadn't consumed a vegetarian meal since the time in Cambridge, but she now wondered whether she might make it more of a regular culinary choice. Her Irish family had always been a meat and potato kind of clan, and as she sipped the steaming soup by the scant spoonfuls, she smiled over the reaction her mother would have to the particular mix of ingredients. Bending over the bowl, she inhaled the aroma.

The soup was amazing—sweet, tangy, delicate, spicy in an apple pie kind-of-way, all rolled into one spoonful. She smiled over the synchronicity—'*mixed form*' again.

Kate dipped her chunk of bread into the soup, savoring the poignant flavor, when from the corner of her eye, she noticed what she thought was movement outside. Turning slowly, she peered out into the dusk. Nothing but darkening trunks. Continuing her gaze, her eyes becoming accustomed to the diminishing light, she saw it. A shape slowly, almost imperceptibly, moved among the trees, blending in with the bushes underneath. What looked like a young black lab, was digging with its paws on the ground, pushing up a small, over-turned log. It used its claws to pull up something underneath before shoving it into its mouth in clawfuls.

Guess I'm not the only hungry one around here. Thinking it must be Channing's dog, Kate continued eating herself, calling out mentally to her visitor, "*Bon appétit*, my furry friend."

As she watched, she realized that her furry friend was not alone. Now there were two dogs, then three, all the same size, each digging under fallen tree limbs and logs. Her eyes widening, she dropped her spoon into the bowl and gasped. *Oh, my God!* A large, *very* large, animal appeared through the trees. It was definitely a bear. A *big* bear covered in matted, black, furry hair, with an enormous, rounded face.

Kate inhaled deeply, feeling frozen to her seat. She had to remind herself that Channing said they wouldn't hurt her. Exhaling slowly, she tried to subdue the rising fear that competed with sheer excitement over the scene outside. What she assumed to be the mother bear was helping overturn larger logs, holding them upright, while the cubs dug underneath. Pushing back her chair to stand, Kate noted with alarm that the mother bear suddenly stopped, looked in the direction of the cabin, and with one quick whistled grunt, the cubs each raced up the nearest trunk, holding on, and gazing down. The mother laid the log down with one paw and remained motionless, except for her head, which moved slowly in the air as if she were trying to smell the source of the noise. She ambled over to the cabin—just outside the window where Kate stood, now absolutely frozen with fear.

As Kate watched, the bear abruptly stood on her hind legs, raising herself to eye level with her. Their eyes locked in a stare of mutual surprise. Kate's heart pounded with an inexplicable mix of terror and exhilaration over the raw experience. *My God! I'm staring into the eyes of a mother bear!*

As she stood riveted to the spot and gazed into the bear's eyes, she felt her intense fear suddenly melt into a pool of understanding. Even in the fading light, she detected intelligence and feelings in the expressive, knowing look of the mother, who was sizing her up as foe or friend to her cubs.

Kate nodded slowly, moving only her head, and offered a closed lipped smile, for she had read somewhere never to bare one's teeth to an animal. She watched in complete fascination as the bear turned away from her, bent over again on all fours, whistled to her cubs, and waited until they climbed down. She then slowly ambled off into the dusk, her obedient children falling in line behind.

Kate sat staring into the darkness, her head cradled by one hand. *What an amazing experience!* She shook her head slowly from one side to the next and back, marveling over those eyes, that expression. Her thoughts wandered, flowing in different directions, before settling on Thoreau, trying to recall what he said about looking into the eyes of a wild animal. Getting up, she searched through her bag until she found her worn copy of *Walden.* She needn't have bothered, as she discovered in a glance at the bookshelf next to the desk, where dozens of copies of *Walden* were stacked, with a few open to specific passages. Shaking her head, she smiled. *Synchronicity at work—yet again.*

Wondering which passages were deemed important enough to Channing to remain open on his shelf, she perused them, scanning several before halting. There it was, her eyes settling on an edition that featured woodcut illustrations. A bird with large eyes greeted her as she read:

> *All intelligence seems reflected in them . . . a wisdom clarified by experience.*

Nodding in recognition, she looked up. That was it—*wisdom clarified by experience.* She realized that through their mutual exchange, the bear had shared her experience with humans, both good and bad, and needed to know, to figure out—and quickly—with which side Kate was aligned. She was delighted to know—and amazed—that the bear had sensed her inner good nature, or she would have run off, or worse, perhaps, attacked. She tilted her head back, gazing up into the air, as a dawning realization came over her. *My first wild animal communication!*

Kate felt a tingling sweep through her as her reflection upon the experience filled her with exhilaration. This was an experience that millions of people on earth would never, ever have—to be so close to such a beautiful, wild animal. She shook her head repeatedly as she contrasted her two experiences with bears—one dead and frightening, the other alive and fascinating. Her thoughts returned to her previous reaction to the scene in the cottage. How could anyone bring himself to kill and eat such an incredible creature—a cousin, as the Native peoples would say, to humankind. To Kate, now, it felt like murder, a feeling that made her shudder in horror.

She glanced down at her meal, grateful that she was not eating meat. She couldn't, not now—*not just now, anyway*—after her experience. As a new understanding of vegetarianism filled her senses, she wondered how long her revulsion to carnivorous cravings would last. The question made her think of Thoreau, whom she vaguely remembered dealt with this very question. While during previous readings of *Walden*, she had dismissed his famous philosophical stance against meat, alcohol, and caffeine as excessive, if not outright evangelical, she now eagerly sought out his account of his shift from being a hunter and eater of meats, both domesticated and wild, to becoming a vegetarian.

Picking up her copy and moving over to the reading chair, Kate curled up with a cup of raspberry leaf tea to re-read "Higher Laws." For the first time in her life, she carefully considered Thoreau's chronicle of the evolution of his philosophical stance on food and drink. Of the many observations and assertions he made, one struck her deeply:

> *I believe that every man who had ever been earnest to preserve his higher or poetic faculties in the best condition has been particularly inclined to abstain from animal food.*

Putting down the book, Kate sank back into the inviting chair. Kicking her feet up onto the ottoman, she reflected on his point. Its impact, she discovered to her amazement, swirled meaningfully within her. For the first time in her life, she found herself thinking consciously about her food choices.

She had never really thought about food before. It was simply something there to fill a nagging void—hunger. When she felt depleted, she ate whatever was immediately available, not even bothering to enjoy the process of preparing food. Tilting her head back, she gazed up at the wooden-framed ceiling. How many rye bagels with cream cheese had she consumed during her doctoral days and nights in the library, she couldn't even begin to count. *And prepared foods?* She lived on them, preferring to spend her time learning, thinking, and writing, rather than on something as trivial as making a meal. A new realization crashed down upon her—*perhaps food is not so trivial, after all.*

Kate got up, and going over to the books on the wall, started to scan the titles. She assumed that with his own fully formed philosophy of food consumption, Channing must have a slew of books on the subject. As she studied the bookshelves, she noticed with amusement that each shelf was labeled. She smiled over further evidence of his philosophical commitment to assist the 'lost,' as he put it, with their journey of self-exploration and development. She looked more closely.

Food consciousness. Scanning the titles on the shelf, she discovered a particularly intriguing title. *Omnivore's Dilemma.* Chuckling, she found the title intriguing. Sounding like the perfect context for dealing with the questions she felt rising within, she pulled the book, almost as dense as *Moby-Dick,* from the shelf. Refreshing her tea, she sat down to read. What she discovered was nothing short of revolutionary to her way of thinking. *Previous way of thinking,* she reminded herself. She read late into the night, mesmerized by the exposé of how food arrives at the table.

Kate awoke with a start early the next morning to a slight noise outside. Wondering whether the bears were back, she sat upright, turning to peer out from the window in the tiny loft where she slept. It was then she noticed Channing walking away silently, his form almost enveloped by the trees. Hastily opening the window, she called out, "Good morning!"

"Ah, I'm afraid I've wakened you."

"You don't have to go—please come in."

Turning to gaze up at her, he slowly made his way back to the cabin door, waiting until she opened it before entering. Though a bit flustered, yet enervated by Channing's unexpected appearance, Kate hastily threw on her Harvard sweatshirt and jeans, calling out, "I'll be right down."

"I've brought a bite to eat for breakfast," he announced when she opened the door for him.

Kate gazed wide-eyed at the bulging basket. "I'll say," she said with a grin. "I'll make some tea."

After setting down the basket on the table, Channing glanced over at the ottoman, strewn with various books on food.

"Ah, I see you have been reading into the politics of food consumption," he remarked.

Kate smiled pointedly. "Yes, my re-reading of 'Higher Laws' prompted me to explore your rather extensive collection on the subject."

He nodded. "There has been a marked shift in consciousness from the philosophy of food choices to the politics, science, and economics of food consumption in cultural studies now for some time," he said.

"After being horrified by what I read in Pollan's book, I moved to figuring out how to eat locally by reading Kingsolver's chronicle." As she poured the tea, she added, "*Animal, Vegetable, Miracle,* indeed—with emphasis on the last bit."

Channing nodded. "It requires regular vigilance, but once one locates appropriate food sources, it then becomes a simple matter of dedication to the principle."

Kate bent over the basket, inhaling deeply. "What have we here? It smells delicious."

"Oh, just something I baked up this morning."

Sitting down, she looked across the table at him. "How thoughtful of you."

Channing began removing items from the basket, setting them on the table. "Unaware of your nascent interest in food philosophy, I brought you some locally made organic yogurt from raw milk, as well as some raspberry muffins and oat farls."

Kate frowned. "Farls? What are they, exactly?"

He just smiled at her, waiting to see whether she could discern their identity.

She studied the triangular shapes. "They look like scones, actually, but a little different."

He beamed. "Right you are." With an intense look, he explained, "'*Farl*' is, I believe, the traditional Irish word for a particular cut of an oaten scone."

"Oh, really?" Kate said with a slight toss of her head. "I don't think I've ever had a scone made from oatmeal, but then again, I probably wouldn't know, since I don't bake."

"Is that a philosophical principle with you?" He studied her closely.

"No," she admitted with a sheepish grin. "I've just never had the time." She shrugged. "Too busy in the library." She took a bite of the warm farl. "Oh, scrumptious."

"Glad you like it. They're made from my oats."

Kate shook her head and gazed at him. "Is there anything you *can't* do?"

He snorted, before locking eyes with her. "Yes, live in the city and teach at Harvard."

Smiling, she quipped, "Well, I guess I have one up on you." She continued eating, before suddenly exclaiming, "Oh! Speaking of comparable experiences, I have an incredible experience to share with you!"

He smiled. "Oh? Since I left you last night?"

Kate broke out in a radiant smile. "It was unbelievable!" She waved her arm towards the ottoman. "It's what spurred my reading into food philosophy."

"Hmm." He nodded, waiting.

Kate's eyes widened. "I saw a *bear*—just as it started to get dark!" She shook her head quickly. "No, actually, *four* bears." She looked at him, her eyes dancing. "It was just an *amazing* experience. Transformative, really—at least, for the moment." She gave a wry, twisted grin.

Channing smiled. "Ah, you saw the new family, I presume."

Sliding back in his chair, he asked, "Three sizable cubs and the mother?"

Kate looked at him in wonderment. "Exactly. You've seen them as well?"

"Ah, I know the mother well. I raised her when she was an orphaned cub." He nodded.

"You *did?*" Kate shook her head. "How did you do that?"

He smiled at her. "I'm happy to share my story, but first I would prefer to hear of your experience." He nodded. "It is only the blessed few who get to experience such a gift of Nature."

Kate just shook her head, her eyes glistening. "It was amazing. After I realized that what I thought were black labs were actually bears, or bear cubs, I saw the mother. Oh, my God," she exclaimed, with a slight tilt of her head. "When she stood up and gazed at me, with only the open window between her and me, I thought I would die," she said with a sheepish grin, "but then, the miracle happened."

"What was that?" He looked keenly at her.

"As she looked at me, *studied* me, really, my fear suddenly changed to awe." She looked over at Channing with a thoughtful expression, before continuing. "We simply regarded one another for what seemed like a long time, she reading my expression, and I intuiting her thoughts. For the first time, I understood, *truly* understood, how intelligent, knowing, and deliberate animals could be."

Leaning back in her chair, she sipped her tea before explaining. "She communicated to me her experiences with people, which seemed, oddly enough, to flow through my mind in images of both cruelty and kindness, while I shared my fear and fascination with her—as well, I suppose, that I was no threat at all to her cubs."

"Ah, yes." Channing nodded slowly before meeting her gaze. "What you experienced was telepathic communication."

Shaking her head slowly, Kate said softly, "It was just an incredible experience." She looked off into the distance towards the pond, before shifting back to Channing. "I was very grateful to be eating your wonderful, I might add, maple squash apple soup—no meat."

He bowed silently.

Shaking her head again, she said, "I thought about my two experiences with bears—the dead one and the live one—which, in turn, inspired me to read about vegetarianism and food philosophy." She shrugged and with shy grin, said, "So far, my time here has been quite powerful—and it's only Saturday morning!"

Channing smiled and offered a slight nod. "Yes, it is through such experiences that we come to discover our inner selves, the '*higher laws*' of our spiritual natures."

Kate smiled. "I used to think Thoreau was just being, well, *excessive,* but now, I'm not so sure."

"Indeed."

Leaning over, she said, "You were going to tell me about raising the orphaned cub. What happened to her mother?"

Channing's smile faded, much like the retreating sun suddenly enshrouded in storm clouds. A slight, though noticeable grimace formed at his mouth, as his eyes turned a steely gray. "It is not a pleasant account," he said, his tone grim, "though the outcome has been positive."

Kate peered at him. "If you don't mind, I'd like to hear it anyway."

"We take our wild animals seriously up here," he remarked. "We either kill them for meat, spending time and money hunting them down, or we side-step the law and engage in animal activism—the latter group even more ardent in their mission, perhaps, than the hunters."

She nodded. "Yes, I have seen the results of the first choice," she said in a caustic tone. "Horrible."

With a glance at her, he said, "Some activities associated with the culture of hunting have resulted in the rise of the second approach."

"I'm not sure what you mean."

Channing looked intently at her. "I suppose one could say that it comes down to two essentially disparate attitudes about the natural world and its various members. In the one case, you believe it is all there for the taking, while in the other, you believe you must share and respect your fellow creatures."

Kate nodded knowingly. "Though not quite the same, a version of that philosophy exists in *Moby-Dick.* Ishmael calls it '*fair game.*'

Channing's eyes flashed. "Yes, and like the cruel assault and massacre of whales that Melville chronicled in his book, some of the activities up here have required and inspired what we call *intervention.*"

She noted his overtly grim expression. "You mean as in a Greenpeace sort of way?"

"Exactly." His clear eyes seemed impenetrable.

"I'm all ears," she said, her body tense with anticipation.

Sitting up straight, and holding his mug between his two hands, Channing began, "There is a particularly vile and insidious activity up here, which involves chasing, or as many of us would say, *traumatizing*, bears with vicious dog packs."

Kate curled her lip. "Ugh. That sounds awful." Shuddering, she asked, "Is that part of their hunting?"

"No," he said tersely. "They euphemistically call it a *sport.*" With a cursory nod, he explained. "They train their dogs to chase and hunt down, sometimes killing, bears during the summer months since they aren't allowed to hunt then." He grimaced. "Of course, this is the very time that mothers are raising their newborns, as well as teaching their yearlings—" and with a glance at Kate, "their two year-olds, that is, how to become independent."

"Doesn't give them much chance for survival, does it?" Kate commented with a shake of her head.

"No." He took a sip of his tea. "This is why it is vital that the mothers remain safe to focus on continuing the population, as well as in engaging in their natural roles as mothers and exemplars."

Kate squinted at him. "I'm not sure I really want to know, but what is involved?"

His steely gaze returned as he explained. "So these people place radio collars on their dog packs and send them into the woods to search out and chase bears." He shook his head. "If you can imagine such an unholy act, these dogs chase a bear continuously through the forests, until the poor bear either drops from exhaustion or dies from traumatic aftermath. Some bears have been known to run over thirty miles in their desperate efforts to escape. Those that do survive are traumatized for life, resulting in a severely reduced life, both in quality and duration."

"But why do people engage in these actions?" she blurted, as she furrowed her eyebrows.

"Under the ostensible excuse of preparing for the fall hunt," he said curtly. "They actually think it is fun."

"My God, how horrible."

He nodded, his eyes measurably sad. "Yes."

"So your little orphaned cub?" She couldn't complete her sentence.

Nodding grimly, Channing said, "Mother killed by a dog attack after a prolonged chase." He met her shocked stare. "Luckily, my neighbors were able to save the poor cub they heard crying up in a tree, waiting for her mother to retrieve her."

"My God—how tragic." Kate just shook her head sadly.

His mouth decidedly grim, he stated, "That incident marked the beginning of the intervention project."

"Oh, God. It gets worse." Her mouth twisted into a rigid line of anticipation.

"Indeed." With a brusque nod, Channing launched into the rest of the account. "My neighbors decided to take matters into their own hands, knowing there was nothing deemed illegal about the bear-chasing activities—at least here in Vermont."

Kate couldn't help but interrupt. "But why not? Vermont seems so, well, progressive, really, about all things environmental."

"*Aye, there's the rub*, so to speak," said Channing with a nod. "Vermonters have been hunting since their first white settler ancestors arrived up here." With a shrug, he admitted, "Most transplants, those who oppose hunting, that is, are frankly fearful of challenging those historical acts—beyond posting 'No Trespassing' and "No Hunting' signs."

"Really?" She arched her eyebrow in surprise.

His lips taut, he said, "Hunting 'accidents' have been known to happen, which makes my account about this particular resistance movement, all the more powerful."

"Well, go on. I can't wait to hear about it—I think," she said, as her mouth formed into a grim twist.

"Well then, my neighbors rounded up some other friends who owned quite a bit of land, land on which the dog runners often trespassed."

"Do they?" Kate asked wide-eyed.

He shot her a caustic look. "Recall how little effect my signs had on your own innocent pursuits of pine-cone gathering on my land."

Kate instantly blushed.

With a half-smile, he continued. "You might be able to imagine the feelings of those who assume an 'historic' right to hunt lands, purchased by some transplant, now posted with menacing signs." He shrugged his shoulder. "They simply walk right past them—though not before shooting up the signs with buckshot."

Kate's eyes clouded over with apprehension.

"So, some of my neighbors posted a set of signs along their property boundaries which announced: *Radio dog-free land. Enter at your dogs' risk.*"

Kate sipped her tea before asking, "And did they stop the bear chasers?"

"Um, not exactly with the signs alone." He looked away.

Leaning forward, Kate asked in a rush, "So what else did they do?"

Shrugging, Channing continued, "When the signs failed to deter the dog owners, who actually responded by shooting up the signs, as I mentioned, or in many cases, just tearing them out of the ground, the intervention team, as they called themselves, moved onto to stage two."

"I can just imagine," she said with trepidation.

"No, I do not think you can, actually." He turned to gaze pointedly at her. "Nothing short of guerrilla warfare, I'm afraid."

"What was that?" she asked.

With a grim expression, he said, "Many of my animal activist friends had been in the Vietnam War, or their fathers had, depending on their age, so they knew firsthand how to stop the enemy advance, so to speak—some of it not so nice."

"Go on," she said with an audible sigh.

"First, they engaged in economic warfare. New signs went up, though, this time," he qualified with a terse nod, "painted in blood red letters on large, wooden boards." He looked over at her before continuing. "They read: *No radio dogs. All radios will be destroyed.*"

"Sounds ominous."

"Of course, that was the intended effect." Scowling, Channing added, "After a few of those were filled with bullet holes, they began trapping the dogs, confiscating the radios, and threatening the owners by yelling into the radios, 'If you do not call off these dogs, we will not only destroy your radios, but we'll kill your dogs, as well.'"

Kate's eyes widened. "Oh, my God."

He shrugged. "Some of this happened, before the bear chasers realized that the resisters were *deadly* serious." With a nod, he continued, "When it started getting expensive for them, truly expensive, as in lost radio equipment, loss of dogs, and 'unexplained' truck and ATV damage, they called off their dogs, and the chasing of the bears stopped." He shook his head. "An unfortunate solution to a terrible problem."

Kate nodded. "That's an incredible story." Shaking her head, she added, "I just don't understand the mentality of wanting to hurt those beautiful creatures."

"Your two authors, Melville and Thoreau, both speak to that question, when, in the one case, Ishmael describes the mania to hunt and kill whales that is stirred up in the hearts of the crew, while in 'Higher Laws,' Thoreau describes the base tendency man has for killing."

Kate nodded. "Yes, that's true, though those thematic points are not usually the subject of focus in the scholarship."

"Outside the realm of theory, I suppose," he said with a glance at her, before settling back in his chair. He said quietly, "It is for such reasons, that humankind must strive to identify with their higher natures."

"Speaking of which," Kate said, "how did you raise the orphaned bear cub?" She shook her head with a smile. "I bet that was an incredible experience."

He returned the smile with a brief nod. "Yes, so much so, that I wrote a book chronicling the experience."

"Really?" she asked. "Heather has never mentioned it."

He stood up, walked over to one of the bookcases, and retrieved the book. "You might like to read this, or at least, look at the photos of the various cubs I have raised to return to the wild."

Kate thumbed through some of the photographs. "My God, they are climbing all over you!"

She looked at him with a mixture of fear and fascination.

Channing smiled. "Oh, yes, I have a few scars from inadvertent claw scratches as souvenirs of those days."

"That must have been scary."

"Not really. They are fascinating animals." Nodding, he added, "It opened up an entirely new way of looking at bears."

"Oh? In what way?" Kate regarded him with some measure of surprise, not knowing until that moment of Channing's professional expertise in bear ethology.

With a nod, he said, "Well, for one thing, we now know, based on the research of Ben Kilham, that bears communicate through a very sophisticated linguistic system, a language that can be learned."

Breaking into a big smile, Kate teased, "Ah, of course, your academic specialization proved instrumental in such discoveries."

With another brusque nod, he continued. "Well, yes, it did. But in the case of the bears, it goes well beyond biochemistry, just as with plants." He gave her a stern look.

"Oh, I'm sure," she said, backing down, realizing that he found nothing amusing about his field of study.

Nonplussed, he continued. "Bears are more intricate, more complex, and more able than we humans have thought. They think, reason, intuit, react, feel, love, share, and understand time, as well as a host of other actions some of us attribute only to humans."

"What was the best part of your interaction with bears?" she asked, now more than intrigued.

His eyes resembled the color of translucent green boughs. "The greatest gift of all—their ability to love."

Though drawn to the depths of wisdom revealed in his stare, Kate felt overwhelmed by its impact and looked away. "I'm looking forward to reading your book." She glanced back at him to see him stand up.

"I should take my leave to enable you to return back to your research and your reading," he said with a tone of finality.

"Well, sure, thank you," she responded somewhat awkwardly. She felt that she could listen to him for hours. "And thank you, again, for breakfast." Half-turning, she added, "I do find your research and lifestyle quite fascinating, really."

"Should you wish to join us up at the house for dinner, we would welcome your company," he said, with his slight bow.

"Well, yes, thank you," she said, though heard the hesitation in her voice.

He instantly smiled. "If not, we completely understand that your work has transported you to places you might choose not to leave."

"What time do you eat?" she asked, looking at him.

"Whenever you arrive," he said with a nod. "We like to adopt the Abenaki practice of not organizing our lives around a sense of hours beyond sunrise, midday, sunset, and night. There is no word for 'time' in their language."

Kate chuckled. "Oh, I like that concept, though I can't imagine living that way in Cambridge."

Channing studied her quietly a moment before speaking. "Perhaps you'll come to have an awakening similar to the grandson of an Abenaki elder, who, while teaching at Columbia, went to meet his grandfather in northern Maine to learn about his ancestral culture."

"What happened?" asked Kate, feeling an acute sense of anticipation.

Channing bowed slightly. "He lost his sense of modern time, instead, learning to rely on the ancestral concept."

Kate turned her head slightly. "But how could he organize and work at Columbia without relying on a conventional sense of time?"

Channing nodded. "He didn't."

"Oh?" Kate looked bewildered.

"He felt so transformed by his experience that he gave up his academic life to live among his grandfather's people."

"That's pretty extreme," she said.

Nodding, he added, "Not really. He continued his cerebral work, but simply shifted his emphasis. He wrote a book about the experience."

"Oh—experience outweighing theory, again," she said thoughtfully.

Walking over to another bookcase, Channing pulled it down and handed it to her. "Perhaps you might find this interesting."

Kate grinned. "I find *all* of it interesting," she exclaimed. "I could spend a month of Sundays here, just reading, thinking, and roaming these woods."

"You are welcome to do just that," he said. With a brief bow and a clasp of his hands together, he stepped out of the door.

"Thanks so much—for everything," she said softly.

As he walked away, Channing said over his shoulders, "Perhaps we might see you later this evening. If so, we will introduce you to the deer."

"The deer?" she called out to his back.

"Yes, we feed the wild animals." With that, he disappeared into the great embrace of the trees.

"Of course you do," she murmured. She stood leaning against the door, not wanting to break the spell their exchange had cast.

At last, with a sigh, Kate walked back to the table. Noticing his book lying there below the others he had set out for her, she picked it up to read the title: *Feeding Bears.* Grinning, she shook her head. She looked out the window, her eyes focusing on the pond. It seemed to her that the inhabitants of Walden North spoke a language different in orientation from hers, perhaps in part due to their lifestyle.

With a slight toss of her head, she walked over to the reading chair, and plunking herself down, opened his book. She smiled, realizing that it was, in fact, a different language—*the language of Nature.* Soon, she was immersed in Channing's account of living with and feeding bears.

Just after six, Kate arrived up at the house.

Heather came out to greet her, her laughter ringing through the air. "I almost did a double-take when I saw you coming along the path. I'm so used to observing you bustling around campus, and to see you here—walking slowly, looking around as if taking in your surroundings—well, it feels *odd*, to say the least."

"Now, that's a fine greeting for your dinner guest," Kate bantered. "Do I really look so different?"

Heather rushed to explain. "Oh, I didn't mean anything by it, really, except, well, I'm used to your *powerwalk*, as you juggle an armful of books and bags, not—" she said, glancing down in curiosity at the handful of cones and evergreen twigs. "What are those?" She regarded Kate through slightly raised, rounded eyes.

"Actually, I was hoping you would tell me," Kate countered, her expression radiating her sense of contentment.

"Well, sure," said Heather easily. "Come on in." She held the door open.

Channing turned from his work in the kitchen. "She arrives laden in gifts," he said with a brief smile. "I see that your interest in forest life has not waned."

Kate smiled. "If anything, I'd say it is flowing with the high tides of the full moon."

Channing nodded. "An interesting metaphor, not, I presume, found in *Walden.*" A quizzical smile played at the corners of his mouth. "You must be reading—"

"Oh, *everything* in that cabin of yours," she interjected. "You've misnamed it, in my opinion, however, since there is no time for meditation—with all those fascinating books lined up, just begging to be read."

"Indeed?" he said with a slight hesitation. "You may have a point there."

She grinned and shrugged her shoulders. "Besides," she said playfully, "I don't actually *know* how to meditate."

"Ah," he said with a slight bow.

With a wide grin, Kate teased, "And not a single book on the topic as far as I could see."

He wiped his hands on a cloth. "At least, you looked. I shall make sure to add some for future reading adventures."

She held out her arm. "Oh, I don't know if there's any hope for me. I'm still wearing my watch."

"Yes, I noticed," Channing said dryly. "Though I wouldn't necessarily take pride in that fact—never mind the disrupting effects on your chakras and energy."

With a shrug, she countered, "How else would I know when to come to dinner?"

He regarded her with a pointed look, as he passed by with some bowls of food. "When you're *hungry* is the usual time."

Kate chuckled. "Hmm. Intuition and common sense, rather than theory, prevail here, I see."

"Indeed, they do," he rejoined, with a pleasant nod.

Over dinner, Kate studied Heather, relieved to see how relaxed and happy she appeared. "And how does it feel to be home, Heather?" she asked with a smile.

"Just great! It's so, well, laid back here," she said, "no assignment deadlines, no place I have to be, and the rest of it." She leaned back in her chair. "And I have really missed hanging with Dad."

As Kate looked on, both smiled fondly at one another.

"I am sure you have, Heather," said Kate. "Delicious dinner by the way," she said, glancing over at Channing.

"We call it Kingdom stew," he said with a sly nod, "since it contains a bit of all representatives from the vegetable kingdom we glean here in the woods."

"And we live in the Kingdom," Heather chimed in.

"For obvious reasons, of which you are well aware," said Channing with a self-deprecating smile, "we try to come up with creative new ways to consume beans."

"And what do you call this," Kate inquired, pointing to a side dish.

With a slight nod, Channing said, "Grilled beans teriyaki."

Kate looked at him in surprise. "You use teriyaki sauce—from Japan?"

He shook his head. "No, no, we make our own."

"You do?" she asked in awe. "But don't you need seaweed, or something like that?"

Both Heather and Channing broke out laughing. "Well, that would be difficult to find locally. Not such exotic ingredients, no," said Channing with a rare twinkle in his eyes.

Kate shrugged. "You know, I wasn't kidding when I said I know little to nothing about food preparation."

Heather said with a giggle, "Haven't I said it before? You're a Harvard professor! You're not *supposed* to know how to cook."

Kate bowed to her. "Thank you, Heather, for understanding my cultural contexts." Smiling, she added, "Besides, my mother seemed to take pride in telling her friends that I couldn't boil water or put a meal together to save myself from starvation, but I could assemble a dynamite essay."

"Indeed," said Channing.

With a shrug, Kate said, "We each have our special talents, I guess," and looking at Heather, with a sideways nod at Channing, added, "Though some appear talented in everything."

"Yep, that's my dad," Heather said, beaming.

Looking flustered, Channing side-stepped the compliment. "The teriyaki constitutes yet another creative use of beans, since, in addition to our maple syrup, it is made from lacto-fermented soybeans, which, as you might recall, we grow here in our fields."

Kate nodded, as she took a bite of the grilled beans. "Though I haven't a clue what lacto-fermentation involves, whatever you are doing, keep it up. This is just delicious!"

"A common practice among rural people for generations," he said only.

Turning to him, Kate said, "By the way, I finished reading your book today. What a fascinating account of your bears. No wonder that mother bear I saw yesterday seemed so, I am almost embarrassed to say, human."

Heather looked at Kate in surprise. "I thought you were researching the history of Walden North."

Kate gave a wry smile. "I got sidetracked by wanting to understand the significance of my various bear encounters yesterday."

"And by collecting evergreen cones, I see," said Channing, as he tried to restrain a burgeoning smile from developing into an ear-to-ear grin.

Kate offered a sheepish grin of her own. "I have to admit that it's a bit embarrassing not to know how to identify the different conifers, though, until now, I've never really thought such knowledge important enough to learn."

Channing and Heather helped her figure out how to identify the different types. Kate listened spellbound to their thorough descriptions, not only of physical characteristics, but their ecological, medicinal, and cultural significances, as well.

At the end of their lesson, Heather leaned over, and with a broad smile, announced, "Okay, quiz time!"

Kate groaned.

Wagging her finger at her, Heather said, "See, now you know how it feels to have a spot quiz!"

Kate grimaced. "Karma, is it?"

Heather giggled. "Your time has come to pay up. So," she began, "which one of these specimens is used for holiday wreaths?"

"Um—" Kate said with a pause, "um, let's see . . . oh, yes, fir."

With pursed lips, Heather nodded. "Yes, very good. And what time of the year does one cut the branches?"

"Um, after several frosts."

"And why is that?" Heather pursued.

"To preserve the aroma?" Kate cast a sidelong glance at Channing, who was regarding her with obvious amusement.

Heather peered at her. "Hmm, that sounds more like a question than it does an assertion, Dr. Brown. Which is it?"

Kate started to laugh. "Do I really sound like that in the classroom?"

Heather said with a wide grin, "Ah, yep."

"It's a wonder any of you listen to me." Kate shook her head.

Heather retorted, "You're the grade executioner."

"Well, I'll have to work on my delivery style," Kate said, "or I'll never be able to look you straight in the face without laughing over this quiz of yours."

Heather suddenly exclaimed, "Oh, look! They're here!"

Kate glanced at Channing in surprise. "Are you having more guests?"

Channing stood up and said, "Only the wild kind." Beckoning to Kate, he suggested, "Come on outside for a better look."

Quietly opening the door, he gestured for them to sit in an Adirondack chair on the back porch, which overlooked a small clearing.

Leaning over, Heather whispered to Kate, "Be perfectly still, so they can pick up your scent and not be afraid of your movements."

At first, Kate saw nothing, even though her companions seemed to be watching something intently among the trees at the edge of the forest. Following their gaze, Kate scanned the tree trunks, looking for any sign of movement. From the corner of her eye, she thought she had detected a blur of action. Cautiously turning her head ever so slightly, she peered in the direction she thought she had seen something. She waited, frozen in place.

After some minutes had passed, she was rewarded. A large, brownish-gray deer timidly stepped out from behind a massive tree trunk, her form blending in almost imperceptibly with the trunks behind her. She was close enough that Kate heard her snort, before raising her head slightly to sniff the air. With her wide ears extended, she turned her head slightly and continued sniffing. After some minutes testing the air, the deer moved away from the protection of the trees, walking with cautious steps toward a long, open, wooden box that lay on the ground along the path.

What ensued delighted Kate beyond all expectation. As the deer bent over the box and began licking its contents, another deer emerged from the trees, followed by another, and yet another—until the path contained well over one dozen. Kate stared wide-eyed at the spectacle. Some deer appeared in pairs, one bigger than the other, presumably mother and offspring, while others arrived singly or in small groups of three. Although there seemed to be certain deer that enjoyed first dibs, the others eventually had their turn at the box—once the first group had consumed their portion and walked away. As the deer became filled, some of the younger ones began to run around in the clearing, chasing one another in play.

Glancing over through the corner of her eye at Channing, she smiled, only to be stunned by his response. Kate hurriedly shifted her gaze, wondering whether she had mistaken his expression in the fading light—had he actually winked at her? She tried to suppress the smile she felt blooming in all directions over her face, but could not. In another surreptitious glance, he noticed her attempts and smiled, before looking away.

As soundlessly as they arrived, the deer took leave, often one by one, or in couples. As the last one disappeared into the trees, Channing stood up. "Who needs television when one can watch that?"

Heather got up and stretched. "I had almost forgotten how enjoyable it is to watch the deer."

"What did you think, Kate?" asked Channing, as they walked back into the house.

Offering a grin, she said, "There seemed to be so much going on. I observed one smaller deer trying to make his or her way into the feeder, but was shoved out of the way by some older ones. Another deer, most likely its mother, came over to where the little one stood behind the others, and looking from side to side, snorted, before using her head to make room for the little one." She gazed at him. "They seemed so *aware,* so intelligent, and knowing—with feelings, as well as a sense of justice."

Channing gazed back at her. With a nod, he said, "Very astute observations. Of course, you are correct about each one of those attributes."

"Back in the northern suburbs of Chicago, people complain about the few deer they see, claiming they were destroying their gardens. There's a movement to . . . what's the word they use?"

"Harvest?"

Kate nodded. "That's it. Quite the euphemism, isn't it?" She turned to him. "They call it mercy killing as well, arguing that it is better to kill them, than let them die from lack of food."

"Nothing very merciful about that." Channing folded his arms across his chest. "And why are their food supplies so compromised?"

Kate looked at him. "I don't know, actually, since I haven't a clue what they eat."

He responded tersely. "They used to rely upon the saplings and twigs from the groves of trees, as well as low-lying shrubs, grasses, and clovers that grew in the meadows in which they roamed—before those meadows were transformed into suburban house sites—replete with fenced gardens and chemically-laden grass."

"I see," she said.

"How 'merciful' of people to take away their food sources, then claim to act mercifully by killing them off altogether," he said, his tone bitter.

Kate glanced out the window toward the forest. "When you describe it like that, it makes perfect sense to support the deer over one's daffodils."

"Indeed." He shrugged, before turning away to make some tea. "A mug before you return to the cabin?"

"Sure. Thanks."

He set down three mugs. Heather stood up, taking hers, and said, "If you guys don't mind, I have homework to do. You see, I have this professor," she said, smiling coyly at Kate, "who not only assigns lots of heavy reading, but follows it up by asking us to record our responses to it in a thoughtful manner. That takes hours and hours of time. So Goodnight, Professor, and Goodnight, Dad."

Kate shook her head. "My God, I'm such a terrorist."

Channing smiled. "No, but you are exacting. That's good."

Kate sipped her tea. "Oh, this is great. What is it?"

"Rosehip tea."

"From actual roses?" Kate asked.

He couldn't help but snort. "Yes, from actual roses." He looked at her a minute, then, with a shake of his head, seemed to dispel the urge to say whatever had been on his mind.

Taking another sip, she commented, "I never knew one could make tea from roses." She smiled over her teacup. "I thought they were simply ornamental."

He gave her a sharp look, augmented by his pointed retort, "How quickly subsequent generations lose the folk and herbal wisdom of their ancestors."

With a confused look, Kate said, "I'm not sure I know what you mean."

Channing turned his head slightly to the side. "Surely, your Irish ancestors were thoroughly proficient in gleaning, preparing medicinal tonics, and the like from the wild." He shrugged. "How soon we lose generations of collective wisdom in one fell swoop when adopting metropolitan lifestyles."

"I suppose," she said, looking away.

"Anyway," he said with a wave of his arm, "I was going to tell you before that some of us up here have started an initiative to feed the wild animals, beginning in late autumn into just before winter, in the case of the bears, and through the winter months, for the deer."

Kate turned back to Channing in surprise. "I thought you weren't supposed to feed wildlife."

When he instinctively folded his arms across his chest, a gesture Kate knew signaled a lesson in thinking outside the box, she braced herself.

"You're a philosopher," he said. "What should we do when we humans invade and encroach upon their habitats, reducing their food sources significantly—should we just let them fend for themselves?" He shook his head slowly. "I don't believe that."

Kate assumed her skepticism showed in her expression. "What about the theory that it is not good for humans to intervene in nature's plan, so to speak, that human interference can actually harm—even when we are trying to create good?"

He looked sideways at her. "Oh, I believe we have long passed the point of non-interference in Nature's ways, wouldn't you say?"

Kate nodded, looking away. "Yes, when you put it that way, most assuredly."

"We feel that it is only just to help feed the animals whose habitats we encroach on, taking away their food sources," he explained. "We have tried to identify areas up here where food is scarce for the wildlife, and help, by either reintroducing those foods and/or recreating those habitats." He smiled. "The state of Vermont even offers tax breaks for landowners to engage in such projects."

"What a place," Kate said with a smile. "So much emphasis on the natural world here." She looked over at him. "It's really like a 'world elsewhere' here, isn't it?"

Channing nodded amiably, though without smiling. "Yes, it is—though we have our issues, as I discussed before. I can understand how it might appear," he said, glancing at her, "unusual, odd, eccentric, even other-worldly, as you indicated, but as Thoreau discussed, life used to revolve around the natural world, as it continues to do so, at least, in this region of Vermont." He stood up to take their mugs, placing them in the washtub in the sink.

Following his movements, Kate turned to make eye contact when she said, "Actually, from the little I have seen, and based largely upon what you have related to me about life here, I would say that little has changed since Thoreau's time—at least, up here."

Wiping the mugs dry, Channing nodded. "Although part of the way of life here stems from the old adage, 'it's the way we have always done things,' particularly among old Vermont families, the deliberately conscious adoption of a more natural lifestyle among newcomers to the area makes it a very attractive location for initiatives related to supporting their mode of living, hence my rationale for locating my Findhorn-Vermont center here."

Kate smiled, trying to suppress a giggle she felt rising. "I can see that Vermont would serve as the perfect site for a center focused on communication with, hmm, plants, animals, and bugs." She offered a bright smile.

Un-offended, even amused, by her remark, Channing readily returned her smile. "What—you cannot imagine Cambridge a suitable place." He said it as if he had already intuited her response.

She twisted her mouth to one side. "You would know better than I, but in a nutshell, no."

"Yes, I believe you are correct in your assumption."

He studied her a moment before speaking, as if gauging the potential impact of his next statement before uttering it, she noted.

"Yes?" She waited, wondering the reason for his hesitation.

"I am, however," he began, "interested in soliciting your input on some of the pedagogical plans I am formulating for the center, though our discussion can wait for another time."

She tried to re-assure him that she was open to new ways of thinking. "Well, sure, Channing. Whenever you'd like to chat about your ideas. I am happy to help in whatever way I can." She flashed him a warm smile.

"Good, then," he said, before turning away. Walking over to the mudroom, he retrieved a flashlight. "Although you might prefer the experience of walking in the night forest, as Thoreau described, you may wish to have this handy." He held it out.

Kate hesitated before taking it. Partially turning away, she said, "Thank you for dinner. It's been, well, an eye-opening experience."

"Ah," he said only.

She didn't move. "Particularly the deer watching, though, all of it, really."

"Yes." He stood with his hands in the pockets of his well-worn jeans.

When she didn't move, he walked back to the door and opened it, holding it for her. Glancing at him, Kate slowly walked toward the open door, but upon reaching it, stopped.

"I wondered, if you—" Again, she hesitated.

A look of understanding crossed his face, as his expression changed from a slight frown, to a brief chuckle, and a firm nod. "I did not wish to presume."

She let out a sigh of relief. "You know, it's one thing to experience a bear in the daylight—behind a solidly built wall and a half-closed window," she admitted, "but the thought of meeting your—however warm and fuzzy—bears at night, while walking alone in your deep woods, is something altogether, well—" looking at him with a shy smile, "absolutely *terrifying* to me."

He almost smiled. "Of course. I can walk with you." He gave a slight bow before saying, "After you."

Once outside, Channing attempted to pass her the flashlight. "No, please, in this case, I would truly rather follow you." Kate gazed around at the darkness, not moving.

"There's nothing to fear," he said with quiet assurance. "We'll just stand here a few minutes and allow the darkness to illuminate the night scene for us."

"Sounds like an oxymoron to me."

"You will understand shortly," he said.

They both stood next to one another, silently taking in the night. As Channing had predicted, after getting accustomed to the light of the night, Kate found that she could make out trees, the clearing, and even the path leading to the cabin. Looking in his direction and now seeing him, she said, "Amazing! I can actually see in the darkness."

"Although it requires a different set of senses to walk in the night, it can be done." He started walking. "Shall we?"

"As long as you lead the way." She added dryly, "Something I do not say easily to anyone, let alone to any man."

He chuckled. "Well, thank you—I think," followed by a hasty qualification, "though I do not presume, nor wish to lead you or any, um, woman. The goal is for each of us to find our own way." He turned back to her. "Wouldn't you like the experience of making your way through the night forest? I'll walk behind you."

Despite his urgings, Kate said, "Not this first time, please. You must remember that I come from a place where walking in the dark among trees is considered very dangerous."

She followed him along the path, timidly at first, taking tentative steps as if with closed eyes. But as her vision became more accustomed to the dim night, she walked with increasing confidence, as if enjoying a day hike through the woods. As she glanced from side to side, she noticed with a mixed sense of awe and relief that she could actually see fairly well around her. Tall trunks lined the path, the faintest glimmer of light occasionally radiating down through the trees. As they continued, Kate was surprised to discover that the setting felt increasingly more serene, despite her initial misgivings.

They soon reached the cabin, though not before an owl startled them by calling, "Whoo-cooks-for-yoo." Channing turned back to Kate and said lightly, "'*I rejoice that there are owls.*'"

Kate smiled into the dark. "I have always loved that sentiment." She looked up at him in the faint light shining above them. "It sounds like one of the simple joys of life, but I now know that the ability to hear an owl in such a woods, is nothing short of an all-encompassing philosophical stance."

He chuckled. "It is interesting for me to see my world through your eyes." He stepped up onto the threshold. "Shall I light the lamp for you?"

"Thanks. That would be great. I don't have much experience with kerosene lamps, oddly enough." Kate leaned against the cabin door, watching him as he twisted the knob and lit the wick. "I wanted to say that I also find it quite intriguing—" she said with a smile, as she sat down at the table, "if not directly challenging, to see my academic world at Harvard through your ideological lens."

Channing turned away from the lamp to look at her, his eyebrow assuming an angle of skepticism. "Do you not think your view of your own life is also grounded in ideology?"

Kate nodded. "Yes, I have come to understand that." She folded her arms. "Actually, the impact of thinking through the underlying premises, upon which my life there is based, is proving to be nothing short of tumultuous, particularly after our discussions on economics."

"Oh?"

She threw him a wry smile. "Not to mention the politics of plumbing, heating, and food." Shaking her head, she said dryly, "Never, will I look at my dinner in the same way."

Channing smiled. "A lot to contemplate, if not mediate upon." With a slight bow and tipped fingers, he said, "Good night to you. May your thoughts be expansive," before slipping out the door into the darkness.

Going to the door, Kate called out, trying to catch a last glimpse of him. "Thank you—for everything." But the darkness had already enfolded him.

Kate slowly closed the door, made a cup of tea, and sat down at her computer, feeling the need to reflect upon the evening. Suddenly changing her mind, not yet ready to confront the white screen, she took her tea and moved to the reading chair.

Looking out to the night, she let her thoughts drift—floating here, rushing there. A pattering moved into her consciousness, as she realized that it was now raining, making the most comforting of sounds against what must be a metal roof. She looked around the cabin by way of the soft light filtering through the shadows. A surge of tranquility and real contentment filled her, as the rain continued its soft drumbeat. *The beat of a different drum. My drumbeat.*

She kicked up her feet onto the ottoman and sunk back into the chair. A stream of notions floated through her consciousness. *Bears. Deer. Fish. Whales. Intelligent consciousness. Higher laws. All part of the great whole, Nature. To look at this matter in every light—weigh it with different scales.* With a twist of her mouth, she started to reflect on the conversation over dinner, when an insight surfaced.

Is there another lens through which to consider Ishmael's philosophy? Setting Ishmael alongside Thoreau's *higher laws*, she shook her head, as she abruptly sat upright. She realized Ishmael was not so different from Channing—a 19th-century Greenpeacer—saving the whales and people from the devastating effects of an economic system based on greed.

Moving back to her computer, Kate excitedly opened her laptop. With insights percolating, she wondered whether there was a way to *look at this matter in every light* as Ishmael so frequently urged throughout *Moby-Dick*. She wrote late into the night, her insights in full sail over an endless, expansive, green sea.

CHAPTER TWELVE

Brute Neighbors

KATE ENTERED THE CLASSROOM with a slow, easy-going gait, unlike her typical, bustling rhythm. Usually juggling an armful of books, along with her laptop, and a bag brimming with notes and papers, she now carried only a worn copy of *Walden*. A few students looked up from their computers when they realized she had arrived, exchanging quizzical glances with one another.

Noticing, Kate smiled easily at them. Instead of stepping behind the lectern and taking a perfunctory roll call before beginning class discussion, she moved over to the other side of her desk and half-sat on its edge, facing the students. A few in the front sat up straight. She started right in.

"Good morning, everyone." She flashed them a warm smile. "Today, I thought we would step back from our usual approach, to explore, instead, which particular themes, ideas, feelings, ways of life, etc., are resonating with you from this book more generally, than our chapter-by-chapter focus has allowed."

She looked around the classroom with an expectant gaze. They seemed a garden of flowers, looking dazed from a sudden storm. She tried to make eye contact with several different students, but no one volunteered their thoughts. "Anyone?" she asked faintly.

After a minute or so, she offered overt encouragement. "Your comments or observations can be based on your reading journals, which, so far, you have been sharing only with me—aside from the anonymous reading excerpts with which I have opened each of our class discussions." The flowers seemed to close for the night, folding their petals downward, as if to escape detection.

Kate waited, looking around with a bright smile. "Any takers?" Again, she scanned the room. With a shrug of her shoulders, she said, "Okay, then, why don't we start by taking out a sheet of paper."

There were a few groans. "Does it have to be paper, Professor?"

"Are we handing it in to you?" called out someone else.

A disembodied voice, sounding hopeful. "Could we e-mail it?"

Another voice complained. "I can't write with a pen—I only use my tablet or laptop."

Kate smiled, determined to remain undaunted by their reticence. "Fine, then. Use whatever method you prefer to write down some of your impressions that have truly moved you—to feel, think, or act in new ways."

"I don't understand," said a voice from the corner.

Kate chose specific individuals with whom to make eye contact. "You know," she said, "a theme, idea, topic, etc., related to your reading, that you find personally interesting—perhaps even moving enough, to act upon."

After some shuffling, the students began tapping away at their keyboards, emitting a sound, thought Kate, not unlike the pattering of rain on a metal roof. She scanned the room with a smile. It made her feel happy to discover a connection between two wonderful, yet wholly different experiences. Staring off into the distance, she could see the cabin now—the soft light, the walls piled high with books, all lulled by the harmonious melody of rain. Her own drumbeat—a reflection that infused her with joy.

Her eyes returned to the students, as the pattering faded into silence. They looked up at her expectantly, to which she responded with a big, warm smile. "Anyone like to share what resonates with you?"

The few in the front instantly slumped in their seats. When no voices spoke up or hands rose in the air, Kate said in a pleasant voice, "You are obviously more comfortable speaking with one another." With a nod, she indicated with her hand, "Why don't you—over there—break into a small group, while you—over there, there, and there—do the same?"

No one moved, staring at her in astonishment. Kate looked at them, waiting. Standing up, she faced them. "You do know what small groups are, don't you? Didn't you use them in high school to generate discussions?"

"Depends on which schools we came from," a voice offered.

Kate nodded. "Oh, I see." With a slight twist of her mouth, she said, "Well, for those alumni of boarding schools, a small group is simply that—a group discussion with one's fellow classmates—no more than five to a group." She smiled, held out her hands, and said, "Shall we, then?"

"How do we begin?" someone asked.

Kate walked back behind her desk. "However you would begin an exchange with another outside of class." With a wide smile, she announced, "All I am doing is providing the subject for a convivial, spirited exchange."

Sitting down behind her desk, she sat back and surveyed the scene. The less intrepid had already moved their desks, forming small circles, while others seemed to create what resembled a collision of cars scattered in ever direction on a crowded, icy interstate.

She glanced back at Heather, who was just in the process of moving her desk to join a group in the back. When they made eye contact, Heather offered a big smile, giving her a quick thumbs up, before sitting down in her new group.

As Kate watched, she thought her students resembled the deer she had observed—first one emerged hesitantly from the protective anonymity of the forest, then another, now both walking with timid steps toward the food, and upon successfully reaching it, and beginning their meal, the others joined in. A few tentative voices, followed by others. Before long, the room reverberated in animated exchange and occasional laughter.

Closing her eyes, Kate heard only the humming of the universal lyre strumming one, long, harmonious chord. Her own thoughts flowed freely. She figured that chanting must feel like that, like the sense of oneness she felt along the bank of the pond that day—*all things into one.*

As Kate emerged from her reverie to observe the scene before her, she noted that Heather had ended up forming a small group with just one fellow, aptly named Forrest, Kate noted with a grin, with whom Heather seemed to be communicating in earnest. She was bent forward, leaning toward him, speaking, it seemed, nonstop, while he leaned back, just watching her with a big, silly grin on his face. Whenever he said something, she flushed and looked away, eventually meeting his unwavering gaze once again.

Kate smiled to herself. "Good for you, Heather. You tell him all about life in Walden North," she mentally called out. Just then, Heather glanced over at Kate, who immediately smiled, nodded, and gave her the thumbs up sign. Heather turned beet red, but with a soft smile, returned to her doting audience of one.

Glancing at her watch, Kate realized that time had sped along. Although she was tempted to reign in the groups to ask for some sort of report back to the class, she noted that they were so engaged with one another, she hesitated to break up the spirit of real communication that seemed to flow through every crevice of the room. When the class had ended, she simply stood, looked around one last time, and walked out—leaving the conversation to continue without her guidance. Now that's *real* education, she thought proudly.

Kate sauntered along the stone paths from one campus green to the other toward her office. Although she held office hours regularly the same day as class, no one actually came. '*The guest who never comes,*' she recalled with a smile, though she waited each time in expectation that today would be different.

She settled into the comfortable swivel chair, leaning her head on her hand and gazing out the window. The last remnants of fall color dropped away almost reluctantly, it seemed, from the trees outside her window, with each breeze that rustled through them. She realized with a start that it was snowing leaves—a phenomenon she had never before that moment actually noticed. Gazing through the canopy, she wondered what they would look like dressed in actual snow. Her thoughts drifted to an image of the deep forest of Walden North. Her vision blurred, shifting to visualizing a winter walk among white pines, glistening in snow.

A knock interrupted her meditation. "Professor? May we come in and talk to you?"

Kate reeled around in utter surprise, offering them a dreamy gaze. "Oh, hi," she said with a smile. "Come on in. You are my first guests. Are you here for dinner?" She grinned.

Heather didn't miss a beat. "I'm honored to be considered your dinner guest, but no, we are not Krishna, but come on a similar mission."

Forrest—a tall, lanky fellow, more legs than anything else—entered without a word, and after a brief nod in Kate's direction, slumped in one of the chairs near the desk. Folding his arms across his chest, followed by crossing his Birkenstock-sandaled feet, he directed his complete attention to Heather.

With subtly raised eyebrows and a special gleam in her eyes, Heather signaled to Kate her excitement over the attention. Every time she turned toward Forrest, her face glowed.

Heather turned back to Kate to explain. "We're here because we'd like to do a joint '*Experiment in Living.*'"

"Oh?" Kate swiveled slowly in her chair.

Heather smiled. "Well, essentially, we want to exchange lives, isn't that right, Forrest?"

He nodded only.

Kate cast a searching glance toward each of them. "Well, maybe you could explain in a bit more detail?"

"Of course," Heather said, while shaking her head. "Well," she started, as she glanced with a huge smile at her companion, "Forrest has never really experienced a true forest like ours, despite his name, so he wants to come stay in the cabin."

"Hmm. Sounds intriguing," Kate said. Glancing over at Forrest, she added, "I've just come from there myself and can vouch for the transformative experience it offers."

Forrest just nodded.

Heather jumped in. "What do you think?" Her wide eyes assumed super-moon status. "Will Dad go for it, do you think?"

"Of course," Kate responded, without thinking. "He'll most likely think it's an opportune experience for both of you." Her glance shifted from Heather to the now smiling Forrest.

"Oh, good!" Heather was beyond enthusiastic.

Kate turned to her. "And what about your '*experiment in living*'?"

"Well," said Heather, with a shy glance at Forrest, "I've never experienced life on Park Avenue in Manhattan, so I'll be going to his house."

He nodded. "She'll get to experience elevator living at its best," he said with a grin. He reached over and touched her shoulder gently, giving it a slight squeeze. "We'll exchange Walden North with Central Park, and—" he said, grinning at Heather, "I'm betting, back again to Walden North."

Resisting the urge to proclaim gratitude that Forrest had finally spoken, Kate said instead, "Oh, my, that's quite an *experiment in living*. But you'll have to do something truly Thoreauvian as part of the project, you know."

Heather flashed a warm smile. "Oh, we plan to watch the dawn rise over Central Park, then fly to Walden North, and watch it from over the pond—to compare the two experiences."

Kate smiled at the pride Heather seemed to intone into the word 'we.'

"Oh, is there an airport nearby, Heather?"

Forrest grinned. "We'll just land in one of those big fields of beans Heather keeps talking about," he said, as he touched her arm, "if not, there's always the county airport."

"So, you fly yourself," said Kate with a nod, "I see. How wonderful." She gave them both a bright smile. "I'm looking forward to reading about your experiences." As they stood up to leave, she added with a slight turn of her mouth, "though you are not required to be completely *thorough* in your account of the entire experience, just *Thoreau-vian*."

Heather giggled over the pun, while flushing over the insinuation. As they stood starting to leave, she turned to Forrest. "I'll be right there," breaking out in a sweet smile. "Will you wait for me?" She placed a timid hand on his arm.

"Always," he said gruffly, looking down at her with a searching gaze. With a brief nod at Kate, he left the office.

Heather flushed pink, her eyes glistening. Leaning over to Kate, she whispered, "He even meditates! Dad will be happy about that, at least." With furrowed eyebrows, she looked more than anxious. "Don't you think?"

Kate smiled and offered a supportive nod. "Oh, I'm sure it will all work out beautifully."

"Oh, do you think so?" Her eyes seemed to float in orbs of shimmering light, not unlike the lily pads on Walden Pond under a brilliant sun. "He even wants to fly me to the Vineyard for one of Mom's retreats! Mom will just love him!"

"Well, it seems this little '*experiment in living*' is taking some new turns for the two of you. How exciting!" Kate smiled.

"We're leaving for Walden North this coming Saturday," Heather said. "Won't Dad be surprised!"

Kate chuckled. "Oh, I'd say so. Oh, that reminds me." She sat upright and began searching through her bag. "Can you bring something up to your father for me?"

"Sure—what is it?" Heather asked. "Another pinecone?" She smiled coyly at Kate.

Kate swatted her arm. "Oh, you. No, it's an article I wrote while in the meditation cabin during my last visit up there." She smiled with pride. "It's just been accepted in a premier environmental journal." She looked away. "I thought your dad might be pleased to read of my, em, new turn, onto a '*less traveled road*' in academia." She handed it to Heather, who scanned the title in curiosity.

"Ooh, may I read it too?" She looked at Kate, who nodded. "It sounds really interesting."

"If you'd like, Heather, sure." Turning to the computer, she printed off two additional copies. Placing one copy in her bag, she gave the other to Heather. "Here you go. Your own copy."

"Oh, thanks." She tucked it under her arm. "I'm sure Dad will be excited to read it, as well."

Kate smiled at her, and squeezing her arm softly, said, "Good luck with the '*experiment in living*'—and the romance that's sure to flow from it."

Heather reached out and gave her a big hug. "Thanks. I'm so excited!"

Just as she started out the door, Heather turned around. "Oh, by the way, I guess Dad's been meaning to talk with you about his own '*experiment in living*' in the planning stages."

Kate looked at her with surprise. "Oh, really? Oh, you must mean his Findhorn—Vermont project."

When Heather nodded, Kate continued. "While he mentioned wanting to speak to me about it, I can't imagine how I could be of help to him. He knows so much more than I, really, about all things Thoreauvian."

Heather smiled. "He wants to discuss what he called pedagogical techniques with you. I've been telling him about how much of a positive effect you are having on our class. I e-mailed him about this morning's class."

Kate's eyes widened. "Your father has really resorted to using e-mail?" She shook her head. "I thought he was joking."

"Well, he can't organize his new life center without it." She shrugged. "Besides, since your visit to him—remember, I told you? He's decided he should keep in more or less daily contact with me."

Kate twisted her mouth into a wry smile. "Glad to help."

"Anyway," said Heather, "everyone raved after class this morning about how awesome it was to talk to each other, and the fact that you actually ask us what we're interested in. They love the reading response journals assignments."

"*Really*?" Kate was surprised by the news. "They weren't very forthcoming this morning."

"*Really*," said Heather with a firm smile. "We have to write, in its other sense, *really* boring papers in all our other courses. Yours gets us thinking, about not only ourselves, but how we live and want to live our lives." She shrugged. "I mean, after all, take Forrest, who grew up with super famous parents in Manhattan—with everything he could ever want and more. And yet he can't wait to spend time without electricity and water in the meditation cabin."

Kate smirked. "Oh, I think it has less to do with my great teaching and more to do with your beautiful smile!"

Heather beamed. "Do you think so?"

"You know it!" said Kate. She enjoyed seeing Heather's eyes brighten.

"Maybe," said Heather with a shy smile, "but it also has to do with your opening his eyes. He's said as much."

Kate laughed. "Oh, not me. It's all Thoreau."

Heather grimaced. "No, not really. We all remember you and your introductory lecture about how quaint Thoreau's ways seemed to you. We have watched you transform as you have been teaching *Walden*. It's really been inspirational. When you shared your story about visiting my dad and meeting the bears, well, the entire class was just so enthralled. Now they all really want to go out and have some amazing '*experiments in living*' themselves."

Kate looked astonished. "I had no idea."

Heather smiled coyly. "That's why my dad wants to talk to you."

"Tell him anytime." She offered a shy smile. "I'm intrigued." Heather laughed. "Aren't we both? Okay, see ya!"

Kate stood watching the two of them, as they walked away down the hall, Forrest's long arm wrapped around the more petite Heather. Although she had discussed in her article Thoreau's concept of '*experiments in living*,' Kate hadn't ever considered that love could be part of either the experiment or the living—until now. She gathered up her things, closed her office door softly behind her, and went outside for a long walk.

Glancing at her watch, Kate realized she was to meet Blake on campus before joining him for dinner. She sauntered along the stone path to his office, enjoying watching the leaves swirl around her, before adding to the rich array of striking hues on the now multi-colored grass. She hoped that Blake would enjoy reading her new article—perhaps even embrace the idea of visiting Walden North with her.

She knocked on his half-open door with a soft tap, poking her head around the door. "Hi, Blake, may I come in?"

He didn't even look up. Waving her in with a brusque gesture, Blake continued typing on his keyboard. Kate thought better of kissing him and instead sat down, waiting for him to finish his work. After some more minutes, he stopped typing, closed his laptop, and looked up unsmiling at her.

Knowing that it always took him some time to become sociable after intensive concentration, she offered him a warm smile. "Hi, are we still on for dinner?"

He sighed. "Yes, I suppose I should take a break. I must return to my work, though, as I have a deadline."

She shook her head. "You're organizing your life almost entirely around deadlines these days, it seems."

He gave her a curt nod, before turning to gather some materials into his bag. "That's what we do, we academics."

"Oh!" Kate said, as she leaned forward. "Speaking of academics, I have some news."

He turned to face her. "Yes? A publisher for your dissertation?" He looked hopeful.

Kate shook her head. "No, not yet, but I just had an article accepted for publication."

Blake stared at her. "Oh? Something from your dissertation? I don't seem to recall you mentioning anything to me about that."

Removing the article from her bag, she walked over to the desk. "Well, not exactly from it. Tangentially related, perhaps. It's basically new material, though I do discuss Melville's whales." She leaned toward him. "Don't you remember I told you I was researching the interconnecting links between Walden Pond and Walden North, Vermont? I brought you a copy."

Scanning the title page, he peered at her as a deep scowl spread across his face. He tossed the article on his desk. "What is happening to you?" Blake gazed at her with overt disapproval in his eyes. "First, you repudiate your ancestry, and now this?"

Kate felt an instant sense of dread drain her enthusiasm. "Oh, Blake, we've been through this before," she said with a deep sadness in her voice. "I cannot claim distantly related people as my direct ancestry," she explained. "That would be like claiming I was a Kennedy—and showing up on the front steps of Hyannis."

"Well, from the genealogical account you have related to me, you do have Kennedy blood flowing in your veins," he shrugged, "however removed, of course."

Turning to her, his voice almost pleading, he implored, "To turn your back on your immediate extended family, the Vermont Brownes, with their impressive pedigree, particularly for their historical connections to Harvard and its mother institution, Cambridge, is, is, well, utterly self-immolating." Blake grimaced sternly. "For God's sake, Kate, the bloody library is named after your family—a link to which is foolhardy not to claim an association."

Kate's green eyes flamed red. "Oh, and I thought it was the quality of my research that counted for acceptance at Harvard."

Frowning, he said, "Kate, we have been through this before." He peered at her. "Surely, you have not forgotten—or dismissed—the insights I shared with you on the indivisible link between culture and intellect."

She said nothing as she folded her arms across her chest.

"Your active re-integration into the Browne family would ensure your survival here at Harvard."

Her eyes blazing, Kate sputtered, "Oh, as it has secured your continued membership? Does the quality of your scholarship not matter?"

"Oh, Kate, my membership here was secured from both sides of my family lines the moment I was born."

She just stared at him, saying nothing.

He gazed at her emblazoned expression and reddened cheeks with increasing concern. "My God, you are a descendant of Sir Thomas Browne, for God's sake, woman! Surely, that matters to you, doesn't it, Katie?"

Kate paced back and forth in his office. "What does my bloodline have to do with my article?"

"I could have got you published in one of the top journals through that bloodline you are so quick to disavow. And to write about this rubbish?" With a deep frown, he asked with even more acidity, "What happened to your interest in philosophy?"

"It *is* philosophy—though from a different vantage point. I moved from the 'philosophy in whales' to the matter of the philosophy of maintaining their continued existence, I suppose you could say." She shrugged. "Someone has to speak for them."

"Listen to you! You sound like a bloody Greenpeace radical!"

With an irritated shake of her head, Kate countered, "I'm simply saying that literary texts do speak to pressing ecological concerns, in addition to their thematic and philosophical points."

He turned to her with sad eyes. "Where, or where has my old Katie gone?"

"Oh, for Heaven's sake, Blake, don't be so dramatic." She folded her arms again. "You'd think it was a bloody sin to develop and grow."

Blake vigorously shook his head, flinging disapproval in all directions, like someone applying fungicide to subdue invading insects. "And to publish in that *rag* they have the utter temerity to call a 'journal'—as if it compared even the *slightest* with the esteemed intellectual journals of our profession."

He now paced the floor, his walk shifting from a gentle padding to pounding within minutes.

"My God, Kate, how could you even begin to compare the Walden of Thoreau's idyll, with that lowlife place among the Billybobs up in the no man's land of northern Vermont?" He glanced over at her, still too furious to cease his pacing. "What's got into you?"

Kate said nothing, her heart dropping like an anchor through the sea of inspiration she had been harboring.

Blake stopped abruptly, and reeling round to her, his eyes now threatening an imminent storm, thundered, "Is it that . . . that, *hippie* disciple of Thoreau that is drawing you to embrace this silliness? That Channing fellow?" He turned away. "*His* ancestors must be turning in their graves in embarrassment over his disavowal and his actions."

Kate stared hard at him. "I'm not sure I should dignify that question with an answer, but no, it is not."

"You are treading through dangerous waters, here, Katie, my dear," he said in a low tone, reminding Kate of the deep growl uttered by a rabid animal before it attacks. She gave an involuntary shiver.

"You have no idea how brutal your fellow colleagues can become when threatened."

Kate studied his smoldering eyes. "Oh, I don't know. I think I can easily imagine." Looking away, she said in a soft voice, "What happened to the intellectual pursuit of knowledge?" Turning back, she met his now furiously knit eyebrows and glaring look. "Is that, too, politicized in some subtle way that only the insiders know?"

"You don't cut away the very foundations upon which the ivory towers have been constructed." He now paced furiously. "It's, it's—"

"Impudent?" Kate shot back, "as in 'impudent upstarts'?" She stood glaring at him. "Is that how I seem to you with this article?"

Blake stopped and stared at her in astonishment. "Well, yes, actually." He studied her face, as if trying to locate an opening into her soul. "How did you know to articulate it thus?"

Turning on her heels, Kate said, "Oh, I had a few lessons in detecting the genuine, from the imposters, trying to gain club membership."

"Just what exactly are you trying to prove?" His voice appeared to her as a series of daggers slicing the air.

Kate almost felt as if she had to dodge each weapon hurled in her direction. "Nothing, nothing at all." She paced the room. "It's just that I feel, well, to borrow from Thoreau, '*awakened*.'"

Blake spit out his words. "Preposterous notion. We are all more than awake here at Harvard—and in the academy." He thrust out his chin in a pout. "We're intellectuals, after all. That is what distinguishes us from the unthinking multitudes."

Kate waved her arm as if to dismiss his attitude. Turning to face him, she explained, "Greeting the dawn, as in '*Only that day dawns to which we are awake*,' is like researching and working here at Harvard. Like that statement, we dwell in theory, in ideas, in philosophical notions. That, in itself, produces a sense of awe when we discover the 'dawn,' shall we say, of each of our research goals."

With folded arms and pursed lips, Blake said, coldly, "Well, yes, so far. Go on. I'm listening."

Shaking her head, she continued. "But the last lines of *Walden* point to the difference."

Blake frowned. "Have you not just quoted the last line? I don't seem to recall any additional statements," he said, his mouth shifting to a decided grimace.

Kate rushed to respond. "But that's just the point!" Nodding, she added in a spirited tone, "Most readers overlook Thoreau's call to action required to differentiate between simply seeing the dawn, versus the need for acting upon the awakening, as in '*the sun is but a morning star*.'" She looked at him with wide, pleading eyes. "Don't you see?"

He returned to pursing his lips. "I don't see anything at all in that last line. Besides, one cannot even see stars during the day." He tossed his head in dismissal.

"But *that's* precisely the point!" she returned. "Since one cannot readily see them, one must experience the notion, the feeling, the idea, always grounded in *experience*." Shaking her head sadly, she concluded, "That's where we academics tend to stop, and where the real philosophers, the poets of life, begin their search for stars throughout the day—through experience." She gazed at him a moment, before saying in a resolute tone, "We academics are students merely, not active participants in what he called the '*experiment in living.*'"

"Utter bollocks," Blake retorted in staccato notes. "I may not be able, nor *want*, to save you this time, Kate. I predict this is not going to go over well with Dean Edwards." He stomped out of his office, slamming the door behind him.

Kate sat and let the stray tears trickle down her face without even bothering to wipe them away. Along with her tears, she felt a new insight flowing through her. *It's time I started really feeling, rather than intellectualizing, life around me.*

She gently closed the door of his office behind her and went outside.

By the end of the week, the students had become so interested in discussing their reading in small groups that when Kate entered the class on Friday morning, she found them already actively engaged with one another. As she moved from group to group in silence, offering only a nod and a smile to anyone who even noticed her, she strained to listen to the exchanges. Not only were they on topic, she heard snatches of heartfelt philosophical discussions regarding the plight of the natural world and their roles in caretaking the earth.

One group Kate happened to overhear was discussing Walden Pond. When she stopped to listen, one of the students, named Sarah, addressed her.

"Professor? Some of us were wondering whether we could all go visit Walden Pond." Others nodded their heads in agreement.

Another student spoke up. "We didn't know if it is okay to have a field trip in college, but it seems kind of crazy not to go visit, when we are studying a book whose setting is located a few miles away."

Kate nodded in agreement. "Absolutely." Deliberately revising one of the dean's statements, she asserted, "Not going to Walden when studying Thoreau's book would be like his studying navigation science here at Harvard without ever going on the water," she turned to point out the window, "down there—to experience his studies."

Some of the students nodded, while another said, "That sounds pretty crazy."

Kate shook her head. "We should blend theory and experience."

Within a few minutes, the news had spread through the other groups that the class was going to go to Walden Pond. Everyone started discussing the particulars, arranging rides for those who didn't have cars, while others figured out the directions. When the din of excitement had abated, they all looked up expectantly, as someone asked, "When can we go?"

Kate scanned the lively faces. She was thrilled to see them so animated about experiencing Walden Pond for themselves. "Tell you what," she said, "It's just after peak foliage this weekend, so why don't we all meet there tomorrow? We might catch the last of the leaf color." Heads nodded in agreement, before the students returned to organizing their rides and emailing directions to everyone.

Kate just watched them, excited by their enthusiasm. "By the way," she said, "let's bring some particularly Thoreauvian foods for a picnic, shall we?"

"You mean like beans?" called out someone.

"And water?"

Kate nodded. "That's right. What about yeast-free bread?"

"You mean like Matzo crackers?"

"Yes, anything that is commercially yeast-free." She thought a minute. "I would think wild-yeast sour dough bread would work, as well."

"There's a bakery around the corner from where I live that makes flatbreads. I could bring some of those," suggested one of the students.

By the end of class, they had made up a creative list of food and drivers. A few students even volunteered to film the event. They left class still engaged in animated exchanges. Kate watched them all leave, shaking her head in amazement. The transformation in her students felt like foreshadowing in a novel, or perhaps prophetic tidings—though of what, exactly, she wasn't quite sure.

By the time of the late Friday afternoon faculty tea, news had leaked out among Kate's colleagues about her new publication.

Blake held court among a group of his colleagues. "Oh, it's much worse than even that," he proclaimed with a sneer. "She's being published in the *Mother Earth* of environmentalist rags—er, did I say, rag? I meant *mag*, though the first appellation equally applies, as well." The others smirked.

As Kate entered the lounge, some heads turned in her direction, while others simply ignored her entrance and continued on with their conversations. Snippets of critique found their way to her, as she walked slowly by a few groups, who obviously had no plans to welcome or include her.

Kate stood at the edge, looking on, while sipping her white wine in small draughts, unsure of which group to join. Although she didn't really feel like mingling, Blake had warned her of the dire necessity to show up religiously each week. As she stared absently about her, she noticed Dean Edwards approaching. She inhaled deeply, holding her breath for what she was sure to be a raging blast.

Without a greeting, he launched headlong into his question. "Is it true you have been associating with the School of Education, Ms. Brown?" He scowled at her. "I thought I had made my '*Great Expectations*' clear in that regard."

Kate looked at him in trepidation. "I'm not sure what you mean, Dean Edwards."

"It seems that you are engaging in *pedagogy* in your course."

"Pedagogy?" she repeated.

"Yes, activities used in elementary schools, I believe." His stare was cold and hard.

"Oh," she said, in a light of recognition, "you must be referring to my small-group discussions." She smiled. "Just a technique, a useful one at that, to generate exchange on how the readings resonate for the students."

"It's not a bloody book club, Ms. Brown. It's a *literature* course and writing seminar."

"Yes, I realize that, Dean, but—"

"They are to focus on the scholarship around *Walden*, not their individual feelings about the book."

Kate looked at him through wide eyes. "But that is precisely what I am doing, Dean."

"You are to prepare them to be scholars, Ms. Brown, as I thought we had discussed," he reproached, after slugging down his single malt. "Unless, of course, you aren't well enough versed in the scholarship yourself."

Kate gave a curt nod. "I can assure you, Dean, that I have immersed my course in the history of research on *Walden*."

"Then be a good girl, will you, and pass on that knowledge to your students, instead of exploring their *feelings* about their readings like a bloody therapy group!" His eyes appeared as fiery slits, inflamed with volcanic wrath. "Frankly, I have entertained serious doubts about your levels of competence, particularly after hearing you are penning articles outside of your area of expertise."

Kate tried hard not to shake her head. "But Dean—" she began, her tone plaintive.

He interrupted her. Leaning towards her, he spoke in a low, threatening tone. "I'll have no activism here in my college, Ms. Brown, environmental, pedagogical, or otherwise. We engage with the leading thoughts through the history of culture, not feelings, and most certainly, not militant action." Throwing one last glare in her direction, he stormed away.

Blake appeared from behind. "I did warn you, Katie, not to rile the man. He has straightened you out, hopefully, in ways I could not."

Without even responding, Kate swept past him, placed her wine glass on the table, and left, making no eye contact with anyone.

Within the hour, she was jogging along the river, trying to shake off the feelings of anger and despair that had overcome her. Increasing her speed, she ran hard until her breathing caused her to slow back down to a jog. Glancing over at the river, she noticed some ducks swimming in a line down the middle. She wondered whether it was some sort of mystical sign for her to adopt the *middle way*.

As her eyes followed their trail, she slowed to a gait that kept the ducks at her watery side. Finally stopping, she stood along the edge, watching them paddle down river. She realized their particular path must reflect their delight in swimming along an endless stream of water—right in the thick of it. Nothing compromising in that, she concluded. They were simply feeling centered. When they had disappeared into the horizon, Kate turned back, resolved to finding a way to feel centered herself.

By the time Kate arrived at Walden Pond mid-morning the next day, several of the students were already there. Two greeted her in the parking lot, armed with a video camera.

"Well, hi," she said pleasantly. "What are you filming?"

Sarah spoke. "It's so cool what we're doing!" She looked at her companion with a sweet smile. "Zach's been filming me going up to people," she said, before waving to some runners packing up their car, "and asking them why they come to Walden Pond."

Kate smiled and nodded. "Oh, really? That would be interesting to know."

Zach broke in. "It gets even better," he said with a laugh. "Sarah then asks them if they have ever read *Walden*!"

Sarah giggled. "And guess what they almost always say?"

Kate smiled. "Haven't a clue. Tell me."

They both looked at each other before breaking out in laughter. "They say, 'Well, I *started* it—'"

"And?" Kate looked from one to the other.

Sarah giggled again. "No one seems to have ever *finished* reading *Walden*!"

"Really." Kate shook her head. "Well, you'll all be the first, then, it seems."

Zach provided an account of their exchanges, concluding, "Sarah then tells them how awesome the various chapters are and urges them to try again." He shook his head. "She should be a professor," and turning to Kate added, "like you—a born teacher."

Kate smiled, glancing at Sarah. "We'll both take that as a compliment, won't we, Sarah?"

Sarah looked at Zach through joyous eyes before turning to Kate. "Um, Professor, we were wondering if we could make a film for our '*experiment in living*.'"

Opening her trunk, Kate turned back to them. "Oh? Tell me more." Removing some of the dishes she brought, she handed some to each, before they all started walking.

Zach started to explain. "We both think it's pretty interesting that Walden Pond attracts so many people who come here to run, walk, go to the beach, and kayak."

Sarah nodded. "Yeah, that's right, and we want to find out how many of them actually come here because this was Thoreau's place, as a sort of pilgrimage or retreat for themselves, or whether—"

Zach continued. "They just come because it's a nice place."

Sarah jumped back in. "So, we want to talk to them about their understanding of the book and its themes, and if they haven't read it, encourage them to do so."

Zach smiled as he jerked his thumb in her direction. "See? A natural born teacher."

"Oh, you." Sarah gave him a playful shove.

Kate nodded. "Well, it sounds like an interesting idea. Will you show it to the class?" Recalling the dean's warning, she added, "Of course, you would need to write up an account of your *experiment*, based on motifs from *Walden*."

"Absolutely," they both said in unison.

"We're thinking of putting our video up on YouTube," said Zack.

"Ooh, not sure about that last one. What if Thoreau finds out?" Kate said, as she gave them both a smile, thinking how gratifying it felt to see her students so enthused over their engagement with Thoreau's book. That's what learning is all about, she thought. She recalled her own sense of inspiration from the literary themes and philosophical implications of her favorite novels that had fueled her passion for further study. She smiled over at them. "Sounds like a plan."

They walked on the path along the pond to Thoreau's original cabin site, now nestled in a stand of young pines. Kate was pleasantly surprised to discover that several of the class had set up a picnic site, having placed large tablecloths on the ground for the meal, while some of the others had arrived by kayak, several of which hugged the shoreline. Zach immediately started filming their arrival and the display, while Sarah asked for an explanation of each dish set out on the cloths.

When it came to Kate's turn, she smiled over at Heather, who was leaning against Forrest's upturned knees, and announced, "Beans, of course! Where would we be without some Thoreauvian beans!"

Heather leaned over to peer into the dishes and exclaimed, "Aren't those my dad's beans?"

Kate grinned proudly. "Yes, they are from that local foods restaurant we dined at," she said with a nod.

"Awesome," exclaimed Heather. Turning to Forrest, she said, "Wait 'til you taste my dad's beans!" He smiled fondly in return, touching her shoulder gently.

Addressing Heather, Kate asked, "Heather, why don't you tell everyone about your beans, your methods of preparing them, and about the restaurant your dad helped start up?'

As Zach filmed, Heather explained the details to the increasingly more enraptured group.

"Wow!" someone exclaimed. "We'll have to all go there for dinner," while someone else chimed in, "I had no idea local food could be so good."

"Another class field trip?" someone suggested.

"Awesome!" another chimed in, as others nodded in quiet agreement.

Within minutes, everyone was devouring the various dishes, while engaged in animated, convivial exchange. Kate leaned back silently, taking in the scene. She was delighted with the positive response of her students to experiencing both the location of Thoreau's former cabin site and the simple foods upon which he relied while living there. When the course began, Kate had never considered for a second that she and they would be discussing the merits of local foods and the philosophy of simple living. She shook her head in wonderment. A true '*experiment in living*,' she thought. *Mine, as well as theirs.*

When every morsel had been consumed, and tablecloths folded up and packed away, some decided to hike around the pond, while a few others started collecting pinecones and particularly colorful leaves. Heather and Forrest suggested an expedition to the original bean field. When a small group followed them, Zach and Sarah joined in to film the event.

Just before they disappeared into the trees, someone called out, "Professor, if you want to kayak, you can use mine—the green one."

With a warm smile, Kate waved in acknowledgment.

Looking around, she realized she was alone. Noticing a trunk of one of the larger pines, she ambled over and sat, leaning against it. Time passed by unaccounted as she continued sitting, and with arms wrapped around her knees, gazed out over the still pond. The tranquility soothed her. It had been an emotionally tumultuous week, with the excitement over getting the article accepted in the new environmental journal, followed by the overflowing enthusiasm the students were exhibiting over reading *Walden*—only to be chastened by her colleagues' censure of her innovative efforts in teaching and research.

Rather than representing the 'higher laws' of the intellect, her colleagues now seemed no better than brute neighbors, unable or unwilling to rise above their critical tendencies to embrace the holistic. Dean Edwards appeared to her as a giant black ant ready to fight to the finish to defend his kingdom against the encroaching, though diminutive, red ant. She folded her face into her hands.

Kate could just imagine the dean thundering, "You've transformed Prescott's seminar into a film studies course? *Film* studies, Ms. Brown?" as he spit out her name.

She shook her head to dispel her negative thoughts. She wasn't just reading and teaching *Walden*—she seemed to be *living* each chapter. But how to reconcile the 'higher laws' experience at Walden North with the 'brute neighbors' of Harvard, remained the challenge.

Kate continued to gaze out over the pond, now an iridescent mirror, reflecting fiery reds, elegant coppers, and lively yellows against the sheer blue surface. She had never experienced anything quite like the simple, though radiant beauty of the place—outside of Walden North, she realized. There she had enjoyed the tranquility of solitude—alone, but not lonely—in the cabin, with nature outside as her companion. She raised her eyes to the sky above. *Odd thoughts for this city girl.*

A whirring sound stirred her. Having never heard it before, Kate had no idea what to make of it. Staring in the direction from where she thought it had emanated, she kept her eyes focused on the thick, lower brush under the canopy of pines at her side. She was soon rewarded for her concentration. A long, duck-like bird waddled out from under a bush, followed by three younger ones. They were dressed in the colors of fall, rich browns and deeply burnished golds, looking more like autumn beech leaves than animals. Kate sat perfectly still, not daring to breathe. She so wanted to see whether the birds would approach her.

The mother made her way through the beds of fallen leaves, all the while looking anxiously from side to side. Kate marveled at how protective she seemed of her little ones, wondering what she would do when she finally detected Kate's presence. The moment revealed itself. Though Kate had anticipated a profound reaction from the bird, she had not expected the depth of emotions it would trigger within her.

Just as the mother bird unknowingly clucked her way toward Kate, she veered in another direction, two of her three chicks following in unison. The last one, however, with head down toward the ground, continued on the previous path, climbing right onto Kate's shoe. When it realized it was no longer on the ground, it looked up, meeting Kate's enthralled gaze. Two rounded orbs, like the glistening surface of the pond, invited Kate's gaze inward, it seemed to her, through ions of time and space. The gaze seemed endless, clear, innocent, pure—and yet inordinately deep—deeper than any other she had ever experienced, outside of the bear's eyes.

Thoreau's words surfaced within her own depths—

> *Eyes not born when the bird was, but coeval with the sky they reflect.*

She had always wondered what exactly Thoreau had meant by those lines, but now she knew firsthand. The '*wisdom clarified by experience*'—referred, not only to the intelligent eyes into which she was gazing so earnestly, but to her own consciousness rising to the surface—buoyant from experience.

When the mother bird realized that one of her own was missing, she turned, and seeing Kate, whirred and clucked, flailing her wing up and down, while her chicks fled under the protective cover of leaves. Within seconds, Kate could no longer discern between the beech leaves and the feathers of the small birds seeking refuge. She smiled and called out softly, "Don't worry. I won't harm you." Remaining perfectly still until the mother disappeared into the bushes, Kate then leaned her head back against the trunk and closed her eyes, as if to record the profound event—and the emotions it inspired in the inner recesses of her psyche.

When the moment had passed, Kate got up, stretched, and decided to walk along the less-worn path around the more secluded side of the pond. With her feet gently crunching against the leaves, she heard birds nearby chirping, as chipmunks called out in alarm, announcing her presence. She continued on through a dense stand of evergreens, whose branches hung low and soft. With a deepening sense of pride, she realized that she was able to identify first a stand of firs, followed by hemlocks. She smiled, thinking how happy Heather would be, and perhaps Channing, to know of her growing botanical literacy.

Coming to a cove, Kate noticed something swimming away from the shore, the water parting, it seemed, on either side of the animal. She stopped to watch. All of a sudden, what she assumed was a duck, dove down into the water, emerging some minutes later, in another spot farther away, but close enough for her to detect the black head and white ringed neck. Just as she gasped in delight over her discovery, the bird emitted a low cry, both haunting and eerily musical. A laugh it almost seemed to her, yet unlike one she had ever heard—except for the odd-looking duck at Walden North. She stood riveted, waiting to see or hear what would follow. Suddenly, another laugh echoed through the air, and before she knew it, another of the ducks sailed out from the cover toward the first. *Loons!*

As she stood watching them dive and resurface, calling out to one another, Kate noticed some kayaks in the distance approaching. The loons were faster than they, however, and diving down, swam away from the intruders. Kate waved frantically to her students, who like Thoreau, vainly tried to catch up to the infinitely crafty loons. With a brief wave, she listened intently, mesmerized by the wild sound echoing among the hills surrounding the pond, before continuing on her way, disappearing herself into the trees.

With a pounding heart, Kate thought of Ishmael's recurrent comment throughout *Moby-Dick*, "*There is meaning in this.*" But how exactly it all applied to her life, she wasn't quite sure. She discovered one bit of insight, though, she realized, as she drove back to Cambridge. After reflecting upon the week's events, culminating in her uncanny nature experiences at Walden, she was determined to find a way to reconcile into a transcendent whole, the two increasingly conflicting sides of her own evolving nature.

One thing she knew for certain, she concluded, as she sat down at her desk and gazed out to the maple beyond her window, there was nothing brutish about animals—*only the human ones.*

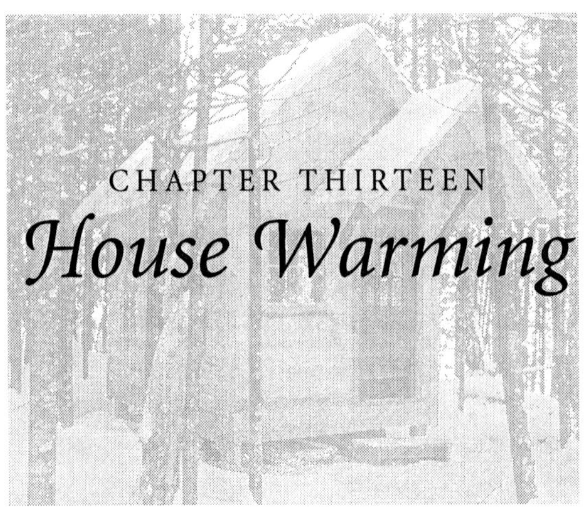

CHAPTER THIRTEEN

House Warming

THE FEROCITY OF THE DEAN'S IMPLICIT THREAT, reinforced by Blake's brutal disapproval, had unnerved Kate, disquieting her Waldenesque reverie, that she retreated from her idyll, instead, dedicating the remainder of the semester to focusing exclusively on her research. She intended to remain *clinched* to her desk while engaging in the arduous task of revising her dissertation into a book—worthy of Harvard.

Outside of class and a brief daily run, Kate retreated to a self-imposed, solitary confinement to focus on her book. Looking up momentarily from her laptop, she stole a quick glance out her window. Besides, she consoled herself, it was late October, and the leaves had already fallen. Time to move inside, she told herself, *house-warming.*

In preparation, Kate headed out early one Saturday morning for her run, laden with several book tote bags. Inspired by the squirrels she observed running up and down the branches with stores of supplies, she resolved to gather her own, thinking she would save time more readily needed for her work if she purchased and stored long-term food supplies. As she ran along the path toward the farmers' market, she thought of Channing's advice to buy in bulk to save time and money.

At the entrance to the Cambridge Farmers' Market, Kate stood rooted to one spot. She looked on at the scene with a sense of helplessness, overwhelmed by table after table laden in freshly harvested produce. Knowing she wouldn't take the time to cook much, she decided to purchase the bulk of her supplies in raw form. Kate ventured down the aisles, buying up bagged salad greens, carrots with their green tops still on, the last of the season's tomatoes.

When she arrived at the fruit section, a huge smile emerged from the anxious clouds of uncertainty that had concealed it. She had forgotten that she was now residing in the region of Concord grapes, her absolute favorite. She approached the vendor, who was in the process of adding more clusters to his already bursting table.

"Tell me," Kate said. "Are these Concord grapes grown near Walden Pond?"

He smiled and nodded. "Not far at all. My farm has been there for generations." He picked up a large cluster of dark blue grapes. "These here come from some vines that have been growing up along the edge of our barn now, for as long as I can remember, and I'm almost seventy," he said with a nod. "They're genuine heirloom Concords, like myself," he said with a smile. "Try one," he urged as he pushed the cluster toward her, "Nothing but clean air has touched those skins."

Kate offered a warm smile in return. "I'd love to try some of those," she said as she put one in her mouth. "Oh," she shook her head in true admiration, "just scrumptious."

Popping one into his mouth, the grower said, "Yep. The perfect combination of tart and sweet. Nothing quite like it in any other grape."

"Why is that?" Kate asked, as she reached for another from the cluster he continued to hold out to her.

"They're wild," he said as he bowed his head in what seemed like respect. "'*All good things are wild and free*,' you know."

Kate arched her mouth into a wide smile. "Oh, I see you've been reading Thoreau."

Nodding, he said, "Well, I read bits of him here and there. He was a great man for collecting wild specimens and replanting them elsewhere." With a twinkle, he said, "Might've even been responsible for planting my great-great-granddaddy's supply of Concords."

Kate smiled. "We can only hope." After she collected several clusters of grapes and paid, she started to leave before turning back. "Tell me, sir," she said, "Have you actually completed *Walden*?"

He looked at her with clear, blue eyes that reminded her of the bird she had experienced at Walden before quoting an extract in a tone approximating a chant:

> *"I learned this from my experiment. Advance confidently in the direction of your dreams and you will meet with a success unexpected."*

With a nod, he said, "It's my personal mantra."

Kate nodded. "You sure know your *Walden*."

His eyes locked with hers. "He inspired me to follow my dreams of taking back our once falling-down farm. Simplified my life and paid off the mortgage, I did." Folding his arms over his chest, he gently rocked on his feet. "I never look back, only ahead. '*The sun is but a morning star*,' you know."

"Yes." Kate smiled warmly. "I do know."

He leaned toward her, pulling out from under his counter a bag of apples. "Here, take these wild apples to remember this conversation by." He added, "The trick is to believe it, and in yourself, so whole-heartedly that you find the way to '*build the foundation under your castle in the air*.'"

Kate was sure her eyes revealed the sense of wistful hopefulness she felt overcome her. "Thanks," she said, and with one last turn towards him, as she walked away, "thanks again for your encouragement."

She walked away lost in thought, meandering through the market until she reached the outer edge. She found herself in the crafts section filled with a variety of sellers. With a quick glance around, her eyes settled on a table covered in words—wooden plaques with individual words and expressions carved into them. It felt like a woodworkers' bookstore, filled with timeless messages painstakingly carved onto each block of wood. After reading a few here and there, she felt her attention drawn to the middle. A small, weathered, whitewashed plaque, with edges more wooden, than white, stood upright in the center. Kate bent down over it. *Simplify*, it read.

"I'll take this one," she said in a firm voice, without asking the price.

The man behind the table studied her a moment before speaking. "I have others that are less expensive, imitations of this original."

Kate peered at him, wondering why he was trying to redirect her. "I'd prefer this one."

"Hand-painted, though not carved," he persisted, before bending over and pulling out one from a hefty pile of plaques. "Like this."

Kate shook her head. "No, thanks, though. I need the real one—hand-carved and all." She studied the man curiously. He was dressed in a leather vest with plaid sleeves rolled up past his elbow. It was then she noticed that two digits of his finger were missing from his right hand. She gazed back up at him in alarm.

He turned his head to the side, as he looked intently at her. "Well, until now, I haven't wanted to give up that one. Cost me two fingers, as you've noticed, but it gave me a new life."

"Really?" Kate asked. She was intrigued by this fellow's story of transcendence.

"Why do you want this one?" he asked, studying her. "It was like you zeroed in right on this one—above all the others. I watched you," he admitted.

"I need the daily reminder in as simple a way as possible," she said non-committally, reinforced by a shrug of her shoulders.

"Uh-huh," he said, not sounding convinced. His right hand, what was left of it, wrapped around the plaque in question.

Kate gazed searchingly at him, ambivalent about confiding in the fellow. "Well," she said, with a sigh, "I teach *Walden* at Harvard, which is causing me to question everything I came here believing in."

"Ohhh." He rolled the word long in his mouth. "That's heavy. Really heavy." He nodded, as he gazed at her.

She met his penetrating stare. "And what about you? How did it change your life?"

One of his eyes flickered almost instinctively, it seemed to Kate. "It led me to a meditation center, whose practices, I have made my way of life."

Kate's eyes widened. "Wouldn't be that one in the Berkshires." She studied his features, his calm disposition. "Would it?"

He nodded. "Ah, so you know it, then?"

Kate shook her head. "No, only about it. I know one of the founders."

"So Channing sent you here." He peered at her. "I sensed it the moment you focused on my *Simplify* plaque."

Kate jumped at the sound of Channing's name. "No, actually, he didn't." She twisted her mouth into a wry half-grin. "Well, not directly, anyway."

"Uh-huh," he said in a tone that conveyed his clear disagreement. "Told you about the farmers' market and buying fresh and in bulk, did he?"

She nodded. "Well, yes he did, actually."

He stared hard at her. "How to simplify?"

"Well, yes, that as well." She twisted her mouth to the side, holding it at mid-point, unsure in which direction to shift—frown or smile.

With his head slowly bobbing up and down, he set to work wrapping the sign in a brown grocery bag. "He sent you here, all right. You can be sure of that. Here, you take it."

"Are you sure?" She looked from the plaque back up to him.

"Oh, I'm sure, all right. Besides, sounds like you need it more than I do." He gave her a slight bow.

"May your thoughts be expansive, your way transformative."

She smiled. "You sound like Channing," she murmured.

"He's my *sensei*," he said, as he touched the few fingers left with those on the other hand.

"Your what?" she asked.

"Sensei. Lama. Teacher," he said. With a slow nod, he added, "Like you, a teacher."

She locked eyes with him, before turning to leave. *Coeval with the sky*. "Thank you. Thank you so much."

As she turned away, he proclaimed, "You know, Channing calls me Elijah—from *Moby-Dick*."

Kate reeled around at the sound of both names. Gazing at him with widened eyes, she said, "I'm sure he does. It fits—perfectly."

He nodded. "Good day to you, Miss." With a slight wave of his remaining fingers, he turned around.

Kate shook her head over what she could only interpret as an omen. *There is meaning in this*. But what, exactly, she couldn't discern—*not yet, anyway*.

She walked in small, measured steps, not wanting to leave the market. It felt as is she were protected there, understood even, though by complete strangers, whose intersecting paths she may never again cross. At last, she stepped back outside into the busy, noisy streets of Cambridge, hugging her plaque. When she reached her apartment, she carefully removed the bag and placed the plaque squarely in the middle of her desk. Images of the ducks paddling down the middle of the river swam through her mind. The middle way, she thought. *There is meaning in this.*

With a bowl brimming in Concord grapes, she opened her laptop and went to work. She and Blake had discussed in depth the changes necessary to transform a dissertation into a readable, scholarly book. Hours, days, and weekends passed. Hard as she tried, Kate could not restrain her thoughts from expanding beyond the arguments she had spent years making in her dissertation.

Though focusing on the topic, *Moby-Dick*, she found herself re-writing from an entirely different perspective. As she wrote about Ishmael's *sea-change*—from focusing on economic gain to protecting the natural world—she felt an internal sea-change alter her own course. Confusion over her divided sensibility regarding her academic research waned with the receding tide of deliberation, as a new focus breeched the surface of her consciousness. Like the great white whale, it ascended into the sky of possibility—before rapidly sailing off into a new, unexplored direction.

Typing with an inextinguishable fervor, Kate set aside her previous research into the philosophy of composition and publication of *Moby-Dick*, instead reaching down to Ishmael's *lower layers* of insights. She picked up her ragged copy, flipping to the last lines of one of the chapters:

> *Ship and boat diverged; the cold, damp night breeze blew between; a screaming gull flew overhead; the two hulls wildly rolled; we gave three hearty cheers and blindly plunged like fate into the lone Atlantic.*

She leaned back into the night. The words of Thoreau came floating along through her thoughts. *Alone, but not lonely.*

Kate scanned the following chapter of *Moby-Dick*, looking for Ishmael's profound statement about the voyage. "*In landlessness alone resides the highest truth.*" She looked up as an insight bubbled to the surface. *Thoreau's Higher Laws.* She reached for her bag and pulled out *Walden*, skimming through it until she found the passage for which she was searching:

Not till we are lost, in other words, not till we have lost the world, do we begin to find ourselves, and realize where we are and the infinite extent of our relations.

Leaving both books open and overturned, she went over to make a cup of tea, her mind flowing with ideas. Her thoughts an ever-expanding sail, Kate started to comprehend the truths behind the great insights of both *Walden* and *Moby-Dick*, which in her mind, formed a new harmony.

What she discovered in the subterranean depths of the essential natures of both books was nothing short of an environmental and existential imperative, a call to action based on experience. She figured that Melville, while lost at sea, both literally and figuratively, discovered the existential necessity to preserve, rather than exploit, when confronting the 'essential facts' of the whale, while Thoreau, lost in the woods, discovered humankind's role as caretaker of nature. As she sipped her tea, she came to what felt like an inevitable conclusion: both transcendentalists, both environmentalists. Different settings, same message. The words of both authors floated along the currents of her consciousness:

Not til we are lost, do we appreciate the vastness of Nature . . .
In wildness is the preservation of the world.

As Kate opened her laptop again and started typing, she realized that, though her work may not speak to the "*Johns and Jonathans*" of her fellow academics, she could not, would not, follow the "*ruts of tradition and conformity.*" Like Thoreau, she felt that she must speak "*without bounds*" in her "*waking moment*" to others in their "*waking moments.*"

As she immersed herself in her writing, Kate realized with a growing sense of calm fortitude that she had passed an "*invisible boundary*" separating herself from her colleagues and their great expectations, leaving behind the old laws in favor of discovering new universal laws of Nature. She felt as if she were exploring undiscovered continents and worlds of new perspectives on the mighty books she was now examining in a *different light*—through which, at last, she would reach the higher latitudes of her own being.

Alone, at last, along the cliff overlooking *landlessness,* came the moment to click on the 'send' button, plunging her book, it seemed, "*like fate into the lone Atlantic,*" as Kate sent her manuscript to prospective publishers. She knew she had chosen a road less traveled, but whether it would make "*all the difference*" she did not know, but hoped to discover.

CHAPTER FOURTEEN

Former Inhabitants & Winter Visitors

CLOSING THE CAR DOOR BEHIND HER, Kate felt the intense cold instantly grip her in its frigid vice, squeezing out the last bits of residual warmth stored from hours of driving in her heated vehicle. Inhaling deeply, she noted that her nostrils seemed to stick together. She shook her head—was she completely mad to embark on this expedition in the depths of winter.

After securing her snowshoes, Kate waddled over to the edge of the woods. Looking ahead, she noticed the path curve and wind through the pine-clad forest. It appeared enticing—idyllic. She repeated her new mantra: *I can do this.*

Already blanketed in heavy snow, the woods uttered no sound, an experience Kate found surprisingly consoling. After the near constant din of Cambridge, the place felt comforting in its complete tranquility. She thought it warm even—though the temperature had dipped into the single digits. She marveled over her newfound sense of delight in the winter landscape.

Kate traveled under a thick canopy of towering pines, their lower boughs, it seemed to her, offering downy pillows of comfort to any animal needing a respite from the chilling cold. As she studied the scene before her, she noticed what appeared to be a bough laden with an extra layer of snow. As she approached, however, the snow mound suddenly moved. To her astonishment, it displayed two eyes and massive white wings that momentarily fluttered, until detecting no threat in her approach, settled back down over the bough. *An owl!* She slowed her pace, while maintaining eye contact with the majestic creature. *How many of my fellow academic colleagues get to experience this?*

Shaking her head slowly, Kate called out, "'*I rejoice that there are owls.*'" Suddenly, the owl stirred, and silently, yet ever so graciously, flew to a more distant bough, higher on one of the pines.

"Off to await the dawning of your day, are you?" she called out to her forest companion. "You and I both."

The owl turned its head in response, resting its eyes back down on her. Kate was sure it watched over her, as she made her way past its perch toward the cabin in the woods.

After continuing along the rutted path she assumed Channing had carved into the snow, she heard a faint sound in the distance, largely regular and repetitive. Not knowing quite what to make of it, she followed the sound, which increased in volume, as she trudged along the path under the snow canopy.

When Kate arrived at the clearing behind the cabin, she stopped in her tracks. She had discovered the source of the sound she had been following. Leaning on her poles, she watched as Channing methodically swung his axe against a log propped up on his wooden horses, time and time again. He slowly made his way down the length of his long log, alternating between swinging and chopping. She observed his method, which seemed more to her like a graceful ceremonial dance of a Native brave beating his drum, than cutting logs with such a big, heavy tool. After finishing one, he simply turned back to what appeared to Kate as an insurmountable pile of logs. She shook her head slowly in wonderment. *And he doesn't call that work?* She chuckled to herself as she slowly made her way towards him.

Kate called out. "And here I thought male New England writers like Thoreau and Frost wrote about their relationships to their woodpiles as metaphors."

Channing reeled around at the sound of her voice, staring at her as if she were an apparition. He was clearly startled, Kate thought with amusement. *Aha!* she thought. *I am not so easily categorized.*

"Well, well, look whom the winter winds have blown in." Placing his axe down, he relaxed his startled expression into a pleasant smile. "That woodpile is certainly no metaphor!" he exclaimed.

"Tell me," said Kate with a smile, "After all that cutting, do you still look at your wood pile '*with affection*' as Thoreau claimed men do?"

He walked toward her in welcome, bowing slightly before her. "The philosopher has come to visit the hermit."

Kate tossed her head. "But wouldn't that mean that I '*have no venture in the present*'?"

"Do you?" He studied her with his usual intensity. "Aren't you still the '*friend of human progress*'—working hard and faithfully borrowing against the present—in hopes of future success?"

Their eyes met momentarily, before Kate turned away with a shrug. She felt his stare bearing down on her back, as if feelings surfaced from his reservoir of thoughts, which he kept to himself.

Recovering her composure, Kate turned and nodded. "I'm thinking you might be more the woodchopper than the hermit," she bantered. "After all, you did leave your solitary life to visit Cambridge."

Not missing a beat, Channing shot back as he turned to her, "Not unlike Thoreau who nonetheless called himself the hermit."

"Guess it depends on which exchange we're about to have," she quipped.

Studying her, Channing asked, "You came all this way by snowshoe, Cáitlín?" He looked impressed, she thought. She felt her cheeks redden.

"Yes, yes, I did, a feat in itself, I must admit," Kate admitted with a shrug. With a shy smile, she added, "Actually, I have *'an appointment with a beech tree and a yellow birch.'*" She looked around into the earthen forest gilded in white. "They must be here somewhere."

His chuckle transformed into a hearty laugh. "Well done," he said with an approving nod.

Turning slightly in his direction, Kate added, "Actually, I was hoping to meet *'an old acquaintance among the pines, but the ice and snow caused their limbs to droop, and so sharpening their tops, have changed the pines into fir-trees.'*" She faced Channing, displaying a sparkle shining in her eyes. "As you might infer, my evergreen cone collection has improved my botanical literacy."

"I see you are walking more of the walk, even if on snowshoes." He folded his arms across his chest and chuckled.

"Hard not to—considering the distance you live from any road." She offered a disarming smile.

Channing looked with concern at her face. "Well, unless you have been tanning in one of those salons in Boston, I think your unusually rosy cheeks indicate you may benefit from a bowl of North Woods stew."

Kate readily accepted.

"Well, come in, then." Gesturing to a chair near the open fire, he said, "Melt the icicles from your hair near the fire there, while I round up some mugs and bowls."

"Do I have icicles?" Kate felt her hair, discovering entire long wisps had frozen solid.

"Your hair with its reddish tones must resemble the colors of the pickerel Thoreau detected under the ice of Walden." He chuckled as he went in search of mugs, evidently pleased with his comparison.

Kate sat back, taking in the interior winter setting of the cabin. A sizable cauldron hung over a bustling fire. She'd never seen a cooking method quite as exotic. She studied it some minutes before speaking. "Do you actually cook in that?" she asked, pointing to the pot.

Channing shot her a sharp look. "As people have done for millennia—most assuredly, your own ancestors in Ireland."

She shook her head. "That's amazing."

"Beats paying the utility companies for the right to eat," he said with a curt nod, "with the added bonus that food tastes infinitely better simmering over a fire than heated on an electrical element."

"Really?" Kate looked over at him. "I never considered that the type of heat source would affect the taste."

"You have no idea."

"That's what Heather keeps saying to me," she said with a slight hint of irritation. "I'd like to find out."

Channing turned to her, shooting her a knowing look. "That desire constitutes the first step along the long road of experience."

"A long road it is—if journeying here is part of the experience."

"Here you are," he said, offering her a plate with a bowl and some slices of bread. "Experience for yourself."

"This looks different from the last bread you served me." Kate gazed at the slices. "Did you bake this yourself?"

"Yes. An astute observation from someone who does not bake. It's rye, actually."

"Another '*experiment in living*,' is it?" she asked, before biting into a slice. "Oh, my God, that's *delicious*!"

He flushed, evidently pleased by her sincerity. Channing said, "Glad you like it. Baked it," pointing over to his wood stove, "in that."

"Really? I had never thought to consider how, exactly, you baked the last loaves you shared with me." Suddenly, she stopped chewing as a thought crossed her mind. "Of course, the woodstove and the open fire—the two methods Thoreau relied on for cooking at Walden."

"As I said, it beats enriching the utility companies." Channing nodded.

"Oh," she said with a gleam in her eyes, "I bet it's much more than that." With a knowing nod, she asked, "It's all part of the '*it's not work, it's a lifestyle*' philosophy, isn't it?"

He openly laughed, despite his usual restraint. "Yes. It certainly is."

"And you didn't use yeast, either, I bet?" she asked with a sly smile.

"Only wild yeast floating about in the air," he admitted, "though I rely on what's called a *clef*, a starter, made from it." He noted her blank expression. "Not much of a baker? You know it, most likely, as sour dough bread."

"Oh, right, of course." Kate took another bite. "Whatever it is made from, it is scrumptious." She smiled appreciatively at him. "Probably made from your own grains, right?"

"I think you are starting to get the lifestyle part," he said with a smile. "Yes, indeed, from my own grains—mostly rye, actually, with some oats, wheat, and a bit of barley thrown in."

Kate shook her head in silent amazement before trying the stew. "Delicious!" She blurted. "Thanks so much for feeding me. I had no idea I was so hungry."

"You did a lot of snowshoeing for a novice," he said. "You needed some reinforcements."

She dipped her spoon into the bowl. "Can't get this in Cambridge," she said after tasting it. She hesitated, before asking, "What's in it?" she glanced up at him. "Tastes different from the last time."

His eyes twinkled as he said, "Afraid to ask, were you?"

Tossing her head, Kate bantered, "Not really, since as a Thoreauvian, you most likely refrained from relying on the remains of some poor animals, like bear, deer, or moose, for ingredients."

"Hardly," he snorted.

"It's not woodchuck stew, is it?" She recoiled in mock horror.

With a chuckle, Channing explained, "No, just a few poor squashes and wild apples, carrots, parsnips, onions, and garlic—"

"None of the famous beans?" she interjected.

He peered at her. "I was coming to those."

Kate laughed. "Of course you were," she said, before eating some more. "Whatever you have put in it, the flavors are amazing."

After completing their meal, and settling down to a large mug of hot-spiced apple cider, Channing looked over at her with curiosity. "Your cheeks seem to have recovered from the cold. So what brings you here on this frigid winter's day?"

"Oh," Kate said, sitting up in her chair, "I've been doing some research at the town hall."

Nodding, he asked, "Are you still interested in the history of Walden North? I quite enjoyed your article on the power of Place."

"Oh, thanks," she said as she blushed. "I've become quite fascinated by the existence of the two Waldens, as you know from my previous article, so I am continuing my research on the settlement of this particular Walden." Smiling, she added, "I figured you could clue me in on details I cannot locate in the town records."

"Oh?" he said non-committally.

"Yes, I was taken with your account of some of your neighbors, their reasons for living here, and their lifestyle choices." She smiled. "So fitting in a town called Walden North."

Channing leaned back in his rocker, which creaked with his weight against the blistery floorboards. With the firelight streaming rays of yellow behind him, she thought he resembled a figure from a rustic painting, perhaps one from 17th-century Holland, depicting rustic farm life in the rural kitchen—with herbs suspended from beams overhead, loaves of bread cooling on a planked table, and a blackened cauldron simmering in the open fireplace. She suppressed a chuckle, as she commented inwardly, not daring to verbalize her thoughts—*a far cry from MIT and Harvard, Dr. William Channing.*

Leaning back, her mouth slightly turned up, she absorbed the tranquil scene.

His eyes settled on her twisted mouth, vainly attempting to suppress a smile, while her eyes flowed with obvious amusement. "What is it, exactly, you find so amusing?"

"You mean beyond your Icelandic-looking moose folk sweater with matching socks?" She tried to prevent her mouth from breaking into a smile.

Channing snorted. "A far cry from the herringbone, bowtie clad colleagues of yours?"

"Exactly what I was thinking!" she exclaimed.

His eyes, picking up the earthy tones of his sweater, seemed like rounded pinecones. He rocked gently. "It truly is a world elsewhere here," he said with a sigh, then with a penetrating look said, "I remain ever grateful to assert."

"Of course," Kate said, without thinking. "Right now, with such tranquility and solitude just oozing about the place, why would anyone want to be anywhere—but here?" She clasped the woolen throw he had given around her. "It's so, well, relaxing."

Nodding, Channing looked at her with a keen glance. "Don't do much of that, I would think in Cambridge."

"No, no time," she said with a shake of her head. "But that's okay. I love being there."

He glanced over. "Do you—still?"

"Well, yes. My work keeps me absorbed. It's my life." She shrugged. "What academic wouldn't love to trade places with me?" she said with a slight toss of her head before breaking into a wide smile. "Except you, of course."

Channing nodded slowly and throwing her a penetrating look, quoted:

> "*Two roads diverged in a yellow wood, and*
> *I—I took the one less traveled by,*
> *And that has made all the difference.*"

Kate smiled. "As spending my days and nights in the library have made it for me." She leaned forward to place her mug on the table in front of her. "So tell me, in the spirit of bridging both our divergent lifestyles, about some of your neighbors, the people who live up here."

Standing up, Channing brought over some more cider to refill her mug. "Shall I '*conjure up some old inhabitants*,' or do you prefer to hear about some of the more recent transplants?" he asked. With an unusual twinkle shimmering in his eye, he added, "And let's not forget you, the visitor, with your undaunted faith, the last of the great philosophers visiting the hermit." Toasting her with his glass, he called out with a flourish, "May we '*build castles in the air with no earthly foundations*'!"

"Cheers," she said in a light tone.

Channing resumed his gentle rocking. "If it were spring," he announced, "I could lead a foundation hole tour." He looked over at her. "You know those references in *Walden* to the merest of remains of the former inhabitants around the pond, which, I'm sure, served as the inspiration for the Frost poem, as well as, perhaps, the John Elder book of his own experiences."

"Oh?" she said, "I don't think I recognize the reference to Frost, or to Elder."

Channing gazed over at her before resuming his thoughts. "You may not appreciate this coming from a relatively new city, but here in northern New England, where so many of the few inhabitants there were, left for largely economic reasons at mid-century," and looking at her sideways qualified, "as in the mid-19th century, that it is not unusual to stumble across—or into," he said with a smile, "the remnants of their former houses."

"Really?" Kate said.

Looking away into the distance, he murmured, "Powerful energy remaining in those old cellar holes. Entire lifetimes' worth." He stopped rocking and looked over at her, his eyes the deep brown of pinecones. "Surely you picked up some of this energy in reading the old accounts of the original inhabitants here?"

Kate nodded. "Well, I don't know if it was energy in the sense you may mean it, but it was very powerful reading, I admit, hence my interest in the modern draw for people who move here."

"It seems as if Walden North serves as a sort of '*thin place*.'" He rolled his head from side to side before continuing. "You know the term?" he asked, looking over at her.

Kate shook her head. "No, can't say that I have read about it."

With a slight nod, Channing said, "Yes, I suppose it was not part of your literary education, though if you had studied Yeats and the Mystics, perhaps." He resumed rocking.

"Yes, well, in that regard I assumed a particularly American cultural outlook," Kate said with a slight toss of her head.

"You'd think that Melville might have addressed the concept, since he certainly must have experienced the phenomenon on the open sea." He looked over at her. "Ishmael doesn't address thin places in his account?"

Kate shrugged. "Not by that term, but since you haven't yet explained what they are, I really don't know for sure."

"In short, it's the meeting place where the two worlds—the material and the energized—meet," he said with a glance at her, and added, "Usually some powerfully raw, pristine, wild place, in the Thoreauvian sense of wild."

"Uh–huh," she said, uncertainty weighing down her tone.

"No passages spring to mind?" Channing regarded her with an inquisitive gaze.

"So you mean Walden North resonates," she responded, with a furtive glance at Channing, "um, that is, acts, serves, as a thin place?"

He nodded. "Did you not feel it as you snowshoed under the stately snow pines, in the deep, majestic, transcendent tranquility of the winter forest? As if you could just step into another time, or that perhaps you had suddenly entered a different world entirely?"

"A place where time stands still, do you mean?" She looked at him with a searching expression.

"Or where there is no word for time, as the Abenaki would say," he said. "A meaningless, trivial concept in the presence of the great mystery of life, as embodied in the juncture of different dimensions."

Kate shook her head gently. "That's pretty profound. I'll have to think about that one."

Channing guffawed as he rocked. "Oh, we're nothing if not profound up here in these ancient woods."

"Yes, I'm beginning to get that impression," she said dryly. Taking a sip of the cider, she asked, "And is it that search for profundity, for some deep, mystical meaning to life's mysteries that draws people here?"

He smiled. "I think the name provides the fundamental draw. Who doesn't want to live in Walden *North*?" He tossed his head. "It resonates a sense of the wild that even Walden *Pond* does not." He sipped his cider. "After all, Thoreau himself escaped to the great *North* of Katahdin to experience true wildness during his sojourn at Walden Pond."

Kate nodded. "Hmm. That makes sense." She leaned forward, placing a leg under her. "So the original settlers, the white ones, that is, sought to transplant here the ideals of Walden Pond that did not exist in the reality there of felled woods, decimated wild animal populations, and pond draining for ice, plumbing, and the like?"

Channing nodded. "Yes, I do believe that was the case, at least with the mid-19th-century settlers, all ardent transcendentalists to boot. It is still that way, I think it accurate to say." Looking over at her, he quoted, "You know, '*in wildness is the preservation of the world*,' so for those who believe that, who live by that philosophy, the more wild, the more free to live life according to the natural laws of Nature."

Kate chimed in. "From my research, I gather that this philosophy transcended natural law to shape social truths, as well, as in all men are equal. Vermont, you most likely know, was not only the first free state in the North, but it also led the fight to free all enslaved peoples nationally. It has always been a place that prided itself on tolerance."

"Oh, yes," he said, extending her line of thinking, his voice reflecting his rising enthusiasm. "Some of the original settlers were people from different ethnicities who bonded, such as Native American and Puritan English, finding that the frontier, so to speak, provided them with the freedom, the privacy, and the tranquility to live out natural feelings in a natural setting."

"Ah, yes, the stories of *Hobomok* and *Hope Leslie,*" Kate murmured. "Such poignant accounts of love across forbidden ethnic lines."

Nodding, Channing added, "Or in our special case, the tale of Injun Joe and white Molly, the daughter of a colonial Army captain."

"Ah, yes. Elizabeth Hill from the Walden General Store regaled me with that account." She smiled. "And later?"

He leaned forward, meeting her gaze. "Not only was Walden North settled by abolitionists weaned on Thoreauvian ideals, but some of them went to jail like he did, refusing to pay taxes to a government that supported slavery." He nodded. "They went on to establish an elaborate, untraceable Underground Railroad after the Fugitive Slave Law was enacted. Of course, until that point, free blacks & Native Americans lived peacefully here in our area of Vermont."

"It was quite a progressive region," she noted.

"Still is," Channing qualified, "Hence the migration of people here that feel in tune with what we call the '*spirit of the place.*'

Kate nodded. "I like the sound of that—the spirit of the place." Smiling at him, she said lightly, "It sounds like something Thoreau should have said." She gazed at him, her eyebrows furrowed, eyes narrowed. "Did he, somewhere, I haven't yet encountered?"

"Not that I know of, but I am sure he thought it." Channing offered a brief grin. "I do, you know, possess a few independent thoughts of my own."

Kate sat back, gazing at the fire. "What was it Thoreau said about the fire in winter?" she asked, shifting her gaze to stare at Channing.

Nodding, he said with a smile, "Ah, you must mean, '*I weathered some merry snow storms and spent some cheerful evenings by my fire-side, while the snow whirled wildly without.*'"

"Yes, that's it." With a slight shrug, Kate said, "Though it appealed to me, not ever having had a fireplace, I couldn't really appreciate that statement, until now." Kate found herself glancing down at her watch. "Oh my God," she gasped, "Look at the time! I need to head back."

Channing shook his head slowly. "It's going to be dark momentarily, and if I'm not mistaken, the temperature has plummeted since we were last outside." He walked over to his thermometer. "It's really cold now—five below."

"Whatever it is, I had better get going." She stood up and faced him.

Channing said, not before looking away, "Perhaps you should stay the night and get a good start in the morning."

She stared at him. "Um, I don't know—"

Meeting her gaze, he said quietly, "You are welcome to stay in the meditation cabin, though since I did not expect you, and it is not insulated, it would be very cold." Looking away, he added, "Heather's room is free, of course. I'm sure she won't mind." With the briefest of glances at her, he added, "I would think you might find some clothes that would fit, since you seem to be more or less the same size."

Kate hesitated. "Are you sure it's too dangerous to venture out now?"

"Look, you were freezing coming here, and it was only mid-day." He stood up and said, "Come, you should decide for yourself."

Shrugging, Kate said, "Well, okay."

Channing rustled through some clothes hanging on the pegs near the door, before thrusting in Kate's direction, a long woolen scarf.

"You better wrap this around your face. I doubt you are accustomed to such cold."

"Thanks, I could use it—I forgot to bring one." Tossing her head, she said, "But I am more than used to cold temps. I am from the 'Windy City,' after all."

Channing shot her a caustic look. "Why, don't they heat the libraries there?"

She shook her head and retorted, "I don't spend all of my time in the library, you know."

He held the door open for her. "No, just most of it, I'm sure."

The cold greeted them with an inextricable embrace, sending instantaneous shivers down Kate's spine. "My test for the temperature is when my nose sticks together," she announced, with a slight smile over at Channing. "It's even much colder now than it was when I started out," she admitted. "You've convinced me. Time to go in." Turning round, she started up the stairs when Channing extended his arm out to stop her.

"Don't go just yet. Experience a sunset here in the cold, north woods. They are indescribably mystical."

Surprised by his touch, she stopped, turned around, and gasped. The setting sun, low in the horizon, cast a yellow light that slivered through the landscape, transforming a series of tree trunks, a spot of snow, a section of frozen pond, into bursts of flames—before slowly receding into the softer hues of the coming night.

Kate reeled round on her heels, looking in every direction. "It truly is magical, isn't it, the last light of the day." She looked up at Channing.

He nodded into his scarf that was wrapped loosely around his neck. "Particularly a winter's day, and specifically, *here*." He shifted his gaze from the pond to her, as he stuffed his hands into the pockets of his woolen vest.

"I've taken to watching the sun set through my maple tree in Cambridge each day," Kate said quietly, as she watched the waning light flicker over the pond. "Just like here, there's something so tranquil, so comforting, about seeing the sunset, hearing the last of the bird songs for the day."

Channing turned away to watch the light fade farther and farther out over the pond, speaking only after it had disappeared into the hills beyond. "Being in tune with the natural rhythms of the day and night brings tremendous joy, as well as inner serenity."

Kate looked at him with unveiled curiosity. "Do you do this often yourself?"

He looked down at her through impenetrable eyes. "Every sunset and every dawn."

She said softly, "Of course you do. I'm not surprised."

Channing cast a somber look at her. "It's part of the point of living here," he said simply.

"Part of the lifestyle, living in harmony with nature's rhythms, as you put it," Kate said more as a statement than as a question.

"Yes, exactly."

"May we go in now?" she asked turning to him. "I'm freezing."

He chuckled. "Of course. Besides, we need to warm you up before returning for star gazing."

Kate shivered involuntarily. "You mean when it plummets to -15."

He smiled as he climbed the stairs. "Oh, much colder than that. Closer to -25, maybe -30. It's during the coldest of nights that star gazing here becomes such a memorable experience."

Once inside, Channing removed the cauldron from the fire and sprucing it up with extra logs, gestured to one of the chairs beside it. "Why don't you sit close by the fire to warm yourself while I prepare some tea." He walked over and handed her the throw she had been using. "You might like this."

She looked up at him and smiled. "Well, thanks."

Soon they both sat warming their cold faces while watching the fire blaze away. Kate sighed contentedly, as she glanced over at Channing. "This is so nice. Thank you for having me."

He nodded briefly. "Of course, Cáitlín. You are '*the visitor at the door*.' You are always welcome."

Kate noted his serious expression, as she flushed from the compliment. He was always so formal with her, even when trying to be jovial. She smiled at him. "You must know that book by heart," she said as she wagged her finger. "It's utterly remarkable what you can quote."

"I have a lot of time up here during long winter nights for reading and contemplation," he said with a slight bow.

Snuggling up in her throw, she asked, "Will you tell me about some of your neighbors? We never got to that part of the story of this intriguing place."

"Yes, of course. I'll start in by regaling you with accounts of my friends, neighbors, and fellow residents of Walden North." Channing looked over at her with a gleam in his eyes. "I admit we are a collection of unique individuals. Shall I start with the Buddhist banker, the afterlife attorney, the veggie grower surfer, or the angels communal moms?"

Kate laughed. "Ooh, I think the angels commune sounds like a great place to start."

As he began his story, she held up her hand. "Wait!" she said. "Although I asked about the angels commune, I'm just wondering about that vegetable surfer."

"Yes?" Channing glanced at her. "He's a good friend and neighbor. Riding the Wave Farm, he calls it," he said with a chuckle.

Kate squinted at him. "Is there something I don't know about Vermont geography?" Tilting her head, she asked, "How is it possible to surf in Vermont?"

Channing snorted. "It isn't. He sells his vegetables at the local farmers' market on Friday morning, hops on his tractor, since he doesn't have a car that works, straps on his surfboard, and away he goes."

"Goes? Goes where?" Shaking her head, she asked, "You don't mean he surfs by way of his tractor, do you?"

Channing openly laughed. "Well, I suppose in a manner of speaking he does, though not in the way you are thinking." He smiled at her as he got up to prepare some food. "No, he drives his tractor to the coast of Maine in order to surf there."

Kate's eyes widened exponentially. "He takes a tractor all the way to Maine? Isn't that pretty far on a tractor?"

Channing nodded, as a wide grin spread over his face. "Yes, it takes him well into the evening to arrive at his destination."

Kate laughed. "I'm trying to imagine the fellow on some rusting, old tractor with a surfboard strapped to it." She looked over at Channing. "That must be quite a sight."

"I told you we all follow the beat of a different drummer up here."

She smiled. "I'm beginning to see what you mean," she said, nodding. "But I interrupted you. You were starting to tell me about the women in the commune who advertised for men to offer their services for propagation, was it, you said?" She leaned back chuckling. "Oh, my God."

"Yes," he said with a nod. "The donor list was quite long, including the vast majority of men up here."

Kate giggled. "I can just imagine."

As he prepared setting out the dinner that had been simmering in the woodstove, Channing related accounts of some of his neighbors and fellow inhabitants. Kate listened with heightened interest as she learned through his narration that people came from all walks of life to live there.

"So many of the organic farmers, were, in fact, not from farming families at all?" Kate asked. "I am surprised."

Channing glanced at her, as he set down a platter of roasted root vegetables, together with baked beans, creamed spinach, and some warm bread. As he sat down after replenishing her cider, he looked at her with sincere, serious eyes. "Hence the need for a

Findhorn-Vermont," he said. "Please help yourself," he added, his tone gracious.

Kate found herself consuming more than usual, assuming the cold had intensified her appetite. "This is simply extraordinary," she proclaimed. "Thank you so much for your hospitality."

Channing nodded and gave a brief smile. "It's simple country food, prepared and eaten by people like us for generations up here." He chewed a piece of bread slowly before resuming his thought. "You know, our present generation has largely lost the folk knowledge that once governed people's lives, even as recently as three generations ago." He glanced at her.

Kate nodded. "Yes, I believe you mentioned something about that last time we chatted." She shrugged. "After all, my own parents probably know about some of the dishes you have prepared but have never bothered to pass on that knowledge." She leaned towards him. "You know, like those oatmeal scone-like breads and that dish you ordered in the restaurant."

Nodding, he said, "Ah, farls and boxty, you mean." He looked at her. "Precisely my point behind wanting to establish a Findhorn-Vermont."

Kate smiled at him. He always seemed to have a pedagogical or life lesson underlying his comments. "I'd like to hear all about it, if you don't mind telling me."

Channing stood up and started to clear away the dishes. "Why don't we adjourn back to the fireside for this part of our exchange?" Gesturing to the kettle, he asked, "Would you like more cider or do you prefer tea?"

Kate smiled. "Tea sounds great to me on this wintry night."

"Right then. I'll bring some over to you."

As she stood to help with the dishes, he motioned her away.

"Why don't you settle yourself by the fire and enjoy your thoughts?"

After a short time, Channing came over, offered Kate a steaming mug of rose hip tea, and sat down across from her. A full smile emerged from behind the somber clouds of his expression.

"Shall we '*build castles in the air with no earthly foundations*'?" His smile lingered as he looked at her.

Kate felt her face warm, but whether by his unexpected, radiant smile or the fire, she couldn't be sure. "Which of us is the philosopher, and which the poet?" she bantered back.

Nodding, he said, "I think we each possess traits of both, wouldn't you say?" Leaning back and thrusting his long legs towards the fire, he added, "Though I surely lay claim to the title of hermit."

Kate shook her head as she swung her legs up under her. "Oh, I don't know. I've been ensconced in my apartment since I saw you last, actually, working on articles and books, leaving only to run and teach my class."

He offered a wry grin. "Isn't that just the point, though? Each one of us possesses traits of one, as well as the other. If I recall correctly, the philosopher always saw the possible in the present, which swings our conversation back to Findhorn-Vermont."

Kate nodded. "Indeed, like the flight of the turtle doves, with their ever increasing arc, returning back, though at a higher state of elevation."

Channing's eyes crinkled upward in approval. "An expansive, multi-valent insight, Cáitlín."

Kate chuckled. "I see you have been talking to Heather about my classes again."

Smiling, he nodded. "Yes, you are improving her—and my—vocabulary."

Taking a sip of his tea, he turned to her. "Actually, that is one of the reasons I wished to discuss with you my ideas for my foundation."

She looked down. "Oh, I have little to contribute."

He regarded her in silence with a searching expression until she looked at him. "You have a talent for making learning interesting."

He then delved into an overview of his plans for the foundation, sharing with her the idea of creating a school for the experiential arts, as he explained it.

"How can I help you in your planning?" Kate said, with a slight tilt of her head. "I know nothing about meditation."

His gaze was intense. "You inspire others through your pedagogical style," he said. "I'd like to incorporate some of your approaches to teaching in my own school."

Kate felt her cheeks warm. "Well, thank you. That's very kind of you to say, but if you consulted with my dean, and most likely the majority of my colleagues, they would argue otherwise." She looked away into the fire.

His voice firm, Channing countered, "That is precisely why I wish to consult with *you* over anyone else." When he noticed her disconcerted glance, he added, "You reach others, whether you realize it consciously or not." He smiled at her gently before continuing, "And whether they, as in the case of some of your, um, colleagues and dean, like it or not. Your example has touched them, and I would venture to say, that a significant part of their unease, even open rejection of your initiatives, stems from their own internal ambivalence over their chosen approaches."

Kate looked pensive. "I've never thought of their negative response to my work and teaching style in that way before—kind of like the resistant learner, who spends the majority of the semester locked in his resistance—only to embrace the new knowledge and insights once he decides to let go." She straightened up and looked at him. "That's why I never give up on those type of students. I just continue encouraging them until they unfold."

Channing nodded. "And you wonder why I wish to consult with you—encourage you to participate?" He leaned toward her as a knowing look spread across his face. "Do assure me that you are not a 'resistant learner' yourself in this regard."

Kate looked at him, before nodding. "You know, you may be onto something. I am reticent to embrace what I feel growing more strongly inside me because I fear changing my life in significant ways—"

"From what you had planned," he interjected with a knowing look. "Yes, the hound on the scent, eyes on the ground."

Kate shook her head. "Exactly so, from what I had planned for myself."

"Ah, the first steps—if not the first one hundred, in the transcendental journey of *awakening*." He leaned back with a soft smile. "I know the rhythm of those initial steps well."

With a nod, he added, "But let's not forget that '*not till we are lost do we find ourselves and the extent of our relations to the world.*'"

Shaking her head, Kate said in awe, "How his words stir my soul into thought."

"Indeed," said Channing, with a knowing nod, "and ultimately, into action. '*The sun is but a morning star,*' let's not forget."

Kate smiled warmly. "Okay, I'm all ears, now that I am opening myself to this new experience. Tell me more about your foundation. I'll do whatever I can to help you think through your ideas."

Looking at her with a somber glance, Channing said, "The goal is simple. I wish to offer an array of insights and skills to educate and thus enable people to live as self-sufficient and as simple a lifestyle as they may choose to adopt."

"Like what?" she asked, leaning forward.

"Oh, for starters, helping farmers and growers learn to communicate with their plants and animals, meditate away pests, and through such knowledge, maximize their self-sufficiency, among other skills." He gripped his teacup in both hands, as he rocked back and forth slowly.

Kate searched his expression. "But how can I be of help? I know next to nothing, as I said, about any of those topics." She twisted her mouth as she looked sadly at him. "I wish I did. It all sounds really fascinating, though."

Channing stopped rocking and leaned forward. "Heather has reported to me that you have shifted your classes to accommodate each of the students' interests. It is that sort of approach to creating learning environments grounded in differentiation, yet which remain all-inclusive, that I would like to incorporate into my school." His gaze was firm, yet expansive. "And let's not forget your abilities with the recalcitrant."

"Uh-huh, I see," she said, as she traced the rim of her cup with her finger. "So you would like me to consult with you about ways you can create learning environments conducive to the topics and skills you wish to offer?"

"Yes, that's right." He nodded. "Precisely."

Kate shifted her head from side to side as she thought. After a few minutes, she spoke. "I might be able to help you," she said in a voice conveying her sense of rising intrigue. "You'd have to tell me more, much more, in rigorous detail, about the school and its format."

"Of course," he said nodding. Leaning towards her, he asked, "So you'll do it, then?"

She looked at him for a minute before speaking. "What, exactly?"

Channing returned her curious gaze with determined sincerity. "I'd like to hire you to serve as a pedagogical consultant, perhaps even head up the educational component to the Center."

Kate envisioned a new fork in the road of her career, her life. "I am awestruck." She smiled shyly. "Being the rigorous planner that I am, I never once thought of this career track." She looked away. "It seems so different from the road upon which I have been traveling."

He gazed at her kindly. "Actually, Cáitlín, if you think hard about it," he said with a nod, "meditate even," he interjected with a pointed look before continuing, "upon your academic choices, interests, and initiatives, I feel confident that you would find an underlying harmony in what may feel at the moment as disparate, even conflicting, paths."

"Really?" She wasn't sure what to think or say, but intrigued, turned towards him now in rapt attention. "Can you explain what you see?"

Channing studied her a moment in silence. "Although it is better for you to intuit the underlying currents of your own soul, I can say this much." He looked intently at her. "Your approach to teaching complements your intellectual interests, in terms of your dissertation research, your current evolving interest in *Walden*, and the direction of your most recent research connecting the two. In all cases, don't they point to an essentially inclusive philosophy, a real sense of an egalitarian community, based on mutual respect for both people and place, rather than on a hierarchical structure, based on social status or prestige?"

Kate shook her head slowly. "I never thought of it at all in that way before, though I have, of late, been reminding myself with ever increased regularity to consider everything from different perspectives." She smiled at him. "I do believe that I am finding a way to balance my instincts with my thoughts and actions. At least in my classroom, students are truly engaged with their learning, as well as committed to acting on their insights to share with others—resulting in trying to make the world, or at least a given place, better for everyone." She offered a shy smile. "It's so gratifying."

Channing nodded. "Yes, that feeling of doing good for others and the earth is precisely the affectional goal of my proposed center—another reason for you to be involved."

Kate shook her head. "It would be nice to be appreciated for my 'pedagogical' approaches to learning, I have to admit."

"Indeed. It forms part of the basis to my request for your assistance and active participation—if not direct leadership."

Kate gazed at him with questioning eyes.

Leaning toward her, Channing said, "We'll work out the details of your participation, whether it is part-time at first, or full-time—should you decide at some point to follow the less-traveled road to Walden North."

Kate smiled at him, feeling oddly at peace. "Yes, I shall think about it all." She looked off into the darkness, saying quietly, with a pensive tone, "I like that concept—the less-traveled road to Walden North. Hmm."

Returning her warm smile, Channing suggested, "In the meantime, we should go outside for a brief star-gazing experience. Though it must be quite cold at this point, I don't think you will regret it."

They walked out under a sky laden in stars. "Absolutely amazing," she murmured.

"Yes. Yes, it is. I find that I feel both humbled and energized by star-gazing."

"I think I know what you mean," Kate acknowledged. "Particularly with this infinite amount of stars. I've never seen so many, ever before."

As they walked back to the cabin, Kate admitted, "You know, Channing, I feel like I am experiencing a completely different side to the world that I never realized existed before coming up here to Walden North."

"You are," he said. "The question is how or whether to integrate the two into a harmonious new level of living, or choosing one over the other."

As Kate lay in bed, she found herself wondering briefly if the visitor '*who never comes*' would come to her door. But he never came. Shifting her thoughts, she fell asleep in the dark, dreaming of a winter dawn.

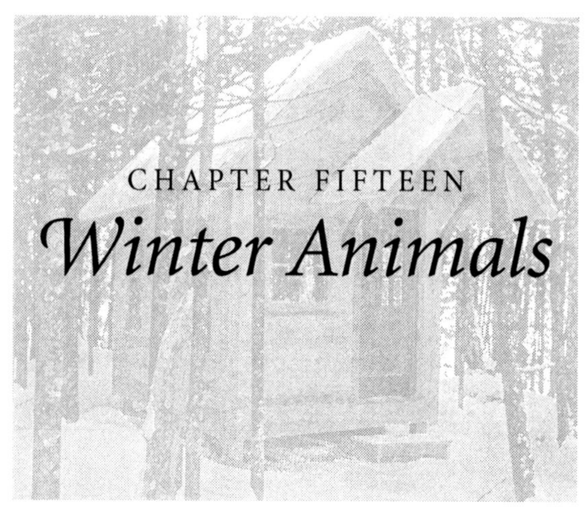

CHAPTER FIFTEEN

Winter Animals

The dawn arrived sooner than Kate had expected. Waking to an insistent knock on her door, she heard Channing call out, "Cáitlín. Cáitlín. Good morning. If you hurry, you will experience something I believe will be of great interest to you."

When she appeared, Channing ushered her with rapid gestures toward the door, an act unusual for him. "Come quickly, or you will miss them."

Kate followed behind. The frigid air shocked her as she emerged from the warm log cabin. She stood shivering in the dawning light, rhythmically shifting from one foot to the other to keep warm.

Channing pointed in the direction of the corner of the field below the cabin. "You're about to experience one of Thoreau's chapters in action."

"Which one?" she asked, her teeth chattering. "I've been feeling lately that I am living each chapter that I'm teaching."

He smiled. "'Winter Animals.' Teaching that, are you?" he asked with a mischievous smile.

She regarded him with surprise. "Coincidentally enough, that is the very chapter we will be discussing next class."

He gave her a wry look. "Indeed."

She locked eyes with him. "You mean my sense is really occurring?"

Channing smiled wisely. "Synchronicity at work—"

Arching her eyebrow, Kate completed his sentiment, "I know, 'yet again.'" She shivered uncontrollably, moving from foot to foot.

"You should try to stand still," he whispered, noting her attempts at warming herself.

"Is it the deer again?" As Kate turned in the direction of his beckoning finger, her eyes widened.

He nodded almost imperceptibly. "That and more."

Over one dozen deer, clothed in their winter coats of dark grey, were bent over the feeder. Another half dozen or so, lurking along the outskirts of the field appeared to be standing guard, sniffing the air as they incessantly moved their heads from side to side, while a few huddled in groups of two, their bodies crossed, each head staring out in a different direction. Kate shook her own in awe.

As she continued to watch, she leaned towards Channing. "Something is different," she whispered. "Why is it they are not competing for the food like the last time we observed them?"

Glancing at her sideways, he almost smiled. "Winter animals," he said. "They are a lesson for us humans."

She turned to him. "In what way?"

With a sly nod, he said only, "You'll see."

After the first deer left the feeder, they retreated together back along the edge of the field, replacing the former sentries. The new group congregated around the grains.

Upon observing their movements, Kate turned back to Channing. "It's like an orchestrated dance."

With a soft smile, he said, "Ah, but our deer are following the beat of an inner rhythm—the beat of the soul of Nature."

"Oh, Thoreauvian deer, are they?" She glanced over at him briefly with a wry smile, before turning back to resume her focus on the deer.

"*Naturally*," he quipped, apparently delighted with his pun. Looking over at her with anticipation, he asked, "What else do you notice?"

Kate watched the new deer, some of which were already moving away. "They don't seem to be very hungry," she said with a glance in his direction. "Maybe it was just my excitement over seeing them the last time, but they seemed to eat a lot more than now."

He nodded. "Precisely."

Turning to him, she asked, "Why—wouldn't the cold make them more hungry than in the fall?"

"You can see for yourself," Channing said with a nod. Noticing that she was shivering, he said, "We can observe from inside if you prefer."

She smiled brightly, admitting in a sheepish voice, "I guess I have spent more time than I admit inside a warm library." She shuddered. "It's really freezing out here!"

He grinned. "Oh, much lower than that—about -15, perhaps, -20, even."

"Oh, my God," she exclaimed, now waving slightly from side to side to warm herself. "You've convinced me."

"We'll watch the parade from inside," he said, as he walked up the porch steps.

"Parade?"

His smile was warm. "You'll see," he repeated mysteriously, as he held open the door for her. "Hurry inside."

Setting Kate up in one of the chairs, positioned next to the window for external viewing, Channing handed her a woolen throw and a pair of binoculars. "I'll make something warm to drink—tea?"

Kate smiled up at him. "Umm. Sounds lovely."

"Fine. You keep me updated on what you observe." Their eyes met briefly, before he turned away.

Kate watched him move to the kitchen area before turning back to the window. His anomalous character struck her. She wondered whether it was simply characteristic of him to be so warm, yet detached, almost simultaneously. She took up the binoculars. Better to focus on the scene outside, than in, she decided.

She noted that the few deer remaining at the feeder picked up their heads, as if realizing she was watching them. It seemed that by some internal communication, they suddenly moved away in unison, disappearing into the gloom of the forest.

"Anything?" Channing's voice called from behind.

"Well, the last of the deer seem to have left, since no new ones are appearing," she reported, as she turned back to address him. "Is there something else I should watch for?"

With a knowing smile, he said, "Yes, indeed. The parade will continue in new form." He walked over, and laying her mug on the table next to her chair, plopped down in the adjoining one, threw up his gangly legs onto the ottoman, and sunk back. "Now, as you'll see, it gets really interesting," he said, with a sidelong glance at her.

Kate looked at him in surprise. "More than it has already?" she asked, before shifting her attention back toward the scene outside.

They both sat peering into the morning light for some time, when Kate announced, "Looks like we have company—a really big deer." She briefly glanced at Channing. "A male, maybe?"

Leaning forward, he shook his head. "It's a male, but not a stag, Cáitlín. Can you tell the difference?"

Kate studied the emerging form as it entered the field, heading straight toward the feeder. "Its walk is different," she commented, "more genteel, even though the animal is so much bigger."

"Yes, indeed," he said agreeably.

She continued watching before crying out, "Look! There's another one, though smaller and thinner. Must be the baby." The animals bent over and ate from the feeder, each raising its head after grabbing a mouthful and chewed before going for more. Kate turned excitedly to Channing. "What—are they elk?"

His eyes looked kind when he turned to her. "No, no elk east of the Mississippi. Those are moose—a cow and her yearling."

"Really? Moose? I've never seen one before now." Her eyes shimmered with her thrill of discovery. Turning back, she resumed her observation. "Their legs seem so thin and wobbly that it looks like they could easily fall right over."

Channing nodded. "Those thin legs of theirs make it possible for them to run through low brush quickly without getting stuck."

"Absolutely amazing," she commented. She gazed at the scene spellbound.

He looked at her with a question on his face. "What do you mean—that they can run easily through the forest, despite their size, or that you are able to sit here and watch them?"

"Well, both, I guess," Kate admitted with a smile. Taking a quick sip of her tea, she continued her observation. "So this is the parade to which you had referred earlier?"

Rolling his mug slowly in his hand, he nodded. "Oh, there should be more."

Kate watched as the moose finished up and glided back into the forest, it seemed to her, almost effortlessly. "They are so dainty for such large animals."

Channing let out a low laugh. "Yes, that is a good word to describe their movements—despite their size."

Kate suddenly called out. "Okay, so what is this new creature?" She pointed over to the edge of the field.

They both watched as the animal made its way through the snow with its head down and tail extended. "Seems like he knows exactly where to go," she noted.

"Oh, he does. He comes around almost daily, these days."

"So what is it? A wolf?" She turned to Channing with a look of astonishment. "This is like National Geographic in real time." Her eyes caught a new creature emerging from the trees. "Another one—no, wait, three more!" she announced with great excitement.

Nodding, Channing said, "That would be the family of coyotes that lives here in the woods close to our house. We hear them singing at night. The parents have been teaching the pups how to catch food all fall."

He looked over at Kate's blank expression. "They howl when they have caught their food. You might have heard them last night." He said it more as a statement than a question.

"No, I don't think so." She turned to him. "But I'd love to hear their singing."

He looked at her with a searching expression. "Perhaps during your next visit."

Kate looked at him in surprise. It seemed like a definitive event to him. "Yes, perhaps," she said, her voice soft, her gaze meeting his.

She turned back to watch as the parents stretched to reach the food, using their noses to throw some onto the ground where their pups sat waiting. She glanced over at Channing. "They show such loving concern for their young ones."

"Yes, indeed," he said, his tone brittle. "More than do many human parents."

Kate looked at him. "That's it—they seem so *human*, despite their appearance."

Throwing her a sidelong glance, he countered dryly, "Or perhaps we humans have more *animal* in us than we acknowledge."

After they disappeared down the field, Kate sat back and faced Channing. "I don't get the parade," she said, with a confused shake of her head. "They all appear so," she stopped, gazing out briefly, searching for the right word, "*considerate*."

With a slight frown, Channing retorted, "More than our fellow men and women might act, if forced to search for food for themselves in such challenging conditions."

Kate gave a vigorous nod. "Exactly. They seem to be cooperating with one another, leaving food for the next group." She shook her head. "Extraordinary. I would never have expected that."

"Yes," he said nodding, "Nature is full of profound insights."

She looked at him before speaking. "I know you don't have a television and all that, but it's so different here from nature programs, which tend to depict animals as voracious predators." She waved her hand at the window. "Not like these genteel individuals."

Channing smiled. "An eye-opening experience, isn't it," he said, "to discover the inner graciousness and generosity of wild animals."

Kate shook her head. "I never knew."

Channing got up, and walking over to a bookcase, pulled down a book. Walking back, he sat on the arm of his chair while opening it.

Kate expression blossomed into a coy smile. "Let me guess. *Walden*?" Grinning, she added, "'Winter Animals,' no doubt, as you alluded to before." She sat up straighter and blurted, "but I don't remember Thoreau describing this parade of deer, moose, and coyotes."

"No, quite right," he said with a nod. "He describes another animal parade he observed, which," he said, with a knowing look, "you may now appreciate all the more since you have gained firsthand experience." His eyes gleamed.

Kate chuckled. "Ah, yes, experience over theory. I get that now."

Channing read the passage to which he alluded. After finishing, he said, "Perhaps if we had only corn kernels, we might just attract the squirrels, blue jays, and chickadees as Thoreau did."

She smiled at him. "I could try that at my bird feeder back home in Cambridge."

Glancing over at her, he added, "Besides, you must recall his lament over the last of the moose, as well as the last deer, having been killed by a hunter some time previous to his sojourn at Walden."

"That's right! I had forgotten that," Kate exclaimed. "So the natural world up here is actually, well, more *natural*, than in Thoreau's time."

Channing nodded. "Yes, indeed. In Vermont most of the trees had been cut, about eighty percent of them, while in Massachusetts, the percentage was even higher, hence Thoreau's call for preserving what remained."

Kate nodded. "Yes, I suppose we do '*need the tonic of wildness*.'" She shrugged and looked at him. "Until my visits up here, I never really knew what that meant." Stretching her legs on the ottoman, she added, "but each time I visit, I feel so, *rejuvenated*—as if I have spent so much more time away, than I actually have."

Channing gazed at her quietly for some minutes before speaking. "Of course, the goal is to reside in one's own Walden every day."

Kate turned away. "I've been working on that." When he didn't respond, she turned to look at him, searching for an answer in his intensity. "Though it seems more theoretical than experiential."

His eyes widened briefly, as they shared a mutual gaze. "I am confident that the poet and the philosopher within you will join forces." He made a slight bow.

She studied his soft eyes that evinced wisdom she did not yet feel herself. "Yes, perhaps."

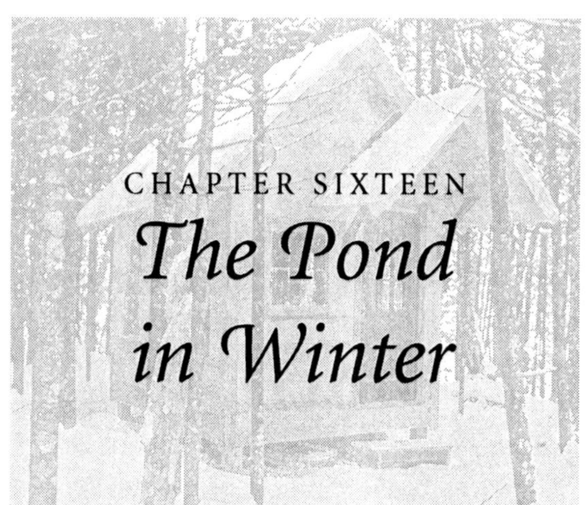

CHAPTER SIXTEEN
The Pond in Winter

WHEN KATE RETURNED FROM HER TRIP TO WALDEN NORTH, she discovered three letters waiting in her mailbox. Scanning the return addresses, she noted two came from the presses to which she had submitted her book manuscript. When she read the return address of the third, the effect instantly sent waves of fear reverberating through her. Office of the Dean, it read. The *Dreadful Dean,* she corrected herself. Her mouth twisted down into a decided grimace, as she bit her lip. Which to open first?

Entering her flat, Kate strode over toward the window and placed each of the three envelopes, side by side, down on her desk. While the suspense was killing her, she succumbed to her sense of disconcerting ambivalence over the conviction that her fate lay in the contents of those letters collectively. Hovering over them, she placed her hand over her mouth in a Munchian moment rare for her, as if to stifle the scream of *angst* she felt forming inside, before shifting her gaze from the desk to outside.

The maple stood covered in the snow that had fallen over the city, blanketing all sound in a downy white. Some chickadees, and to her surprise, two juncos were perched at the feeder, picking at the last few seeds scattered among the drifted snow. Astonished, she noticed, that like the deer, moose, and coyotes of the north woods, each of the birds took its share, before darting back for cover under a larger limb, leaving food for the others. No fighting, no struggle for dominance—just a simple necessity, a consensual cooperation seemed to guide their decisions, their actions.

Forgetting her own concerns for the moment, Kate opened the window and poured out a bucket of seeds to replenish their food. Leaving the window open just above a crack, followed by stepping back into the shadow of the room, she watched, delighted over the ever-increasing numbers of birds now flocking to the feeder, each diving in for a seed from various directions, only to take flight again, leaving space and food for the others. They moved in such rhythmic regularity that Kate felt as if she were watching an orchestrated dance—a ballet of birds twirling and leaping, before melding into the encircling arms of outstretched branches. As she stood gazing at the scene, even the desk with its tuft of white blended into the setting—brown folding into white, white shifting to brown—a harmonic symphony.

She continued watching, her eyes glazing over at the scene, with its blurred bits of brown and white transforming into an impressionistic painting of winter. And then she heard it. The sound startled her with a jolt from her reverie. Although she had never heard it before, she identified it instantly. Her eyes flickered to stare outside.

There it was again—the simple sound of a bird's wings—as it took flight. Though she stood motionless, listening intently to the subtle music of *birdwing*, the effect moved her, like the sound of the wind breathing through pine needles in the woods of Walden North. In that moment, she realized what Heather had been communicating, what Channing had endeavored to share of his own journey along the road, as she now conceived it—*from here to up there.*

Kate turned, and with a dismissive glance at the letters, walked away—her thoughts barely perceptible waves rippling softly upon the shore of the pond. As she made some tea, she felt waves of deep conviction gathering momentum, with each flap of birdwing she heard. In that moment, Kate realized, with a tremendous sense of relief, that she had been right, despite what the publishers, the dean, and even Blake, might think. Her book felt to her like the perfect articulation of her evolving sense of the exact location she wished to stake her place in academia. She was excited about sharing the insights she had discovered in Melville and Thoreau regarding a simpler way to live in the world—revolving around the rhythms of the natural world. With a glance out to the birds flying here and there, she realized now, with the same ironclad conviction she had felt for the primacy of academic ways, when she first moved to Harvard, that the sage voice of the simple woodchopper resonated more deeply, more movingly, more meaningfully, in *birdwing* than in the bellicose sound of expertise.

Bending down to greet her fate, Kate knew that she would find a way to continue along her own road, however less traveled, following the beat of birdwing in the air. Scanning the three, she decided to open the Harvard University Press letter first. With the dance of birds behind her left shoulder, she read the conditional acceptance of her manuscript—provided she made substantial revisions.

As she scanned the areas of concern, Kate smirked. Of course, she noted, they want me to write *out* everything I recently wrote in. The result would return her back to the academic track upon which she had begun—back to rigorous, intellectualized theory. She dropped the letter on her desk, watching it fall as a last leaf in autumn, before turning away to observe the birds. Words from *Walden* floated by:

And where will the birds live if their groves are all cut down?

She couldn't recall many commentators discussing that point in their analyses, she thought, with a resolute toss of her head.

Kate's thoughts flashed through the contents of the letter. She should be thrilled, darting in joy, as so many birds on the wing. Her book would be "ground-breaking," the editor had predicted, if only she would omit the sections on ecological proselytizing. *No environmental jeremiad necessary, as the rigor of the philosophical argument stood firmly on its own theoretical, hallowed ground*, he had written.

As she gazed outside, her eyes alighted on the presence of a new bird unknown to her, arrayed in the colors of a summer dawn, despite the season, which was now energetically gathering a few seeds into its large, pouched bill. Kate felt an instant kinship with it—both delighting in the prospect of reward. The lure of advancement appeared in her consciousness like a fishing line dropped through a hole in the ice to the fantastical, watery world below—enticing any unsuspecting taker to bite— before being reeled up and out onto someone's dinner plate.

The image of the view to the invincible summer beneath the ice conjured up recollections of Thoreau's delight in discovering the pickerel of Walden. How he had waxed poetically over the colors of the lowly pickerel, proclaiming them superior to the highly prized cod and haddock! And yet, he had forsaken his delight in pickerel, and all animal foods, to live according to the higher laws of his inner nature. With a glance out the window, she found herself applying Thoreauvian maxims. Heaven is *out there*, the transcendental *thin* places in Nature, as well as above our heads.

Kate reached for the second letter—from Dean Edwards. She grimaced, as she opened it, fearing a new set of '*Great Expectations*'—or worse, she thought with an involuntary gulp, or perhaps, *unmet* expectations. She figured that he must have heard about the individualized learning goals she had initiated, she thought with an involuntary shudder, or perhaps the impending "*My Walden*" student exhibit at Walden Pond she had organized. She shook her head, hoping he hadn't heard about the Walden film project and the Harvard Green website her class had created. Those initiatives will send him right over the edge of rationality, she thought with an unusual mix of dread and satisfaction.

Reading through the letter as she held her breath, Kate threw it down in disgust. Another set of expectations, with the additional threat of conditional employment, based on returning to a more acceptable teaching format, in concert, he had said, with the "honor" of being part of the select few to teach at Harvard. She shook her head, as she folded her arms as if to shield herself against the attack. *More conditions.* She leaned against the window frame and gazed out through saddened eyes as waves of remorse crashed against her sense of resolve, spraying blinding ice foam in her line of vision.

At last, Kate turned away from the window. *'The winter of our discontent,' indeed.* Walking past the third letter, she reached for her bag, took out her phone, and called Blake. He was sure to set her right.

"Hi, Blake, am I disturbing?" she asked timidly, in response to his detached greeting.

She could hear him sigh. "Yes, Katie, lately you have, indeed, been quite disturbing. Calling to make amends, are you?"

Shaking her head, she countered, "I'm sorry, I didn't know I was being disruptive to your sense of equilibrium." She wondered if she had been successful in hiding the sense of outrage she felt over his comment.

"Well, Katie, I might consider giving you another chance, but only if you re-focus your attention, to your work—and to me."

Jesus. More conditions. She exhaled deeply, before responding. "Actually, Blake, that's why I am calling—to talk to you about my work," she said, before impetuously adding, "on which I have been focusing."

His response was curt, even cutting. "I am referring to the work you came to Harvard to do—not some Harvard Green project, of all such silly endeavors. It's not the sixties, you know."

"Oh, so you know about that student project, then," she said, her voice downcast, as she felt her resolve fading into the grey sunset outside.

"Oh, everyone does, Katie," he snapped. "What's got into you—besides the lure of the hippie life up in Vermont?" His tone was even more caustic than she had remembered. "What would your Browne family say? After all, you have a name and a serious reputation to uphold."

Kate sighed more heavily than before. "Oh, Blake, you're worse than Dean Edwards with his triple-decker set of expectations and conditions."

"It's for your own good, Kate. No one knows what to do with you anymore—including me."

Kate bit her lip before responding. "Listen, Blake, though I probably know what you are going to say, I'd like to talk to you about this. I've just received two letters, one from the Harvard Press, and one from the unfailingly proscriptive Dean Edwards."

"And what did they say?" his tone taut.

"Well, in a nutshell, so to speak—" she began.

Blake cut in. "Oh, for God's sake, Kate, will you desist from employing those nauseating nature references? Speak in the language you learned at Northwestern, and sound like the academic intellectual you are—or once were."

"Oh, Blake." Kate felt the sigh escape from the now murky bottom of her own internal Walden.

"Well, then, has the book been accepted, or not?" he asked in his officious, and, she noted, quite annoying tone.

"Well, it's conditional," she said with a twist of her mouth.

"On what?"

"Well, upon substantial revisions," she confided, not bothering to disguise her bitterness, "essentially cutting out what I had added last fall."

Ignoring her acridity, Blake's icy tone melted into summer. "But that is fantastic, Kate, utterly, bloody fantastic!"

"Oh?" she asked, feeling unsure of her own response to the letter.

"A few revisions aside, and you'll be published with Harvard!" He rattled on.

Kate could imagine him opening the little notebook he carried everywhere and jotting down his points.

"I'll just make a list of people to contact about your book, including your extended Browne family, when it comes out, to assure a positive reception, and you are on the road to tenure! What utterly delightful news."

"Well, thanks," she said, her voice hollow. "I didn't know about having to make all those revisions, essentially changing the nature of the book."

"Oh, nonsense," Blake countered, with a dismissive finality, before lapsing into rebuke. "Besides, there is no 'nature' to your book—only a sound, cohesive argument." Without waiting for her to respond, he continued. "We all make the necessary revisions we need to get published. It's a given. Part of the '*Great Expectations*'—the rite of manhood one endures to achieve the award of club membership through tenure. You're well on your way now, Katie, love."

Kate noted with a grimace that she was back to 'love' status. "I suppose," she stammered. She bit her lip, before twisting it back and forth.

"Indeed you are, most assuredly," he countered. "And I'll help you see to it."

Without waiting for her to respond, he added, his tone coy, "Now, what about a late bite—or perhaps a bit of dessert—this evening?"

Blake had transformed into his old, charming self. To be expected, Kate thought with a sigh. He was nothing if not utterly consistent, both in his outlook and corresponding manner.

"Could we make an evening of it tomorrow night, Blake? I had thought to review the revisions requested by the editor in order to map out my direction."

"Good girl!" he applauded. "Right-o, until tomorrow, then."

Kate turned off the phone with a sigh. No plotting necessary, she thought. The route, grid-tied and straight, was paved with future rewards—if only she would choose that road.

Sitting down at her desk with a refreshed pot of tea, Kate decided to review both letters again. Glossing over the dean's relegation of her tenure-track status down to the level of "conditional instructor," he went on to lay out his list of expectations—assign term papers, focus on critical readings based in existing scholarship, and publish in academically *esteemed* journals and presses. Upon proven evidence satisfying his expectations, he would re-instate her position to tenure-track status. Kate grimaced when she came to the part, "quite *simple*, really," evidently a sarcastic reminder of their first meeting when he had addressed his expectations for the Thoreau seminar. But the last line seared her through and through. "We expect you to follow the beat of the *Harvard* drum, Ms. Brown."

Casting the letter down, she muttered, "Conform, conform, conform." Such a far cry, she realized with a growing feeling of despondency, from "*Simplify, simplify, simplify.*"

Grabbing her mug of tea, Kate tipped back in her chair, placing her feet over the stacks of papers on her desk. She sipped her tea, looking out into the night. The darkness outside seemed a reflection of what she felt inside. She shivered uncontrollably. It was cold, really cold—the frost carving intricate designs along the edges of her windowpane.

As she sat looking at the frosted paintings illuminated by the desk lamp, whose glass shade cast hues of blue, then green, Kate recalled a passage from the chapter she was teaching about the ice cakes of winter skimmed from the "skin" of Walden Pond. She felt herself as exposed as the poor pond in the harsh winter. How odd, she remembered thinking, that the frozen blocks could remain so for five years, retaining their shape, while the fresh water soon lost its sweetness. Was there a message—for her—carved into the icicled shapes?

Kate recalled that Thoreau compared the different modalities, as the distinction between the intellect and feelings. Closing her eyes, she imagined water flowing, making its way through field and forest to find a new union. If given the choice, she concluded, she preferred the fresh, pure Waldenwater, which, after thawing, flowed freely into the sacred water of the Ganges and far into other sacred streams, known only to the few.

With that acknowledgment, she reached over and opened the letter from Dewey College Press. Upon reading the first line, Kate sat up abruptly, nearly spilling her mug, and raced through the remainder of its contents. Each line seemed more re-affirming than the preceding.

Tears filled her eyes, as she read the comments of the reviewers, one of whom praised her book as "the perfect mix of intellectual rigor, environmental activism, and enlightened pedagogy"—a particular mixture, the reviewer noted, that reflected their college mission. They get it, she thought. *They understand.* Leaning back, she closed her eyes, letting the news of her book acceptance flow through her, washing away her previous sense of despair.

Feeling re-invigorated, Kate placed the letter gently down on her desk, opened her laptop, and copied the website address from the ending of the letter. Scrolling down through the site, she clicked on each of the new books published with the press, delighted to discover that they were *her* kind of books. On impulse, she clicked on the college website, only to discover another door thrown wide open—an opening, it felt to Kate, tailor-made for her.

In that moment, Kate finally understood the significance for her own life in light of one of Thoreau's concluding insights in *Walden*. For the first time in her year at Harvard, Kate detected—and saw—the current of an underlying harmony to seemingly disparate entities, the "*seemingly conflicting, but really concurring laws*" guiding her path in life—just as Channing had intimated. Without a moment's hesitation, Kate responded to the letter of acceptance—before turning her attention to writing a letter of application for the advertised position she had discovered there.

After sending off both letters, Kate leaned back in her chair, her eye resting on the photos of the two Walden Ponds she had framed together after her last trip to both special places. As she gazed at them, she recalled Thoreau's conclusion that the pond was made deep for a symbol. It was a depth, she realized, that she could only experience by swimming among pickerel, in the blended currents of Waldenwater and the sacred Ganges of Walden North.

CHAPTER SEVENTEEN
Spring

THE STUDENTS DECIDED TO HOLD THEIR FINAL CLASS of the year at Walden Pond. It was spring, after all, they had argued, and in keeping with the themes of Thoreau's last chapter, claimed it could only be truly appreciated at its source—along the shores of Thoreau's Walden. They planned everything, from the meeting time—at dawn—to the last meal they would share as a class.

When Kate arrived in the parking lot in the semi-darkness, she noted with surprise that several cars were already parked. Must have spent the night here, she thought with a chuckle. Placing her large thermos of raspberry tea in her backpack, she thrust it over her shoulder and sauntered off in the direction of the pond.

She jogged along the now well-known path to the Thoreau's original cabin site where they agreed to assemble. No longer feeling apprehensive when alone in the woods, she followed the mulched trail cut into dense stands of hemlock and fir just above the pond.

The pre-dawn air was cool, almost frosty, with patches of crusted snow still here and there, yet Kate felt an unexpected warmth rising within. Although she could never have envisioned, when first assigned the Thoreau seminar, that her teaching would lead her along the path to where she now found herself in the dawning light, Kate felt the assurance of conviction rise with each step.

Despite what the dean and some of her colleagues might think of her pedagogy, Kate remained convinced that her less-traveled road provided the perfect route for her to remain true to the spirit of *awakening in Walden*. After all, she reasoned, as she caught sight of a group of the students sitting along the edge of the pond waiting for dawn, what is the point of studying Thoreau, if not actively engaged in the "*business of living,*" or, in this case, to experience, firsthand, the poetry of the "*living earth*"?

Looking up at the waves of vibrant hues of rose and gold, now undulating across the morning sky over the violet waters of the pond, Kate felt as if this dawn would prove prophetic in some fundamentally transformative—and transcendent—way. Kate glanced back with pride at the students who had transformed through their reading, from being "*students merely*" to "*seers*" in the Thoreauvian sense. She smiled to think that, like the jailer, the judge, and the preacher of *Walden*, in opening the door of her classroom to the great outdoors, she and her students were able to "*witness their limits transgressed,*" discovering the "*tonic of wildness*" in the natural world around them—and within.

Kate knew now—the feeling stretching out and up in every direction, like the grape vines encircling the trees in their journey heavenward in the legendary Vínland—that she had crossed that 'invisible boundary' separating herself from her colleagues, perhaps, even, of traditional academia itself. Though unsure exactly of what "*new, universal laws*" would appear, she was willing and determined to discover.

Kate entered the dean's office with her head held high. "Hello, Ms. Watkins. I'd like a few minutes with Dean Edwards, if that's possible," she said firmly.

She met with an even firmer stare, cold and superior. "Meetings with the dean require an appointment, Ms. Brown."

Kate firmly stood her ground. "Would you mind checking his schedule for his availability tomorrow, then?" She could just glimpse the Master himself sitting at his desk through the half-closed door. "I just need a few moments."

"Given the circumstances, Ms. Brown, I am happy to transmit any message. Really I—" retorted the woman with open disdain.

"It's quite personal, actually." Kate managed to assume her sweetest smile. "I should think he would prefer to hear it from my lips."

Now more than agitated, the flustered receptionist could only muster, "Indeed," followed by a stare that would sear frozen flesh. "I don't know quite what to say, given the new turn of events." She tapped on her now closed schedule book.

A voice bellowed from within. "Oh, just let her in," commanded Dean Edwards. "Let's get this over with."

With a triumphant smirk at the woman who tried to stand, Kate swept majestically past her into the office, firmly closing the door behind her.

Furrowing his bushy eyebrows and removing his pipe from its perch at the corner of his wide mouth, Dean Edwards stared through smoldering eyes at the unexpected intruder. Kate nodded, before sitting in front of him. "Thank you," she said graciously without a trace of irony, "for clearing up your busy schedule to see me."

"And what matter is 'private' between us that you felt compelled to abandon all sense of decorum to take up with me?" His formidable brows formed one long, obstructive hedge. Grimacing, he tossed his head slightly, muttering, "It will be a long time coming before I hire another Midwesterner."

Kate ignored the slight, choosing, instead, to remain on course. Coaxing a warm smile from within, she said, "Dean Edwards, I came here to discuss briefly my employment with you."

Leaning over his desk, he thundered, "Surely you are not considering suing for discrimination. Your conditional status has nothing to do with your, your—"

"Sex, do you mean, Dean?" Despite the plethora of retorts rising within her, she offered only a taut smile, however skeptical it made her appear to him.

Waving his finger in her direction, he stammered, "If you even think about doing so, I warn you—" leaving the actual warning hanging in the air like a dead weight.

"No, Dean, nothing of the kind," she said with a dismissive toss of her head. She met his eyes. "Actually, I came to thank you."

He leaned back in his oak chair as if avoiding a direct hit. "Thank me?" His widened eyes conveyed his sense of bewilderment. "Is this some kind of warped joke?"

"Oh, no joke at all." She countered, her tone light.

Recovering his composure, he sat upright, eyeing her with a cold stare. "If so, Ms. Brown, the joke is sadly on your shoulders."

She said nothing.

With a stern shake of his head, he said in a clear rebuke, "You do not appear to grasp the gravity of your situation." He leaned back, gently swiveling in his chair, while tapping his folded fingers together over his chest. "Should your probationary status result in your dismissal, it will preclude your seeking a tenured position in any esteemed university or college in New England."

"Actually, I am here to discuss that very notion with you."

"Indeed," he muttered. "Perhaps your mentor at Northwestern may take you back—if only to restrain you." He sneered. "Oh, did I say, restrain? I suppose there's that to it as well," he said, chuckling, "though, of course, I meant re-train you—until you have internalized the ways of the academic world."

"Oh, no need," Kate responded, her tone clipped. "I believe my experience teaching *Walden* has re-trained me, as you called it."

Now fired up, Dean Edwards continued. "I am dismayed, thoroughly dismayed at the mockery you have made of the Freshman Seminar." With a deep sigh, he shook his head, looking completely crestfallen. "How shall I explain this to Prescott, when he returns from Oxford?"

Nonplussed, Kate leaned forward, and placing her folded hands on the edge of his desk, began. "That is why I am here, Dean. I wanted to thank you for assigning me the *Walden* seminar."

With a violent shake of his head, he stormed, "Reading response journals of all useless drivel, Ms. Brown?" His voice rose. "And filmed *interviews* and nature journals to replace the semester term paper?" Shaking his head, he muttered, more to himself, than to her, "I had no idea they were so lax out there at Northwestern. And they call themselves an Ivy League." An unrelenting flow of disdain poured from his shoulders, flooding their exchange in mutual resentment.

Despite her overflowing sense of anger, Kate smiled sweetly. "Actually, Dean, if you study the history of composition of *Walden*, you would discover that David Henry, as you prefer to call him, wrote his *magnum opus* from his own journals—both reading response and nature excerpts—as I believe Professor Prescott has examined."

He only glared.

"If it weren't for the extraordinary opportunity you offered me in teaching the *Walden* Seminar, and the transcendental *experiences* it presented," she said, pausing to ensure her emphasis was noted, "Well, I would be still be dedicating my life trying to secure life-long membership into the esteemed Harvard Club." She offered a coy smile. "As well as, of course, trying to satisfy your '*Great Expectations.*'"

"What do you mean?" He scowled with such fervor, that his now deeply furrowed brow reminded Kate of the famous description of the obsessive Ahab—filled with rage against the uncontrollable, white whale. Another accusatory, enraged stare caught her eye as she briefly glanced behind the dean's head, from a portrait of an eminent Harvard father, whose frozen glare eerily resembled the dean's. Kate realized there was no free will possible on any of their parts—beyond seeking a new life to live.

"I wanted to offer you my resignation in person." She smiled. "Assuming, by now, of course, that this act must certainly constitute one of your '*Great Expectations*' for me."

"You are *resigning*?" he asked, his eyes wide. "From *Harvard*?" He stared hard at her. "No one in my tenure as dean has ever willingly resigned his position here."

With a toss of her head, she said, "Oh, I know of one other." Kate's smile spread, as she tried to suppress a rising need to laugh. "As Thoreau said when he left Walden Pond, '*I am leaving here for as many reasons as I came.*'"

"You have made a mockery of our ways." He turned away in his chair.

"Not at all, Dean," Kate countered. "It's simply that I have '*many more lives to live.*'" She twisted her mouth into a wide grin. "Though, unlike my literary mentor, I am actually taking to the woods," she added with a chuckle.

Dean Edwards turned away in his chair. "I have heard enough."

Kate reached out to shake the utterly astonished man's hand.

"Thank you, Dean," she said, as she grasped his half-extended hand, and shaking it vigorously, added, "Thank you for opening my eyes."

"I fail to understand what great insights you think you are looking at," he sputtered.

As she started to leave, Kate suddenly turned back. "Remember, Dean:

'*It's not what you look at, but what you* <u>see</u>.'"

She regarded him sincerely. "And I have seen, truly seen, that—again to borrow from the worthy Thoreau—'*the preservation of the world*,' lies not in replicating the culture, but in promoting '*the wild and free*,' through listening '*to the beat of a different drummer*.'"

Dean Edwards only shook his head, before turning away with a mumble, "Good day, Ms. Brown." Kate thought he sagged his usually proud shoulders more than just a little.

As Kate sauntered across the campus for the last time, she looked eagerly ahead, whispering to herself, "There *is* more day to dawn."

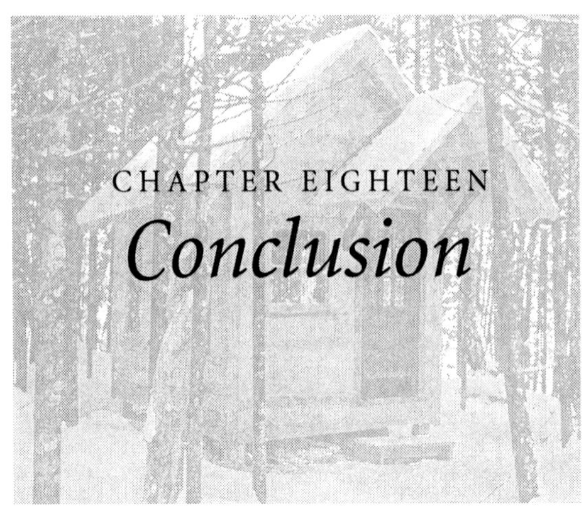

CHAPTER EIGHTEEN
Conclusion

"You did *what?*" thundered Blake. He stared hard at her through blazing eyes.

Kate had never seen him so angry. Lifting her head, she turned away slightly, as if to ward off any verbal blow that might follow.

"It isn't that I am not cut out for Harvard and traditional academic life," she explained. "It's that I do not wish to be boxed in with that particular paper and wrapped with your ribbon."

"Ouch," he said, thrusting his head back, as he visibly reeled from her curt statement.

"Oh, Blake, it's not meant to hurt," she said, as tears pooled in her eyes.

He gazed at her with a searching, though sad expression. "Haven't I given you everything you could want."

"Yes, Blake. Everything that money, prestige, and social status can buy, apparently."

"Then, what is it you want?"

"My freedom."

He tossed his head up into the air. "Oh, for God's sake." He turned away. "Your parents misnamed you. You should have been called Nora from '*A Doll's House.*'"

Kate gazed at him through glistening eyes. "Yes, I guess it does feel like that."

"That's utter *bollocks,*" he retorted.

Kate twisted her mouth. "To have all your actions and life shaped and contained within a pre-determined, circumscribed set of acceptable action." Looking at him, she added, "It's just not for me anymore."

"The great New England philosophy is not called *predestination* for nothing, you know," he said, his tone openly bitter. He thrust his chin out in a pout, while folding his arms across his chest.

Suddenly Kate clapped her hand over her mouth in astonishment. "Oh, my God! I had never made the association before!"

"Whatever are you babbling on about," Blake asked crossly.

"Predestination, the '*Great Expectations*' of Dean Edwards!" she blurted, staring at him wildly. "He must be a descendant of the philosophical master of Predestination himself—Jonathan Edwards!"

Blake waved his hand dismissively in the air. "Well, of course, he is a direct descendant. Haven't you seen the famous portrait of the old boy hanging on his office wall? What of it?"

Kate shook her head slowly, as the portrait she had glimpsed in the dean's office rose to consciousness. A smile spread across her face, much like the light of a clear dawn above the earth's horizon. As new insights welled within her, she started quoting Thoreau:

> *"New universal, and more liberal laws will*
> *begin to establish themselves . . .*
> *old laws be expanded . . .*
> *the license of a higher order*
> *. . . simplify."*

Blake stared at her as if she were mad. "Whatever are you on about?" He glared at her with rising impatience.

Kate announced excitedly, "Jonathan Edwards, for all his belief in predestination, led the '*Great Awakening*'—just as his descendant, however unintentionally, has initiated mine." She shook her head in awe. "The new liberal laws of transcendentalism at work."

Blake turned away muttering, "I've really come to despise that eccentric Thoreau."

She looked knowingly at him. "Oh, Blake, you wrote the multiple Shakespeare book. Why don't you come with me and write another book—of your own choice, on your time, according to your own dictates?"

"What, and leave Harvard behind—to go live in the woods like a Billybob?" He turned around with a deep scowl on his face.

"Yes," Kate said encouragingly. "Leave the world of Harvard, with its predestination and '*Great Expectations*' embedded, both in those lifeless portraits and their descendants, behind—for the more liberal laws of an *awakened* life."

Blake scowled at her, a ferocious glare, not unlike the dean's. "Not on your life—or mine." A look of horror crossed his face. "I was tight-roping too far out along a precarious limb as it was."

Kate tossed her hand with a dismissive thrust. "You—we, could live in the house in Woodstock. God knows, you have life-long funding for a different lifestyle."

"If I were to venture north with you, I'd be cut out without even a good-bye, don't you know, Kate?" He turned away, before turning back impulsively. "You are just going to throw away all your hard work, the pride of your family in your success, your chances for advancement, both with Harvard, and, and—with me?"

"Oh, Blake, I am simply following the dictates of Ishmael. I am looking at this matter in different lights and weighing it on different scales."

He peered at her through storm clouds of emotion. "And whatever happened to the scale of normalcy, of received wisdom, of the '*Great Expectations*' of everyone who has believed in you?" He shook his head.

With bent head, Kate turned away. "What about the '*Great Expectations*' I've set for myself? Should they be subordinated to everyone else's expectations for me?"

Blake reeled her around. "Truly, Katie, have you gone utterly mad to give all this up, for some, some pastoral *ideal*?" He regarded her through cold, hard eyes. "Have you not learned anything while here at Harvard?"

She stretched out her hand to touch him. "But that's just the point, Blake! I've learned the importance of experiencing the world, not remaining content simply with theorizing it."

He nodded brusquely. "How terribly ironic. You have learned from your time here at Harvard, the premier theoretical institution perhaps in the entire bloody world, to choose *field trips* to Walden over exacting scholarship." With a thunderous scowl, he added, "It's simply unthinkable—and utterly unacceptable." Turning on his heels, he walked briskly away, slamming the door behind him.

The exchange continued to elicit waves of sadness whenever Kate thought about it, even as she drove north with tremendous anticipation. Halfway over the bridge, she glanced down at where the Mystic flowed into the harbor. The setting triggered a rush of memories of her nervousness over that first meeting with the dean, her run earlier that morning when she could not embrace the dawn—single-mindedly absorbed by succeeding in academia.

And now she was leaving it all behind, to move to Vermont—to educate those interested in communicating with and living surrounded by the natural world, both at a college truly committed to such ideals, and at the learning center Channing had founded.

She shook her head with a smile. Not that she really knew or understood how to do that, exactly. Channing said it would flow naturally from her, bloom from within, he had claimed, once she left Cambridge behind and *transplanted* herself in more fertile soil conducive to abundant growth. A wide smile spread across her face. He was always speaking in botanical metaphor. She couldn't wait to experience the reality in which those metaphors were grounded.

Once past the New Hampshire border, Kate could feel her shoulders relax, her shallow breathing slow down. She glanced regularly at the miles and miles of sprouting maple and birch leaves shimmering among dark evergreens. Opening her windows despite the chill of the day, she inhaled the sweet aroma of Spring. With each passing mile between Cambridge and her, Kate felt the waves of sadness that had overcome her, swirl up and float away, beyond even the towering summits of the White Mountains, and past them, into the uncontained vastness of the ether.

Just then, Kate spotted the sparkling burnt-orange orb of the sun just breaking above the mountain summit, casting swirls of red and yellow along the violet mountaintops. With an impulsive turn, she wheeled over to the side, so she could get out and experience the dawn. Snow still clung to the sides of the sheer mountainsides, while the tops glistened in a vibrant white against the now rainbow of color, radiating its exuberant celebration of a new morning to the world.

Kate whirled around to witness the light cascading among the mountains, before striking its brilliance into the gorge where she was standing. "'*Only that day dawns to which we are awake,*'" she sang out to the rocks and waterfall beside her.

Getting back into her car, she continued north, at last reaching the point where the mountains of New Hampshire folded into the cascading green hills of Vermont. Kate shouted out the window when she crossed over the Connecticut into Vermont:

"*The sun is but a morning star—*"

She took the turn northwest past swerve of rock and bend of river, to drive down the *less traveled* road to Walden North.

The End

&

A New Beginning

Acknowledgments

In thinking back upon the many people who have inspired and encouraged me in this literary endeavor, I start with the students with whom I was fortunate to study the pages of Thoreau's *Walden.* Their questions, insights, enthusiasm, and their own transformations while reading (and completing) *Walden* inspired me to shift from *talking the talk*, to *walking the walk*—leading me to 'saunter' along the decidedly 'less traveled,' though endlessly enriching, *Road to Walden North.*

I express gratitude to Thoreau scholars who have dedicated their academic lives to studying *Walden*, generously sharing their insights through their research—too many to name individually, but who collectively have inspired me throughout my own academic and writing career to remain true to the spirit of Thoreau and his ever-timely themes in *Walden.* Among the Thoreauvians, I'd like to signal out Executive Director, Michael J. Frederick of the Thoreau Society, as well as Editor, Mark Gallagher, of the *Thoreau Society Bulletin*, for including me among the contributors to the Annual *Gatherings* at Walden Pond and as a reviewer for the *Bulletin.* My thanks, too, to the folks at Walden Pond Reservation for allowing me to host a "My Walden" exhibit of student projects, inspired by their own readings of *Walden.*

Fellow writers and scholars took much needed time and attention from their own pressing publishing deadlines to read and comment upon my manuscript:

- John Hanson Mitchell, whose wonderful books I have taught in my college courses alongside *Walden*;
- John Elder, who showed how 'way leads onto way' in his *Mountain of Home;* and
- the utterly inspirational, Frank Howard Mosher, whose early book, *Where the Rivers Run North,* enkindled my passion both to live in and write about the Great North Woods.

In the spirit of the Transcendentalist notion of the 'great whole,' I have referred directly throughout the pages of this novel, to the ever-inspirational research and writings of selected authors, including Barbara Kingsolver's, *Animal, Vegetable, Miracle;* John Elder's *Reading the Mountains of Home;* Benjamin Kilham's *Among Bears;* Jack Becklund's *Summers with the Bears;* Michael Pollan's, *Omnivore's Dilemma;* Warner Shedd's, *Owls Aren't Wise & Bats Aren't Blind,* and Paolo Freire's, *Pedagogy of the Oppressed.*

More oblique, though significant influences (and references) include: Annie Dilliard's *Pilgrim at Tinker Creek;* bell hooks, *Teaching to Transgress;* Diane Beresford-Kroeger's *Arboretum Borealis,* Bernd Heinrich's *Winter World, A Year in the Maine Woods,* and *The Trees in my Forest*; Elizabeth Marshall Thomas' *The Hidden Life of Deer;* Bill McKibbon's *Wandering Home* and *Deep Economy*; Ben Hewitt's *The Town that Food Saved & Saved*; and Peter Tompkins' and Christopher Bird's *The Secret Life of Plants.*

I remain forever indebted to—and humbled by—the inspirational folks living close to the land in the hills of Walden, Hardwick, Greensboro, and Craftsbury, Vermont, through whose examples, and often direct guidance, helped me to *experience* firsthand, the joys of living *simply.* Likewise, author friends there—Nancy Marie Brown,

Joyce Mandeville, Denise Brown, Sara Dillon, and Brett Stanciu—provided a stimulating mix of encouragement, friendly critique, and collaboration.

Publisher *extraordinaire,* Dede Cummings, of Green Writers Press, transformed these pages into a beautiful book on every level. Her intrinsic sensibilities as a writer herself have shaped her unwavering spirit of collaboration in editing, book design, and book promotion. I was proud to *place* my two novels with a press that exhibits a missionary fervor for both local lore and earth-wide conservation.

Former academic colleagues engaged in years of discussions over pedagogical strategies and ideal learning environments, which, in turn, shaped my own pedagogical *experiments in living*. May these pages help them understand and perhaps appreciate my reasons for choosing the *road less traveled* to Walden North.

Friends and family—who have both questioned and championed my evolving philosophy of *Simplifying*—have served as deep sources of inspiration and motivation, and to whom I remain forever grateful.

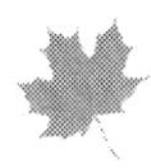

Sheila Post, PhD, taught college American literature and nature writing in New England for over a decade before deciding to write her own. A prolific academic author and place-based novelist, Sheila is the author (as Síle Post) of *Your Own Ones*, also published with Green Writers Press. She resides in northern New England, overlooking the forested mountains of her own Walden North, as well as at her Walden-by-the-Sea in Prince Edward Island.

CPSIA information can be obtained
at www.ICGtesting.com
Printed in the USA
LVOW12*0138030916
502741LV00002B/2/P

9 780996 135764